# THE NIGHT VISITOR

◇◇◇◇◇◇◇◇◇◇◇◇◇◇◇◇◇◇◇◇◇◇◇◇◇◇

In horror, Sigurd saw the dark shape of the dead but reanimated wizard Vigbjodr blocking the doorway. Then the draug lurched forward on leaden feet, advancing on the bed where Sigurd lay. It advanced to the foot of the bed and looked down. Sigurd slowly shrank himself to the smallest lump possible, feeling like a rat in a trap.

The draug took another dragging step, and Sigurd felt it groping at the foot of the bed. Then it drew back with a rumbling growl.

Still muttering, it turned its eyes upon Sigurd. Two dull, red lights regarded him from a face that seemed more bone than flesh, with matted tufts of beard hanging down to the draug's breast like strands of filthy wool . . .

Also by Elizabeth Boyer
*Published by Ballantine Books:*

THE SWORD AND THE SATCHEL

THE ELVES AND THE OTTERSKIN

THE THRALL AND THE DRAGON'S HEART

# THE
# WIZARD
## AND THE
# WARLORD

## Elizabeth Boyer

A Del Rey Book

BALLANTINE BOOKS • NEW YORK

A Del Rey Book
Published by Ballantine Books

Library of Congress Catalog Card Number: 82-91149

ISBN 0-345-30711-9

Manufactured in the United States of America

First Edition: August 1983

Cover art by Laurence Schwinger

Especially for Allan, who dreamed the Hross-Bjorn;
who continues to look for dreams,
and loves no walls but canyon walls.

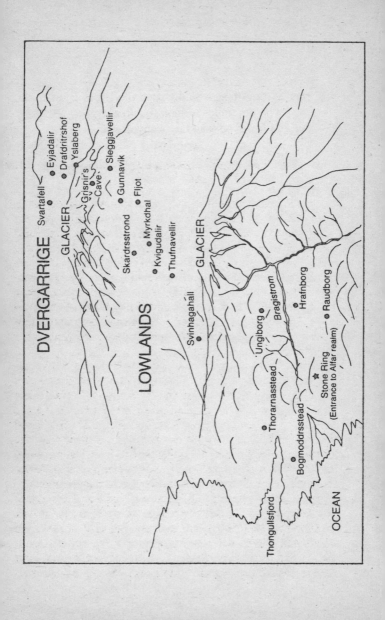

# Chapter I

◇◇◇◇◇◇◇◇◇◇◇◇◇◇◇◇◇◇◇◇◇◇◇◇◇◇◇◇◇

The persistent rain began turning to snow. Sigurd sat on a mossy rock to glare down into the little valley where his grandmother's house was disappearing behind veils of rain and mist. Since spring, he had been trying to expand the tiny hut into a fair-sized longhouse, but the weather had been wet all summer and he had no spirits for cutting turf in the rain. Morosely, he doubted if he would get the house finished before the fall freeze-up, particularly since both of his thralls had run away. They had been frightened by the talk that his grandmother Thorarna was a witch and was directing sendings against her neighbors to cause bad luck.

Sigurd scowled toward the lower valleys and the settlements. Old Bogmoddr, their nearest neighbor, had found a colt dead yesterday and loudly blamed Thorarna—and after living more than twenty years as her neighbor, since the time she had arrived at Thongullsfjord alone, except for a small, red-haired child. Sigurd himself had seen nothing to convince him that evil magic was plaguing his neighbors, and not just the usual bad luck that was certain to strike even the best of men. When the settlers of that remote bit of hospitable land came together, however, all they could talk about was cattle and sheep that had fallen to their deaths over cliffs or into fissures, driven mad by some supernatural force, or the milk and cheese in the dairies that had been fouled and spoiled by an envious spell. The fishing was worse than anyone could recall, and most damning of all the evidence against Thorarna was the weather,

1

which remained damp and mizzling most of the summer so that the hay spoiled before it could dry; it never failed to rain directly after someone cut his hay. Thorarna was even reputed to have turned the land-vaettir against the settlements, as evinced by the great rat that had attacked the largest toe of Bera of Alfgrimssynrsstead, shaking it with a fury most unnatural even in the fiercest of rats.

Thinking about his neighbors' accusations made Sigurd hot with fury. No one wondered that a lone and very ancient little woman could accomplish such diverse tricks as inflicting chills and fevers at the farthest south holding, at the same instant drying up the milk of the cows twenty miles to the north. Neither did they question her ability to break the necks of fifteen sheep in one night or to gallop her horse over the roofs of distant neighbors from dusk to dawn without stopping once to rest. Sigurd suspected that someone was doing the mischief and afterward blaming it on Thorarna's spells. Thorarna was nearer eighty than seventy, a gnomelike little creature so fragile of limb that Sigurd could lift her easily onto her horse, since she was no heavier than a child.

Sigurd yearned to put a stop to some of his neighbors' malevolent gossiping; indeed his considerable presence was enough to silence the boldest of them and send them skulking away, remembering urgent errands they had barely begun. Sigurd was neither stout nor particularly tall, but no one liked to cross his proud and warlike disposition. Where he had learned such a dreadful proficiency with weapons the settlements could not guess and he never told that it was from Thorarna. From his earliest days, she had taught him how to wield a small sword and axe and had made him run up the steep fells until he thought his heart would burst and his exhausted legs would turn to paste. By the time he was old enough to find other boys to fight with, he had learned enough from Thorarna to compensate somewhat for the lack of a father and older brothers to teach him. His haughty determination to admit no superior and very few equals had won him a great many fights he ought to have lost and earned him respect not unmingled with fear among the inhabitants of the isolated Thongullsfjord. As long as Sigurd stood between his grandmother and the gossip, no harm would come to her while he could grasp an axe in her defense and dare anyone to accuse her openly in his presence.

Sigurd pulled his hood further over his eyes, knowing it was senseless to sit brooding and getting wetter by the minute, but it suited him to become thoroughly miserable and angry before he took action. He found himself resenting being an orphan of one-and-twenty and wishing he had a father and plenty of family to admire and encourage him, but here he was, virtually alone against the entire world. His few friends had learned early on that Sigurd brooked no teasing about being raised by his grandmother.

No one knew how he cherished the secret hope that his fate would be as lucky as that of a perfect dolt named Hemingr, whose natural father had honored the old tradition and sent for his son when he was sixteen years old. Sigurd had feigned lofty indifference; having an absentee father was common enough in a settlement where vikings and merchants landed. No one dared taunt him about it; he had seen to that by making swift and horrible examples of any boy who tried to mock him or the parents he had never known. Sigurd's hopes hadn't died easily—Sigurd never relinquished anything without a fight—and when he was eighteen he was still hoping, although he was far too proud ever to admit it, even to himself.

Until that period of his life, he had besieged Thorarna mercilessly with questions about his parents, but she was as stubborn as he was and refused to do more than say, "When I am on my deathbed I shall tell you, but until then I shall carry the secret locked within me. I have learned to live with it, but you aren't prepared yet to bear the burden." Then she sent him away on some complicated errand to tire him out with exertion and perhaps make him forget his troublesome questions.

As he passed his eighteenth year, Sigurd's inquiries about his parents decreased; he found immediate concerns that were more interesting, such as his first lengthy sea voyage with an amiable viking who had designs upon the islands to the south of Skarpsey. When Sigurd returned, he was a man in his own right, and Thorarna was pleased to see him assume the master's responsibility over their small holding. He bought some thralls to help expand the hay tuns and tend more sheep and cultivate more ground. Thorarna thought the parentage question safely dead and breathed a sigh of relief.

Sigurd himself put the question in the back of his mind for several more years, until the ugly rumors about Thorarna surfaced like sharks in the peaceful Thongullsfjord, just when he had begun to make a name for himself as a viking and a fairly competent farmer. Such gossip put him into a bad humor, since it pointed up what his neighbors must be saying about him and his grandmother. A man's life could be mercilessly ended in battle or shipwreck, but his reputation lived on in the form of gossip or praise. His situation was tenuous, and if the men of Thongullsfjord decided to banish Thorarna, either he would die fighting them or he would become a landless, lordless wanderer, outlawed and outcast. It was a sentence of lingering death by starvation and exposure.

He glared gloomily at the toes of his boots and was not at all surprised or dissatisfied when the stitching suddenly parted under his gaze. Calamities great and small had followed him all his life when he was in this sort of humor. A strange influence broke plows, harnesses, and tools; oars fell overboard, sails ripped, and anything else occurred that would further exasperate him. Cursing his bad luck, he started to get up to leave, but suddenly realized that a man on a horse was standing just above him on the steep fell. He freed his sword immediately. A friend would have hailed him; only an enemy would creep up so close and sit staring so rudely.

"Who's there? Speak your name!" he commanded with a flourish of his sword, striding two steps closer to get a better look at the intruder.

The stranger, closely cloaked, made no move. Sigurd halted and returned the man's intense stare, suddenly wondering if he were seeing an apparition. The stranger edged his horse sideways up the hillside, still keeping his eyes fixed on Sigurd. The rain began descending with a vengeance. As Sigurd shook the water from his eyes, the image of the horseman faded into the mist and was gone.

Sigurd blinked. "An Alfar!" he said to himself, forgetting his wet condition for a few moments in his awe. Then he hurried downhill to tell Thorarna, who seemed to know almost everything a Scipling could know about the old legends. She held her beliefs with passionate fervor, in spite of the growing tendency to disbelieve in the unseen realm and its inhabitants. Sigurd sheathed his sword with a smile, confident of astonishing her when he told her what he had seen.

Thorarna, however, seemed in no mood for his news when he arrived home. She was carding wool, an occupation she took up when she was particularly piqued at someone or something. Today she scraped the fibers back and forth as if she were carding the heartstrings and sinews of a cherished enemy.

"Bah!" she declared, her eyes burning with an aggressive gleam when Sigurd announced his discovery. "Alfar! You must have fallen asleep and dreamed it. A man on a horse, you say, came and stared at you? A rude thing to do, knowing Alfar aren't welcome in this realm. I wouldn't have wondered if you'd been kidnapped and carried away. But look at you, wet through and cold as a fish. Imagine a grown man without the wits to get out of the rain. A fever more than likely inspired you to imagine you saw a man and a horse."

"I don't feel that I have a fever." Sigurd hung up his cloak and sat down by the fire, where his fleece slippers waited. With a twinge of uneasiness, he noticed that Thorarna carded the wool away to nothing, allowing it to fall unnoticed at her feet. Her hands were shaking and her eye was too bright and fixed, gazing away at unpleasant scenes that were miles away.

"Grandmother? Is anything wrong?" Sigurd asked.

"Wrong! What would a boy like you know about it?"

"I'm not a boy," he reminded her gently, but she only pshawed such a notion. When it suited her, she conveniently reduced Sigurd to the status of a boy of twelve, with all the accompanying aggravating defects. Nine years ago she had been quite stout enough to intimidate him with a willow switch and she frequently reverted to those glorious days even yet.

Now, as he looked at her with considerable consternation, it struck him that she was much reduced from those past days.

No longer robust, she looked more like an old twig with its bark dried around it.

"Haven't I warned you enough about strangers who might tell you they once knew us?" she went on in her lecturing tone. "It's not safe for you to talk to strangers!"

Sigurd tried to make her laugh. "To be sure, Grandmother, I ought to be frightened—a great fellow such as I am, who has gone viking three summers now and ought to know how to take care of himself. Come now, Grandmother, what are you so upset about?"

"I'm not upset. You're the one with the fever and chill, and you won't stop pestering me about your father and mother, so it's no wonder I've gotten into a state!" Her hands trembled so much that she dropped her carders and scarcely noticed, plucking distraitly at her hair and gown as if she didn't know what she did.

Sigurd leaped up in alarm, seeing what a tremble she had fallen into. "Grandmother, you're not well. Something has excited you. I decided long ago not to trouble you any more about my parents, who by now are surely dead and gone. You ought to lie down; let me help you." He picked her up gently and deposited her on the narrow shelf of a bed with great solicitude.

"Dead and gone!" she exclaimed to herself in an odd voice, looking around fearfully, as if she had forgotten where she was.

"Shall I make you some tea to steady your nerves?" Sigurd tucked her eider around her awkwardly. "Your hands are like ice and your poor little feet, too. What did you ever do to get so shrunken and tiny, Grandmother? Don't tell me it's just age; old Grelod is twice your age and fatter every year."

Thorarna glared at him helplessly, but her voice was grateful. "You great ninny, do you think I can't care for myself and you, too, as I have done for all these years? With precious little help from anybody else, too," she added emphatically. "Now brew me some tea, Sigurd. My wits need clearing. I've had something of a shock today, that's all. Nothing you should concern yourself about just yet. A visitor from as well as beyond the grave, she added in a sleepy whisper, but Sigurd caught the word visitor.

"Was it that brainless Bogmoddr, accusing you about his wretched colt? If he was here on such an errand, I'll break his head for him. I've heard enough idle gossip. I'll go and—"

"Sigurd, hush." Her voice was weak and tired. "Stop stamping around and pay attention to the tea. Talk won't hurt such a tough old boot as I am." She opened her eyes, which held a flicker of their old fierceness. "But it will hurt you. I want you to leave here before your name is too damaged to repair. I can't allow my bad reputation to tarnish yours."

Sigurd snorted, scalding himself with the hot water. "Now she's raving out of her mind. She thinks I would desert her when she's sick and old. She must think I'm not much of a man, to abandon my own grandmother to the trolls in the fells and to vengeful neighbors!"

Thorarna lifted one hand for silence. "At least I don't talk to myself yet," she snapped. "Now listen to me and stop trying to jolly me along as if I were a feeble old woman and you were a grown man. You think you're protecting me, but there's not much left any more for you to fuss about. It's simply not worth it any longer. I want you to leave Thongullsfjord at once, Sigurd. Tonight or tomorrow at the latest. It isn't safe here for you any more."

Sigurd handed her the tea. "Didn't you begin training me to fight early in my life, Grandmother? You told me one day I would have to use my weapons to save myself and you. Why were you so intent, if I'm only to run away after all?"

She shook her head impatiently. "Can't you see, you fool, that you can't fight sendings and trolls? That's what has been terrorizing the settlements, Sigurd, and most of these fools must soon realize that an entity far more malignant and powerful than old Thorarna is behind the misfortunes of Thongullsfjord. After today, the troubles will grow worse; and the cause of it, Sigurd, is inside this house. It is you and me, and a certain carved box in that trunk by the loom. Our doom has been following and searching for us these twenty years. It can have me—I don't mind dying now—but you must escape, Sigurd."

"Escape? No, I'll fight, Grandmother! I'll not give up our home to sendings and trolls!"

"You don't understand. These things come from the other realm. I see now that there's not much we can do against them—against a certain one who would like to possess that box and its contents." Her eyes flashed and she propped herself up a little straighter. "I've outwitted them all for more than twenty years. I bear them the greatest of malice, Sigurd, and I wish you to continue it. For that reason I've kept you and that box from them."

Sigurd stared at her without understanding. He seated himself on a stool at her side and demanded, "Who, Grandmother?" He was so uneasy that his glance caused the cup to leap out of her fingers and spill on the packed earth floor. A long black sausage dropped from its moorings in the rafters, and the broom fell over with a crash into a nest of buckets and kettles.

Thorarna looked at the mess and pressed her hand over her eyes. "Go away, Siggi, I'm too tired to tell you anything else. Run outside and play, won't you?" Her voice trailed away sleepily, and all Sigurd could do was pace up and down, clenching his fists and wondering who had visited his grandmother that day and who had stared at him on the fell. Finally he put on a cloak and saddled a horse to fetch a woman from Bog-moddrsstead to sit with his grandmother.

When that was done, it was nearly dark, and old Grelod, a great friend and ally of Thorarna's, was installed beside the hearth like a protective dragon, swathed in shawls and various smelly charms done up in little bags. She had a charm, a petrified foot or claw or some ghastly object, for every illness and occasion of life, from a birth to a burning. Sigurd thought her quite a sorceress, and there was something awful and inevitable about the way she took charge of Thorarna, banishing Sigurd contemptuously as a mere male who was of no consequence in the unfolding drama. Thorarna's fate lay in the hands of Grelod, which were soon busily mixing and powdering things and simmering small pots that made an abominable stink over the fire.

Sigurd kept out of the way, feeling absolutely worthless.

He made his bed in the barn and spent an uneasy night listening to the strange creatures that had come to inhabit the fells of Thongull—trolls, with bellowing voices like bulls or seals, whose noises kept the livestock restless all night. Knowing that they had followed him and Thorarna was not a thought that lent itself to composing a mind for peaceful slumber.

To his further dismay, Grelod's presence threatened to become a permanent institution beside his hearth. Thorarna got no better. Sigurd soon abandoned the hope that her sickness would convince the hardheaded neighbors that she was innocent of the supernatural crimes of which they suspected her. The depredations worsened in frequency and destruction. The trolls no longer took the trouble to hide themselves from view in the twilight after sundown, and the nighttime hours became a period of terror. Many people reported that the dead were no longer quiet in their graves, but stalked about, doing unspeakable acts of malice against both man and beast.

Two families packed their boats and departed for the south, barely in time to miss the winter freeze-up of the fjord. The long, dark winter found many settlements with half enough wood and peat, a fraction of the usual food laid by, and hard knots of fear in the hearts of those who listened to the trolls in the fells mocking their desperation with assorted depraved roars and screams.

In the spring, the survivors made note of the grim toll taken by winter and the trolls and packed their boats or begged the unwilling sea traders to carry them south. Desolately, Sigurd watched them go, finding Thorarna's vindication a hollow consolation. His only comfort was the loss of old Grelod, who had had enough of scratchings at the door and unfamiliar tracks in the snow.

Thorarna to the last refused to be cajoled into a ship and berated Sigurd daily for staying with her. Bleakly, he watched the ships sailing out of the harbor, pelted as often as not by the unseen watchers in the cliffs on either side. His sword never left his side and he longed for a clean shot with his bow at one of the lurking marauders. He knew they were hiding in the lava flows, waiting for their opportunity, especially after sundown.

He began to feel that he and the other busy Sciplings were the intruders on Skarpsey's ancient soil, and it was not a pleasant experience at dusk with shadows filling all the ravines and creases in the fells.

By midsummer, all the farms of Thongullsfjord were deserted except for Sigurd's and those of two other families who had waited to see if the situation improved. The trolls and sendings rampaged with greater tenacity than ever. Sigurd urged the others to stay, despite the fact that they possessed only a handful of sheep, cows, and horses, and that no traders dared risk the capricious wrath of the trolls guarding the cliffs that overlooked the fjord.

"We have to go if we want to stay alive," Bogmoddr declared; he was not quite as fat and red and complacent these days. Sigurd knew he'd hoped to take up all the deserted holdings for himself, but he'd lost his courage. "We can't survive another winter like the last one. I've learned to hate this unnatural, cursed place." He glared around at the rotting hay and his pitiful, sad-eyed sheep.

Snjolfr grunted in agreement, twitching his shoulder toward the fells. "Well, they can have it. I've lost everything I've worked for and all my fathers gained before me. The trolls won in the end. Always knew they were here, just waiting." He blinked at Sigurd half apologetically and added, "You and your grandmother are welcome in my boat. We can't go off and leave you here to die."

Sigurd nodded and sighed, not even bothering to point out, as he usually did, that the land to the south was all taken up and they would be tilling other men's fields for them instead of their own. All he said was: "You'll regret leaving your farms behind, one day."

"Not if I live to see my children grown, which I won't do here," Snjolfr retorted, seconded by a sharp sniff from his wife. "I don't know how you and Thorarna have survived as long as you have, alone up there so near the trolls. Not to say she has spells to keep them off," he added hastily as Sigurd suddenly bristled with anger. "That's all bygones, I hope. I never thought it was her, really. This misfortune is

something much more—" He spread his hands to encompass
all of the island, and left off what he was going to say with
a depressed sigh. "You and Thorarna be at the boatstands
tomorrow. We're setting sail at evening with the tide."

"We won't keep you waiting," Sigurd said, prodding at the
baskets and bundles the women were resolutely packing with
their household goods. He knew he and his grandmother couldn't
survive alone, not with the trolls openly prowling the deserted
pasturelands and ransacking the empty houses. "It's my grandmother there's no convincing. She wants me to leave her behind
to die."

"We can't do that," Bogmoddr declared. "She always was
too stubborn for her own best interest. But you'll have to be
more stubborn, Sigurd. You must bring her to the boatstands
tomorrow if you have to carry her all the way, kicking and
struggling, I have no doubt."

The women shook their heads and shuddered. "Imagine
being left here alone to die!" one exclaimed.

Sigurd strode homeward well before dark with the flour he
had traded for, but the watched feeling made him uncomfortable
until he was safely at home. As he approached the barn, the
two remaining geese came to meet him, cackling hungrily, as
if Thorarna hadn't already fed them. The penned sheep blattered
demandingly, wanting the scanty hay left in the barn. Sigurd
fed the animals and stepped into the house with a greeting, but
it was empty. With mounting alarm, he looked from the dead
fire to the bread and cheese drying on the table and on to the
empty peg where Thorarna's cloak usually hung. With a shout,
he plunged outside to search for her. Pausing a moment to
listen, he heard a faint cry from the hillside above the house.

He found her where she had lain on the hillside all day in
the rain and wind, unable to muster the strength to rise.

"That wretched spotted lamb got away from me this morning," she said, very pale and weak. "I fell down and couldn't
get up. The trolls will have it before dawn."

"Hush," he said, trying to stop the quiver in his voice. "Let
the trolls have all the stupid sheep. You shouldn't have come
up here alone. What if you've broken something?"

Ignoring her protests, he picked her up in his arms and carried her to the house. He was horrified to feel her bones so fragile and birdlike beneath her skin. She had once been stout enough to carry huge loads of hay on her back after working all day, and easily able to lift a sheep and throw it down for shearing. Scarcely anything was left of his grandmother, and suddenly he felt terribly alone with the darkness of the fell pressing hungrily at his back.

When he had locked the door, started the fire again, and lighted the whale-oil lamp, he told her about Snjolfr's offer to take them to safety. "We have to go, Grandmother," he finished firmly. "You're not well, and the southlands are far more pleasant in the winter, they say. After you're strong and fat again, we'll come back to this little house. We can live like the foxes themselves on the berries and birds and hares and whatever else nature offers, and I can go with the vikings in the summers."

Thorarna was shaking her head with great weariness, pulling her eider up under her chin. "Not I, Sigurd. You can see I'm dying, can't you? This is the place where I intend to molder away, and the time is not far distant. Something happened to me this morning—half my body seems to be dead already, and I can't seem to think." She sighed and closed her eyes. "So sleepy. There's something I have to tell you, as soon as I remember what it is. But I do know that you must go with Bogmoddr and Snjolfr. Go south with them. Now, tomorrow."

Sigurd sat down and folded his arms. "I won't go without you, Grandmother, and that's the end of it."

She shook her head, as if it were very heavy, and her eyes opened. "I think it is finally time I told you about your father and your mother. Your history—a sad story."

"No, no, you're far too tired," Sigurd said hastily. "You don't need to tell me about it now. You've had a fall and you're chilled. It's nothing serious, Grandmother."

"Silence, child. I know what I know. Today I saw an old sheep dying—my fetch. This time Grelod isn't here to hold me back with her spells and charms. She'll be angry that I cheated her so, the moment her back was turned. Hah—she was a true friend, Siggi. If I leave you anything, I hope it's the ability to know a true friend from a false. But to the meat of the matter—before this old husk is too tired. Your mother— I wronged her, Sigurd. She was my daughter, and her name was Ashildr." The name brought a spasm of pain, and Thorarna fell back, gray-faced and gasping. "I renounced her for marrying—as she did. I haven't spoken her name for more than twenty years—but now I must forgive her."

Sigurd knelt beside her in alarm, seeing that her condition was indeed serious. "Grandmother, can't I do something for you?" he whispered. "Are you in pain?"

She opened her eyes reluctantly. "Yes, pain—jealousy. He took her away from me—but not you, if I can help it. Two of them—I can't remember which married her and which killed her—but I hate them both." Her faint voice dwindled into senseless mutterings.

"Go on, Grandmother," Sigurd encouraged her. "Tell me about my father." He could scarcely speak.

"Father—the man on the fell—yesterday. Or was it last year? I told him—no son, you'd died in the fire. You'll forgive me one day, Sigurd. Couldn't let him take you to that other place. The other one watched you, too—he's the one—trolls, sendings. I told him—no son. He didn't believe me. Mustn't let him take away Ashildr's carved box—Ashildr's wedding present from—from—he took Ashildr—she died—in the fire—"

Sigurd struggled to understand; but his wits were already benumbed by the fear of her dying. "Then my father came here? He sent for me?"

"Sent for you! Sendings! He'll kill you, Sigurd!" She clutched his arm in her cold little claw of a hand, glaring past his shoulder wildly. "Keep Ashildr's box away—the warlord wants it— evil, evil man—burned your mother—"

"My father did, or this other? Do you remember his name?"

"Name—name—" Her eyelids fluttered, and her breathing was so faint that Sigurd feared it had stopped. "Ashildr— Ashildr, oh forgive me! I tried to keep him safe—keep the box away from them—wizards and warlords both. Ashildr, are you still here? Let me take your hand."

Sigurd held her hand gently in his own, letting her murmur on to Ashildr, mostly nonsense, until she fell quietly asleep, breathing small, shallow draughts—but still it was breathing. He hoped she would be strong enough to tell him more tomorrow in a more connected fashion. He still knew almost nothing about his father and mother; and, of course, he remembered nothing useful except some childhood nightmares about fire. Sadly, he thought these might have been a veiled memory of the fire which had killed his mother. Thorarna had told him it was a sad story, and he began to suspect that she was right.

He sat beside her watchfully all through the night. She slept quietly, except for a few querulous calls for Ashildr, but he was able to reassure her and soothe her back to sleep. Near dawn, which came early in the north country, she opened her eyes with perfect clarity and exclaimed, "Ashildr, fetch my best apron and brooches, your father is home!" She moved as if to rise and collapsed softly in Sigurd's arms, breathing her last.

# Chapter 2

By the time Sigurd had torn enough wood from the house and barn for his grandmother's pyre, the day was far advanced. With a numb feeling, he watched the tremendous fire leaping high into the gray sky. At midday it still burned, lifting a column of black smoke into the sky like a banner.

At last he gathered a few possessions, remembering Bogmoddr and Snjolfr waiting at the boatstands. Knowing he was probably too late, he hurried anyway, hoping they had seen the smoke and guessed that Thorarna had died. Leaving her unburned and unburied would have been unthinkable. But perhaps they had thought trolls had burned the house.

After hurrying the four miles to the harbor, he found his hopes were dashed when he reached the empty boatstands. Bogmoddr and his boats were gone, leaving nothing behind except an old basket which had burst. The thrifty housewife had transferred the contents to another container, wasting only one seed cake that had fallen in the wet sand. Sigurd turned away with an effort, knowing he was not likely ever to see another trace of human occupation on the grim shores of Thongullsfjord. As he gazed out to sea in bitterest desolation, he heard the voices from the cliffs begin a chorus of hoarse chuckles, as if they possessed a great secret, warning Sigurd that the day would soon be spent. He looked around in sudden uneasiness at the familiar scene, which was now deserted and somehow menacing. The hopelessness of his fate staggered him. He turned away from the vast emptiness of the sea, which only reminded him what a trifling speck he was in such an overwhelmingly huge and desolate scheme.

They might have waited, he told himself a hundred times that night; surely they weren't that afraid. Outside the abandoned house in which he sheltered, the depraved howlings and roarings of the trolls rose in fierce exultation from the cliffs of the fjord. Whatever unnatural forces had been sent against Thongullsfjord, they had succeeded. Sigurd did not sleep, listening with a species of paralysis as something sniffed vigorously under the door and battered at the planks with uncouth grunts and growls.

In the morning he returned to his house and found it ransacked. The sheep and geese were gone, little to his surprise. Silently he examined the tracks in the soft earth. Neither man nor any beast he knew could make such a track. He shook his head and began to scowl. The grief of Thorarna's death and the shock of his abandonment were clearing from his brain. He glared around at the sad shambles of his home and down the mountain toward the deserted settlement; then he began to

burn with outrage. He stalked around the buildings, studying
the tracks as intently as a hunter following his prey. On the
knob of hill where he had burned Thorarna, he found the tracks
of shod horses and a few marks of men's boots where they had
dismounted to look at the ashes. Sigurd clenched his axe and
glowered around him at the fells that were shrouded in mists
and cloud, wondering where his enemies were hiding—behind
a waterfall, in the shadow of a crag, or inside a cave in the
lava flows?

"Come out, you cowards!" he roared in defiance. "Nith-
lings! You don't dare to fight me!"

The imperturbable silence finally quelled his furious rav-
ings. With a last muttered curse, he returned to his defiled
house and looked around numbly at the wreckage. Everything
had been dragged out and smashed—kettles, crockery, and
furniture. The clothing Thorarna had made with spinning wheel
and loom during the dark days of winter was in shreds everywhere, and her faithful implements were likewise torn to pieces.
Nothing was spared, and Sigurd's sense of outrage swelled.
The only object that escaped violation was Thorarna's large
carved trunk, which had been battered at with axes but remained
miraculously intact. Perhaps the arrival of the men on horseback
had had something to do with its salvation, since the creatures
that had done the damage certainly weren't human. Sigurd
paused, staring at the trunk as he pondered, wondering who
the horsemen could possibly be. Outlaws, he finally decided,
who were probably feeling emboldened by the removal of the
settlement. What an unpleasant surprise for them awaited on
the fjord cliffs, Sigurd reflected with dark satisfaction.

He took the key to Thorarna's trunk from his pouch and
used it to open the heavy lid. Immediately, the fragrance of
herbs and the perfect orderliness of the trunk's contents struck
him with such a poignant remembrance of Thorarna that he
could scarcely bear his losses. Gently he searched through her
finery and keepsakes, resolving that he would burn them all to
send their essences after her to the place where she had gone
to meet her ancestors. She would be most indignant with him
if she didn't have her best dress.

He discovered the object of his search at the very bottom of the chest, stowed away as if Thorarna hadn't wanted to see it very often. Lifting out the small carved box, Sigurd took his first good look at it. Thorarna hadn't been able to keep many secrets from a small, inquisitive child, but she had always refused to let him examine the box as closely as he would have liked. It was made of unfamiliar dark wood and its carving was beautiful, but he took no time to appreciate it in his anxiety to open it and ascertain if it held any clues to the identity of his enemy or his father. To his consternation, the box seemed to have neither hasp nor hinges. It was cunningly carved indeed, he thought in amazement, searching in vain for the crack that denoted the lid. He shook it and heard something rattle softly inside—documents made on sheepskin, perhaps, and probably containing all he needed to know. For a moment, he debated smashing the box to get at its contents and even gave it an experimental tap, but the carvings of twining serpents made him think it might be unlucky, and the carved faces of the figures seemed to look at him warningly. It was a rather small box, not much longer than a loaf of bread, so he didn't imagine it would be too awkward to carry with him, wherever he decided to go. The sad ruin of Thorarna's house and the desecration of his childhood memories convinced him that he didn't want to stay any longer at Thongullsfjord than it would take him to assemble his possessions and decide where to go.

He spent the rest of the day burning Thorarna's belongings and gathering the remaining bits of her bones, which he buried safely beneath the huge black stone where she had often sat to rest herself and where she could look down at her house and buildings and spy upon small Sigurd to see if he was doing his work or not. Many times she had chased him around the rock with a switch in her hand, training him and teaching him to defend himself against the enemy she had known would appear—the warlord.

Since the trolls had stolen everything remotely edible in the house, he spent the afternoon hunting for a bird or a hare. At once, he learned that the game was either too wary for him to approach or it was frightened completely away. He also found the place where the trolls had eaten his sheep. The fleece and much of the meat were shamefully wasted. At the end of the day, he returned to his ravaged house with a tight knot of apprehension in his empty belly.

Somehow he managed to sleep a while, curled up beside the fire in the rubble of his past. He was exhausted, but he awakened instantly when light feet ran softly across the turf roof. He'd barricaded the place as well as he could, and the turf walls were ten feet thick. Still, he armed himself and waited, listening to the creatures scratching and battering at the stout timbers of the door and digging at the turves on the roof. Dawn put an end to their labors, however. Looking at the evidence of their attack, Sigurd wondered if he would survive another night. He found a small parcel of dried meat Thorarna had stowed under the eaves which the trolls had somehow missed and went to work repairing the worst of the damages.

The trolls returned in greater numbers the following night, but they did not break through his roof until the night after. Sigurd waited below the hole with his axe, watching the earth crumble away beneath their eagerly scratching claws. They jostled and snapped at each other in their fury to get at him, with a sound like dogs worrying a rat to death. When a paw or head appeared in the opening, Sigurd slashed at it with his axe, sending its imprudent owner howling. His resistance to being murdered and the advent of dawn diminished the trolls' ferocity by slow degrees, ending with their ultimate retreat in grumbling twos and threes. When sunlight shone through the hole in Sigurd's roof, he peered out warily and saw four heaps of stone where the sunlight had touched the carcasses of four dead trolls. He was too exhausted to be much astonished at anything and spent the day sleeping and refortifying his tottering fortifications. When he climbed onto the roof, he saw that the trolls had finally hit upon the idea of digging a second hole through the turves. When they got through, it would be short work for a dozen of them to dispose of one lone defender. Not without penalty, however, he told himself grimly and made certain his weapons were honed to the utmost sharpness.

The trolls returned about midnight. It took them nearly until dawn to break through the second hole, which they did with horrible, triumphant snarling. Sigurd, however, had inspired them with enough respect that the brutes did not immediately rush through the breach to attack. They hung back, shoving one another and squabbling, as if trying to thrust down the lesser trolls to be cut to ribbons first as a diversion for a co-operative attack on Sigurd.

Sigurd hacked at them determinedly, and finally retreated from the loft when they continued to show reluctance in attacking him. He barricaded the little loft entrance from below as best he could and waited for the trolls to break through from above. They would make particularly vulnerable targets squeezing through the small opening.

During the interval, he thought he heard someone blowing a horn high in the fells. More likely it was his ears ringing from the cumulative effects of fatigue and suspense, he told himself. Then he noticed the sudden silence from the loft. The trolls were motionless for a few moments, then began a scrambling rush back onto the roof and outside. Silently they poured over the side of the low eaves and galloped away. Peering through a crack, Sigurd had a glimpse of hulking hairy shoulders, ungainly arms, and large pricking ears tufted with hair. With a last nervous cackle, they vanished into the shadows behind the empty sheepfold.

Sigurd opened the door and listened warily. The dawn was not far off, lighting the sky and making the earth seem all the darker. He saw nothing and heard nothing unusual, so he closed the door again and sat down to gnaw abstractedly at the stale dried meat, trying not to think about the coming day or anything in particular. His dazed brain was incapable of making any intelligent decisions. He could leave, but he knew the trolls would track him down mercilessly and kill him easily once he was without the scant protection the house still offered.

While he sat, he must have dozed; the next thing he knew, he was startled awake by a sudden noise at the door. Seizing his axe, he leaped up and stared at the door, which was shuddering under a thunderous knocking. Outside he heard the snorting and pawing of horses and the rattle of their bridles. He also heard muffled voices, then the authoritative knocking resumed.

"Is anyone there?" a deep voice demanded, and the latch shook. "It's locked from within, so someone must be inside."

"Not likely," another voice said. "The last of the Sciplings left several days ago. You might just find a troll holed up in there, I should think."

"The trolls were trying to dig someone out of here. I think there must be a survivor. Someone burned a corpse on the hilltop." The door creaked on its hinges as someone shouldered it experimentally. Again the voice called, "Hulloa! Is anyone inside? You've nothing to fear from us."

"You'll never convince the old woman of that, I fear," someone said. "She's hid herself pretty well from you these past twenty years." A muffled conversation ensued on the other side of the planks, and Sigurd crept closer in an effort to hear what they might have to say about Thorarna and possibly himself.

Someone suggested blasting the door open, and another predicted that some kind of trap awaited them. Yet another boomed, "Well, it's far more likely the poor wretches have starved to death and there's nothing inside but corpses. The trolls have taken everything essential to life. I suggest you give it up, Halfdane."

The door creaked and shuddered again. "I've searched too long to give it up so easily. We'll have to use magic to get the door open. It looks as if the old woman has prepared us an unfriendly reception."

Sigurd's anger took fire again. The sendings, the trolls, and the final desertion of Thongullsfjord were the preparations for this meeting. He knew now that the man or wizard or whatever he might be who pounded so impatiently on the other side of the door must be the warlord Thorarna had prepared him to challenge one day—the warlord who wished him dead for no apparent reason.

Sigurd jerked back the bars and flung open the door. Axe in hand, he stared at the strangers, who stared back in mutual surprise. They were heavily cloaked and hooded against the chill of night, and Sigurd could tell little about them, except that they were about fifteen altogether and they all carried weapons.

"Who are you, and what do you want with me?" Sigurd demanded. "Isn't it enough that people have died and the settlement is deserted except for me? What is this grudge you've been carrying for twenty years?"

The foremost of the strangers, the one who had done the knocking, half-raised his axe. He was a burly fellow with a dark mane of beard framing his scowling face.

"Who are you?" he demanded gruffly, advancing a step.

"My name is Sigurd, if it's of any concern to you. My grandmother told me about you, and I've seen enough of your works in this past year to make me glad to meet you now. You caused the sendings and the trolls and the deaths of many Sciplings. I hold you accountable for these crimes and I challenge you now to defend yourself, it you regard yourself as a man." Sigurd took a strong grasp on his axe and braced himself in a defensive position.

The strangers gasped and murmured excitedly. The leader called Halfdane threw his cloak out of his way and unsheathed his axe. "I have no wish to insult your manhood by refusing to fight with you, nor do I intend to appear a coward by seeming unwilling, but your accusations leave me no choice but to defend my honor. You must remember that any misfortune that befalls you is of your own manufacturing. But first I would like to know the name of the old woman who lived here and if that was her pyre on the hilltop."

"I don't know what business it is of yours," Sigurd retorted. "Don't attempt to dishonor her; she was my grandmother, Thorarna."

Halfdane looked at him for a long moment. "Was that her real name? What was her father's name? And who are your parents?"

"I heard her use no other," Sigurd snapped, "and she told me nothing of my parents before she died—nothing I would care to tell to a stranger and an enemy. Now, are you done with your questions?"

"Not quite. Does the name Halfdane of Hrafnborg mean anything to you? Perhaps you have heard it as Halfdane the Warlord." The increasing dawn light illuminated his grim, lowering countenance.

"If that is your name, the only thing it means to me is that it is the name of my enemy," Sigurd declared. "My grandmother told me that a warlord intended to destroy me and she laid the blame of the sendings and trolls on him. It must be an old and bitter feud for you to stalk my grandmother and me for so many years, but I believe this will be the end of it now." He swung his axe impatiently and measured his opponent.

Halfdane raised his axe and advanced a step. "Your grandmother has done an excellent job of teaching you to hate a man you have never seen. If I tell you she was mistaken, you'll be insulted, will you not? Perhaps you yourself have made a hasty and ill-formed conclusion about what I have done."

"My grandmother never lied to me," Sigurd replied angrily. "You can't change my mind. I know you're the warlord she spoke of, the one who caused all the misery of Thongullsfjord out of your spite against us. You're an evil being, and I challenge you to a holmgang." He made a menacing move with his axe.

"And you're a hasty, ignorant being, but I'm always glad to oblige a fool in throwing away his life," Halfdane answered. He allowed Sigurd to take the first swing at him, deflecting the blow with ease. After that, he took command of the fight, allowing Sigurd to expend himself in desperate and futile attempts to get past his enemy's defenses. Sigurd fought like an army of one, but his fury was no match for Halfdane's cool, collected skill in parrying his rushes. Each of the warlord's moves proved to Sigurd that he was capable of ending the fight quickly at any time he chose, which only made Sigurd the more furious.

"Now you've lost your common sense," Halfdane said and felled Sigurd with a single sharp rap with the handle of his axe. "You're not a bad fighter, but you need teaching and practice. I can see you've had some experience. No, don't look for your axe, the fight is finished for now." He put his foot on

Sigurd's axe. "Dagrun, we can't leave him here for the trolls. We'll put him up behind Skeifr. You see to it while I look inside the house."

Sigurd sat up unsteadily. His skull felt absolutely split, and they had taken away his axe, but he was still defiant. "I don't like this talk of being carried off. I'd rather take my chances with the trolls than with outlaws. This is my house, and I intend to defend it and the ashes of my grandmother." He rose and clenched his fists as Halfdane returned from his inspection of the house.

"Don't be absurd," Halfdane replied. "You won't last another night. It was fortunate for you that we arrived when we did to frighten off the trolls, or they would have had you by now. I suggest you gather the possessions you'll require, so you'll delay us no longer. Dagrun, accompany him and be watchful, in case he's got a sword hidden somewhere." The warlord turned away, dismissing Sigurd with a last glance of his contemptuous, fox-colored eyes.

Dagrun stepped forward with a crusty glower. "Come along. We can always use a good man with an axe. Do be a sensible fellow. Only a fool would deliberately prefer to become supper for a pack of stinking trolls. You won't be needing much; Halfdane provides us with everything we need."

"There's only one thing I must have, if I'm forced to come with you," Sigurd growled, stalking into the ruins of his house. He knelt beside the hearth and reached into the secret hiding place dug into the earth under one of the stones where he had hidden the small, carved box. He ignored the curious stares of the men as he accompanied Dagrun to the horses and glared resentfully at the fellow who had taken his axe.

"We'll be keeping your weapons for just a short while," Dagrun said. "That's Skeifr, the one you'll be riding behind. You can't be sorry to leave this desolated place, can you?" He spoke grudgingly, as if he were hopeful Sigurd wouldn't embarrass him. With a sigh, Sigurd put on his cloak and took a last look around at the house and the fells.

"It isn't so bad at Hrafnborg," Dagrun continued. "I think you'll like it, if you like to fight. As soon as Halfdane thinks you're good enough, you'll be able to ride with us, hunting trolls and raiding the hill forts of our enemies. It shouldn't be long; you're well begun with an axe. Rolfr isn't nearly as good with an axe and he's an endless nuisance besides."

"What's that?" a strident young voice cried out. "I'm not an endless nuisance! Expecting as I do to be murdered at any moment by Bjarnhardr's Alfar, I certainly wouldn't say I'm an endless nuisance. The end is definitely foreseeable. By the way, that was a splendid fight, Sigurd. My name is Rolfr, and I'm much looked down upon as the youngest and least experienced and I'm always being thrust into the background, holding the horses and fetching the firewood, but I'm more than pleased to make your acquaintance, anyway. You don't have to ride behind that old drone Skeifr when you can ride with me. Come, give me your hand."

"Do be quiet, Rolfr. Halfdane's instructions were to—"

Rolfr leaned down from his horse, sticking out his hand with a friendly grin. "I foresee we'll become fast friends, Sigurd. Let's shake hands."

Sigurd extended his hand reluctantly. "Pleased to meet—" he began, just as Rolfr gave him a terrific haul upward and onto the horse behind him.

"I think I shall call you Siggi, if you don't mind," Rolfr said. "I've got great plans for you."

"No one except my grandmother ever called me Siggi in my life without repenting of it," Sigurd declared hotly, but it was all he could do to hang on as Rolfr whirled his horse around and jabbed its ribs with his spurs. The beast crouched for a mighty spring, launching itself into a breakneck gallop over rocks and underbrush in pursuit of the solitary dark figure of Halfdane, who was riding ahead, outlined against the silver morning sky.

Sigurd didn't feel much like talking, but Rolfr kept up a lively conversation without much input from Sigurd. Rolfr possessed the gift of endless speech—with himself, the horse, or the terrain. Finally Sigurd broke in with a question.

"Where is Hrafnborg? I've never heard of it."

Rolfr laughed, letting the horse slow to a bone-rattling trot.

"I'd be surprised if you had, you know. But of course you can't help being a Scipling. I'd almost forgotten it. This promises to be great fun, if you're as uninformed as other Sciplings I've heard of. Just tell me who you think we are. I've told you all our names, so that doesn't count."

Sigurd scowled at Rolfr, who was looking over his shoulder with a sly grin. "I don't know what you mean, you fool. Outlaws, I suppose. Perhaps you've been hiding inland, preying upon travelers and isolated houses—"

Rolfr interrupted with a delighted roar of mirth, causing several of his companions riding nearby to glare at him and motion for silence. "Then you have no idea who we are and where we are going. How delightful. I hope you won't be frightened, Siggi. Have you ever heard of the Ljosalfar and Dokkalfar?"

"Well, of course I have. We have hundreds of legends—"

"Legends! That's some consolation, I suppose. But you don't really believe there were already people on this island when the first settlers heaved their doorposts overboard and arrived on these fair shores?"

"There may have been; but if there were, where did they go? I hadn't noticed any of them still lingering," Sigurd replied testily.

Rolfr laughed again. "Where indeed, Siggi? Where indeed! They had to go somewhere. Where do you suppose they all went?"

"I don't know and I don't particularly care," Sigurd snapped. "I'm in no mood for games. I've been beaten and kidnapped by strangers or outlaws already, so I don't need to be tortured by your stupid riddles. If you've got something to say to me, say it and then be silent!"

"You've had a rough time of it, and I'm sorry for it," Rolfr said soothingly. "But we're all you've got now, since your people have abandoned the settlement, and the nearest Scipling habitation is far to the south, a good long ways in a boat. We'll be at Hrafnborg in less than two hours. You never suspected you had neighbors so close, did you now? I see by that scowl on your face that you're still trying to puzzle it out. Look up ahead where Halfdane is waiting for us. I believe that will begin to explain who we are and where we have come from."

Halfdane waited alone on a windy hilltop, surrounded by a circle of ancient, staggering stones. Sigurd had seen such places before, and Thorarna had warned him away from them, saying they were places of great evil and misfortune. As Sigurd watched, Halfdane beckoned impatiently to his men. They rode up the hill in pairs and threes, passed through the circle of stones, and seemed to vanish into a wall of mist on the far side. Sigurd blinked his eyes, thinking it was a trick of the sun and the fog. They did indeed vanish right while he was looking at their stalwart backs, quivers, and bows.

"Wait," he muttered as they approached with the last group of three, but Rolfr only laughed, assuring him there was nothing to fear, as if disappearing were a commonplace event with him.

Halfdane fell into the rear position and followed them through the ring of stones. Sigurd turned to watch him warily, not trusting at all to have him at his back, and thus missed the instant when he and Rolfr passed through the circle. Although he looked back quickly for the weathered stones, he saw nothing of them—only a barren hilltop covered with a rubble of stones and moss. Attentively, Sigurd looked around at the landscape, realizing it was different from what he was accustomed to. It had a rugged, blasted look, as if the sparse covering of earth and grass had been clawed away, leaving only the bits of green turf and stunted trees that could scrabble out a meager living in small sheltered nooks. The high fells were capped with ice and veiled with waterfalls. Streams and small lakes made a silvery lacework of the black, rocky earth.

"Beautiful, isn't it?" Rolfr demanded cheerfully. "I'm always glad for this first sight of it whenever I have occasion to leave it for a while."

"Leave what?" Sigurd asked suspiciously.

"Why, the Alfar realm, of course. It isn't the moon, you fool. Your people might have called it the hidden realm, so that makes us the hidden people—hulderfolk, elves, whatever you call us—but we are properly called the Alfar. Ljosalfar and Dokkalfar; we, of course, are Ljosalfar, or we wouldn't be out here in the bright sunlight and we wouldn't be troubling ourselves with you, for certain. We'd have left you to the trolls." Rolfr favored Sigurd with a wide grin and a devilish wink. He was about the same age as Sigurd, with a sharp, ferrety face and deep-set, twinkling eyes, a sparse rusty beard, and a bony, elongated frame. Sigurd couldn't help staring at him, capable of thinking only that here was a genuine elf, alive and substantial.

"Can you do magic?" he inquired, awed in spite of himself.

"Magic? To be sure! I was born with magic in my blood," Rolfr declared. "Life would be terribly awkward without it. You must suffer dreadfully, blundering on blindly as you Sciplings do."

"We manage just fine," Sigurd snapped, "until someone starts making sendings against us and bestirring the trolls to attack us and all manner of evil tricks. I can't imagine a man or an Alfar following so willingly in the course of a monster like Halfdane."

Rolfr chuckled nervously and darted a quick glance at the warlord, who was riding not far ahead. "Warlords are a different species, I'll be the first to confess," he said in a low tone. "Halfdane is as fair as you could ask, as long as you don't cross him, but he won't tolerate insubordination. It's very strange, this business of Thongullsfjord; I don't understand why such an insignificant place has become such a bone of contention between Halfdane and Bjarnhardr, and why in particular they are both so keen about you and your grandmother. I know nothing about it. I'm only a warrior, but somehow I understand that something important for Halfdane has happened tonight."

"My grandmother told me that a warlord was my enemy," Sigurd said bitterly, "and I've seen the havoc he caused in his search for me. I'll not rest until I've finished my holmgang with him."

"But Halfdane wouldn't destroy Thongullsfjord. That's more the style of Bjarnhardr, the Dokkalfar warlord. At least I don't think he would—" Before Rolfr could continue, Dagrun rode alongside with a threatening expression on his face.

"Don't chatter, Rolfr," he said. "We don't know yet if this

Scipling should be a guest or a prisoner. You know you should learn to be cautious."

"No, I don't know it," Rolfr returned airily. "Dagrun, you are such a great toad of a fellow sometimes! I intend to befriend Sigurd, since he has lost everything familiar to him, except that little box he carries under his arm. That carving is too elegant to be done by a Scipling hand, Siggi. Wherever did you get a box so obviously carved in the Alfar realm?"

Sigurd looked at the box suspiciously, but before he could demand an explanation from Rolfr, Halfdane suddenly brought his horse sharply alongside and thrust his lowering face into Rolfr's and said in a threatening tone, "Rolfr, you talk far more than is good for you—or Hrafnborg. If you don't keep silent, I'll make you walk the rest of the way home."

With a final glower, Halfdane moved his horse away, but not out of earshot. Rolfr heaved a martyred sigh and hunched his shoulders; but whenever he thought Halfdane wasn't looking, he threw Sigurd a wink, and the expression in his eye was not daunted. Dagrun kept close, muttering worriedly to himself and shaking his head.

"I ought to have known better than to permit a stranger anywhere near Rolfr's jabbering," he lamented to Skeifr. "Halfdane will blame me for it. I wouldn't mind, if it weren't my fault."

Rolfr was hard put to remain silent for long, so he hummed bits of songs and would have whistled, but Dagrun silenced him after the first two notes.

"What a magpie you are, Rolfr," Dagrun said. "If you weren't the best bowman in the entire hill fort, Halfdane wouldn't tolerate you for half a day."

Rolfr grinned and preened himself proudly, keeping one eye on Halfdane all the while. Sigurd almost smiled, glad for the distraction Rolfr offered from his worries about his future.

When they finally came into view of Hrafnborg, Sigurd would not have recognized it as a hill fort if Dagrun hadn't pointed it out to him. A cluster of longhouses blended into the rocky knob of a windswept hill. Steep crags protected the hill on two sides, and an extensive earthwork encircled it on the other sides. Plumes of smoke curled lazily into the sky, and Sigurd heard an infrequent and faint bit of conversation or the clank of metal as the wind blew the sounds to them. It was like any Scipling settlement, he told himself, sternly refusing to confess to a sharp twinge of homesickness, mingled with the glad expectation of food and a safe place to rest.

Halfdane led the way through the earthwork, halting the procession at the doors of the firehall. Sigurd observed more men who looked like warriors and a large number of horses grazing on and around the earthwork. The wives and children of the warriors were waving from doorways, plucking geese and doing other homely chores, while the children did their best to get under the horses' hooves, and all the dogs came out to bark a welcome.

The riders dismounted before the hall, shook hands with their companions, and began to disperse, some homeward to their families and some into Halfdane's hall. Dagrun directed Sigurd into the hall, a dark, spacious place with raised platforms along the sides for sleeping, a great hearth at either end, several annexes for the kitchen, and other private quarters. Benches and tables were arranged down the center, and women were in the process of setting out a generous meal for the warriors who shared Halfdane's hall. Rolfr remained near Sigurd during the meal, grinning and winking at him and making faces at old Dagrun, who seemed determined to prevent Rolfr's talking much to Sigurd.

"Don't worry," Rolfr whispered, when Dagrun had to turn away to speak to someone else. "Alfar mutton is just as tough and greasy as Scipling mutton, I'll warrant. You needn't worry about eating an enchanted feast and falling forever under our power."

"As if I had a choice," Sigurd growled, darting a venomous glance at Skeifr, who hadn't seen fit to return Sigurd's weapons yet. "I'm starting to feel more like the prisoner and less like the guest. When can I talk to Halfdane again? I want to know what he plans to do with me." And whether Halfdane's reasons for bringing Sigurd to Hrafnborg were humanitarian or vengeful, he added mentally.

Rolfr nodded and winked at Sigurd in a manner meant to be reassuring. "I shall befriend you, so you've nothing to fear," he announced, ignoring the baleful eye bent upon him by Dagrun. "I shall see to it that you're quartered with me, instead of in this drafty old hall, and I'll be your teacher in the fine arts of weaponry and magic."

"And a worse teacher you'd never find anywhere," Dagrun interrupted irritably. "I'd turn you out on your ear, Rolfr, were I Halfdane, and think myself well rid of a nuisance. Why haven't you got it into your head yet that we're fighting for our very survival and for the very existence of the Ljosalfar as a people? You seem to think it's all an entertaining game invented specifically for your amusement. Either that or you're more than half mad."

Rolfr only grinned the merrier. "An excellent speech, Dagrun. I drink to you for your great tact and delicacy, and I—" He happened to glance up just as Halfdane came stalking through the hall, still clad in his dusty traveling garb. A wake of silence followed the warlord as he approached the table where Sigurd sat. He lowered at Rolfr, who suddenly seemed to remember an important errand he must run at once; he excused himself quickly and hurried away. Halfdane then looked at Sigurd.

"I trust you have refreshed yourself by now and rested somewhat?" he inquired in a gruff tone, fastening his eyes sternly upon Sigurd's resentful countenance.

"I have," Sigurd replied. "I hope you'll trouble yourself to explain further to me the meaning of what has happened to Thongullsfjord—and to me, also."

"I came for the purpose of fetching you away," Halfdane said. "Follow me and we shall talk, I hope. And bring your carven box with you."

# Chapter 3

◇◇◇◇◇◇◇◇◇◇◇◇◇◇◇◇◇◇◇◇◇◇◇◇◇◇◇◇◇◇◇◇◇

Sigurd's hand closed protectively around the box and he rose and followed Halfdane, with Dagrun treading at his heels. The young man scowled at the staring Alfar, knowing he looked like a guilty prisoner, an atrocious villain in ragged clothing stained with the blood of trolls and dust from traveling. He straightened his shoulders, resolving to maintain his pride at all costs.

The warlord's private quarters were near the end of the hall, behind a stout door studded with nails. A fire burned in a hearth, reflected a thousand times in the bright metal of weapons hanging on the walls and in the bright eyes of a pair of wolfish hounds, stretched at full length before the flames.

Halfdane pointed to a chair. "You may sit there, if you choose to relax your guard for a moment. I assure you we mean you no harm. On the contrary, we may be able to benefit one another, if I can convince you to forget your ill-informed prejudice against me."

"My grandmother was not ill-informed," Sigurd declared. "She told me I had enemies who were looking for me and would take me away somewhere. You don't deny that you have been looking for us for a long time."

"No," Halfdane said, "I won't deny it. Your grandmother hasn't been helpful in the least to my efforts, either. She's done her best to conceal from us the fact that a male heir has taken possession of that box you carry."

Sigurd glanced at the box, and its carved faces seemed to leer at him menacingly. "Am I to understand that there is something of considerable value inside this box which you wish to obtain?"

Halfdane eyed him darkly, his rugged features betraying no

emotion. "Whether I wish to obtain it or not isn't the question. But yet, it is rather valuable. If it fell into the wrong hands, much damage could be done to our cause. Many Ljosalfar could be destroyed. We are few and scattered, but we still fight and we desperately need what is inside that box."

"You'll never take it from me while I'm alive," Sigurd retorted. "I don't know what your cause is, but what I've seen has led me to suspect that you're all outlaws and you're hiding yourselves in hill forts for good reason. I don't have much sympathy for outlaws, particularly after what happened to Thongullsfjord. I can't believe that men of principle would destroy a settlement merely to take possession of one individual—or an object in a box." He looked at it with growing curiosity and a certain amount of alarm. What had his grandmother to do with outlaws and an object of such great value to them? He shook his head slightly as he tried in vain to puzzle it out.

Halfdane cast aside his cloak and paced up and down before the fire for a few moments, the firelight glinting on the nails in his belt and sword sheath. "You are a stranger to us and our ways," he said at last. "We are the Ljosalfar, or what was left of them after the Dokkalfar of Bjarnhardr overwhelmed Snowfell and scores of Ljosalfar hill forts. Yes, we are outlaws, because we are the remnants and we refuse to surrender. We strike back at Bjarnhardr at every opportunity, holding a very tenuous line between destruction and survival. We keep mainly to the high fells, where few Dokkalfar dare to approach. We are hunted and despised, but one day we hope to gain enough power to rout these usurpers from our homes and fortresses. We are desperate and we are few; there are only thirty-two hill forts left of a once-great kingdom that covered Skarpsey from end to end. Our enemies now hold all the lowlands and all the island except the highest fells. While we live, they cannot rest, knowing that the Ljosalfar never accept defeat easily.

"Thus it is that they, with their sendings and trolls, have destroyed your settlement in an effort to find the possessor of this box and kill him. The box and its contents would be used to finish the annihilation of the Ljosalfar, which would be speedily realized if Bjarnhardr possessed the object within.

"I sense my disadvantage in appealing to you, as an outsider, after you have seen the misfortune of Thongullsfjord—and after your grandmother unknowingly fortified your reason against us. She had good cause, but her message has been confused. Hrafnborg is not the origin of the sendings and Thongullsfjord's misfortunes, and you would know that, if your grandmother had been able to tell you the truth. I expect she kept the box a secret, and the first time you heard my name was when I told it to you myself. Am I correct?"

Sigurd maintained a stony silence. If they thought to discredit Thorarna in his eyes, they were bound to fail. Her last words had been spoken to warn him about the warlord, and he would bear her warning with him to his death, if necessary. Besides, he had begun to learn suspicion and knew that liars could be the most eloquent of speakers. He was also tired, overwrought, and in no mood to be convinced of anything.

Dagrun sighed impatiently. "I told you he'd never believe a word of anything we tried to tell him, Halfdane. Why is it that the emptiest heads are the most stubborn against anyone who wants to enlighten them? Why couldn't that old woman have done her duty, instead of trying to cheat us and deceive us—"

Sigurd made a sudden angry move that silenced him. "I won't listen to a stranger speaking ill of my grandmother. Whatever her reasons were for not telling me about the box, she must have thought they were good ones; and they no doubt were, since she was a person of rare good sense. I don't wish to hear anything more about it now and I prefer to form my own opinions about who is good and who is evil, whether it be Dokkalfar or Ljosalfar. For all I know, the Ljosalfar may be the most treacherous of fiends and the Dokkalfar the sensible people."

Dagrun shook his head with dismay and muttered under his breath, "I could convince him, if I had a heavy enough club, I'll warrant. The Dokkalfar sensible! I've never heard such a crock of foolishness—"

Halfdane looked scowlingly from Dagrun to Sigurd. "Then he'll have to find out for himself, if that's the way he wants it. It shouldn't take long for him to learn, if he survives the lessons. Very well, Sigurd, you are free to decide for yourself on whom to bestow the contents of that box. I won't burden you with any more unwanted advice, but allow me to say that the safest place for you right now is Hrafnborg. I won't keep you for nothing. You'll have to work to earn your bread and shelter. You'll have to be trained and outfitted before you're worth anything to us. Is that agreeable to you?"

"In the absence of alternatives, yes, I'm forced to say it's agreeable to me," Sigurd said, managing to convey the meaning that he thought quite the opposite.

"Good. We'll have no further disputes between us. I'll not be so foolish as to ask you to leave the box in my safekeeping, so I'll warn you to keep it well hidden." The furrows in Halfdane's dark brow revealed his displeasure as he gazed at Sigurd. "Dagrun, you shall find him a place in the hall and see to it that he has what he needs."

"That skittish Rolfr has offered to take him under his wing, but I don't think we ought to encourage it," Dagrun growled.

"To forbid it is to make it a certainty," Halfdane answered with a scornful curl of his lip. "Let him go with Rolfr then, but you make certain that some of Rolfr's excesses are hampered whenever possible. See to it our new comrade gets the instruction he needs, and presently we'll learn if he'll be useful to us." His eyes rested on the box under Sigurd's arm a moment as he made a gesture of dismissal. Dagrun started to withdraw, but Sigurd stood his ground.

"I have some questions I'd like answered," Sigurd said, returning Halfdane's disapproving scowl. "First I'd like to know what is in this box, and then you may tell me how you know it. Since it is my property, I think I should know as much about it as I can."

Halfdane's expression became thunderous and he stalked away, muttering a ferocious oath under his breath. Turning, he glared at Sigurd and said, "In spite of your own good opinion of yourself, you are yet rather green in skill and experience, as well as years. It would be wise for you to abandon such a haughty attitude, or you'll be humbled in ways that might not be pleasant. The contents of this box, which you so arrogantly lay claim to, will remain a secret until you or someone else is able to open it.

You see that the box is designed in such a way that it won't be opened by ordinary means. I won't tell you what is in it, because I can't trust you. All I shall say is that the box has returned to the people who made it, and you'd know what I'm talking about if your grandmother hadn't been a fearful and rather short-sighted old woman. Take it with you and begone; the next time we meet, I hope you'll have a little more sense." He nodded to Dagrun and sat down in a large chair before the fire with his back to his visitors.

Dagrun propelled Sigurd from the chamber and closed the door, muttering, "That's a fine show of gratitude, even for a Scipling. A worse case of conceit I never saw. Whatever is in that box, I'm sure you're not worthy of it. I hope you're not thinking of maybe running away from Hrafnborg. If you are, you'll have to match your wits against mine, and I'm a clever old dog, I assure you. I'll see to it everyone here knows your inclinations. You shall be restricted to the area within the earthwork to start with, unless you'd rather begin by being locked up for a while. How much freedom you continue to enjoy here depends upon your actions."

Sigurd surveyed Dagrun's authoritative posture and the menacing look of command in his eye and decided he had underestimated the man's authority, as well as his cunning. It would be difficult to escape with Dagrun so suspicious of him, but it was apparent that escape would be Sigurd's first priority, since Dagrun was already threatening him with imprisonment. The threat was likely to become action at a capricious whim of Dagrun's.

"I shall attempt to be sensible," he replied, with a touch of sarcasm. Dagrun raised one gingery eyebrow, but decided to let it pass for the present.

"Time alone will prove it," the Alfar answered gloomily and beckoned to Rolfr. "Come here, you jackdaw; I have an assignment for you."

Rolfr looked dismayed for a moment. "What have I done now? I thought I was reasonably blameless for once, Dagrun. Unless it was that witch Ragnhild," he added in a murmur.

"Never mind, you great calf. This Scipling is your assignment. I want you to billet him near you, and you're to keep both your eyes upon him so he doesn't foolishly wander into mischief.

I know I'm telling the goat to guard the grain, but you're the low man on the roster, and we can spare you the most easily from the patrols. It's senseless to try to advise you not to discredit Hrafnborg and Halfdane to this stranger, but I order you to win him over to our side and make him understand the desperate threat the Dokkalfar are to civilization in general. You do comprehend, don't you?"

Rolfr's expression changed from one of woe to astonishment and elation. He turned to Sigurd and shook his hand. "Well, then! You see, Siggi, I knew we'd become great friends. I'm sure we have a natural sympathy for one another. It will be a pleasure getting you settled. You'll share with old Adills and me, if you've no objection to a moldering cellar of a room, and old wizard, and sixteen dozen bats—and me, of course."

Sigurd had no time for any questions and managed only a parting scowl for Dagrun before Rolfr led him away on a tour of inspection over the entire hill fort. The houses and barns ranged from small wattle-and-daub huts to expansive longhouses where several families resided together, often accompanied by their horses and other livestock at one end. Sigurd observed watchmen everywhere on the earthwork and the cliffs; no approaching enemy could escape detection—nor could anyone conveniently depart by stealth.

Rolfr's quarters were in the sunken remains of an old round tower that had probably been on the site long before the hill fort. Most of the roof was gone, but that was no matter to Rolfr, since he lodged in what seemed to be a cellar beneath it. Plenty of light filtered through a large rent in the stone flooring overhead, where the supporting posts had rotted away and collapsed. Rolfr explained that he hung something over it in the winter; otherwise it was very convenient for letting out smoke when he wanted a fire and for looking at the stars.

Sigurd stumbled down a short flight of shifty stone steps and knocked his head on a beam, causing a sifting of dust to fall on him. The place seemed more like the inside of a well, furnished with beds, a table, and a tangled disorder of saddles, bows, and cloaks and boots. Seated at the table was a very old man, sitting primly upright and fast asleep with a book in his hands. The end of his beard lay across the book, and a cat was curled inside out on it, twitching in its sleep.

"Well, here it is. I hope you like it. You'll sleep over there," Rolfr said, pointing to a heap that might have concealed a straw tick. "Plenty of fresh air and light, lots of room if we move some of Adills' lumber around a bit, and nobody will bump you out because they've been fighting more years than you have. Nobody wants to share quarters with old Adills, and he's been here longer than anything, not to mention the bats."

"This is the wizard?" Sigurd lowered his voice and looked at Adills with awe.

"No need to lower your voice; when he's like that, he's deaf as a post. Older than the roots of Yggdrasil and forgetful as the middle of last week, but he'll still show you a thing or two. He's helping me study to be an apprentice to a wizard. Those are the bats." He nodded upward at the high gloomy recesses of the ceiling, where the bats hung in sober festoons. Their tiny eyes winked at Sigurd in the darkness.

Sigurd stepped back. "You must be crazy to want to stay in a place like this. It would be better to sleep on the floor in the hall than with all those bats. And that wizard—what's the matter with him? Are you sure he's not dead? A person can't sleep sitting up like that." He looked around him in contempt, feeling another clutch of homesickness as he compared the disorder to Thorarna's orderly way of doing things.

Rolfr shrugged, undisconcerted. "I'd rather have my own place, even if it is rather unusual, than no place of my own in Halfdane's hall. Sometimes I even do my own cooking down here; and in the winter, it's quite cozy. No drafts, you know. Adills doesn't mind the company, although the bats aren't friendly and sometimes they get noisy at night. I expect they've been here as long as Adills, and he's nearly fossilized. He won't bother you. He's very seldom awake. I haven't seen him move for over a week." He saw Sigurd's outraged expression and hastened to add, "Oh, don't worry about it, that's just the way wizards are sometimes. You know how bears hibernate, don't you?"

"How?" Sigurd demanded truculently, but Rolfr chose not to hear him and went on chattering about some sort of nonsense, constellations and falling stars and eclipses of the moon. Sigurd sat down experimentally on his bed, after shoving off some boots and an old horse cloth. He lay down, keeping the box under his arm, astonished at how wonderfully comfortable he suddenly felt. In a moment he was asleep, leaving Rolfr rattling on about cooking up a huge mess of something on their own fire, just the way it ought to be done, and not murdered the way Halfdane's cooks would do it.

When Sigurd finally awakened, he looked around at the unfamiliar room, trying to remember where he was. His reason struggled to deny that he was actually inside an Alfar stronghold in the hidden realm, but his eyes beheld the strange evidence in the form of old Adills, still sleeping bolt upright over his book at the table. Rolfr sat on the other side of the room, polishing a saddle and some boots.

As Sigurd watched, Rolfr pointed to a boot brush on the floor beside Sigurd and the brush promptly slithered across the beaten earth toward Rolfr. With a twitch of his shoulder, Rolfr closed the door behind him, which was making a draft, and a slight nod urged another stick of wood onto the small fire crackling invitingly in the center of the floor. He whistled softly to himself without looking up. In a moment he said, "Now that you've slept away a day and a half, don't you think it's time to get up and start learning to be an Alfar, Siggi? If you're going to stay with us, you may as well become one, don't you think?"

Sigurd sat up stiffly, stretching his exhausted muscles. "A day and a half I've slept? Well, I'm not surprised. I didn't get much rest with those trolls digging at the roof every night. If you think you can make an ordinary Scipling into an Alfar, you're perfectly welcome to try, but I don't think I'll ever be able to do the things I just saw you doing."

Rolfr's mouth fell open. "What? You mean polishing boots? There's nothing to it, Siggi. You just—"

"No, no. I meant all those little tricks you just did. Like shutting the door without touching it and making the brush come to you. That's rather spooky, Rolfr."

"Those are nothing," Rolfr exclaimed. "You should see some of the old Alfar, and Adills, and the other wizards. An infant can do these simple things, but it takes years of study and practice to get your power in your control, so you can do wonderful things like shape-shifting, treasure hunting, and repelling spells and curses. Or better yet, casting spells and curses. I should be an apprentice right now, but my family was too poor to get me articled, so I joined Halfdane. I am a tolerably good shot with a bow. When I've learned enough on my own, perhaps I can beg a decent wizard to let me work for my keep."

"What about Adills?" Sigurd nodded toward the old wizard.

"He's very helpful, but he spends most of his time in his fylgja form, spying upon the Dokkalfar. He teaches me when he can, and I pester Mikla to show me what he learns from Jotull. You'll have to get to know Mikla. He's not much older than we are and an admirable little fellow, when he can escape from Jotull long enough to have some fun."

"I'm simply starved, Rolfr. I'd rather have something to eat," Sigurd said a little irritably. "And you might remember that I'm not an Alfar, and I doubt if you can teach me much."

Rolfr pulled on his boots. "Halfdane's got a decent meal tonight, for a change. Sometimes he's too heavy on the bread and cheese and a little close with the meat, but last night's patrol killed a bear, so there's plenty of fresh meat for a while. You're not very pleased to be here, are you, Siggi?"

Sigurd averted his eyes, wondering if Alfar possessed the ability to read thoughts. If so, Rolfr would know that his only desire was to escape from the restrictions of Halfdane.

"No, I'm used to having my freedom," Sigurd replied. "No one has ever told me where I can't go or what I can't do. I get the idea that all of you men here are nothing but Halfdane's puppets. You certainly jump when he or Dagrun says leap."

Rolfr lost his benign expression for a moment. "Siggi, one important lesson you must learn in this realm is not to bite the hand that feeds you, or vice versa. I know the Sciplings have their earls and rulers; surely there was someone you owed fealty to."

"No, never, not even with the vikings," Sigurd replied proudly. "Thongullsfjord had no need of governors. We were all equals."

"I don't mind having Halfdane for a lord," Rolfr said, "although I do complain about the food and accommodations sometimes. In a desperate situation such as the Ljosalfar are in now, it's wise to ally yourself with someone far stronger. I know it must seem like a frightful loss of freedom to you, but it works out best in the long run for everybody."

Sigurd put on his cloak. "Let's go eat, shall we?"

They left Adills and the cat still sleeping soundly. A night patrol was leaving as they emerged from Rolfr's grotto. Twenty riders cantered past, exchanging insults in high spirits and bidding farewell to their companions who were staying behind. Sigurd looked to see if it was Halfdane leading them, with the notion that perhaps he might not be so well watched if Halfdane and Dagrun were gone.

"That's Alfgeirr's patrol," Rolfr told him. "It goes out six days and then rests here for six days for five turns; then Sjaundi's and Toki's patrols take five turns while Halfdane's and Alfgeirr's guard the hill fort. As soon as I'm off home duty, I hope you'll ride with Halfdane. I'll see to it you get a decent horse."

The hall was crowded with men noisily enjoying the company of their friends and the huge haunches of roast bear meat, charred black on the outside and pink and succulent on the inside. Rolfr cleared a space for them to sit, amid much good-natured banter on both sides and friendly nods to Sigurd from the others, who knew that nothing was more unwelcome to a stranger than questions and too much curiosity. The food and drink were excellent. As soon as Sigurd dispatched one slab of tender meat, someone flung another piece onto his plate with gruff generosity. The mitigating effects of the ale soon convinced him that the Alfar were the finest, jolliest fellows he had ever known. Once he glanced toward the dais where Halfdane and Dagrun and other important Alfar sat and met the warlord's baleful gaze with a haughty stare. It was then that he discovered a girl sitting among the grizzled warriors and wearing the same arrogant expression as Halfdane. She was richly dressed in red, with a fine shawl over her shoulders fastened with a large brooch; she wore her hair in a coil of braids around her head.

"Who's that? His daughter?" Sigurd asked Rolfr.

"No, you dolt, that's a cousin of his. She's here because the rest of her family is dead and Halfdane is her only relation. Her name is Ragnhild, and I'm madly in love with her, although she does have the worst disposition you can imagine. If she were a berserkr, she'd have all of Skarpsey quivering in terror. Her temper makes all the milk in the dairy go sour if she just walks past the open door. I think she had a troll for a nurse to learn such savagery." Rolfr smiled and sighed in admiration. "She hates me from the depths of her very soul and never fails to do me the most abominable tricks. She's done me a particularly grievous wrong lately, Siggi, and I want you to help me get even with her. I happened to commit a regrettable mistake last week and she was tattling to Halfdane almost before I knew what I'd done. She is delighted whenever she can get me into trouble. You see, I'm also a poor and distant relative of Halfdane's, and she thinks I'm not quite as good as the dirt under her feet."

Sigurd shook his head. "You must be crazy, Rolfr. You say you're madly in love with this creature?" He looked at Ragnhild and found her unfriendly gaze fixed upon him, as if she had guessed what Rolfr was saying. Sigurd had never encountered such an alert and terrible gaze since Trygvi's vicious old bull had chased him.

"Yes, indeed, Siggi. One day she'll tire of abusing me and begin to admire me for my persistence. But in the meantime, you've got to help me humiliate her. I have an excellent plan."

Sigurd looked away from Ragnhild's challenging glare. "I don't think I want to get involved in your petty broils with Ragnhild. It sounds like madness to me."

"Nonsense. She's a very clever opponent. It will be well worth your while matching wits with her." Then he changed the subject to Mikla, the apprentice to the wizard Jotull. Before Sigurd was quite aware how it happened, he was trudging up the steep hillside behind the rest of the longhouses and huts toward the solitary house where Jotull lived.

"Now, I may as well warn you," Rolfr said, stopping to catch his breath after the rather steep climb. "Jotull is about as disagreeable a fellow as you'd care to meet anywhere. He can't abide nonsense of any sort, which is why he hates me so much, I suppose. He keeps Mikla working late hours almost every night and can scarcely bear to let him off for an hour. What I hope is that

Jotull isn't here tonight. He goes off prowling, much like old Adills, and Mikla and I have had some merry times in his absence. Once we got into some books of spells Jotull keeps locked away and we learned how to raise a corpse out of the grave. It took us all night to wrestle the creature back in before it killed us."

"And that's what you call fun?" Sigurd demanded. "I want no part of anything to do with draugar!"

"Oh, it was just a passing fancy. Necromancy and the evil arts are best left alone. We were just being mischievous. Now hush and let's creep up on the house and try to look in for Jotull. If he's there, we won't be visiting Mikla." He beckoned, leading the way around the corner of a low turf house.

They paused beside the door, which was open a crack to let in some cool air. A fire blazed inside, illuminating a young man beside the hearth, reading in a thick book.

"There's Mikla, and not a sign of Jotull," Rolfr whispered. "But just to be certain—" He scratched softly at the door, and Mikla looked up intently.

"Who's there?" he called, taking up his staff warily.

"Just me," Rolfr whispered. "Is the old dragon gone? I've brought the Scipling for you to meet."

Mikla opened the door in two strides. "Come in, come in. I heard about Halfdane bringing back a Scipling. How do you do? I'm Mikla and I hope you'll like it in Hrafnborg for as long as you decide to stay."

Sigurd liked his quiet, serious demeanor. "Thank you. My name is Sigurd. Hrafnborg is a different place from what I've been accustomed to, but otherwise it seems very pleasant. Not as much freedom as I would like, and I'm not quite sure what the difference is between Ljosalfar and Dokkalfar yet, but I'm sure I shall learn quickly."

"Worlds of difference! Come in, and I'll tell you whatever you want to know, and a good deal extra besides." Mikla pointed out chairs to sit on and began passing around a clay bottle of something that turned Sigurd's legs to lead and his brains to fire. He felt he had never understood anything so clearly as Mikla's words about the Ljosalfar and Dokkalfar, but when Mikla paused for him to ask questions, he couldn't remember a thing.

"I'm still not convinced," he heard himself say stupidly—stubbornness was a good camouflage for ignorance, he had discovered. "I don't even know what that thing is inside the carven box, so how am I supposed to decide who should have it?" He knew he was talking too much, but the effects of the fire and the ale and whatever was in the clay bottle combined to make him rattle on willy-nilly.

"I suppose it's something very valuable, but not gold because it isn't at all heavy. What I wonder the most is how my grandmother came to possess something belonging to the Alfar realm. When she was dying, she tried to tell me about something, but all I learned from it was the name of her daughter who's dead twenty years, and I suppose she must have been my mother. She might have known where the box came from, if she had lived. Strange to think she was about my age when she died. Her name was—"

He was seized suddenly by a yawn, and Mikla looked apprehensively toward the door and thrust the bottle under his cloak. Sigurd finished, "Ashildr." He felt too sleepy to continue, but his drowsiness fled when the door suddenly creaked open and the wizard Jotull stepped into the room.

Rolfr leaped up in fright. "Sorry to have disturbed you, Mikla, we were just leaving. Pleasant to see you, Jotull. Hope you've had a jolly trip. We won't trouble you any longer with the nuisance of our presence, if you'll kindly—"

Jotull remained in the doorway, blocking it effectively. He silenced Rolfr by thrusting him aside with his staff so he could take a better look at Sigurd.

Sigurd looked back at him, fascinated by the thought that he was face to face with a practicing wizard. The wizard was a tall, imperious-looking fellow, black-bearded and elegantly clad in black from head to foot. His eyes held Sigurd's with an expression of glad recognition. Jotull closed the door, dropped his satchel in a corner, and flung off his cloak.

"No, no, you needn't leave just yet," he said with a smile. "Sit down and let's become better acquainted. I've long had a great regard for the Scipling realm and its inhabitants. Mikla, bring us something to make our visit a little more pleasant and our house more hospitable."

Rolfr shrank into a chair, making no attempt to conceal his astonishment as Jotull commenced to chat comfortably with Sigurd. Sigurd soon lost his awe of the great man, and before their hour-long visit was over, he was convinced that he had found a friend and an ally in Hrafnborg.

# Chapter 4

Jotull took an amazing interest in Sigurd's welfare. In the days to come, he saw to it that Sigurd received the best teachers to instruct him in the crafts of warfare and promised to be Sigurd's teacher in magical skills. Rolfr could scarcely contain his amazement and glee, immediately extorting the promise from Sigurd that he'd promptly teach Rolfr everything he learned. Rolfr had established himself as Sigurd's satellite and basked in the reflected glow of Jotull's favorite at every opportunity.

"I'm not sure I want to learn magic," Sigurd said uneasily when he presented himself for his first lesson from Jotull, with Rolfr accompanying him. "Sciplings don't possess any magic by nature, as you Alfar do. I fear you'll be rather disappointed with such a slow and stupid pupil as I suspect I'll be." He looked around Jotull's workroom, which was cluttered with the substance of many experiments. Mikla nodded at him encouragingly and went on grinding something with a mortar.

Jotull folded his arms and shook his head reprovingly. "That's not the attitude to begin with, or you're defeated before you try. There's nothing supernatural about magic, as you Sciplings believe. It's merely the physical evidence of your own powerful belief in your own capabilities. I think you'll be astonished at how easy it is, once you try it. You'll be able to move inanimate objects, find lost objects, remove or resist spells and curses, blunt the weapons of your enemies, or transport yourself through space. Or change your form at will. But those are highly advanced skills for wizards, and occasionally the apprentices of wizards. Most average Ljosalfar don't get much beyond casting very simple spells, and their idea of resisting curses is to carry a collection of amulets and the most popular talisman—a dried hawk's foot or some such nonsense."

Sigurd observed Rolfr going through his pockets and pouches and throwing away his amulets and dried charms with disgust. "I'll do my best. I covet the skills of magic, and they would make me less dependent in this realm if I learned even the basic ones."

Jotull looked pleased. "Yes, you've no need to be dependent if you learn your lessons well."

Sigurd wondered if he was referring to the carven box. He would speak to Jotull about it soon and ask him his advice, when Rolfr wasn't around to carry tales back to Halfdane.

The first lessons in magic were dull enough. Jotull taught him how to write in runic, as well as how to read what he had written.

"You learn very quickly," Jotull said, when Sigurd had mastered the scratchy figures. "I can't recall a more promising student. If you continue as you've begun, I shall hope for great success for you."

Mikla and Rolfr looked at each other in silent wonder. Neither of them would dream of receiving such praise from Jotull, knowing well he wouldn't deign to notice them unless they had done something absolutely stupendous, like floating Hrafnborg in midair for a week or more.

"I think we've done enough with the runes for now," Jotull continued, taking up his elegantly carved staff and giving its silver knob a quick polish, much like a cat giving its coat two or three quick licks to reassure itself how handsome it was. "Let's go outside now and we'll talk about some direct effects.

Perhaps you can even try a few for yourself. Mikla, I want you to come along for the exercise. You need some fresh air in those Guild-pickled brains of yours and some color in your book-blanched face, so you'll look more like a man than a vegetable that's been kept down cellar too long." He smiled at his joke, but Mikla took umbrage at once and looked sulky. "Takes himself far too seriously," Jotull muttered to Sigurd as they left the house. "The Wizards' Guild is a very good school, but its graduates tend to think a great deal more of themselves than they ought to."

Rolfr cleared his throat apologetically. "I don't mean to interfere, Jotull, but Halfdane doesn't want Sigurd to leave the hill fort. Maybe we ought to inquire first if—"

"Inquire?" Jotull asked in an odd tone, fixing Rolfr with a sharp stare. "If Sigurd is safe with anyone, it ought to be me. I am teaching lessons in magic and I don't want the petty demands of a mere warlord interfering. I hope you have the good judgment not to earn my wrath and disappointment by carrying tales to Halfdane." He said it very jovially, with evident good humor, but Rolfr was effectually silenced as they descended the hill toward the earthworks.

Jotull strode past the guards without a glance at them and led the way through the opening in the earthworks to the meadows and fells outside. Sigurd was delighted to see something else besides the same views of barns and longhouses inside the earthworks. The last light of the sinking sun lingered on the steep, green fells, softening them with shades of blue, and the rising mist made them seem almost transparent.

When they were about a hundred yards from the earthworks, Jotull stopped and leaned upon his staff, gouging its point into the soft, green moss. "We'll begin with a demonstration of power. Mikla, I hope you can oblige us with a simple example of your art. You don't need to astonish us with your extraordinary Guild education; just an easy demonstration will suffice."

"I am glad to comply with your wishes," Mikla said, with a solemn and deferential nod; "but you must surely be aware

that Halfdane gave orders for Sigurd to stay within the earthworks and boundaries of the hill fort."

Jotull merely sniffed and shrugged. "Can the Scipling be in
any danger as long as I am here? If I need to, I shall explain
to Halfdane that I am conducting lessons and I don't tolerate
interference and interruptions. Now, sir, are you sufficiently
disburdened of your useless admonitions so you can proceed?"

Mikla patiently levitated a few rocks, sent for some sticks
and set them afire without benefit of a tinderbox, found a gold
coin that Sigurd hid, and performed other schoolboy tricks, as
Jotull disdainfully called them. Then, for good measure, Mikla
conjured a fire show, a dazzling production of multicolored
flames shooting from an upright stone as if the bare, black
surface were exploding with flowers.

"Very pretty," Sigurd said admiringly, looking at Mikla with
new respect. "That's real fire, isn't it, and not just illusion?"

Mikla crisped several mossy boulders and set a small bush
ablaze, which Jotull promptly extinguished. "A Guild apprentice never loses an opportunity to show off," he said. "That's
quite enough, Mikla. We shall now allow Sigurd to attempt a
spell."

"I'd like to learn the formula for fire," Sigurd answered.
"I've spent many a night shivering and freezing, wishing I
could make a fire from nothing."

"Fire is better left to the experienced," Jotull said sharply,
just as Mikla began to say, "It's very easy—" A glance silenced
the apprentice. "Now, Sigurd, I shall teach you a simple formula for summoning objects to you. You shall write it in runic
in the sand and use your powers of concentration to make it
work, as I have taught you."

Sigurd tried and tried repeatedly, despite the fact that he
felt rather foolish mumbling over some scratches in the dirt
and staring hopelessly at a small rock that he hoped to move.
The rock did not budge, little to his surprise. He thought he
detected a glint of mirth in Mikla's eye, which made him
suddenly furious.

"I can't do it with everyone staring at me!" he flared, starting
to stamp away, but the rock suddenly flew up in the air and

came down nearly on Rolfr's head. Rolfr sprang away with a yelp, and even Jotull looked astonished, gaping around to see if someone hiding nearby had thrown the rock as a joke. Mikla permitted himself an injudicious chuckle. Sigurd was embarrassed and hastened to apologize.

"Things like that happen when I get into a black mood," he said gloomily. "Sometimes I think I'm followed by an evil little sending with a strange sense of humor. When I was a boy, it helped me win a lot of fights, however." He sighed and shook his head. "I'd rather hoped it wouldn't follow me into this realm, whether it's a sending or simply bad luck."

"It's your power trying to help you," Mikla said excitedly. "All you have to do is get control of it and persuade it to act in your best interests. You say it's been with you all your life?"

"Silence, sir," Jotull interrupted sternly. "I am the practicing wizard here, you might recall. If Sigurd needs any advice, I shall be the one to give it to him. I've seen this sort of power before and it's not the right sort at all. We'll have to capture it and put it in a safe place where it won't trouble you any longer, Sigurd. It could be quite dangerous, you know." He glanced around suspiciously for more dangerous symptoms of Sigurd's unlucky follower. "Come, it's time we went back inside."

He led the way, and Mikla and Rolfr trailed behind, holding an intense whispered conversation. Sigurd took no notice of them; he was listening to Jotull's plans for capturing his unruly power and disposing of it. Jotull assured him it would not be painful and that he was better rid of it, since it would only get in the way of his future studies.

Mikla lingered at the old round tower, allowing Jotull to proceed up the hill to his house alone. "I haven't had a look at old Adills in quite a while," he said to Rolfr. "Is there any change in him yet?"

"No, indeed," Rolfr said. "Come in and see for yourself. He's been gone so long he's getting dusty." He led the way into their dingy quarters and lit a candle. Mikla closed the door securely and muttered a spell over it.

"You'll have to teach me the eavesdropper spell sometime,"

Rolfr said with an envious sigh. "There's so much that I'd like to learn, if we only had the time."

Mikla seemed to be thinking of something else. He paced around the table several times, bending anxious looks upon Adills, who looked as peacefully and mildly at rest as any carven statue.

"I wish Adills would come back," Mikla said with a frown. "He doesn't know how we need him now. Sigurd, you admire Jotull very much, don't you?"

"Somewhat," Sigurd answered guardedly.

Mikla rubbed his hands together while he was thinking and laced his fingers when he spoke. "Jotull is new here. I came here as Adills' apprentice, but, as you can see, Adills isn't the most attentive master, so I puttered around by myself and enjoyed it tremendously until Halfdane decided to summon another wizard to watch over the affairs of the hill fort while Adills went a-roving. We don't know where Jotull came from, but I can tell you he's no Guild wizard, the ones who are the best and most loyal to the Alfar of Snowfell. He might be from one of the smaller fire wizards' schools, but I don't think so." He paused to let Sigurd question him, fixing his listeners with his most solemn stare, which would be impressive on an older, stouter frame, but now looked rather top-heavy on his slender form.

"Well? Where do you think he came from?" Sigurd demanded.

"I can't say for certain, but I have my suspicions—Halfdane being who he is."

"Who is he, then?" Sigurd found Mikla's ponderous, portentious attitude annoying.

Mikla folded his arms to explain. "Halfdane made a vow with his own blood that he would kill Bjarnhardr; if he failed, someone of his kin would do it. Bjarnhardr killed Halfdane's wife and family when he destroyed the original Hrafnborg, which used to lie far to the east and north of here. Halfdane has a pair of gauntlets made for him by the Dvergar—the black dwarfs, who can make almost anything magical. He'll use the gauntlets' power to help him kill Bjarnhardr, and everyone knows how desperately grim Halfdane is once he has sworn to do something. If the Dokkalfar were worried about their leader being killed by Halfdane, they might endeavor to destroy Halfdane first by spies and treacherous means."

"And you think Jotull may be a spy?" Sigurd chortled. "For a moment I thought you had something intelligent to say, Mikla. I know you hate Jotull, but I think your imagination or resentment is working overlong and late. He's a great wizard, even if he is rather hard on you and anyone else inferior to him. Unless you've got proof, you shouldn't make accusations like that. If he ever hears about it, you'll be obliged to duel him, and I daresay he'll cook your goose in half an instant."

Mikla smiled a strange, dark smile. "Not if he's a Dokkalfar, Siggi. Dokkalfar don't do fire spells."

Sigurd thought of Mikla's fire demonstration a moment. "But Jotull says there's no real distinction between Ljosalfar and Dokkalfar any longer. He says they're all Dokkalfar, and it is true that Halfdane does all his prowling and patrolling at night, not in the daytime."

"Bjarnhardr's men are out at night," Rolfr said. "Why should he search for them in the daylight hours?"

Sigurd shook his head. "Then that sounds to me like you're all Dokkalfar—dark elves—and there are no longer any light elves."

Rolfr and Mikla exchanged a startled glance. "No, it can't be," Mikla said, conjuring a knob of glowing green flame on the end of his staff. "If I were a Dokkalfar I couldn't conjure fire."

"Many of your so-called Ljosalfar can't conjure flame," Sigurd said. "A good many of them know scarcely any magic at all, except for the simple spells like those Rolfr does. I think Jotull is more correct than any of you like to think. He tells me that the Alfar of Bjarnhardr live in beautiful halls and possess a great deal of wealth. They don't worry about attacking and destroying anyone, as Halfdane does, and they're not required to hole themselves up in wretched places like Hrafnborg, where we live in suspicion and fear from day to day. Jotull says there's no real reason for hiding; the other Alfar wouldn't harm you if you did wish to abandon this windswept place and move to the lowlands. The exile seems to be voluntary on the part of Halfdane and the other outlaw chieftains hiding in these hills."

Rolfr and Mikla looked at each other in dismay. Mikla spoke. "I can easily see how the situation might look that way to an outsider, and you are still an outsider, Siggi, although we don't hold it against you. I'm not going to try changing your mind, but I hope you will at least remember that some things are not as they might appear. Just when you think you have the truth in your grasp, it suddenly changes to something else. You are now in the springtime of your friendship with Jotull, and everything looks best in spring, we all agree. But think of autumn and winter. I've never known Jotull to cultivate the association of any man; he's far too haughty for that. I think he wants something from you, Sigurd. You'd better be sure you want to give it to him."

Sigurd gazed reflectively at the loose flagstone in the floor, which, unknown to anyone except himself, harbored the carven box. "I think that Jotull only wants to help me make a respectable life for myself in your realm. Perhaps as his apprentice you wish he would regard you with the same good friendship."

"No, no, I don't want him for a friend," Mikla said quickly. "I think I'd better leave before he gets suspicious and comes looking for me. The last thing I wish to say to you, Siggi, is to guard that rowdy power of yours, and never let anyone take it away from you. They won't be doing you any favor, I promise you."

Sigurd shrugged, feeling uncomfortable with such earnestness. "Oh, it's nothing except an amusing nuisance. It doesn't really trouble me that much, so perhaps I'll just continue to live with it. Say, Mikla, if you've got the evening free, you ought to come to the hall and watch Rolfr lose something gambling. He lost his saddle last night; and if he doesn't win it back, he's going to get saddle sores from what he's issued when he rides out again."

Rolfr groaned. "I'd nearly forgotten. Come, what do you say, Mikla? It'll be highly amusing, no doubt."

Mikla shook his head. "Jotull doesn't believe I have any time of my own to waste. I'll see you tomorrow, Siggi. Remember what I've said." With a last earnest scrutiny of Sigurd's countenance, he took his leave.

Even Rolfr looked solemn, subdued perhaps by the seriousness of his friend. Sigurd shrugged his shoulders and began to feel better the moment Mikla was gone. He spent the remainder of the night gambling, or watching Rolfr gambling away more of his possessions. Before many hours had passed, he had almost forgotten Mikla's peculiar warning and his admiration for Jotull remained unabated.

He had adjusted rather well to the Alfar schedule, which consisted of patrolling and socializing mainly at night and using the daytime for sleeping, when less vigilance for their night-prowling enemies was required. Thus it was that Sigurd was sound asleep when someone began pounding on the cellar door shortly after dawn, and no amount of ignoring would dissuade their unwelcome visitor.

"Go away!" Rolfr shouted angrily. "Can't you see it's broad daylight and everyone's asleep?"

"Halfdane wants to see the Scipling at once," came the hoarse reply. "He won't tolerate waiting, so you'd better hurry yourselves out of this wretched hole before he gets impatient."

"Halfdane!" Sigurd muttered in annoyance, finding his boots with difficulty. If the Alfar were adept at anything, it was the art of dissipation. Drinking and gambling occupied almost everyone's off-duty hours, although Halfdane attempted to keep free time to a minimum, knowing well the propensities of his followers.

When Sigurd and Rolfr presented themselves at the hall, Jotull greeted them in a solemn, kindly manner. To Sigurd's surprise, Rolfr flushed crimson and angrily turned his back, saying, "You don't need to patronize me, Jotull. You know who it was that told Halfdane about your taking Sigurd outside the hill fort against his orders. I'm not fooled by your pleasant manners."

Jotull looked aggrieved as he smoothed his beard. "I wouldn't have thought it of you, Rolfr. Haven't I always been perfectly

civil to you and to everyone since I came to Hrafnborg? Surely
you didn't think I would do Sigurd any harm, did you?"

"Well, no, not really, but Mikla thought—I mean, it seems
to me that you shouldn't tamper with Sigurd's natural power.
It's unusual for a Scipling to have power, true enough, but, if
he were an Alfar, you wouldn't dream of trying to capture his
natural powers, unless you wished him ill. Even a Scipling is
entitled to his powers."

Jotull sighed and raised his eyes to the sky. "It seems to
me that a spiteful young apprentice and an unproven novice
warrior are no judges of wizards' business and ought to keep
their noses out or they are likely to get burned."

"Or frozen." The words escaped Rolfr's lips involuntarily,
and he looked alarmed at his ill-advised speech.

Jotull shifted his staff to one hand. "Whatever do you mean
by that remark? Do you think I'm a Dokkalfar wizard, standing
here in full sunlight and not harmed?"

Rolfr glowered back at the wizard. "Not only Dokkalfar
serve the Dokkalfar, as you well know. I didn't mean to accuse
you of any disloyalty to Halfdane, but Mikla—well, never
mind Mikla. He's a fool sometimes and I'm another," he added
quickly as Jotull tapped his staff on the ground a few times.

Sigurd scowled disapprovingly at Rolfr. "How can you say
such things about Jotull? No one else but Mikla speaks ill of
Jotull in all of Hrafnborg. Didn't he heal Holti of that dreadful
chill? And what about last week when he had the premonition
to warn the patrol not to use the river crossing?"

"Enough, Sigurd, I can bear a little false accusation," Jotull
said, bestowing a wounded glance upon Rolfr. "Let's go inside
and confess my misdemeanors to our chieftain. Halfdane must
always be correct, you realize." He opened the door and motioned Sigurd and Rolfr to enter before him.

"But I thought Jotull had some authority around here," Sigurd said. "Not to mention the fact that he'd protect me if any
hostile Alfar should appear."

Halfdane, Dagrun, and the other leaders stood before the
fire in the great hearth. Halfdane looked around and demanded,

"What's this I hear about your leaving the protection of the hill fort, Sigurd? You recall I expressly forbade it."

Sigurd bridled immediately, but Jotull put a hand on his arm before he could speak. "I will explain," the wizard said, averting his eyes from Halfdane's rather frayed riding cloak and worn boots with a delicate shudder. "The fault is entirely mine, but I don't wish to be reprimanded with half the fortress watching. Can't we talk more privately?" He glanced politely at Dagrun and the others, who were listening and staring with all their might.

Halfdane nodded, turned, and stalked into his adjoining quarters, where he took a stance before the hearth, bending his dark, lordly gaze upon his visitors. "When I give an order, I expect no abrogation from anyone, and the order stands in its entirety until I declare otherwise. The Scipling is not to leave the confines of the hill fort under any circumstances, except a total rout if we were under attack. Perhaps you did not know of my wishes, Jotull. I prefer to think you were merely ignorant, rather than willfully insubordinate." His voice and his expression were scornful as he added, "I don't see the need for Sigurd to be taught much magic. Your time is better invested elsewhere. Let your apprentice show him a few tricks, if he can learn them."

Jotull knit his brows and came a step closer. "As you wish, of course, but Sigurd has a natural power which plagues him with its capriciousness. It is only a matter of time until it becomes dangerous to him and perhaps even to the rest of us. I would like to capture it and get rid of it."

"You'll do nothing of the sort," Halfdane replied, turning sharply to look at Jotull. "Leave his training to me and attend to your own business of wizarding us away from extinction at the hands of the Dokkalfar. There will be no more of your lessons. You may depart, Jotull. I'm finished with you."

Jotull clasped his hands around his staff and darted a look at Sigurd. "My lord, I think you are making a mistake. Consider the might and power of Bjarnhardr for a moment and how small our chance of repelling his winter campaign again this year. I happen to know the secret you're keeping from Sigurd and I think you should tell him at once what you know."

"Wizard! Keep your silence!" Halfdane commanded in a tone that made everyone flinch.

"I shan't," Jotull replied earnestly. "It's in the best interest of Hrafnborg that Sigurd knows who—"

Halfdane had listened with his hands clasped behind his back, but suddenly he brought one hand forward and pointed at Jotull. Sigurd staggered back as a great force thrust against him in passing, catching Jotull off guard and flattening him with a heavy crash. Gasping, the wizard recovered his dignity quickly, making a quick plunge to retrieve his staff, but Halfdane blasted it across the room with a flick of his finger. Sigurd stared at the black gauntlet he wore, remembering Mikla's mention of it. The cuff was heavily embroidered with gold and silver thread and studded with silver nails.

"You may leave, Jotull," Halfdane continued steadily. "I shall send a boy up later with your staff."

For a moment, Jotull's face was a mask of rage and humiliation; then he composed himself to his customary steely grace. "Very well. I shall thank you for it. I won't soon forget your kindness." With a slight, stiff nod he departed.

Sigurd and Rolfr gazed at each other in silent amazement. Sigurd was transfixed by the utter hatred he had glimpsed in Jotull's eyes. He knew better than to inquire what secret Halfdane withheld from him, but he was certain it concerned the box.

Halfdane removed the gauntlet and put it under his belt. "I trust that you neither one will hasten to carry tales to the men that Halfdane and Jotull have quarreled. For your own assurance, I shall tell you that Jotull and I frequently disapprove of one another and engage in matches of wits that uninformed observers might construe as battles." He beckoned to Jotull's staff and brought it to his hand, examining it with minute interest. "The only way to win the respect of a powerful and haughty wizard is to frighten him periodically. He overreaches as a matter of course, which brings us to you, Sigurd."

Sigurd eyed Halfdane, disliking him more than ever for

humiliating Jotull in front of him and Rolfr. "I suppose you mean to say that learning magic is forbidden to me now?"

Halfdane glared at him from under a hedge of beetling brows. "Mikla can show you what you need to know for everyday purposes. What I have in mind for you is something quite different. You've been wasting too much time with the Alfar—very good fellows, all of them, but they'd be lost in a day without someone to tell them what to do almost every minute of their lives. So I've decided to forbid you to the hall beyond an hour after the evening meal. It won't be of any consequence to you; you'll be far too tired after your daily schedule of lessons in weaponry. I also think it expedient to assign you to a daily stint of guard duty. That should keep you busy and out of mischief, as well as out of Jotull's way."

Rolfr shot Sigurd a commiserating glance. Assignment to the day watch was a great disgrace for a warrior. Old women and young lads usually watched in the daylight hours, and often it was hot and always it was dull. The worst part about it was the fact that one could not stand watch all day long and expect to hobnob with his cronies at night or to ride patrol. No punishment affected the lighthearted Alfar more adversely than the curtailment of their social life.

"Then I'll take the day shift also," Rolfr said, after only a slight hesitation. "Don't worry, Siggi, I won't mind it."

"It was good of you to volunteer, Rolfr," Halfdane said. "It spares me the necessity of ordering you to do it. You'll spend your mornings with your instructors and your afternoons on the earthworks. One day in ten for liberty and one hour every night after the meal. Sigurd, I won't expressly forbid your friendship with Jotull, but neither will I encourage it, understand? If so, you may go to Skefill now for your first lesson."

Rolfr's mouth fell open. "But—you mean for us to begin right now, after only a few hours' sleep?"

Sigurd nudged him sharply and said in a bitter tone, "Why not, Rolfr? We're not children and we won't complain."

"Not half as much as old Skefill will," Rolfr muttered as they left the hall. Sigurd looked back at Halfdane, who glowered after them in his own peculiarly disagreeable manner.

Nothing matched the dreariness of the day schedule of Hrafnborg. Once their lessons with Skefill were over, there was nothing to do but watch the shepherd boys tending their sheep on the neighboring fells, the hobbled horses grazing around the earthworks, and a little girl whose job it was to tend a flock of geese. Sigurd learned to beguile the time by practicing his limited knowledge of magic. Much against the better wishes of Rolfr, Sigurd spent his free hour at night with Jotull, who taught him a short lesson in power each night. As a result, Sigurd was plagued more than ever by the malicious ill luck that followed him. Whenever he was uncomfortable or near someone he didn't like, such as Halfdane, straps and strings had a way of breaking, hanging objects fell to the ground, flies made the horses kick, and anything in his hands seemed to leap away on a mission of destruction and embarrassment to Sigurd.

Ragnhild was as good as a magnet for untoward occurrences. She began to take notice of Sigurd the day after Halfdane's chastisement and subsequent assignment to the day shift. She walked past Sigurd on the earthworks each day as part of her constitutional. For eight days, she only looked at him coldly and marched on, like a queen looking at a low specimen of bog creature. After withering him with her silent scorn, she walked to the stable, where her particularly fine horse awaited her. With the attendance of three archers, she left the hill fort for a ride to the end of the valley. Bees seldom failed to appear, making her horse skittish, or small rocks pelted her or her horse or the attendants. At the very least, a wicked little gust of wind buffeted her hair and tumbled her cloak. Sigurd didn't particularly wish it, but he couldn't help feeling flustered and uneasy when she made such a point of presenting herself to his notice. He couldn't imagine any attachment on her side, and he had no delusions about trying to win the kinswoman of Halfdane, even if Rolfr hadn't already claimed that dubious privilege. But she was handsome in her arrogant fashion, he had to admit.

On the ninth day, she stopped to glare at him and Rolfr. "I know it's you that annoys me every day when I ride out," she said to Sigurd. "I want you to stop it immediately or I shall tell my cousin Halfdane you're being a nuisance."

Sigurd felt his hackles rising at her commanding tone. He tried to stare her down, but she only lifted her chin and looked down her nose with freezing disdain. "It has nothing to do with Sigurd," Rolfr declared. "Your difficulties probably arise from your own deficiencies. Jotull says that a naturally evil personage attracts misfortune the way a lodestone attracts iron."

Ragnhild scowled at Rolfr, then reached out and pinched his nose hard enough to make him shriek. "You've a long nose, Rolfr. Next time I might twist it off if you dare to grin at my expense again." With that, she turned and stalked away, leaving Rolfr to rub his afflicted nose and blink his watering eyes. Sigurd leaped up to look after her, marveling at her casual audacity.

"You see, Siggi? She's a villainous little witch," Rolfr said with a wry smile. "We've got to get even with her somehow. Wouldn't I love to see her embarrassed and all that arrogant pride mortified almost to death? What I want most of all is just to laugh and laugh and laugh at her. I want something that will humiliate her for the rest of her life. I rather think that would improve her character markedly."

Sigurd began to smile. "I think I know how we can do it." He hesitated, looking after Ragnhild as she advanced upon the horse paddock but relishing Rolfr's impatient exclamations. "I'll ask Jotull for his advice."

Rolfr's expression changed. "Jotull? Do you think you should? I mean, do you think you dare?"

"Certainly. He's a very amiable fellow once you get to know him. I think he'd do almost anything I asked him."

Rolfr frowned and rubbed his chin, where young whiskers grew in untidy tuffets. "Well, it can't be anything too hard on her. She's Halfdane's cousin, after all, and I am supposed to be in love with her." He felt the end of his sore nose cautiously. "When will you speak to Jotull?"

"Tonight after we eat."

# Chapter 5

◈◈◈◈◈◈◈◈◈◈◈◈◈◈◈◈◈◈◈◈◈◈

Jotull did not laugh scornfully, nor did he get angry, as Rolfr had predicted. The wizard looked thoughtfully into the fire and puffed at his pipe, which had a carved face on it that either sneered or laughed in the flickering firelight.

"I think I can help you humble the arrogant creature," he said finally. "The only way to do it is to frighten her somehow, although there will be no real danger. The little minx has a birthday in another ten days. Someone is going to give her an amazing present."

"Who?" Rolfr inquired with interest.

"You, stupid, but she won't know that, or I'm sure she'd suspect a trick. She'll think it's from Halfdane and thus be totally unsuspecting." Jotull gazed into the fire with a mirthless chuckle, and his eyes flashed when he mentioned Halfdane. "Leave me now to think about it. Take Mikla with you."

Mikla gaped in amazement at the idea of Jotull granting him some free time. Quickly he put away the spells he was working on and hastened Rolfr and Sigurd out the door, before the wizard had time to change his mind. Exulting, they tumbled down the steep path in the dark. Rolfr busily described their plans to mortify Ragnhild, and Mikla gave but faint approval to them.

"You shouldn't have involved Jotull," he said seriously. "He has a grudge against Halfdane, and I wouldn't be surprised to see him do some harm to Ragnhild to get even."

"Oh, nonsense!" Rolfr exclaimed. "He's going to conjure a snake on her plate or something funny like that, so all the hall can laugh at her. I tried it once, but snakes seem to elude

59

me somehow. All I got were worms, and the cook was nearly dismissed over it. Mikla, tell me how to conjure snakes."

Mikla began to protest that he wasn't about to spend his free time teaching magic to Rolfr. Sigurd preceded them down the hill. Rounding a small cow byre, he halted suddenly and stepped quickly backward. Rolfr collided with him and exclaimed, "What's the matter with you, Siggi? It's just one of the cows got loose from the barn, not a—" He stopped suddenly, drawing in a long breath. "That's no cow of ours!"

A hulking shadow lurked in the lee of the barn, an enormous thing—or things, if it were more than one creature. Sigurd thought he could see three heads in the dark. He moved a step closer, and something set up a menacing growling that chilled his blood worse than any rival he had ever fought. When he moved, it moved too.

Mikla lit his staff and thrust it forward. Three pair of eyes gleamed redly in its light. The bulky shadow lunged forward with savage snarling and a chopping of three sets of wolfish, white teeth. Sigurd glimpsed three horselike faces with sharp pricking ears and wisps of matted mane. Eyes, teeth, and flaring nostrils glared with a blue, unnatural light as the thing sprang forward with a chuckling neigh of evil anticipation.

Mikla threw himself in front of Sigurd, a fire spell exploding from his fingertips. With a savage bellow, the creature reared aloft on two hind legs and pawed at the wall of flame with its enormous front hooves. Sigurd staggered back, appalled, unable to comprehend what his eyes were seeing. He reached for his sword, an old practice weapon Rolfr had given him, but he knew it was worse than useless against such a creature.

Mikla hurled spells at it until it backed away, shaking its heads in annoyance. With a last threatening growl, it turned and trotted arrogantly away, keeping its baleful eyes fixed on Sigurd until it vanished into a ravine behind the barrow mounds.

The three friends immediately rushed toward the hall, tearing open the door and piling inside helter-skelter, with no thought for making a dignified appearance.

Several of the Alfar looked up from their gaming and drinking in consternation. The light and safety of the hall acted as a swift restorative to Mikla's wits. He gripped his staff and hurried toward Halfdane's quarters. Dagrun rose up protectively beside the door, demanding, "What do you want? Halfdane doesn't need to be disturbed over every small broil."

"This is no small broil," Mikla retorted. "We just fought off a fearsome sending by the cow barns. It looks like something sent by Bjarnhardr. I think Halfdane would like to know about it immediately, rather than discover it for himself."

"Then I shall tell him," Dagrun began, still barring the door, but the door opened behind him and Halfdane pushed him aside to scowl a moment at Mikla, Rolfr, and Sigurd.

"Another sending from Bjarnhardr?" he rumbled. "It doesn't surprise me. He used to send one every winter to enliven the long, dark days. I shall send word to Jotull, and he shall work his magic on it, if he has a mind to." He smiled wryly, a bitter twist of the lips, as he mentioned Jotull.

Mikla shook his head. "I don't think it's a sending directed against yourself, my lord. The thing seemed to take a sinister interest in Sigurd, in my opinion."

Halfdane looked at Sigurd sharply. "Is that so? I might have known it would not take Bjarnhardr long to find you here. It's the box that he wants. I trust you have it in a safe place?"

"Why would Bjarnhardr want to kill me with a sending?" Sigurd demanded. "He's not the one who destroyed Thongullsfjord. He and I have never even seen each other. Why would he want to kill a perfect stranger?"

Halfdane replied with a snort of contempt. "Why are you so anxious to jump to his defense, if he's such a stranger? You are as ill-conditioned and unwise as a young man can be, Sigurd. All it takes to open that box is a key, once you are out of the way, and if Bjarnhardr had been the one to find you on that deserted fell, you would not be alive now. Very likely none of us in Hrafnborg would have survived this long. You think I am a cruel taskmaster and a tyrant, and therefore Bjarnhardr must be kind and gentle. I assure you, you couldn't be more wrong, Sigurd."

"I'm not wrong about being little better than a prisoner here," Sigurd flared. "I was brought here against my will and

I'm being kept here against my will. All I can assume is that only an enemy would keep me here as a prisoner!"

Dagrun interposed himself with a furious scowl. "That's a fine, ungrateful speech! What a headstrong young begger! I won't stand here and listen to such impudence. Go on and sit down and see if you can mend your manners before you trouble us again." He gave Rolfr a shove backward and glared murderously at Sigurd. Mikla also looked at Sigurd with dissatisfaction.

"I believe Jotull's company isn't doing him any good," Mikla said. "It would be wise to keep them apart."

"But not practical," Halfdane replied.

Sigurd turned away from Mikla, smoldering. "A fine friend you are, Mikla. It seems that no one is on my side in this place. That sending could kill me and take the box and no one here would raise a hand to stop it." He was angry enough that his natural power began rattling the weapons on the walls and knocking a few of them to the floor.

Halfdane spoke to Rolfr, struggling to keep his temper. "You and Sigurd had better stay here until we're sure that beast isn't outside waiting. Dagrun, send someone for Jotull." With a last black look for Sigurd, the warlord retired to his usual corner alone. In a few moments, the nervous chatter in the hall had regained its normal peak of jollity as the men relaxed, reassured by the presence of their warlord.

Sigurd was not reassured. It seemed to him that he had enemies both within and without. He thought Halfdane looked at him speculatively, trying to judge Sigurd's reaction to the sending, perhaps.

The door opened rather hastily, and Jotull stepped into the hall with his usual graceful flourish. His manner lacked its normal composure, however, as he slammed the door shut and barred it with a flick of his hand. All merry chatter ceased instantly, and all eyes dwelt upon the wizard in helpless fascination as he spent a long moment peering outside through a small hole bored through the door.

He turned triumphantly, sweeping the crowded hall with an imperious gaze until he found Mikla, Rolfr, and Sigurd. "I am relieved to see that none of you were injured by that creature lurking out there," he said in a tone that blanched the ruddiest faces and sobered everyone instantly. To Halfdane he continued, "I recall warning you about something of this nature, but now you see that I was right about the Scipling's natural power. It is not a harmless, whimsical creature any longer. Listen." He raised one finger for silence, and someone outside on the earthworks uttered a terrified scream, echoed by others.

Halfdane and most of his men leaped to their feet, seizing their weapons. "What do you mean, Jotull?" Halfdane snapped. "Explain, and quickly!"

"Don't rush outside too quickly, or you may regret it," Jotull called to the men. "The Scipling's power has taken a most unfavorable material form. It may kill anyone that gets in its path. I would have captured it before it gained such strength, if I had been permitted." He cast Halfdane a sharp glance.

Halfdane strode to the door and unbarred it to look out. A rumbling growl greeted the opening of the door, and the Alfar nearest the door fell back in alarm. "It looks more like a sending to me," Halfdane said, taking a lance from someone and thrusting it into the darkness. A savage three-toned roar announced the beast's attack on the hall, and Halfdane slammed the door and locked it in the nick of time as the creature hurled itself forward. With furious squeals and bellows, it thundered at the heavy door with its hooves, then leaped onto the roof. Mikla immediately fanned the fire into a roaring blaze to discourage any attempts at coming down the chimney, if the beast were so inclined.

"I'm sure it's a sending," Mikla said, as the thing trampled around on the roof, causing dust to sift down and timbers to groan and creak protestingly. "Sigurd's natural power is still here with us." He gestured to the relics and weapons leaping off the walls one by one with a dinning clamor, raining down around Ragnhild, who had taken refuge under a nearby table.

"Stop! Stop!" Sigurd commanded distractedly, but his unruly power started shoving the gold cups and basins off a shelf, to add to the confusion.

"Great gods!" Dagrun exclaimed over the clamor of excited voices. "We had troubles enough without this Scipling!"

"Jotull!" Halfdane roared furiously. "Do something to stop this nonsense!"

Jotull alone was calm, even smiling faintly at the discomfiture of the Alfar. "I shall try. But I don't know who might have conjured such a dangerous sending against Sigurd. I saw how it singled him out. But as soon as I find out who made it, I can begin to make a counterspell. It's quite apparent to me that someone wishes Sigurd ill." He glanced up as a clod of earth fell from the rafters above almost at his feet.

"You're supposed to be the wizard of Hrafnborg," Halfdane rumbled, glaring at him through the curtains of dust and smoke. "I don't care how you do it, just do something to get rid of that sending, no matter whom it's against! You, Sigurd, stop those tricks at once!" Everyone in the hall cringed at his tone.

"I can't," Sigurd retorted, wincing as a particularly fine beaten kettle crashed to the floor. "This always happens whenever I'm upset or nervous about something. You don't need to assume I enjoy it, either."

Jotull gazed around the hall. "I'm going out to confront the beast. I guess I needn't ask for any volunteer to accompany me." His eye gleamed with scorn.

"I shall go with you," Halfdane said contemptuously. "I want to take a better look at it anyway."

Jotull made a mocking half-bow of acknowledgment, and they went outside together. Immediately everyone inside the hall rushed to peer out the few apertures in the old turf hall. The sending continued to roar and trample around on the roof for a short while; then it was gone, after a menacing cackle down the chimney, as if to warn Sigurd that it would be back. To Sigurd's relief, his power abated its destructive activities and Ragnhild crawled out from under the table with a haughty glower at him and marched away to her private rooms indignantly.

When Halfdane and Jotull returned to the hall, they quarreled bitterly over getting rid of the sending. Jotull declared that nothing short of a major purging of the entire fortress would suffice and that the removal of Sigurd to another location where he could be better protected was essential. Halfdane refused to listen to any such ideas and finally banished Jotull with unconcealed bad temper. Rolfr speedily took the hint and hastened Sigurd away to their quarters in the old tower before Halfdane noticed them and brought his wrath to bear upon the cause of his griefs, which was Sigurd.

During the following week, Sigurd observed to his surprise that Halfdane declared an all-out attack on the sending. It soon learned that open aggression earned nothing but a hide full of arrows, so it skulked around cautiously, watching in vain for an opportunity to get to Sigurd. Sigurd felt grateful to the warlord, but he couldn't bring himself to say so. Jotull also attempted many conjurations to lure the horse-bear to its demise, without success. Ignoring Rolfr's protests that it was absolute folly, Sigurd continued his nightly visits to Jotull's lonely house on the fellside. Strangely enough, Jotull's flattery and patronage began to pall, and Halfdane's rough, impartial manner began to appeal to Sigurd. Halfdane treated everyone alike, grimly insisting upon upholding discipline in all circumstances, but everyone agreed that he was scrupulously fair, unimpeachably generous, and far more concerned with the welfare of everyone in Hrafnborg than with his own weal or woe. Several times Halfdane's morose manner seemed to Sigurd a camouflage for hidden, less taciturn feelings. Almost simultaneously, Sigurd began to think that Jotull's suavity was a camouflage for something far less agreeable.

"I don't wish to appear unduly gloomy," Jotull said one night, looking into his fire in a gloomy and sinister manner, "but I fear greatly for your life, Sigurd. I can't do anything against this Hross-Bjorn, and Halfdane refuses to let me take you someplace safer. He won't let you out of his power as long as you possess that box. He covets whatever is inside it, and I know he'd do anything to get it away from you." Jotull smoked his leering pipe and studied Sigurd from his place in the shadows. "And you have no idea what it contains or how your grandmother got it?"

Sigurd shaded his eyes from the bright flames on the hearth.

"No, nothing. All I know is that it must be something dreadfully valuable to Halfdane—or Bjarnhardr."

Jotull leaned back. "Yes, you must never forget it, or forget that you must never surrender it to anyone you don't trust entirely. Neither must you forget what happened at Thongullsfjord."

Sigurd no longer liked to dwell upon it. He felt depressed when he thought of Thongullsfjord and the death of Thorarna. If not for the distress of the disruption of the settlement and the suspicion of her neighbors, Thorarna's life might not have ended when it did. Perhaps she would have told him about the carven box and its contents and how it had come to her from the Alfar realm. Sigurd might have gone to his father, instead of waiting for the trolls and Alfar to carry him off.

Jotull continued to watch him and puffed solemnly on his pipe. The smell of the smoke made Sigurd feel slightly sick. "I only hope this precious object you're concealing is in a safe place in the event of your death. Sorry to startle you with such unpleasantness, but it must be thought of. If you've got your box hidden in your bed straw or in the rafters or under a hearthstone, the sending will certainly find it and carry it to its maker."

Sigurd gaped a moment at Jotull, unable to speak. Unless hiding something under the hearthstone was an especially obtuse blunder, the wizard had read his mind. "I don't have a very safe place for it," he finally managed to answer. "I thought I might ask if you would—"

Across the room, Mikla made a sudden gesture, and Sigurd was seized with such a fit of coughing and choking that the tears ran down his face and he could scarcely breathe. Rolfr thumped him on the back, taking his breath away further. Mikla brought him a drink and led him to the door for some fresh air.

"I think you'd better go home," Mikla muttered with a scowl. "You didn't remember what I said. Take your box and find another hiding place for it, but whatever you do, don't bring it here."

Sigurd replied with a wheezy snort. "I'll do with it what I

please. You nearly strangled me then, Mikla. I won't forget that."

"Good. I hope you don't. Maybe you'll be more sensible if I choke you now and again. Good night, Rolfr. I'll watch you until you get safely home."

"I might have died," Sigurd grumbled as Rolfr laboriously unlocked a cumbersome old lock he had affixed to their door as a precaution against the sending. As he stepped inside at Rolfr's heels, Rolfr suddenly fell back against him with a shout of alarm. A huge black shadow rose up against the faint red glow of the coals and made a pounce at them. Sigurd dived for the door, but it was hopelessly jammed shut with Rolfr's complicated locking device.

"Hullo, Rolfr! Did you forget me in such a short time?" a strident voice cried, adding a rusty cackle of mirth. "And who's this? A Scipling, by my soul and buttons! I knew I had good reason to hurry back so precipitately. My, isn't it cold in here!" Briskly rubbing his hands together, Adills blew on the fire and brought it into a blinding, scorching bonfire.

"Adills, I'm glad you're here," Rolfr greeted him, while Adills moved his chair closer to the fire, winking like an old salamander at Sigurd. "It's a good thing you're back. Sigurd has a sending after him, Mikla's saying some strange things about Jotull, and Jotull and Halfdane are quarreling dreadfully. Everyone's nerves are wrung so tight there's bound to be an explosion. And Ragnhild is perfectly insufferable. She stole a fine shirt one of the servants made and gave it to Halfdane as her own work, and I haven't decided yet how to let her know that I know—"

"I'm glad I came home when I did," Adills said hastily. "I had the feeling something was wrong. Is Sigurd the disturber of Hrafnborg's shaky peace?" He beckoned Sigurd closer and looked into his face with a harmless smile, but his sunken eyes were as hard and bright as garnets. "Hah! You're not happy here, I see. Is it such a bad place as all that?"

Sigurd tried to stare down the old wizard, but he had to look away. "It's pleasant enough, although I'm rather bored with endless lessons and the day watch. Except lately, that is.

Without the sending to add some excitement to our lives, I don't know what I'd do." He glanced uneasily at Rolfr and back at Adills, who hadn't removed his friendly gaze from Sigurd or abated his congenial smile one degree.

"You might try escaping," Adills said. "Have you never thought of that, my friend?"

"I've thought of it," Sigurd confessed uncomfortably. "Jotull seems to—no, never mind. But the sending makes it difficult to stay, endangering all the hill fort. If I left, it would follow and I might find something more exciting than lessons in archery. No, what I meant to say—" He tore his eyes away from Adills and tried to formulate some half-truths to screen himself.

"Siggi, you wouldn't leave, would you?" Rolfr demanded reproachfully. "Is that what you and Jotull talk about when I'm not listening? I hope you wouldn't think of going without me."

Sigurd clenched his teeth, wondering how he had ever let out his and Jotull's unspoken agreement. Something about the gentle old wizard Adills made him confess his inmost thoughts. It was a spell, he thought suddenly, looking at Adills attentively, determined to resist with all his might.

"It was just homesickness for Thongullsfjord, I suspect," Adills said. "A way of passing the time. Yet there's nothing to go back to, is there, Sigurd?"

Sigurd relaxed. Adills thought he wished to return to Thongullsfjord, and that suited his plans exactly. Jotull had told him of Bjarnhardr's fine halls and liberal jarls who gave away gold rings by the hundreds to those who were loyal to them.

"No, nothing," Sigurd replied, "but it was home to me for more than twenty years, and my grandmother's bones lie there."

"Bones, indeed," Adills said. "I saw gold in your eyes. Rolfr, stir me up something to eat and drink; I'm almost perishing. You've no idea how hard it is to beg your way around Bjarnhardr's jarls. They're as close and frightened as a pack of sheep with the wolves howling in the crags above them. And the worst wolf is Halfdane."

"That's splendid," Rolfr said. "We've seen his gauntlet, Adills. He blasted Jotull halfway across the hall with it."

"Did he now! Serves that upstart right." Adills rubbed his skinny knees and put his toes a little nearer the flame. "What was the cause of this stupendous argument?" His bright little eyes fastened themselves upon Sigurd knowingly.

"I was," Sigurd said unwillingly. "Jotull wanted to teach me magic—or rather, he wanted to catch my natural power and confine it. What they actually were fighting over lies right under your feet. Adills, you sly old trickster, take this spell off me so I'll stop telling you all my secrets." He glared at the old wizard, more than half angry.

Adills raised his eyebrows and clasped his hands together. "Oh dear, surely you don't think I'd put that sort of a spell on you? I'm not at all an unscrupulous wizard; in fact, I abhor the sort of wizard who picks people's brains without their consent. If you're telling me your secrets, it must be because you trust me with them. Secrets are sometimes rather unpleasant to keep, like slivers, and one feels better once they are out from under one's skin. If you think you'll feel better, you can show me whatever it is you've got hidden under the hearthstone, but you needn't produce it if you'd rather not."

Sigurd knelt and pried up the stone. "I have to move it anyway. It seems that everyone in Hrafnborg knows where I've hidden it."

"Very likely," Adills said, leaning forward expectantly as Sigurd uncovered the little box, wrapped in an old shirt of Rolfr's. "What a nice bit of carving you've got here. It looks like something done by the Dvergar. Wherever did you get it?" He took it and admired it, looking closely at the carved figures.

"My grandmother had it hidden in a trunk when she died. It was the only thing I took with me when I left the Scipling realm. I don't know what's in it, I don't know why she had it, and I don't know how she got it. I don't know anything about it, except that Halfdane would like to have it and so would Bjarnhardr, if Halfdane is to be believed." Sigurd stared at the box, thinking suddenly that Jotull wanted it, too, if he had read his suggestions properly that night.

"I believe Halfdane is truthful," Adills said. "I taught him to be straightforward when he was a child and a young man.

A difficult life has made him rather gruff and grim, but I think he is honest. He could have simply taken it from you, you know."

Sigurd shook his head and scowled. "It's mine. It was my legacy from my grandmother. Whatever it is, I won't give it away. What I'd like to do is open it and see what I've inherited that has the Alfar realm in such an uproar."

Adills turned the box over several times, looking at it closely. "Well, you won't be doing that unless you have the key to its lock. It's magical, dwarf magic at that, which makes it next to impossible to force. You'll have to take it to the jolly old fellow who made it, Bergthor of Svartafell." He held up the box and tapped significantly at the runic signature on the bottom.

"Bergthor of Svartafell! Do you think we could find him, after all these years?" Excitedly Sigurd took the box and stared at the signature. It had never seemed significant to him before.

"Where has he to go? Svartafell is his home," Adills said, looking perplexed.

"He might be dead," Sigurd said. "My grandmother has had this box for at least twenty years."

Adills smiled and smoothed down his beard so the cat could curl up in its usual place. "Twenty years is almost nothing to a dwarf. Of course, we don't know how long the box has been in your family though, do we?"

Sigurd paused to think. "My grandmother said it belonged to my mother, Ashildr, so it must not have been an heirloom—"

Adills overflowed the cup he was pouring tea into, spilled the hot fluid on himself, and scalded the cat. With a trembling hand, he set down the pot. "Will you look at this mess! My eyesight certainly isn't what it once was. Ah, poor Missu, she'll never forgive me." He looked vaguely under the table for the cat, then stood up rather unsteadily. "Rolfr, I think I shall pay a call on Halfdane while you're fixing more tea and toast. He hasn't been blessed with my presence for a very long time. Not long enough to suit him, no doubt; we always disagree frightfully with one another, but we're bound by mutual re-

spect, despite it all. I daresay he's in more than one muddle
without me here to advise him. He—he, ah, my wits are
obfuscated. I'll be back shortly."

Sigurd rose, handing Adills the staff he seemed to be ab-
sentmindedly searching for. "You might mention Bergthor to
him, Adills, and inquire about the possibility of going to find
him."

Adills was tapping his way toward the door through a maze
of saddles, lances, and chairs. "What? Oh, yes, Svartathor of
Bergfell, I shall mention it to be sure." He fumbled with the
door, muttering wrathfully at Rolfr's lock. As Rolfr plunged
forward to explain its intricacies, the old wizard blasted it with
a small gout of fire. Bits of hot metal showered around Rolfr,
and acrid black smoke roiled around him, smothering his indignant protests. Adills vanished in the smoke, waving his staff
to clear it before him.

"That's a wretchedly inefficient lock, Rolfr. I suggest you
clear it away immediately," Adills growled huffishly.

Rolfr busied himself making feeble attempts at the mounds
of tack and lumber obscuring Adills' bed. Sigurd sat looking
at the box and the signature on the bottom with renewed zeal.
"I never guessed this bit of runic scratching might mean the
answer to my great riddle. I feel certain that once I open this
box, I'll know who my father was. He must have been someone
important if he possessed something so valuable that men even
now are trying to get it. I'll never rest until I solve the mystery."

Rolfr quit his work and came to look at the box, reaching
out to touch it and quickly changing his mind. "Those carvings
look as if all the figures have the bellyache," he said. "I don't
like the look of them. In fact, I don't like that box at all. It
gives me a dreadful feeling, Siggi."

"A bellyache?" Sigurd asked with a grin.

"No, no, you idiot. Just a bad impression. Pay attention,
this may be the only time you see me in a serious mood. We
Alfar are entitled to our premonitions, you know." Rolfr looked
at the box and shook his head. "I don't think you'll be very
happy when you finally get it open, Sigurd."

Sigurd looked at the box and felt a trembling chill in the

pit of his stomach. "Nonsense," he said, to himself as much as to Rolfr. "There's nothing I want more than to see what's inside this box, whether or not it answers my own personal questions. Maybe I'll never know who my father is—maybe it would be better not to know," he added in an attempt at a joke, but Rolfr didn't smile.

Rolfr said, "Put it back under the stone. I'll ask Adills to put a spell on the stone so forty men couldn't lift it. How do you like the old fellow, by the way?"

"There's no deceiving him," Sigurd said slowly. "Nor does he attempt to deceive anyone else."

When Adills returned, Sigurd and Rolfr were waiting for him by the fire. They had his chair within roasting range and his fleece slippers were almost fried. The old wizard winced pleasurably as he thrust his aged toes into his slippers and accepted a cup of stewed tea from Rolfr. Sigurd waited politely for as long as he could, then he impatiently demanded, "Well? What did Halfdane say to our idea of going to find Bergthor?"

Adills looked considerably less happy. "He didn't like the idea. In fact, he would hear nothing of it. I'm dreadfully sorry, Sigurd, to have led your hopes on as I did."

"I can't confess to any great astonishment," Sigurd said with bitter sarcasm. "Halfdane wouldn't for a moment let that box out of his control, he's so anxious to get it for himself. He's the creator of that sending against me, intending for it to kill me, just as his sendings and trolls drove the people out of Thongullsfjord and even killed a few of them. He keeps me here, little better than a prisoner, waiting for his opportunity to kill me and seize that box. I knew from the beginning that he wished me no good. My grandmother warned me about a hostile warlord, and my grandmother never lied to me."

"Perhaps not," Adills replied, elevating one eyebrow, "but she didn't tell you everything she ought to have told you, and therein lies our problem. Are you certain Halfdane is the warlord she had in mind? There are hundreds of them, both Ljosalfar and Dokkalfar."

Sigurd stubbornly shook his head. "It has to be Halfdane. He's the one who was there, and he's the one who's holding me captive and making sendings against me, so that's all the proof I need, and very good proof it is, too."

Adills sighed and rubbed his temples with both hands. "We shall talk at length about it later. Right now I'm rather tired."

Rolfr too was nodding and yawning. "Well then, good night, Adills. You'll be glad to know you're back in time for Ragnhild's birthday."

"Indeed. What shall you give her, a bottle of vinegar and a garland of nettles? You still cherish her dearly, I suppose?" Adills asked with a smile.

Rolfr achieved a grin of pure spite. "Oh yes, more than ever. We've got a splendid present for her from Siggi and me. It promises to offer a lot of sport."

"Not nearly as much as a sending would," Sigurd muttered blackly.

His gloom lasted for several days, relieved only slightly by the anticipation of Jotull's gift to Ragnhild. On the day before her birthday, a pack train from another hill fort arrived with supplies and a fresh string of twelve horses, which the riders had been desperately needing. Rolfr eyes them covetously and said, "You can bet they won't go to underlings like you and me. I'll be lucky to have passed down to me a horse only half as broken down as my own nag. The best horses for the best men is the rule." He sighed gloomily. "I remember stories about how fine our Alfar horse herds used to be, before Bjarnhardr."

"At least you have a horse of your own," Sigurd said, remembering his stout little piebald horse that the trolls had taken. "I'd be glad for the opportunity to ride out. You must be as resentful of being confined to the hill fort as I am, and here I am to blame for it. You must hate me, Rolfr."

"What foolishness," Rolfr answered. "It will be worthwhile if you help me mortify Ragnhild. Tomorrow is the day; I wonder what Jotull has for her?"

Later the new horses were judiciously parceled out, better horses were passed down to deserving riders, and the most unfit of the horses were retired, either for a much-needed rest or, in the case of the most hopeless, to be fattened for slaughter.

The advent of new horses was an occasion for much joking and laughter in the horse paddock, as well as groaning and complaining. Rolfr was delighted to learn that he was eligible for another horse, but as it turned out, he was awarded one notorious for pitching its rider off suddenly and cantering homeward unencumbered by the nuisance of a man in its saddle. The horse greatly begrudged anyone climbing onto its back and usually did its best to discourage such an attempt at the beginning of every patrol by biting and kicking and bucking. It was quite a famous horse at Hrafnborg, having passed from rider to rider. It was not a fast horse and certainly not lovely, but it was apparently indestructible. A vicious temper seemed to have added years to its vitality.

Rolfr at once became the center for much good-natured banter, which did little to prevent him from feeling sorry for himself. Rolfr's old horse was retired to pasture, and Sigurd looked at it longingly, thinking it would carry him at least part of the way to Svartafell. Halfdane's voice calling out his name startled him from his morose thoughts.

"Sigurd the Scipling, come forward and get your horse," Halfdane called over the voices of the others. Sigurd scrambled through the bars into the mêlée of horses and men and toward Halfdane, scarcely believing his luck. Halfdane looked up from his list of horses and riders and pointed to a large gray horse. "That's yours, and it's your responsibility to care for it. You'll speak to the horsemaster about it. I'm going to try you out on a day patrol near the hill fort with a dozen or so of the youngest lads who are just beginning their training. Rolfr will stay with you, and old Borgill will give you your orders. He's too splendid a fellow to leave idle, and he can't see well enough in the dark anymore for night rides. I hope you'll be satisfied with the assignment." Halfdane looked at Sigurd with a trace of a scowl.

"I shall," Sigurd replied, more delighted than he cared to show Halfdane. "Do we start today?"

Halfdane waved him toward Borgill, who was assigning the young lads to some of the least debilitated old nags. "I see no reason why not. Speak to Borgill about it."

Borgill was willing. Sigurd took a great liking to him at once. He was a tall, thin old Alfar with a flowing silver mustache that he was inordinately proud of. It lent him an air of dignity and distinction as he directed his rackety young troops. He spoke quietly and remained calm under the most trying of circumstances. Boys fell off horses, horses bolted, horses refused to move. None of them had saddles except for Borgill, Rolfr, and Sigurd, who used Rolfr's old saddle, a thing that might have been worse than no saddle at all, as liable as it was to falling apart at any moment. Still, Sigurd was happier than he had ever been at Hrafnborg. His horse was a pleasant mare, sedate and middle-aged, but she galloped willingly—not fast, to be sure, but many of the other horses the young fellows had were much worse. Almost all had been pitched off several times or run away with, but they were still game. As they rode into the hill fort, the night patrol was riding out, well-equipped and well-horsed, setting up a frightful contrast with Borgill's outfit, which made it a source of good-natured merriment for everyone concerned. Sigurd burned with embarrassment when he saw Ragnhild laughing from the hall, and he grimly hoped that Jotull's suprise for her would be a most unpleasant one.

Jotull reappeared after sundown on the eve of Ragnhild's birthday when Halfdane's patrol was gone. He rapped on the low door of the tower room with the end of his staff. "Come! It's here," he called, when Rolfr opened the door. "The gossip of something unusual will soon reach Ragnhild's ears, so you'd better hurry if you want to see it first. It's in the stall where she keeps her nag."

Adills pushed the door open to confront Jotull. "I hope you're not up to any unpleasant tricks, Jotull," he said warningly.

"It's only for a joke," Sigurd hastened to say. "I asked Jotull to help us. It's nothing to worry about, Adills. Let's go have a look at it."

"I certainly shall," Adills declared, seizing his staff.

"There's no need," Jotull said with a condescending smile. "I fear the walk to the barn would be too much for you. Your knees look definitely wobbly these days."

Adills lifted his staff. "Then we shall dispose of knees altogether. When will you learn, Jotull, that the wizard's body is only a poor shell for the wizard's spirit?" With a few words, the wizard Adills vanished in a puff of light and reappeared in the shape of a small red hawk. It bobbed its head up and down, the better to see them, looking amazingly wise in the process, and whetted its beak on the post where it sat. With a shrill whistle, it spread its wings and glided toward the distant barns.

# Chapter 6

By the time the others arrived, they found Adills sitting comfortably in a chair the horsemaster had kindly brought him and sipping at a cup of something hot and fragrant.

"I have seen it," he greeted them, "and I do not approve." He nodded to a nearby stall, where a horse was reaching out its muzzle to sniff at the newcomers. It was a delicately formed white horse with large, dark eyes and sharp, inquisitive ears. Sigurd rubbed its neck in considerable amazement and envy.

"It's too beautiful to give to Ragnhild," he said. "What we should give her is a nag like Rolfr's."

Jotull chuckled indulgently and flicked some straw away from the toe of his boot. "No, no, this horse isn't a bit too good for Ragnhild, and once you learn what its habits are, I think you'll hasten to agree."

Adills snorted. "I know what it is and I don't think it's a good idea at all. I'm tempted to put an end to your scheme and I could do it by saying a single word." He rose to his feet and glared at Jotull, much like a tiny sparrow hawk hissing and snapping its beak at an eagle.

"No, it will be perfect!" Rolfr exclaimed. "Tomorrow we've planned an exhibition of riding skills and games and races in honor of the great birthday. Ragnhild will be very haughty with her new horse, which is obviously the finest and fastest in the hill fort and completely useless to a good fighting man who has need of such a horse. In the middle of all the festivities, one of us will ride up near her and whisper the word ever so gently in this lovely creature's ear, and away it will go like an arrow, straight for the nearest water where it will plunge in, right while everyone is watching. Ragnhild and her fine new clothes and new saddle will all get completely soaked, and so will that arrogant little nose which she keeps in the air. She'll be so humiliated she won't show herself for a month. You know how she boasts about her horsemanship. I wonder if it should be the horse pond we duck her in or the lake at the end of the valley. The horse pond is frightfully muddy and full of leeches, so perhaps we ought to use it."

Sigurd looked warily from one friend to another, not wanting to appear ignorant by asking foolish questions. Adills caught his expression at once and explained, "This is not an ordinary horse; it's more of an evil monster. It appears tame and willing enough and will gladly carry a rider, but just mention its name and it will bolt away to dive into the nearest body of water. Such creatures have been known to roll on their riders and drown them, too. Imagine trying to explain your clever trick to Halfdane if something happens to Ragnhild."

"We'll make certain nothing happens to her except a good drenching," Rolfr said amiably. "Siggi and I will stay with her, mostly so we can get the first laugh at her. Perhaps we can be in the race to the lake and call the word just as she gets there."

Adills shook his head resolutely. "It's too dangerous."

"But half the hill fort will be there to pull her out," Rolfr said. "Besides, that lake isn't very deep. Siggi and I could be waiting there to shout the horse's name if you prefer, and then we can jump in after her instantly if she requires it. I'd prefer to let her flounder around awhile first and swallow a lot of water and get thoroughly soaked."

"I shall speak to Halfdane about it the instant he gets back in the morning," Adills said indignantly to Jotull. "This is your doing and I have a feeling it will turn out evil."

Jotull only shrugged and turned away to leave. "There's no convincing you otherwise, I see. Do as you think fit, Adills." His eye met Sigurd's briefly, and Sigurd had the sudden assurance that Jotull had no intention of being thwarted by Adills.

Ragnhild and a troop of Alfar descended upon the barn to confirm the rumors that a very special present from Halfdane awaited her there. Ignoring Sigurd and Rolfr, she swept forward to admire the horse, and Adills was jostled quite out of the way by the Alfar crowding forward to have a look, so he had no chance to warn her. Rolfr took command of Adills before his fragile bones were accidentally crushed. Being rather small and bent, the old wizard was easy to overlook. Indomitably, he settled his cap on his head, plunged into the crowd of taller Alfar, and nearly reached Ragnhild's side, when suddenly Sigurd saw him double over, clutching his back in pain.

Rolfr spied the mishap instantly and sprang after Adills, catching him and gently lowering the old wizard to a heap of clean straw before he collapsed.

"Wretched back!" Adills gritted, his face gray with pain. "I fear you'll have to carry me home, Rolfr. This will take days to cure. I won't be able to move a finger."

"Do you have these seizures often, Adills?" Sigurd inquired, still staring at the doorway, where only a moment ago he had seen Jotull hidden by shadows, making some gestures that looked very like the moves essential to a spell. He was on the point of telling Adills about it; but after a moment's consideration, he decided that would be carrying tales on Jotull, and Jotull wouldn't like it if he found out.

"I never have them when it's convenient," Adills growled, as they placed him aboard a plank to carry homeward. "It feels like knives sticking into my flesh. Blast it, I won't be able to do anything about that wretched nikur you're giving Ragnhild as a horse. Rolfr, if you truly cared about me, you wouldn't permit Jotull to carry out this foolish plan. But I can see you're determined to have your fun, no matter what I say. Don't say I didn't warn you, when something goes wrong."

"Nothing will go wrong," Rolfr soothed him, as they carried him down the steep steps into the tower, head foremost. "I only regret you'll miss out on the joke."

Sigurd remained silent during the administration of herbs and poultices that made his eyes water and great steaming compresses that threatened to broil the little wizard alive. When nothing seemed to have the desired effect, and Adills was in a thoroughly irascible temper, he casually suggested it might be an evil spell.

"Well, of course!" Adills declared. "Send for Mikla at once— but not Jotull. I don't want him anywhere near me."

Mikla looked more solemn than usual when he arrived. Without saying much, he went to work on the spell, between times looking at Rolfr and Sigurd with displeasure.

"This is a complex spell," he said at last with a sigh. "It will take a long time to unravel it, and Jotull won't permit me much free time—especially when it will be to his best interests if Adills' back remains crippling."

"That miserable nikur is to blame for it," Adills growled. "Jotull won't permit me to banish it before it does some harm."

"I don't think it's such a great idea, either," Mikla agreed, with another frown on Rolfr and Sigurd. "I'll be watching, but there's little any of us can really do once Jotull has made his mind up to interfere. I wish you hadn't asked him to help you with this stupid plot, Sigurd."

"It's not stupid," Sigurd snapped at once, with more vehemence than real conviction, but he felt the need to defend himself. "Rolfr thought it was a good idea. You don't see him trying to put all the blame on me, before anything has even happened."

Mikla put his magical apparatus into his satchel. "I shall come back when I can to resume our treatment, Adills. I'll find someone to sit with you until you're back on your feet. I expect tomorrow may be rather lonely for you, with almost everyone watching the riding games." With a last severe glance at Rolfr and Sigurd, he departed, closing the door firmly behind him.

Later, when Adills was either asleep or absent in his fylgja form of the little hawk, Sigurd asked Rolfr, "Are you worried about something very bad happening to Ragnhild tomorrow? Maybe I shouldn't have asked Jotull's advice."

"Well, I'm a little concerned. But I tell myself Jotull won't do anything too dreadful, or he might lose his hold over you by frightening you completely away from him."

"Me, frightened of him? Hah!" Sigurd paused a moment, staring at the coals in the hearth. "Why should I be afraid of him? And what sort of hold does he have over me?"

"Once you ask a favor of someone, he can ask one of you," Rolfr replied, rather sleepily.

Sigurd pondered quite a long time, before asking, "Well? What do you think he would ask of me?" His eyes rested on the hearthstone, which still concealed the carven box. "Rolfr? Are you awake?"

Rolfr was not, and Sigurd was left to his own uneasy thoughts as the room grew darker and darker and more chill as the night advanced.

In the morning, the preparations for the games and races in honor of Ragnhild's birthday began before daybreak. Borgill's mismatched troop of young lads planned a grand parade, relay races, and demonstrations of their rather unskillful riding skills, which promised, as Sigurd and Rolfr watched, to offer the most comic entertainment of the day. The other patrols planned jumps and maneuvers to show off their talents, as well as a mock battle. Prizes would be awarded for the best in each event, and also for the worst performance, since the Alfar loved a good loser almost as much as a winner. The last events of the day would be the races, beginning with heats for the least experienced riders, which included women and girls from the community. Ragnhild scorned to race with them. She would consider nothing less than the last race of the day, which was among the greatest rivals in the hill fort, the four patrol leaders and several others whose horses were fast enough to make it a good competion. Halfdane's huge iron-gray stallion was the favorite to win, if Halfdane returned early enough in the day to let his horse rest for the race at sunset.

During the circus atmosphere of the day, Sigurd thought

more often of Jotull than of Adills, although he heard from Mikla that Jotull would not attend the games. He managed to lose his apprehensions in the festivities and even to carry away a prize in his category for jumping, where anyone who stayed on his horse's back for the entire course was awarded a prize.

By noon, when everyone stopped for a tremendous dinner, hopes of seeing Halfdane's horse win the race were dimming. Halfdane's patrol had not yet returned, and the most pessimistic Alfar were beginning to worry. Delays were not uncommon, however, so the spirit of the celebration was not much diminished, as long as there was plenty of ale to drink in Ragnhild's honor. She was twenty now and of an age to marry when she chose, but Ragnhild had spent a good many years assuring everyone that there wasn't a male in Hrafnborg that was anywhere near her mark.

At last the games, races, and general silliness were over, and the final racers were loping their horses in circles to warm them up before the race. Ragnhild was clad in a fine, red outfit, stiff with embroidery from the high collar of her short jacket to the elegant stitching on her deerskin boots. The white nikur capered and pranced, fanning its long tail and tossing its mane like seafoam. As the sun descended toward the horizon, everyone took a place along the course of the race, and Rolfr and Sigurd rode to the small lake which the track encompassed. There a low cliff rose almost directly out of the water, and the race course lay along the top of that.

No one else cared to come so far from the hill fort. With the lengthening shadows and cool evening breeze, Sigurd suddenly realized how alone they were. The lake looked dark and definitely cold. He couldn't see the bottom.

"Here they come!" Rolfr chortled, hiding himself among the rocks that lay along the cliff a short distance opposite the edge. "Half the hill fort is following. They'll all see her ignoble splash."

The horses came pounding along the narrow track on the cliff, with Ragnhild well in the lead of the others. Their reflections pursued them in the water below. The mounted spectators galloped farther behind, cheering on their favorites. As

Sigurd watched, the white nikur suddenly tossed up its head and began to rear and plunge in an unmanageable manner. The other horses thundered by on both sides, narrowly avoiding dangerous collisions. The spectators gave a shout of alarm from the other side of the lake where they had halted to watch the horses race around the water. The nikur stood on its hind legs, whirling and plunging despite Ragnhild's skillful attempts to get it under control.

Rolfr and Sigurd scrambled from their perches in the rocks to help her. The water below the cliff edge was too great a drop for safety and jagged with black boulders that could break both horse and rider. They reached her, dodging the flying hooves of the nikur, and tried to catch the beast's bridle. In the midst of its snorts and evil-tempered grunting, Sigurd heard a faint voice shouting. "Nikur! Nikur!" it called, and the nikur redoubled its efforts to plunge off the cliff. Sigurd grabbed one of the creature's ears and twisted it in the accepted manner for pacifying an unruly horse, but the nikur gave a final powerful spring, carrying Sigurd with it. Ragnhild screamed as they sailed toward the rocks and water below; in the next instant, the black water closed over Sigurd's head. By a miracle he missed the rocks in his descent. When he floundered his way to the surface, he saw Ragnhild struggling for a precarious handhold on a rock. The shoreline offered little purchase because of its steepness, and the turbulent water battered at them mercilessly in their efforts to save themselves. Sigurd pulled Ragnhild to a slightly sheltered place where they could hold on long enough to be rescued. From his place above on the cliff, Rolfr was bellowing for help at the top of his lungs, unable to do anything more constructive to aid his friends. As far as Sigurd could judge, no one else would be much use either, without a rope long enough to reach them.

"So cold!" Ragnhild gasped through chattering teeth. "I can't hold on much longer!" Her hands were blue with cold and raw from clawing for handholds on the rough rock. "Do you see my horse anywhere, or is he dead?"

Sigurd risked a quick glance around them and saw no horse. All he saw were increasing waves, driven by the wind, and the sun sinking prematurely under a thick blanket of black cloud. In a very short while, their would-be rescuers would not be able to see them in the water below.

"We've got better things to worry about than that cursed beast," Sigurd replied, hoping his voice didn't sound as frightened as he felt. Occupied with the agony of his cold, battered fingers and his determination not to let Ragnhild slip away into the rough water, he hadn't time to dwell on the voice he had heard shouting "nikur" in the cliffs above the lake, but the remembrance of it haunted him with a very nasty premonition. He looked up at their rescuers, who were shouting encouragement and risking their lives and limbs trying to climb down to them while someone rode to the hill fort for ropes. It would be full dark within a matter of minutes.

"What's that?" Ragnhild cried suddenly. "There in the water, almost behind us. It looks like my horse floating up to the surface again, the poor creature."

Sigurd twisted around to look. It was indeed a horse's long, slender head, with the eyes still open and the pale mane floating softly around it. Then Sigurd saw two other heads not far behind and a coiling mass of scaly necks and twisting tentacles. Ragnhild also saw the monster and screamed, hurling herself away from the protecting rock and floundering toward a more distant one farther from the shoreline. Sigurd swam after her with difficulty, weighted down by his sodden clothing and the axe in his belt, which seemed to pull him down like an anchor. He overtook Ragnhild and caught the back of her jacket as the voluminous mass of her clothing thwarted her efforts to stay afloat. She flailed and clawed at him in terror, half-choked with water, but he held onto her securely, knowing she could drown them both in her panic. He reached the rock and looked back for the sending. It circled, keeping between them and their rescuers. One head reached its muzzle out of the water to bare its fangs in a grisly snarl, and Ragnhild shrieked, cringing against the rock, not wanting to see the thing but yet unable to stop staring at it. With a burbling chuckle, it floated gently closer, its six eyes glowing with a watery light beneath the surface.

"It's me that it wants, not you," Sigurd panted, unsheathing his axe. "Slide around to the other side of the rock and stay out of sight. I can hold it off quite awhile, I think, if I can get solid rock beneath my feet." His toes found a slight, slippery purchase on the rock, and he gripped the axe double-handed, but his enemy presented no target better than a shapeless dark mass in the black water.

"Don't be absurd," Ragnhild said sharply, with a sob. "It won't be content until it has killed both of us. I don't want to be left here alone, so you'd better let it kill me first. I can't bear the sight of—" She ended with a scream of horror as a slimy tentacle flicked across her shoulder and brushed her face. She and Sigurd struggled toward another rock outcropping, and Sigurd thought his feet touched the bottom once. Rolfr had mentioned that the lake wasn't much deeper than the horse pond—except for the area by the cliffs. The sending still had plenty of water to maneuver in. As it drove them from the protection of each rock, and space between the rescuers and the victims became even greater. The lake was surrounded now by small fires, and almost everyone in the hill fort was shouting himself hoarse, making it difficult for anyone to hear cries coming from the lake.

At last Sigurd and Ragnhild reached a final pinnacle. They could retreat no further. Sigurd managed to shove Ragnhild out of the water onto its sloping top, where she dug in her fingers weakly, unable to do much more than moan each time she slipped downward a bit. The sending's eyes gleamed in the dark, knifing toward the rock where its victims waited. Sigurd held his axe in one hand, clinging to the rock with the other. When the first long, pale face came within range, he threw the axe with all his might. The sending heaved itself half out of the water with a terrifying roar, lashing its snaky limbs in a writhing mass that glistened in the last blood-red glimmerings of the sun. As it savored its fury and triumph, churning the water to foam and bellowing savagely, a slim dart of flame suddenly hissed from the darkness and lodged in the neck of one of the three heads. With a screech, the sending attempted to extinguish the fire by submerging, but the flame subsided into a sullen, burning coal, eating into the monster's flesh.

"Halfdane!" Sigurd shouted into the windy darkness. He had been thinking of the warlord and his gauntlet since the creature had begun driving them from rock to rock.

As if in answer, a halo of pale flame burst around the image of a horse and rider across the lake. The horse plunged into the breast-deep water, plowing it before him like the prow of a ship, leaping clear of the water several times in powerful showers of spray until the horse and rider seemed to be flying across the surface. The rider was swinging an axe in a gleaming arc, plunging almost into the swirling maze of snakelike tentacles before hurling the weapon with deadly aim. The sending engulfed the axe with a furious roar and retreated, except for a few lashing appendages which Halfdane parried away with his sword. Sigurd recognized him by the gauntlet, which seemed to glow with an aura of power as he wielded his weapons.

The sending retreated further, nursing its wounds with sullen growls and chopping sounds of its three sets of teeth. Halfdane's horse stood unsteadily on a submerged ledge while its rider peered into the dark at the sending's eyes.

"I don't think it will attack again," Halfdane said. "It knows now what a taste of the gauntlet will do for it, but its courage won't be long in returning, I fear. Put Ragnhild in the saddle and you ride behind her. When you get to the shore, send Atli back for me. He's a brave horse, but he can't carry the three of us at once."

Sigurd lifted Ragnhild into the saddle, but then he said, "Only a nithling would leave a man alone in the middle of a lake to face a sending. I can hold to the horse's tail, or to the stirrup and let him pull me along."

"No. I order you to take Ragnhild and go."

"I won't do it," Sigurd retorted, his teeth chattering. "I can swim to shore. Look at Ragnhild; she's freezing. We can't argue about it any longer."

Halfdane looked at her swiftly, sagging in the saddle with her face in the horse's mane. "You're right. But you shall ride, and I shall swim. You've had enough water for one night."

The return journey was considerably slower than Halfdane's mighty advance. The horse Atli swam strongly and steadily instead of plunging and flying across the water. Halfdane held to one stirrup and kept a wary eye turned backward. In the silence behind them, they heard soft splashes and the hiss of water parting around something large following them.

The sending did not make another appearance. They reached the shore, where a group of Alfar waited with dry blankets and mulled drink. Ragnhild, barely conscious, was bundled up more securely and Sigurd allowed someone to drape a cloak around his shoulders, but he impatiently demanded to carry Ragnhild back to the hill fort and rather presumptuously appropriated Halfdane's Atli for the purpose, knowing it was the fastest horse available.

He was not content until he had delivered Ragnhild into the hands of her attendants, who could be trusted to raise a great fuss over her and coax the life back into her cold, gray face. Sigurd returned only as far as the hall, where he stood before a crackling fire and steamed, rebuffing all offers of dry clothes, food, and drink to banish his shivering. His physical discomfort was nothing compared to the thoughts that raged in his mind.

Halfdane entered and passed by him, without a word, to see how Ragnhild fared. After a short interval, he returned in dry clothes and peremptorily bade Sigurd to go change before he caught his death of a chill.

"I won't go until I hear that Ragnhild is in no danger," he answered shortly, disregarding the friendly concern of the listening warriors who had returned to the hall.

Halfdane scowled. "Well, if you're determined to be so foolish, you can come and drip on my hearthstone where you'll be near enough to hear word of her. She's cold and chilled, but the shock is the worst of it, I suspect." He beckoned, and Sigurd silently followed, again refusing anything to make himself more comfortable. Halfdane sat in his chair close to the fire, smoking his pipe and keeping his thoughts to himself.

"I suppose you still think that Hross-Bjorn sending is something I ordered against you," the warlord said abruptly.

"I thought so at first," Sigurd said after a long pause. "But

I can't really believe that even you would risk the life of an innocent girl to get at your enemy. I thought it seemed suspicious that you were gone when the accident happened." He looked sharply at Halfdane, the doubts not entirely dead yet.

"And my return was very well timed," Halfdane continued, as if reading his thoughts. "Ragnhild came to no harm, after all. It would have been easy for one of you to have perished. Maybe next time you won't be so lucky. If you would just let me keep the box safe for you, Bjarnhardr's plots and schemes and sendings would be directed against me, instead of you, and I am far more capable of defending myself in this realm than you are." Seeing Sigurd's suddenly alert and wary expression, he arose with a muttered curse and stalked away. "I see there's no getting around your grandmother, is there? Nothing I can do will ever appear favorable in your eyes."

"It does no harm to consider both sides of every question," Sigurd replied guardedly. "I honestly can't tell if you're trying to threaten me with this sending or not."

"It can't help appearing that way, it seems," Halfdane replied in a bitter tone, looking up as someone tapped on the door.

Rolfr looked in timidly. At a grunt and a nod from Halfdane, he scuttled miserably inside and stood beside Sigurd.

"It was all my fault," he said. "It was my idea to embarrass Ragnhild because she thinks, quite correctly, that I am such a nithling. If it hadn't been for me, Jotull wouldn't have brought his wretched nikur to her; and the worst of it was that you weren't here to put a stop to him. Adills' back seized up in the most extraordinary manner just as he was about to warn Ragnhild; very strange, now that I think about it. He could have sent someone to warn her, and that someone should have been me, but I was too intent on this odious scheme. I doubt if he'll ever trust me again—"

Halfdane lifted his hand slowly. "You say Jotull brought the nikur to Hrafnborg?" he inquired sternly.

"Yes," Sigurd said, "and it was more my fault. I was the one who asked Jotull for his advice; after that, we seemed to lose control of the matter. It was bad that you weren't here."

"Yes, indeed," Halfdane mused. "We were plagued by a run of bad luck. Two horses became lame, and we couldn't leave them, nor could we leave two men to ride home alone. When we were yet several miles from Hrafnborg, I began to have the feeling that something was dreadfully amiss, so I rode ahead alone. I thought I heard Ragnhild calling me from the direction of the lake. The rest of the tale you are acquainted with.

"But I am concerned about Jotull's part in this escapade. Perhaps it was plain and simple bad luck that the horses went lame. They may have been unsound when we bought them. It could have been more bad luck that the nikur jumped into the worst part of the lake. Maybe even old Adills' backache was perfectly natural. We've known that a sending is following Sigurd; and being changeable creatures, they can assume whatever shape suits their purposes. But what puzzles me the most is why, then, would a great and dignified wizard like Jotull stoop to ridiculous tricks like this? If I hadn't heard that call for help, this adventure would have turned out very grim indeed."

Sigurd silently agreed as he scowled at the sodden toes of his boots, thinking of the voice he had heard calling "nikur." He knew he should tell Halfdane about it, but he was curiously reluctant. A nagging thought that it must have been Jotull kept annoying him, and he kept burying it just as persistently, along with the notion that making trouble for Jotull might not be a healthy occupation, as evinced by Adills' back.

Halfdane rose to pace back and forth, making a huge, shaggy shadow on the wall behind him. "Jotull and I don't like one another, which is no great secret. I'll have to suppose that he used the nikur to try to frighten Ragnhild—or worse. I absolve the two of you from the worst of the blame. You were only the tools of his vengeance. To you, Sigurd, I owe my gratitude for preserving Ragnhild's life at the risk of your own."

"I wouldn't have been there to be carried over the cliff with her if I hadn't been plotting a mischief against her," Sigurd answered gloomily. "You don't owe me any thanks. My luck is bad enough that others catch it from me. We all know the sending was waiting in the lake for no one but me."

"But who else knew that you planned to go for a swim in it to rescue a very wet and humiliated Ragnhild?" Halfdane asked with a curling of his lip and a flash in his eye. He paused in his restless prowling back and forth and took down an axe from the wall. "Since you lost your own defending Ragnhild, the least you can do is accept a replacement from me."

Sigurd hesitated, then accepted it. "I think I've been rather ungrateful," he began very stiffly, and didn't know how to finish. He examined the axe, which was a fine one, and said, "I think I shall go home and get dry now, if Ragnhild is in no serious danger."

Halfdane shook his head. "She's not a delicate creature. You can inquire after her in the morning. But before you fellows go, I am sure you are aware that in a case like this, where there might have been serious injury, there ought to be some punishment of the perpetrators. It is expected, in order to maintain discipline. Therefore I am certain you won't complain too desperately if I return both of you to watching on the earthworks for one week from today. Mischief of this sort must be discouraged."

"It could have been worse," Rolfr sighed, when they were outside. "Maybe it ought to have been worse. I feel absolutely terrible, Siggi. I owe you a most heartfelt apology. What if Halfdane hadn't come to save you and Ragnhild? The two people I care the most about in all Hrafnborg would both be gone, and it would have been no one's fault but my own. After tonight, I'll be a changed elf, Siggi."

"But Halfdane is the same," Sigurd replied bitterly. "Discipline must be upheld. That's what really matters the most to him."

"You don't really mean what you say," Rolfr said. "Halfdane was very easy on us and you know it. He might have sent me completely away to Raudborg or Ungiborg, and you might have been locked up. I don't think you've much cause for complaining, in spite of everything Jotull suggests to you."

Sigurd bristled for a stinging defense, then shrugged his

shoulders. "I know, I know. I thought I had to put on a great show to prove my independence. I thought Jotull was wonderful for daring to oppose Halfdane. Now I don't think he's so wonderful and daring. I think—" He paused, knowing Jotull had means of listening. "I think he's the one who sent Ragnhild's horse into the worst part of the lake. He knew we'd go in after her to save her and he knew the sending would be in the water waiting." His voice sank to a whisper.

"That's exactly what I think, too," Rolfr whispered. "And I would wager a year's pay that Jotull conjured Hross-Bjorn, also."

Sigurd rubbed his aching temples and shivered. "What should we do, Rolfr? He's got so much power. I don't mind admitting to you that I feel—well, frightened for my life."

Rolfr too looked worried. "The best thing you can do is to trust Halfdane, as the rest of us do. He'll protect you from Jotull and his clever scheming. You'll be one of us, Siggi, when you accept Halfdane as your leader."

"I'll try," Sigurd agreed determinedly. "You'll see a real change in me, Rolfr."

# Chapter 7

◇◇◇◇◇◇◇◇◇◇◇◇◇◇◇◇◇◇◇◇◇◇◇◇◇◇

When Sigurd no longer sought out Jotull's company, Jotull came seeking Sigurd. With a mildly injured attitude, Jotull accused Sigurd of shunning him, and Sigurd had no defense except to promise to renew his evening visits, although he would have preferred the good-natured company of the Alfar in the brightly lighted hall. Nor did he relish creeping around after dark, not knowing when Hross-Bjorn might lunge out of hiding, blaring a challenge, eyes gleaming and murderous hooves thudding.

When Sigurd and Rolfr arrived at Jotull's house, Mikla looked at Sigurd darkly, without the least glimmer of welcome. Jotull was quick to take up Sigurd's old favorite topics of conversation.

"Well, I hear you're no more of a favorite than you ever were," he began. "I overheard someone remarking about it just recently, saying you were no worse than many others, but Halfdane punishes you more than anyone and still hasn't assigned you to a real patrol in spite of your skill at weapons. You're very good, you know, and it's a dreadful shame for you to waste your time with Borgill and those young sprats on their worn-out nags. I suspect somehow that Halfdane is afraid of you, Sigurd. When you discover what's inside that box, you won't need to be subject to him any longer."

Sigurd poked at the fire. Thanks to Rolfr's misguided efforts at using the most inept of spells to thwart the sending, Sigurd and Rolfr always managed to keep themselves under censure for something. Sometimes they were simply lazy and disobedient. Sigurd learned to accept his punishment stoically, knowing he had done his best to earn it. At present he and Rolfr were under reprimand for pretending to get lost from Borgill's squad as a pretense for doing some exploring on their own; that had cost them the use of their horses for the week.

"I don't think Halfdane concerns himself much with me or with the box," Sigurd replied. "He's got more important things to worry about."

"Ah, that's what you think." Jotull sighed, toying with a silver chain around his neck. "He knows he has you frightened of him, so you'll stop asking about taking that box to Bergthor of Svartafell. When I tried to urge the idea on him, he became furious and warned me not to continue interfering. Interfering, indeed! If it weren't for me, I'm sure you'd be dead by now. He's cold and calculating and cruel. Look at that sending he made against you."

He pointed to the little window, just as a long, pale face glided by, peering in. After assuring itself that Sigurd was within, the sending stationed itself on the roof, peering down through the smoke hole and periodically trying the edges with its teeth.

Sigurd looked up at the sending, and his hand strayed to the fine axe Halfdane had given him. "I find it hard to believe that Halfdane could have conjured such a creature as Hross-Bjorn. Halfdane's no wizard, except when it comes to warfare."

Sigurd met Jotull's gaze briefly, and his defense of Halfdane had nettled Jotull exceedingly. "You'll be sorry if you give that box to Halfdane. I alone know how sorry you'll be."

"I'm not ready to hand it over to anyone yet," Sigurd said. "But if Halfdane were entrusted with something valuable, I don't think he'd misuse it."

Jotull rose to pace the floor. "You've no idea how it pains me to hear you talking like a fool. I never thought Halfdane could subvert such a clever mind as yours, but I see you're beginning to fall into his trap. I'd hoped I could help you, Sigurd. I'm the only one who will take you to Svartafell, the only one who has tried to warn you against Halfdane, the only one who is willing to help you. One day you'll discover by yourself that I am your only true friend."

Sigurd only shrugged. "I've made more than a few friends here. I feel I'm reasonably safe, in spite of the sending. What else can I do, in view of the present circumstances?"

"Escape!" Jotull's eyes glowed with fervor. "Get out of Hrafnborg, away from Halfdane and his sending! Haven't we talked about it often enough?"

Rolfr turned to Sigurd, aggrieved. "Sigurd, you wouldn't leave Hrafnborg without me, would you? You'd have to take me along, and I daresay you wouldn't like that for long. Besides, after all Halfdane has done for you, it would be a nithling's deed to run away so ungratefully."

Jotull whirled to glare at Rolfr, gripping his staff as if he wished to do something with it that would wreak havoc on Rolfr. Sigurd stood up quickly to intervene. "I think our hour is almost over," he said carefully. "Come on, Mikla, you'd better walk with us, since our old three-headed friend is waiting."

Jotull leaned on his staff. "You weren't always in such a hurry. An hour is a relative length of time."

"Not to Adills," Sigurd said. "He waits for us and gives us a bloody harangue if we stay too long."

Jotull coughed contemptuously behind one hand. "Adills might once have been enough protection for you against that sending, but he has grown far too old to be practicing magic. This is a good, stout house with a solid roof and door and it is yours, if you don't feel safe in that crumbling old tower. I've seen a weaker sending tear a stronger house to pieces to get at what it wanted."

"The old tower is stronger than it looks," Sigurd replied.

"And so is Adills," Rolfr interrupted, edging toward the door. "If we need help, we'll go to Halfdane."

"Halfdane! Am I the only one who sees him for what he really is?" Jotull demanded. "He's more clever than most wizards. Go to him then, but I wager you'll change your mind about him one sad day."

Sigurd was glad to make his escape. Mikla's spirits were so elevated by Jotull's discomfiture that he couldn't restrain himself from some most uncharacteristic demonstrations of glee and plotted with Rolfr and Sigurd a complete overthrow of his master. For the first time, Sigurd began to regard Mikla as a friend. The three of them swore a great and dreadful oath that they would be friends and comrades forever, united in the cause of the confusion of Jotull and ousting him from Adills' rightful position as wizard of Hrafnborg.

To Sigurd's relief, Ragnhild's health was not impaired by her icy dunking in the lake, and it was not long before she again took her customary inspection of the fortress by walking from one end of the earthworks to the other. Sigurd viewed her first appearance with guilty apprehension, wishing he had someplace to hide, but he could not very well abandon his sentry position, even though he suspected it might be death to remain. Ragnhild, of all those he knew in Hrafnborg, had the keenest appreciation of the art of revenge. Each day that she had kept to her chambers, he had discreetly inquired of one of her thralls or serving women whether she was doing better or worse, partly in an effort to mollify her temper. He knew the servants would instantly tell their mistress he had asked about her health. Most likely she would only be more offended, unless her soaking had somehow softened her haughty pride.

He kept his eyes on her warily as she approached, pretending not to notice him. She was dressed in red, which was an uncomfortable reminder of that unlucky day at the lake.

"What, no Rolfr?" she greeted him, after looking around.

"He's got a toothache today, and Adills is curing it," Sigurd replied, still wary. "I suppose you've come to avenge yourself on me for that horrible trick we played on you. It was inexcusable."

Ragnhild turned her face away to hide a slight blush. "Yes, I suppose it made quite a spectacle. My cousin Halfdane assured me I looked like a drowned cat. He still chuckles over it."

Sigurd winced at the tone of her voice. "I don't blame you for being angry. You've got plenty of cause. I don't often apologize, but this time I have to say I'm very sorry and I wouldn't have wanted such a misfortune to befall anybody."

"The misfortune was intended for you," she said. "I was of no consequence to whomever it was who wanted to harm you. But I didn't come out here to hear you apologize to me. I wish to thank you for saving my life, when you probably had little inclination to do so. I was a very unpleasant creature to Rolfr and you, but I've resolved to change. I hope you still don't hate me. I've asked Halfdane if you might join us of evenings once a week, if you'd care to. He wasn't opposed to the idea."

Sigurd was struck dumb by the honor being offered to him, to visit on equal standing with important people like Halfdane and Ragnhild. "I'm honored, but—"

"Good. Tomorrow night then. I suppose Rolfr will be frightfully offended, so perhaps you'd better bring him, if he wants to come. I know he's rather in love with me, but I don't like him very much. He's made himself silly trying to get my attention. He must realize that I wouldn't be permitted to make a match with a perfect nobody, such as he is."

"He's a good-hearted fellow, though. I suppose Halfdane has a list of jarls' sons for you to take your pick of."

"He may, but I have established a long tradition of doing as I please; so if he has a list, he may as well forget about it. How would you like to be told whom to spend the rest of your life with?"

"I don't suppose I'll ever have to worry about it, unless I somehow find my way back to my own realm," Sigurd answered, with more gloom than he really intended.

Ragnhild surveyed him with her cool, blue gaze and sat down on a nearby rock. "Then you've never thought of marrying an Alfar woman and staying here to live? It has happened before, you know, and it's not anything so remarkable. The people who have done it might astonish you, if you only knew."

Sigurd paused a moment to consider the idea of spending the remainder of his life in the Alfar realm and letting the memories of Thongullsfjord and its inhabitants grow as distant and unreal as the Alfar realm had once seemed to him. "I can't think it would be a very good thing, if the person from the other realm had left a large family," he said thoughtfully. "It would be difficult to visit back and forth, and the grandparents would never get to see their grandchildren."

Ragnhild brushed some ants off her skirt and stamped on them. "Oftentimes grandparents can cause trouble. Perhaps a mother didn't want her daughter to wed an Alfar, so she made herself disagreeable. I know of one such marriage, which might have been happy if not for a bitter old woman who thought her grandson should be raised as a Scipling, not an Alfar. It was a very sad story, but perhaps I'll tell it to you sometime. You were very fond of your grandmother, weren't you?"

Sigurd nodded reluctantly. "She was the only family I had, and I left her dead, with the ghost of a settlement and the ruin of the farm we worked so hard to build. Everything she worked for came to naught. Even I failed at the last, and that was perhaps the most important to her." He gazed around the earthworks and the neat squares of longhouses inside. Thorarna's warning about the warlord had certainly done him no good.

Ragnhild folded her hands inside her embroidered sleeves and continued to gaze at him. "Well, she wouldn't want you left for the trolls and Dokkalfar, I should hope. What else was

Halfdane to do with a lone survivor? I'm sure he knew there would be difficulties in transplanting a Scipling to Hrafnborg. As for myself, I can't see why you're so unhappy here."

Sigurd stood up uncomfortably, looking down at the tower and hoping to see Rolfr cured of his toothache and coming to rescue him from Ragnhild's questions. "It's not as simple as whether I want to stay here or not," he said stiffly. "It's a question of who are my friends and who are my foes. Before she died, my grandmother warned me about certain things and she gave me a box which doesn't seem to have a key. When I can open it, I'll know more about myself."

"I see," Ragnhild said, rising to her feet and pulling a large bundle of keys from her belt. "Do you think any of these would fit the lock? They're my housekeeping keys, but many of them are for locks I never use."

Sigurd looked at them and shook his head. "I'm afraid more is required than a key."

"Oh! It needs magic, does it? Bring it to me and I'll make it open then. Adills has taught me magic all my life and he says I'll be as adept as Mikla, without going to the Guild school."

Sigurd gazed over the lifeless landscape, where even the birds and hares must have been dozing away the daylight hours. "I was advised to take the box to its maker, a dwarf smith, but unfortunately Halfdane won't permit it."

"He won't? I wonder why not. I think I shall ask him."

Sigurd started in alarm. "No, I wouldn't do that if I were you. I suspect he'd get rather angry, mostly at me for talking so much. I shouldn't have mentioned the box to you." Angrily he told himself he was a gullible fool, ready to blurt out all his secrets to the first listening ear, expecting sympathy for his complaints and advice he had no intention of taking.

Ragnhild seemed to read his thoughts and smiled. "It shall be a secret, then, if that's what you want. You ought to beware of those you entrust secrets to, because you oblige yourself to them. Jotull will spare you tomorrow evening, won't he?"

Sigurd noticed the connection she made between Jotull and

entrusting secrets and frowned. "I'm not obliged to Jotull for very much. I can do as I please with my free time."

She nodded, satisfied, and began to descend the steep slope of the earthworks. "Farewell until tomorrow, then. Do your best to humor Rolfr, if he's at all disappointed."

Jealousy was an idea that had never occurred to Rolfr. He rejoined Sigurd on the earthworks shortly, after spending the entire time watching Ragnhild sitting and talking with Sigurd. His eyes went round with amazement when he learned that Ragnhild hadn't threatened him violence. He had fully expected a fiery, vituperative attack. As to his invitation to Halfdane's hall, Rolfr whistled and shook his head, declining to accompany Sigurd when he went, assuring him he had no desire for refined society and protesting that, after nearly drowning the object of his love, he had lost interest in the relationship and was quite willing to give Ragnhild to Sigurd. There was another girl, the daughter of Borgill's brother, who was showing signs of not absolutely detesting him, which was indeed encouraging.

In spite of Rolfr's predictions to the contrary, Sigurd enjoyed the evenings at Halfdane's hall, particularly since Halfdane had the unusual courtesy to absent himself each time, if he was not gone on the night patrol. Sigurd was treated to a better supper than he was accustomed to in the main hall, and the evening was spent playing chess to the accompaniment of a very elderly harpist and the busy knitting sounds from several of Ragnhild's women attendants. When Sigurd had lost enough chess games, they talked and toasted inflated cracklings on long forks over the fire. Mostly they discussed horses and hunting, until one of the duennas politely suggested the hour was getting late. Then Sigurd left the good cheer and order of Halfdane's hall for the bats and dust of the old tower, which always seemed greatly the worse by comparison.

Before Sigurd could imagine where the time had gone, summer was on the wane and the nights were getting longer and colder. The Alfar cheerfully promised him he would be seeing more Dokkalfar and trolls as winter approached. The most critical time would be the months of darkness when the sun failed to appear. Swords and axes were sharpened with loving care, and new shafts were fitted to spears and arrows. Sigurd waited anxiously for Halfdane to assign him to a patrol where he could expect to do some real fighting, but the first heavy snow of the winter fell, and still he was stuck with old Borgill and the young boys. His skills so far surpassed any of the others' that he and Rolfr had become the instructors. Rolfr began each day by solemnly observing that it was likely to be the last they would spend in such idle amusements; Halfdane would surely assign them both that very day.

One morning the patrol returned looking more ragged and jaunty than usual and reported that they had engaged with a large number of trolls during the night and had killed most of them. The first successful encounter with the enemy was cause for celebration, but Jotull did his best to sour Sigurd's hopes by tauntingly predicting that he would be left at home with the old men, women, and children while all the real warriors were defending Hrafnborg—a most ridiculous position, considering his possession of the carven box.

Despondent and inclined to agree, Sigurd wandered outside the hall to find a quiet place to think. After peering cautiously around for evidences of Hross-Bjorn, he decided that the merry noises of singing and roistering had kept the sending sulking in the old barrow ground beyond the earthworks, which was its favorite haunt. Still vigilant, Sigurd slogged to the tumble-down stable where he kept his horse with several other young fellows' nags. He was perfectly accustomed to the beams and walls inside the old barn, so he had no need of a lantern. Speaking soothingly to the horses, he slipped into the gray mare's stall and knelt down to feel the hoof where she had stone-bruised it the day before.

The injury was still warm with fever, but cooler than yesterday, he decided with satisfaction. He was about to stand up to leave when the door opened again and someone came in. He thought it must be some of the boys coming to look at their horses and was meditating some sort of surprise attack to startle them, when he heard Halfdane speak in a low, impatient voice.

"What is it you need to say that requires such privacy, Dagrun?" he demanded.

"Only this: when are you going to do your duty, Halfdane? You know what I'm talking about—and whom."

"The carven box and Sigurd—yes." Halfdane's tone was expressionless. "I knew you'd begin to think of him when the fighting started."

"Well? Haven't you delayed long enough in getting that box? I can't understand your softness in keeping us waiting for so long. Everyone knows he's got something, but only you and I know what it is. You should have taken charge of it long ago, even before we left Thongullsfjord. The cheeky young devil has been here nearly half a year, and from what I've seen of his temper, I'd say he's not just going to hand it over to you, no matter what you say or do."

Sigurd steadied himself against the wall, scarcely breathing as he waited for Halfdane's answer.

Halfdane paused, and Sigurd could hear him honing his knife against his boot, a most unpromising sound. "You needn't work yourself into such a rage over it, Dagrun. You know I could possess that box and its contents at any moment I chose, if I thought Hrafnborg was in any danger. I've been biding my time, hoping Sigurd would begin to see the justice of our cause without being told. When I've earned his trust, the box will come into our hands without a struggle."

Dagrun spat into the straw. "Trust! I say take it now and make your excuses later. You've got to think about Hrafnborg first, or we may have dreadful problems. What if he runs away with Jotull and falls somehow into Bjarnhardr's clutches? He could come back against us, and that's not a pleasant picture to imagine. He was frightfully partial toward Jotull for a while, you remember. When I think of the power being juggled in those treacherous, skillful hands of Jotull's, it makes my blood turn cold. Jotull is the one who can decide our fate, far more than Sigurd. The longer we wait to get that box, the more chances Jotull will have."

Halfdane sighed, still stropping the knife. "What an evil star Jotull has been since Sigurd arrived. I knew he was weak in loyalty to Hrafnborg, but Sigurd and this box have awakened Jotull's avarice. Would that I knew a way to make a malefactoring wizard behave or some way to make old Adills young and fiery again. Jotull's powers far exceed Adills', and it is Jotull who stands between me and Sigurd."

"Then get rid of Jotull. He's not working for the best interest of Hrafnborg if he's trying to get Sigurd away from us. Mikla says very little, but I think he's afraid of his master. If I had just a bit more of an excuse, I would discover a very bad accident for Jotull."

"You may be right, Dagrun. Perhaps Jotull must go. But that's not likely to help us much with Sigurd, if he still admires the wizard. He might think he had lost his only possibility of escape."

"All to the better for us, then. Sigurd must discover that life is often short and far from ideal when he is playing at holding such a power as that box."

Halfdane remained silent a moment, and Sigurd counted three icy runnels of sweat trickling down his back. He had no doubt that Dagrun hoped to make his life as short and as far from ideal as an axe or sword could accomplish, if he didn't give up the box when it was demanded.

"Sigurd is beginning to trust me somewhat, I think," Halfdane said. "The time is better now than it ever has been, if we are to approach him. It has been an upward struggle, thanks to Jotull, but I've done everything I could, short of assigning him to a patrol. I know that would win him over completely—"

"No, no, don't do it. It's too risky. Far too many opportunities to pretend to get lost. You don't know what Jotull might do. Keep Sigurd safe in Hrafnborg where one of us can watch him."

"That was my inclination also. We can't lose him now, not after searching twenty years for him. Too much is at stake, Dagrun."

"I couldn't agree with you more. That's why we've got to stop wasting time. Enough has been wasted already." He pulled the door open and they went out, still talking in low voices.

Sigurd waited a long time before straightening his aching knees and darting for the small door on the other side of the barn. After remembering to look for the sending briefly, he dashed across the snowy interval to the old tower, arriving at the door with a slithering plunge. He had hoped to be alone, but Rolfr and Adills both greeted him amiably through a pall of smoke, sitting with their feet almost in the fire and smoking enormous pipes.

"Hallo, Siggi!" Rolfr shouted. "What's wrong? You came in as if the sending had its teeth in you."

"You look rather upset," Adills observed, as Sigurd brushed by to fling himself on his bed without speaking.

"Oh, it's nothing," Sigurd replied lightly. "Just a small matter of misplaced trust."

Rolfr fanned some of the smoke away. "I'll bet that hairless rat Ari forgot to poultice your horse again, right? You ought to make matchwood of his ribs, Siggi, or he'll never remember anything."

Rolfr chattered on about the benefits of punitive aids to the memory, which Sigurd hardly heard over the uproar of his own inner turmoil. If he had never begun to admire and trust Halfdane, the pain of his betrayal would not have been so great. He had considered his trust in Halfdane only a small and rather doubtful thing, but its death left him in blackest misery and resentment. His former anger boiled into new life, more virulent than before, and he renewed his resolution to escape from Hrafnborg before Halfdane and Dagrun had a chance to spring their trap on him. There was nothing he regretted leaving behind. Now that his eyes were opened, he could see that everything was lies and bribery, from Halfdane's axe to those cozy evenings by Ragnhild's fire, and even Rolfr's friendship fell under suspicion. He had been blind and stupid to think that these Alfar valued him for anything except the box.

Sigurd, in his disillusionment, wasted no time in taking refuge in Jotull's association once more, much to the bafflement of Rolfr and Mikla. Sigurd avoided Ragnhild and Halfdane's hall to the extent that he missed half of his meals, and he quarreled fiercely with anyone who crossed him. He even quarreled with Jotull, who perversely refused to abandon Hrafnborg instantly at Sigurd's whim. The wizard knew he had the upper hand again and saw no need to hurry.

Although he knew it was useless, Sigurd decided to approach Halfdane and confront the warlord about his assignment to a patrol. He waylaid Halfdane one snowy morning as Borgill was patiently conducting his untidy troops outside the earthworks. Sigurd knew he looked as much like a warrior as anyone as he halted his horse within speaking distance of Halfdane and waited until the warlord rode closer to him.

"I know what you're going to ask me," Halfdane greeted him, looking displeased. "Borgill has told me you're getting quite too good for his patrol, and I suppose there is a bit of truth in the matter. You have been progressing well, until lately. Rolfr tells me you've gone back to Jotull now and he's afraid of what Jotull may be telling you."

Sigurd smiled wryly to think that his suspicions about Rolfr's spying upon him were correct. "I didn't come here to talk about Jotull. What I want to know is why I haven't been assigned yet. I can fight as well as almost anyone and I'm getting tired of staying inside the earthworks. Sometimes it's hard for me to believe I'm not a prisoner here."

Halfdane's eyes flicked over Sigurd's weapons and horse. "We have different ways of treating our prisoners than arming them and teaching them all our ways. I hardly think you've been treated badly; if not for the sending, you'd be better off here than you were in Thongullsfjord. It's partly because of that sending that I won't assign you to ride out with a patrol. You're safer from it here within walls, and we have problems enough with the trolls and Dokkalfar without the sending stalking us also."

"A pity I can't open that box of my grandmother's and use whatever is inside to defend myself," Sigurd said calculatingly.

Halfdane gazed at him a moment, totally arrested, too startled to remember to scowl. "There is a way—perhaps. But no, the time isn't right, not with Jotull interfering. Has Jotull told you anything he suspects about this box—or yourself?"

"Only that I needn't be subject to anyone, once I get it open," Sigurd retorted sharply. "Why, is there some secret that

I don't know? Is that the reason that everyone attempts to deceive me and trick me into giving the box away? I'm no fool; I can see what you've been trying to do and I don't need Jotull to tell me when my trust is being bought." Sigurd's poorly controlled temper awakened his mischievous natural power, and it tweaked at the ears of the horses and buzzed around their heels like wasps until they pranced nervously in circles.

"Bought!" Halfdane repeated as his horse snorted and pawed impatiently. "Is that what you call our friendship and our attempts to make you one of the Alfar of Hrafnborg? If anyone else had found you and that box, I daresay you'd be dead by now or far more miserable than you are. You're weak, Sigurd, and you're allowing that box to get control of you, instead of your controlling it. You're further now from seeing what is inside than you were a month ago, and I wouldn't help you now to open it if you asked me, which you will never do as long as Jotull is here to advise you."

Sigurd twisted his horse's neck around unkindly. "I won't ask, so you don't need to worry!" He spurred his horse and it leaped away, glad to escape the increasing manifestations of Sigurd's power. Halfdane rode off in the opposite direction, and neither looked back.

Sigurd caught up with Borgill's patrol, which was proceeding raggedly across the frosted meadows toward the lake. Rolfr looked at him and wisely said nothing until Sigurd broke the silence.

"Well, if I wait for promotions from Halfdane, I'll be here until I'm older than Adills," Sigurd finally said, still seething. "He told me I won't ride out because of the sending, and I can't open the box because I'm far too stupid, and he won't help me open the box because I can't control it. But if he won't allow me to open the box, how can I ever get rid of the sending? If I can't get rid of the sending, I can't ride out, so it looks as if I'm stuck here until I rot."

"Good, I shall rot with you," Rolfr replied.

"I'm in no mood for joking. You don't really mean it, anyway. I know that all of you are scheming to get the box away from me, and I no longer trust anyone or believe anything you say."

"Except Jotull," Rolfr added. "Jotull, who called that nikur into the lake with you and Ragnhild clinging to it. Jotull, who must have known the sending would be waiting there for you. Jotull, who put a spell on Adills to seize up his back, and Jotull, who has poisoned your mind against Halfdane from the start, while Halfdane has given you food and shelter and protection under his own roof."

Sigurd rode in silence, struggling to reject what Rolfr had said. "Well, I know Halfdane wants the box. I heard him and Dagrun talking about it and how they would take it away from me once they got me to trust them enough. All this so-called kindness is just bribery," he declared bitterly.

"Jotull wants the box just as badly as Halfdane does," Rolfr said. "The only difference is the methods used and your chances of survival afterward. I can see you sharing this hidden power with Halfdane, but Jotull isn't the kind who likes to share."

Sigurd shook his head stubbornly. "I don't want to share my birthright, with either Jotull or Halfdane. I know all this about Jotull, so you don't need to nag me about it. But I need Jotull to get me away from here and take me to Svartafell so the box can be opened as soon as possible. Halfdane has some notion that I'm not ready to know what the thing is yet."

"I see. Then all you'll have to worry about is getting free from Jotull, once you get away from Halfdane," Rolfr observed. "A nice exchange, Siggi, something like the fire and the frying pan."

"You're being disagreeable today, aren't you?" Sigurd glared at Rolfr and didn't speak to him for the rest of the day. His own miserable doubts kept him excellent company, with the result that by nightfall he was in the depths of wretched indecision. Rolfr's easy good spirits were unimpeded by scowls and moody silences, and he was whistling cheerfully over a pot of boiled mutton when Adills came in with momentous news. The old wizard thrust the door open with his staff and hobbled in quickly on a gust of wind that blew him along like a dry leaf.

"It's happened at last!" he exulted, throwing his staff in the corner with a splutter of sparks. "Halfdane has banished Jotull. Ordered him to pack up and leave Hrafnborg before Midwinter or suffer the consequences. I hope he opts for the consequences. I think Halfdane could kill him with his gauntlet." He collapsed into his favorite chair, cackling appreciatively. "Oh, I've waited a long time to see Jotull get his comeuppance. Serves him right for thinking he can flout Halfdane's rules."

Midwinter isn't soon enough for me," Rolfr said, with a troubled glance at Sigurd. "I wish he were gone today."

Sigurd maintained a cold silence, wondering what Jotull's next action would be. All he knew for certain was the fact that, when Jotull left Hrafnborg, he would go with him. Staying in Hrafnborg was going to get him nowhere. Already many of Borgill's young troops were returned to wall-watching, and many of their horses had been put on the list for possible emergency rations for the hill fort when the food supplies ran low. Sigurd's fortunes had turned full circle, and he was again at his low point, perhaps worse off than he had been when he had first arrived at Hrafnborg. The weather was cold and the days almost sunless. Rolfr had told him he could look forward to nothing better than many wretched hours of standing guard on the earthworks, roasting his toes in the coals to keep them from freezing off, with no company more exalted than the most ancient of the fighting men, stout-armed housewives whose ferocity was equal to any troll, and the other members of Borgill's patrol, if their mothers would let them go.

"But Halfdane needs Jotull's magic to assist him, if he's going to survive the winter," Sigurd said. "The Dokkalfar outnumber us twenty to one and maybe more. In years past, from what I've heard, Halfdane has relied upon spells and tricks, such as moving the stones from the safe river crossings to deep parts where anybody who goes in gets washed away and drowned, or spells to frighten the Dokkalfar. What's Halfdane going to do without Jotull's power?"

"We don't need Jotull," Adills snapped. "I've wizarded Hrafnborg through worse winters and I've fought Dokkalfar with Halfdane's father while Jotull was still torturing cats and frogs. A feud between the warlord and his wizard is a dangerous thing, and I say good riddance to Jotull. While there's life in this old carcass, Halfdane won't be without a wizard." He poured a cup of aromatic fluid from a blackened pot and swallowed half of the scalding mixture, which Sigurd had first mistaken for horse linament.

Rolfr edged another bit of peat onto the already hot fire. "Sigurd has a point, Adills. There's not as much fire in your blood as there once was, and it takes a lot more tea and firewood to get you unthawed than it used to. And I've never seen such chilblains as the ones on your toes. You're a tough old reptile, but we're all compelled to admit that you're getting old."

"Bah. Once I get my legs straightened out again, I'll be ready to go. Jotull won't ride out with Halfdane after being sacked, I expect. The Dokkalfar are pushing at Bedasford again and they're liable to get across tonight unless we do something extraordinary to stop them. Svinhagahall Dokkalfar, mind you, so that means Bjarnhardr, Halfdane's oldest and most hated enemy."

"Bedasford, is it?" Rolfr frowned and looked at his weapons rather longingly. "He's getting too close for comfort, particularly this early in the winter. It's not even Midwinter yet."

Adills darted a sly glance at Sigurd. "Perhaps this year he thinks he's got more incentive, and I'm certain he's got more information. He seems to know what Halfdane is going to do almost before it's attempted."

Sigurd interrupted angrily, "If you're hinting that Jotull is spying for Bjarnhardr, why don't you come out and say so?"

"Because saying outright that Jotull is a spy, a traitor, and a beastly, slinking troll's offspring is a good way to make him angry," Adills replied, motioning for his boots with one hand. "I know he had something to do with Hross-Bjorn, and he's using that sending to frighten you, Sigurd, and terrorize Hrafnborg. I could destroy that sending or turn it back against its maker, if I were a bit faster and hadn't forgotten so much." He paused in the midst of their combined efforts to jam his swollen feet into his boots. "I hate to leave you two here with that thing sniffing around the door. It acts worse when I'm not around to defend you. Maybe I should stay here tonight. I have a feeling that something may happen if I'm not here."

"We can take care of ourselves," Rolfr assured him. "Halfdane needs you. If we get into trouble, we'll have plenty of help. We'd gladly trade you places if we could, wouldn't we, Siggi?"

"We certainly would," Sigurd answered with a sigh.

Adills gave himself a brisk shake and reached for his cloak. "It can't be helped. I must go."

He almost changed his mind again when he saw that Jotull had decided to ride out with Halfdane to the fighting, but Adills' hesitation was momentary. He climbed onto his shaggy old nag and positioned himself at Halfdane's side, pointedly shouldering Jotull and his fine horse and trappings aside. Adills waved to Sigurd and Rolfr as the cavalcade trotted toward the earthworks.

Sigurd and Rolfr joined the other wall-watchers and observed Halfdane and his warriors riding across the snow in the half-gloom of the northern night. Sigurd looked at his companions and suppressed a shudder. They looked like the Norns, the three sisters who endlessly spun out men's fates and cut them off when their lives were finished, like threads of wool. The three old women nodded to Sigurd and Rolfr and silently made room for them around the fire.

By noonday, in the unrelieved darkness of the long winter night, the news arrived that the Dokkalfar had crossed the river and were advancing at a determined rate toward Hrafnborg. Several Ljosalfar were dead or wounded, and one was missing. When the messengers returned later with the casualties, Sigurd and Rolfr learned that the missing Alfar was the old wizard Adills.

# Chapter 8

◆◇◆◇◆◇◆◇◆◇◆◇◆◇◆◇◆◇◆◇◆◇◆◇◆

Hross-Bjorn wasted no time in taking advantage of Adills' absence. It began to stalk Sigurd with a vengeance, following him around the earthworks just out of arrowshot on the far side, growling and lashing itself into a fury of destruction. Then it rushed at its quarry, snorting phosphorescent clouds into the air and snapping its teeth in a vile frenzy. Sigurd and the other wall-watchers drove it off the best they could, but their best efforts scarcely dampened the creature's resolve. It lurked around the buildings in the shadows until no one dared to move about the enclosure alone.

Sigurd stubbornly refused Halfdane's curt offer of the protection of the main hall, although he and Rolfr got very little sleep in the old tower. The sending launched its assaults at frequent intervals, with no daylight to deter it and no Adills to singe it with bursts of crackling flame. When the tower threatened to fall down around their ears, Sigurd gathered his possessions and informed Rolfr that he was going to stay with Jotull and Rolfr could go with him or go to Halfdane's hall.

"I'll go with you," Rolfr said, "although I don't expect to like it. At least we won't have to share his company past Midwinter."

Sigurd made no reply for a moment. "When Jotull was talking about my leaving Hrafnborg, did you mean it when you said it was your duty to go with me?"

Rolfr looked around the tower room in sad farewell. "Halfdane ordered me to watch out for you, and I'll do it whether you want me to or not. In fact, I'd do it even if he didn't order me to. It's not going to be easy for you to get rid of me, Siggi.

Now that Adills is gone, you're all I've got, except Mikla, and he's apprenticed to Jotull."

Jotull greeted them with no signs of surprise. "I'd expected you sooner, after old Adills was out of the way," he said. "It will be somewhat crowded quarters, but it will only be for a few days until Midwinter. You've brought the box, I trust?"

"Of course. I'm not a complete ninny," Sigurd snapped. "You must have known all this would happen. When are we leaving?"

Mikla stopped grinding at some bones he was powdering and looked at Sigurd menacingly. Jotull shrugged and said, "Since we're not mincing any words, I'll say we leave when I'm ready."

Sigurd waited impatiently for two days, enduring Mikla's scowls and recriminations. "I won't change my mind," he told him sharply. "I'm going to do what I think is best for me, and there's no other way than leaving Hrafnborg and going to Svartafell."

"No other way!" Mikla snorted. "Try the sensible way. But I suppose that might be too difficult for a person with no sense."

Sigurd did not speak to him again until Jotull announced one morning that he was ready to depart for Svartafell. Heartily sick of living among Jotull's unsavory powderings and sinister collections, Sigurd gladly agreed to get ready. Rolfr said nothing, staring into the fire abstractedly until Sigurd jostled him impatiently.

"Let's get going, Rolfr. Or have you changed your mind?"

Rolfr shook his head, and Mikla's look consigned them both to the depths of Hel's cold kingdom of the dead.

Rolfr sighed heavily. "I have no choice but to go with you. It is my duty as assigned me by Halfdane and also my duty as a friend." He looked uncertainly at Jotull and added, "You'll be glad enough for an extra pair of eyes and ears and arms that can wield weapons in your defense."

"Glad indeed," Jotull replied, offering his hand to Sigurd and then to Rolfr. "Particularly since I intend to leave Mikla here to soothe the indignation of Halfdane at losing two wizards

in one week. Perhaps you can make yourself useful, Mikla,
with that prodigious Guild education you have."

"I'll welcome the opportunity," Mikla replied snappishly.
"Some Guild magic around here might not be amiss. We hav-
en't seen any since Adills died."

Jotull narrowed his eyes to fine glittering points. "Don't be
sure that I won't be coming back—assuming there will be
something left of Hrafnborg to return to, that is. I hope your
native impudence won't carry you too far in my absence, you
young upstart. It will be your unworthy self who advises Halfdane in my absence, so I advise you to tell him not to attempt
to follow us in an effort to regain his property, or things may
go exceedingly bad indeed for that same property." He glanced
almost imperceptibly at Sigurd, who was still holding the carv-
en box.

Mikla replied with bare civility, "I shall allow a reasonable
delay before I inform Halfdane of your disappearance. I needn't
manufacture any clever lies on your behalf; Halfdane will know
at once that the bargain is mutual." He refused to look at Sigurd.

Under the direction of Jotull, Mikla, Sigurd, and Rolfr made
all the preparations for the journey. They finished just as a
very battle-weary patrol rode into Hrafnborg for replacements
and reprovisioning. Halfdane, however, had remained in his
windy camp in the fells, overlooking the activities of the Dokkalfar. Sigurd was grateful for his absence, in spite of Rolfr's
low spirits. The only thing that gave Sigurd a brief moment's
uncertainty was how to say farewell to Ragnhild, who obviously
cared about him to a more than ordinary extent. He had never
liked farewells, but he would have liked to have a last look at
her. His most recent memory of her was observing her wringing
the neck of a chicken for a young kitchen girl who was too
stupid to do it properly. In addition to seeing Ragnhild one
more time, Sigurd also wanted to ask her to lend him her gray
stallion, so that he wouldn't be forced to steal a good horse
from the fighting men.

Jotull disparaged his motives and thought Sigurd overpolite,
but Sigurd eventually won the dispute, and Jotull accompanied
Sigurd to Halfdane's hall. The sending circled at a safe dis-

tance, a looming black shadow composed of indeterminate shapes and an aura of menace that raised gooseflesh. Sigurd could scarcely take his eyes from the creature as it followed in the dismal light of the distant stars, its three sets of teeth grinning in merry anticipation.

Ragnhild showed no surprise at the appearance of Sigurd and Jotull in her house, and looked up only once when Jotull commanded her servants to leave the room. She went on with her weaving until she had finished the row, and then put down her heddles and beater to speak to her guests.

"I've been thinking about you, Sigurd," she said in her matter-of-fact way, "and it came to me in a dream last night that you are going to take a long journey. I won't say a dangerous journey," she added with a glance at Jotull, "because all journeys are dangerous, especially in the eyes of those who are forced to stay behind. I'm glad you came for my blessing before you went."

"You're a clever little witch," Jotull said in dark admiration. "But I hope you're clever enough to know that Halfdane desires our departure to remain a secret. If the others knew the danger was so great that Halfdane would send Sigurd away, they might lose their courage. I shall reward you for the smallest silence."

He reached for his money pouch, but Ragnhild only eyed him in silent scorn. With a scowl, he produced another bag and reluctantly pushed it across the table toward her. "It's a very potent charm I made for myself against the walking dead. You should prize it quite highly before the winter is out."

Ragnhild accepted the charm with a nod. "It should be fairly tolerable. I have no doubt that no one will know you are gone until it is too late to retrieve you." She spoke the last words to Sigurd with particular emphasis. "When we meet next, I expect to find you greatly changed. I have a charm for you to carry with you and I hope it will bring you good luck—and protection." It was a small gold ring on a braided cord made from her own hair, which she hung around his neck. "You can untie the ends and you'll have an extra bowstring, if you ever get into such a predicament, and the ring was one I wore on

my finger. The runes will protect you against the evil powers
of your enemies."

"I don't like to say goodbyes," Sigurd said, uncomfortably
aware of Jotull glowering at him and Ragnhild. "I regret leaving
Halfdane so ungratefully, but you haven't seen him as I have
come to know him, which makes it vital for me to leave
Hrafnborg. I don't care if I never see Halfdane again, but I
don't want to leave as a thief, either, taking a good horse and
a good fighter with me as I am doing."

"Rolfr goes with you then? I'm glad of that," Ragnhild said.
"But what shall you do for a good horse? It seems to me that
you'll have to take one of mine—the gray stallion is the best.
You shall take Elfradr; he suits a warrior the best of any. I
suppose Jotull has provided for the rest of your needs, so you
may go now with my blessing and my assurance that I'll do
my best to confound Bjarnhardr. I have no wish to suffer the
afflictions that Adills suffered." She bent a last hard look on
Jotull and calmly went back to her weaving.

Jotull paused a moment, then opened the door with a shrug.
"She's a curious, cold creature," he muttered to Sigurd as their
boots squeaked at each step in the snow. "She had better heed
my warning. I didn't like that wise expression in her eye, as
if she knew I lied. Yet I know she's had no instruction in
magic."

Sigurd opened his mouth to tell Jotull about her lessons with
Adills; but with rare discernment, he said nothing except, "I
hope her Elfradr isn't fat and out of condition. She has three
horses of her own, while the men are lucky to have one that
can be safely relied upon."

They saddled the horses without arousing any comment from
the watchmen and stopped by Jotull's house, where Rolfr waited
anxiously. Mikla stood at the door and refused to say farewell
or good luck as they rode away under the starlight. Sigurd
could scarcely believe it would be so easy to leave Hrafnborg
behind, pausing only long enough at the guard post to identify
themselves and riding on again as if in search of Halfdane.

"There's your last view of Hrafnborg," Jotull finally announced, as they paused on the shoulder of a fell to rest the

horses and look back. A few dim lights twinkled in the vast darkness of winter and vanished promptly when they rode around the curve of the hill.

The lowest point for Rolfr was passing near the contested area of Bedasford and seeing the tiny watchfires, spread out far below and dotting the sides and crowns of rugged hills in an effort to make the Dokkalfar think they had a great many more Ljosalfar to contend with than they really did. Most of the fire tenders were solitary and valorous old fighters who would rather perish in the snow with sword in hand than peacefully at home.

They camped three times in the snow, close by the foot of a sheltering crag or rock, which never seemed as beneficial as Sigurd had thought it might have been. Safe and snug inside a house, with only periodic excursions into the dark, he had never before felt so oppressed by the unrelieved blackness of the winter night as he did huddling beside their wretched fire and gazing bleakly into the endless darkness that surrounded them. Jotull's maps gave him little hope; they were mazes of runic writing in illegible hands, crisscrossed with ley-lines intersecting the known points of power. Jotull alone seemed undismayed by the prospects of finding so small a thing as a mountain named Svartafell in the dark of winter. He located the directions with the assistance of a dowsing pendulum and assured Sigurd and Rolfr that they were directly on course and could expect to find Svartafell in another four weeks, allowing for the slowness of winter travel and the stops they would have to make along the way to buy provisions. Dispiritedly, Sigurd noted on the maps that the Ljosalfar hill forts nearest Svartafell were still a long distance from it, but he was too tired and low to wonder whom they would be bargaining with in the interval.

On the fourth night, the trolls discovered them and became their constant companions. Rolfr's arrows soon taught them enough fear to keep them from boldly attacking in a wholesale onslaught, and Jotull amused himself by inflicting dreadful spells on them, such as conjuring an image of a sheep, which, once eaten, turned to broken glass shards, proving beyond a doubt that there were substances that disagreed even with the stomachs of trolls. Sigurd killed a few trolls to satisfy his need for vengeance, but even the novelty of that wore off after a week of trekking through the snow and the dark.

"We are going more slowly than I had imagined in my worst estimates," Jotull announced as they huddled around their fire in a vain attempt to get warm. "I hadn't dreamed the going would be so dreadful in these fells. The snow is deeper than I've ever seen it, and the trolls are as thick as fleas. What we ought to do is descend to the lowlands where the traveling will be easier."

"The lowlands belong to Bjarnhardr," Rolfr said dolefully. "We can't go down there to travel, or we'll be captured. Maybe we ought to go back to Hrafnborg. This is madness. Nobody travels in the winter, except the Dokkalfar and other creatures who relish it." He bent a sinister look on Jotull in his fur-lined cloak.

"I don't imagine Halfdane would welcome us back like old friends," Jotull said. "His character is an unforgiving one, I fear. Once he supposes he has been insulted or injured, he is your enemy until death. As you know, Halfdane is always anxious to make an enemy."

"That's not true at all," Rolfr growled. "If anyone has done anything to try his temper, it has been me. If we went back, we could expect punishment, to be sure, but he won't regard us as his enemies. Right now, I think I'd rather be in disgrace at Hrafnborg than in a troll's cooking pot tomorrow." He glowered around at the patiently waiting trolls, who crouched in the snow just beyond easy reach. A couple of old troll-hags, cradling a huge, rusty kettle, had acquired a particular fondness for Rolfr and kept their gleaming eyes riveted to him as they lovingly sharpened two worn-out knives in preparation for some future event that must have given them endless delight in the anticipation.

Jotull threw a small scrap of fish at the trolls for the satisfaction of seeing them tearing themselves apart to get at it.

"Well, Sigurd, do you wish to go back with Rolfr and humbly accept whatever punishment your lord Halfdane decides to mete out to you? I doubt a deserter would ever gain anything but contempt from the men of Hrafnborg—to say nothing of Ragnhild, if you came crawling back to her now as a failure." Jotull lit his pipe and settled himself comfortably to smoke, keeping a careless eye on the trolls all the while.

Sigurd pondered. "No, I wouldn't like to go back to Hrafnborg without whatever is inside this box, and I know you wouldn't either. We've all burned our boats, so there may never be any going back. Is there a favorable route to Svartafell by the lowlands that won't be too near the Dokkalfar strongholds?"

Jotull unfurled a collection of maps to show him not only one route but half a dozen, all equally safe and relatively unencumbered with drifts of snow, hungry trolls, and lurking Dokkalfar. They decided on a course that skirted the questionable area between fells and lowlands, which was claimed by both Ljosalfar and Dokkalfar. If difficulties arose, they could easily retreat into the fells and perhaps locate an outpost of the Ljosalfar for protection. The Dokkalfar would not pursue them far into their own fells, it was hoped, and thus they could avoid crossing the lowlands, curving their course in a northwest direction toward Svartafell.

As they descended from the high country, Rolfr looked back more frequently at the fells towering behind them in the starlight, bathed in the eerie and unexplained lights in the sky. The snow was not as deep, but the trolls were more numerous and more cunning. Jotull was not always able to deceive them with his traps and spells and resorted to killing them with blasts of power until they learned to be more cautious. Sigurd hated them worse than the scruffier, smaller trolls from the mountains. The lowland trolls sat in dark clumps on the hillsides, plainly visible in the starlight reflecting on the snow as they conferred in low voices. They had leaders who dispatched messengers back and forth. After a few days, it was apparent that the trolls were merely watching, following, and reporting on the progress of their prey. Signs of such unexpected intelligence made Sigurd more uneasy than the unpremeditated ferocity and hunger of the mountain trolls.

Rolfr was not at all reassured by their behavior and repeatedly urged a retreat to higher country. Jotull shook his head

and said, "Much as I regret to say it, we couldn't if we wanted
to. I've miscalculated somehow, and we're on the wrong side
of a river for escape back to the fells. I'm rather ashamed to
have made such a mistake, but there you see the river to the
east of us, exactly where we'd prefer not to have it. I must
have taken a wrong tack at that last standing stone."

Sigurd looked eastward at the curling mists rising from the
river, which flowed deep and steaming from its springs under
a glacier capping the fiery vaults of molten stone at the restless
heart of Skarpsey. They had crossed the river further down,
after the water had cooled sufficiently to freeze.

"We can backtrack," Jotull continued, "or we can go on.
This river will doubtless disappear into the fells where it comes
from, which will save us a crossing later. We aren't in much
trouble, if the truth be known."

"Unless those trolls decide to attack us," Rolfr added. "If
they do, we'll have no convenient retreat into the fells, where
all good Ljosalfar know there is safety. I don't like these lowlands. We're too close to Muspell, in my opinion, when the
water comes out of the earth boiling hot."

"But it makes it ideal for bathing," Sigurd said. "A long,
hot soak is what we need to get the ice out of our bones. And
look, there's still green grass and moss around the hot springs
for the horses, which will save our grain supply. I don't think
coming down from the fells was such a bad idea. Once we get
around this river, that is."

The river did not immediately oblige them by turning back
into the fells, but led them deeper into rougher country, where
cliffs of lava overhung their course. It was so pleasantly sheltered from wind and snow that the travelers delayed leaving it
as long as possible. The horses could easily paw away the
shallow snow to eat the dried grass below, and the lava cliffs
offered a variety of caves and hollows for camping, with perfectly dry, sandy floors. The only disquieting factor for Sigurd
was the voices of the trolls on the cliffs around them. He had
not heard that sort of howling and screeching since Thongullsfjord—high, eerie whistling screams that echoed from cliff to
cliff, just as they had over the waters of the fjord, accompanied

by a deeper grumbling bellow like a gruff bull's voice. The racket of the mountain trolls was entirely different. Frequently Sigurd awoke in panic, thinking for a moment he was back in his grandmother's house with the trolls tearing at the roof.

He was almost glad when Jotull picked a low spot in the cliffs and led the climb upward. When they reached the top, the wind snatched at them with a whoop of triumph, welcoming them back. Rolfr pointed toward a gap in the mountains to the south, where a faint gray light tentatively touched the lowering blackness.

"Look at that. It must be almost Midwinter," he declared. "I'll never be so glad to see spring again."

The light soon vanished, but it was cheering, nonetheless. The horses sighed at the return to deeper snow and forged ahead with sure-footed caution over the hidden rocks. For a long time, they heard no trolls and saw none flitting ahead over the white hillsides. Jotull looked from side to side, wondering what it could mean.

"It means they've lost us," Rolfr chortled. "We fooled them when we left the riverbed. I hope we left them all down there."

Entirely too soon for Rolfr's liking, the high headland they were crossing ended abruptly in a steep descent into the river bottom again. It looked dark and uninviting, with a young snowstorm gathering force around the travelers, but thoughts of the pleasant, dry lava caves overcame even Rolfr's reluctance. Wearily, they set up their camp for the night, and Jotull scratched runes and rings around the entrance and prepared a few spells to trap unwary trolls. Then he sat beside the fire, smoking his pipe and gazing through the opening into the storm outside. After their meager supper of dried fish and tea, Sigurd lay contemplating the firelight dancing on the rusty lava cave walls, thinking sleepily that it was almost pleasant and he wouldn't really be anywhere else, even if he could choose it.

Half-dozing, he listened to the gruff voices of the trolls outside, too lazy even to remark to Rolfr and Jotull that their companions had found them again. He opened his eyes once or twice, as Rolfr picked up his bow and arrows and stepped over him to take a position by the entrance. Several sharp shrieks from outside announced that Rolfr's arrows had found their marks, and Jotull's voice rumbled in approval. Then pandemonium erupted in the cave. Rolfr suddenly tumbled backward over Sigurd with a yell, clutching an arrow protruding from his shoulder. Jotull began cursing and hurling spells into the darkness, shouting at Sigurd betweentimes to bestir himself and make himself useful. Sigurd leaped up in horror to see if Rolfr was wounded or dead. He found his friend bleeding a great deal, but otherwise was relieved to discover that the arrow had gone into the fleshy part of his shoulder instead of finding some vital organ.

"It could have been much worse," Sigurd assured his friend as he quickly bound up the wound to stop the bleeding. "Another handspan and it would have missed you altogether. You've been extraordinarily lucky, you know; a handspan the other way and it would have caught you in the throat."

Rolfr ground his teeth against the pain. "Oh yes, I know I'm very fortunate. This way I won't be able to use my bow for who knows how long? I've seen small wounds like this become putrid and kill the fellow with much more pain and inconvenience than one clear shot to the heart. I've got everything to be thankful for, indeed." He closed his eyes, looking desperately pale. "Blast and burn those trolls. Who would have thought they could shoot like that? Let me see that arrow." Sigurd gave him the arrow, which he had broken into two pieces to remove from the wound. Rolfr pounced on the fletched end with a fierce exclamation. "Look at this! Red and black feathers mean this is Dokkalfar manufacture! There are not only trolls out there, Siggi; the Dokkalfar are with them."

"I fear you're right," Jotull agreed from his kneeling position beside the entrance. "I can see their horses and recognize their helmets easily in the starlight."

Sigurd smothered the fire with one of the few spells he had managed to learn from Adills. "You must have made a perfect target with the light behind you, Rolfr. I wonder how long we can hold them off in this cave."

Jotull replied, "We'll last as long as our food lasts and then we can eat the horses, if you want to carry it that far. We could even starve to death, but that's not my idea of a noble way to die, nor do I relish the thoughts of throwing myself grandly on their spears and perishing as a martyr or a berserkr. If I am to be taken captive, let it be while I am at my best." He flung his cloak over his shoulder and stepped to the entrance, raising his arms in a peaceful gesture.

"What? We're surrendering and only one of us wounded?" Rolfr demanded, rising weakly to one elbow to glower at Jotull. "It would look a lot more heroic if everyone were bleeding, Siggi. You know you can't write scalds without blood."

"Hush, you're out of your mind," Sigurd snapped, keeping his eyes on Jotull, more than half-expecting another arrow to find its target.

"Halloo!" came a shout from outside. "Is it a peaceable surrender you want, or a fight until you're all dead?"

"We'll surrender, if you're Dokkalfar from Svinhagahall," Jotull answered. "You may approach. You have my word that we are done with fighting."

With a businesslike rattling of weapons and harness, the Dokkalfar strode up to the cave and stared in at its occupants through a fence of swords and lances. Sigurd was astonished to see so much gold hammered into their helmets, sword hilts, and axeheads, if they were only common soldiers and not earls. Their helmets were a far cry from the functional, conical helmets of the Ljosalfar. The Dokkalfar helmets were wonders of craftsmanship, but Sigurd had the sense to wonder if they hadn't been constructed more for beauty than for protecting their owners' skulls from desecration by an enemy axe.

"Where have you come from?" the leader of the Dokkalfar demanded. He was a handsomely clad fellow with an arrogant bearing who would have looked striking if not for a narrow face like a fox and a furtive expression in his eye. "Raudborg isn't far from here. Are you deserters, perhaps, from the Ljosalfar camps?"

"We're not deserters." Sigurd spoke up promptly when he saw Jotull take his usual stance for circumlocution. "We come from Hrafnborg and we're not doing anything of any concern to the Dokkalfar of Bjarnhardr."

"Hush, Sigurd, and let your elders do the speaking," Jotull said severely, his eyes alight with displeasure.

"Anytime three Ljosalfar are caught prowling in the lowlands, it is of concern to the Dokkalfar," the Dokkalfar chieftain said. "I suppose you are spies, in which case we shall take you directly to Svinhagahall. Bjarnhardr is particularly interested in spies and deserters. I know how he deals with Dokkalfar deserters, so it will be interesting to see what he does with you."

The Dokkalfar behind him muttered their agreement and exchanged some significant glances. Under their watchful eyes, Jotull directed Sigurd to saddle their horses and assemble their possessions again. Rolfr leaned against the rock and watched, trying to start up a conversation with his captors.

"Who was it that shot this?" he finally asked, holding up the broken arrow with his good hand. When one of the younger Dokkalfar toward the rear admitted that it was his handiwork, Rolfr snorted and said, "It wasn't a very good shot at all. If it had been you in this cave and me shooting into it, I'm certain you would have been dead by now. However, I'm grateful to you for your ineptitude, so I'll be able to see what Svinhagahall is like and see your warlord face to face."

"Hold there, what's this?" the chieftain suddenly exclaimed. His jealous eye had watched every move Sigurd made until Sigurd reached for his box to put into his saddle pouch. Sigurd's hands closed around it protectively as the chieftain approached, grinning avariciously. "It looks as if it might hold something valuable. I shall carry it for you, I believe."

Sigurd looked at him coldly. "I believe you won't. It's of no value to anyone but me." His eyes never left the mean, dark face of the chieftain, but he knew exactly where his sword and axe lay behind him.

The chieftain only grinned wider and raised his sword. "I say, if it's valuable to you, then it's valuable to me also. Hand it over or you'll not live long to regret it."

Jotull glided a few steps nearer. "The box is nothing to you. I don't advise your touching it," he said smoothly but firmly.

"There's power loose here, and I wouldn't vouch for its being under absolute control if you should touch that box."

The chieftain hesitated, while small gusts of power nudged at him and tweaked his beard and cloak almost playfully, but when he took a decided step nearer, Sigurd's power leaped at him in a bright crackling arc, knocking his sword across the cave. Cursing, the chieftain clutched his hand and shook it, glaring at Sigurd in fury.

"Well then, you'll have to give it up to Bjarnhardr," he growled. "Come on, make haste! Let's get going. I'm not going to wait until spring for you. Bjarnhardr won't be deprived of his entertainment in your cases, I'm certain. You'll soon see how he treats deserters and spies."

# Chapter 9

❖❖❖❖❖❖❖❖❖❖❖❖❖❖❖❖❖❖❖❖❖

When they arrived at Svinhagahall after approximately two days of hard traveling, they immediately recognized Bjarnhardr's method of dealing with deserters and spies. The earthworks surrounding the hill fort were dotted with bonfires, which half-illuminated a row of gibbets.

"A new batch of deserters must have been captured," one of the Dokkalfar observed in a low tone to a companion as they rode past the grisly gateposts of Bjarnhardr's fortress.

Within the walls crouched the massive ruin of an ancient hall at least as antique as Adills' round tower. Small fires burned in dark niches throughout it, like a multitude of eyes glowing in hollow sockets. Knots of Dokkalfar peered out over the parapets at the newcomers, but Sigurd heard none of the roistering greetings that would have welcomed a Ljosalfar patrol. The Dokkalfar attended strictly to their duties, scarcely

sparing a glance to either side as they stood at their posts or
hurried on errands.

Their captors took them solemnly through the main entrance
of the ancient hall into what had once been an expansive court,
where now most of the roof had collapsed; the hollow shell
furnished a good location for stabling horses. The captives'
horses were left there, and the Dokkalfar pointed the way down
a dark tunnel, lighted at intervals by small, smoky fires, where
a few watchmen crouched over the handful of coals, trying to
capture some of the warmth before the icy wind whistled it
away.

"You'd be warmer in your underground halls, instead of
this drafty ruin," Jotull observed to the chieftain as they waded
through a small drift of snow sifting through a broken wall.
"I'd always thought the Dokkalfar had a better eye to their own
comfort than this place suggests."

The chieftain's dismal snort sounded as if he would like to
agree, but he replied, "You won't catch me complaining. I'm
of rather low rank around here and I have no need for comforts,
besides. When the Dokkalfar rule Skarpsey, our wizards will
rediscover the source of the eternal winter, so this will be a
pattern for things to come." He heaved a sigh and slogged
through another snowdrift. "It will be glorious times for the
Dokkalfar—if we don't all freeze to death first. We lose at
least one guard every watch." He looked sharply at the guard
beside the door where he halted his party, but the poor, stiff
fellow still possessed enough life to stand up and salute shiv-
eringly. "I am Gunnolfr. Open the door, you sluggard. You
can't complain of the cold with such a fire as that."

Sigurd and Rolfr looked at the wretched handful of coals
expiring on the frozen earth. The ragged creature hastened to
hammer on the door, which opened a small crack after a very
long interval. A suspicious voice demanded to know what was
wanted. When the message was imparted, the door grumbled
open a little wider, and someone summoned them inside impatiently and slammed the door shut with a clattering of bars
and bolts.

"Now then, what's your business that you think Bjarnhardr

should be interested in it?" The speaker was clad in a fur cloak and hood, muffled up so that hardly anything of his showed, except the end of a blue nose and two hard, bright eyes under a hedge of beetling brows. "It had better be good, Gunnolfr. You didn't acquit yourself well at Bedasford, not at all. Bjarnhardr has his eye upon you, after your debacle."

Gunnolfr shifted his feet uneasily. "But I have something here to redeem myself. These are spies I captured from Hrafnborg. I don't doubt even Bjarnhardr will be astonished and pleased—enough to forgive us for being so wildly slaughtered at Bedasford. You needn't say that, of course. You won't mention that I said such a thing, will you, Slyngr?"

Slyngr looked at Jotull, Sigurd, and Rolfr, so far amazed as to pull back his hood slightly for a better look, revealing more of his sharp features and a neatly braided beard. The hand that pushed the hood back bore a glittering collection of gold and jewels. "Come with me, then, all of you," he said with an impatient sigh. "We needn't stand here in this drafty hallway, chattering about it, when Bjarnhardr can decide for himself what to do. They admitted to being spies, did they?" He glanced anxiously at Jotull, whose stern, calm presence commanded attention.

"No, indeed," Jotull answered. "I am a wizard, not a spy, and I've wanted to see Bjarnhardr for quite some time. I shall welcome the opportunity to deliver my greeting to him in person. Lead us to him, Slyngr, and we shall follow right willingly."

Slyngr muffled himself inside his hood again with a last disbelieving glare at the strangers and turned to lead them down a passageway by the faint light of a small oil lamp. It was narrow and icy, although the whipping breeze had been shut out, which made it seem somewhat warmer than outside. They descended several flights of crumbling steps and passed earthy-smelling rooms where the doors had been torn off for firewood. At last, the twisting passage led them to the final low door where two guards dozed over their small fire, weapons in hand. Slyngr stirred them up viciously with his staff and harangued them for sleeping before he opened the door and led his procession inward with a pompous air of triumph, as if no one but he had captured the spies and brought them thence.

"Halloa, my lord!" he called, marching into the chamber with an important pattering of his feet. "That ne'er-do-well Gunnolfr has surprised us and brought us three captives. They're spies from Hrafnborg, my lord," he added in an anticipatory whisper as he bent conspiratorially toward a large hooded chair placed before a roaring fire.

At once, Slyngr was thrust aside, and a tall, dark shadow loomed before the fire, almost swallowing its light with a billowing cloak.

"Spies from Hrafnborg!" a mighty voice boomed with a nasty chuckle. "I've looked forward to this occasion for many a year, many a year indeed. Who is this forward-seeming fellow with the wizard's staff? You'd better learn to look at me with more humility and fear than that, my good man. I think I see insolence in your face, and for that I shall make you pay. Who are these two young vermin with you, wizard? Thralls or your apprentices in magic? They look as if they could both use a good flogging, and a prompt hanging would improve them far better, in my opinion." He lay back in his chair and laughed unpleasantly.

Sigurd glanced at Jotull in alarm, but the wizard motioned him to stay silent. Jotull leaned on his staff and loosened his cloak. "I know this foolish game amuses you, Bjarnhardr, but I've come a long way and I'm too tired for nonsense. This is the Scipling from Thongullsfjord—the one Halfdane stole from under your very nose. You could have found him yourself if you'd been a bit more clever."

"That's what you're supposed to do. Supply me with cleverness, but you don't," Bjarnhardr snapped, darting a venomous glower at Jotull. "I notice the Scipling still has the box besides."

"I thought it would be safer to get him away from Halfdane," Jotull replied quickly. "Halfdane has kept him under his eye almost every instant, trying to get the box away from him. Isn't that so, Sigurd?"

Sigurd clutched the box and looked from Bjarnhardr to Jotull. "Yes, that's true," he said warily. "I won't allow anybody to touch it, if I don't trust him. Jotull, you never told me you were disloyal to Halfdane."

He looked down on Bjarnhardr with revulsion. The Dokkalfar was crooked in the back; on closer inspection, Sigurd discovered he had a peg for a foot on his right leg.

Bjarnhardr chuckled, as if reading his thoughts. "You think I'm a worthless thing, don't you?" he demanded, hitching his misshapen shoulder to emphasize his deformity and rapping the stone floor with his peg. "You wonder how the leader of so many could be so unfit, right?"

Sigurd only looked at Jotull in great discomfiture, but Jotull offered him no explanation. The wizard tossed aside his travel-worn cloak and sat down with a weary sigh beside the fire, exchanging his boots for fleece slippers as if he were quite at home at Bjarnhardr's fireside. "You may as well relax, Sigurd. You too, Rolfr. Our journey is over for the time being. I trust you'll continue the course of our friendship, Sigurd, and not despise me for this small deception. I thought it was easier this way. I hope you're not sorry. You must continue to trust me now and follow my instructions just as you always have done, as if nothing has changed."

"Sit down, sit down!" Bjarnhardr exclaimed. "And stop looking so stricken, as if I were some sort of monster instead of merely an ugly old Dokkalfar. You're not afraid of me now, are you?" He grinned horribly, as if making an effort to make himself look worse.

"No, I'm not afraid," Sigurd replied as he sat down reluctantly, trying to conceal his distaste for the misshapen creature. He was also conscious of a sharp disappointment, now that he had met Bjarnhardr face to face. Somehow Jotull had made him sound far more imposing.

Again Bjarnhardr seemed to know his thoughts and found them highly amusing. "Not quite what you expected, am I? Didn't Jotull prepare you adequately? Perhaps you're thinking you'd prefer to be back at Hrafnborg with Halfdane, who at least has a fine beard to cover his face, while mine is sadly naked. With that gauntlet of his, he blasted me with flames, cut me down with his axe, and chopped off my foot. His rage was so great that he would have killed me if not for the intervention of my faithful Dokkalfar. Jotull, if you had been with me then, I might not be such a deformed creature today."

Sigurd turned to look at Jotull questioningly, and Rolfr's face was drained of color. "Then Mikla was correct in his suspicions," Sigurd said cautiously. "But I never thought you were a Dokkalfar, Jotull."

Jotull remained in the shadows, a dark figure holding a staff. "I'm not a Dokkalfar born," he replied coldly. "I don't need to explain my shift in loyalties. Suffice it to say that I have brought you here as a result of much planning and thinking and talking. If you so choose, you can be a part of our scheme for Halfdane's destruction. All our careful plans are now within our reach, as soon as we find a way to open that box. After all I've done for you, Sigurd, I know you won't refuse to help us with our plans for Halfdane and the rest of those confounded Ljosalfar. You've got no reason to attempt to protect Halfdane," he added sharply, seeing Sigurd hesitate. "It's my belief that Halfdane is the warlord who burned your parents in their hall. He has no claim to that box or its contents and he doesn't want you to discover the truth before he gets power over you. If I hadn't seized the opportunity to escape from Hrafnborg, you would never have survived to see that box opened."

"I know he bears me nothing but ill will," Sigurd said, still struggling with the feeling that he had been tricked somehow. "The sending was enough proof for me. I have no regrets for Hrafnborg or Halfdane, if you want to destroy them."

Rolfr uttered a choked roar of rage and made a staggering rush at Sigurd, as if he would strangle him with his bare hands. Sigurd was taken completely off guard, and Rolfr carried him to the ground in his fury, yelling, "Traitor! Don't sell yourself so cheap! I won't let you betray Halfdane!"

In his weakened condition, he was no match for Sigurd, who promptly pinned him on his back with as much consideration for his injury as possible, whereupon Rolfr fainted away with no further commotion.

"Jotull! Can't you do something for him?" Sigurd exclaimed

in dismay, adding for Bjarnhardr's benefit, "He's been wounded, and he's out of his head, or he wouldn't have attacked me. No one could have a more loyal friend than he is to me."

Bjarnhardr motioned to Slyngr. "You and Gunnolfr carry him out of here and have him attended to with all haste and respect due an honored guest, do you hear?"

Slyngr and Gunnolfr hastened to do as they were ordered, not without looking rather puzzled and, on Gunnolfr's part, considerably disappointed. Honored guests were not half as interesting as prisoners.

Bjarnhardr turned again to Sigurd. "Sit down, sit down and be comfortable. I daresay you haven't seen a fire like this in a while, not since you left Hrafnborg, eh?"

"We didn't burn so much wood in Hrafnborg," Sigurd answered. "Supplies were always rather pinched there."

The news seemed to affect Bjarnhardr so agreeably that he could hardly resist bursting into laughter. "Pinched, you say! What could be better for those outlaws, those brigands and thieves? Every horse, every sword, every bite of mutton they devour, all is stolen from me. Even the firewood which Half-dane is so begrudging with is probably stolen from one of my hill forts or, at the very least, cut from the fells and forests which I claim as my own. It's one thing to steal, but quite another to be stingy with what you do steal. I say it shows a meanness of spirit, a lack of open-hearted generosity. Never trust a tuft hunter, or you'll find yourself empty-handed every time. If ever an Alfar was secret and selfish, it must be Half-dane. You say he even went so far as to put a sending against you?"

His manner seemed so sympathetic and genuine to Sigurd that he soon relaxed his defensive attitude and told Bjarnhardr about the sending and his many wrongs at the hands of Half-dane. Jotull stood beside the fire nearby, nodding in agreement and offering further bits of evidence against Halfdane.

"Shameful, shameful to treat a stranger from the other realm so discourteously," Bjarnhardr declared. "What an ill impression you must have of Alfar hospitality. We shall do our best here at Svinhagahall to assure you that the Alfar do possess good manners, fine and plentiful food, and beautiful surroundings. At least the food and fires are plentiful, but if you want to see comfort and beauty, you'll have to accompany me to Bjarnhardrsborg. I'll be the first to admit Svinhagahall is rather rough quarters, but one can't expect an army camp to be very luxurious."

Sigurd had been observing the thick fleeces spread on the floor, the richly carved furniture, and the fine woven hangings covering the walls, all of which made Hrafnborg seem very rough by comparison. If Bjarnhardr considered Svinhagahall uncomfortable and crude, Sigurd wondered what Bjarnhardrsborg must boast in the way of gold and carvings. Never having seen much elegance in his life, he was greatly attracted by the idea of seeing Bjarnhardrsborg.

Jotull, however, cleared his throat. "I fear you'll never persuade Sigurd to join you there, because he's got an errand to attend to first in Svartafell. The dwarf that made the box has a forge there and he'll be the one to get it open. I propose to take Sigurd there myself to make sure nothing happens before he joins you in Bjarnhardrsborg."

Bjarnhardr's eyes kept straying from Jotull to the box Sigurd carried. "And what makes you think I can trust him out of my sight, once that box is opened?"

"You needn't worry," Sigurd said. "I've defended it from Halfdane from the moment I arrived in this realm, but without the help of Jotull I might have lost it and my life. I owe him much, and he has my complete confidence. Still, I wish you had told me we were going to come here, Jotull, instead of going straight to Svartafell."

The wizard seated himself near the fire, keeping his staff across his knees. "You don't need to know everything that is going on in my thoughts, Sigurd. You're still young and inexperienced in the ways of this realm. If you'll look to me and not ask too many questions, I'll tell you all you need to know."

Bjarnhardr leaned forward in his oversize chair. "Yes, we are the best friends you've got now. We shall protect you from the avarice of Halfdane, you and that little, precious box which you hold so suspiciously under your arm as if you don't quite trust me yet. I assure you I won't try to take it from you against your will. I'll do everything in my power to help you reach Svartafell to get it unlocked for you. I wish I had been the one to rescue you from your hapless plight at Thongullsfjord. A lot of time has been wasted that could have been spent so profitably. Halfdane will be distressed by the loss of his opportunity." The idea set him to chuckling until he had to hold onto his chair for support.

"Do you know what's inside the box, then?" Sigurd held it out hopefully, ignoring the disquieting presence of his natural power flitting through the room like a malicious little breeze.

Bjarnhardr started to reach for the box; but as he looked at it, he changed his mind abruptly and knit his black brows over his sharp nose. "No, I've no idea," he said quickly as Jotull turned to him attentively. "No idea at all, except that it may be something wonderful and powerful. The events concerning it happened a long time ago, you see, and very few people are able to recall much about this box."

"But you and Halfdane must have been nearby," Sigurd persisted. "My grandmother talked about a burning and two warlords at battle with each other."

Bjarnhardr waved one hand wearily. "Oh, there were scores of burnings in those days. All the hill forts were in flames at one time or another, with varying degrees of damage. Any one of them could have been your father's."

"But I never thought my father was an Alfar!" Sigurd protested, and his natural power responded by shoving a set of gold-inlaid cups from the table. "I'm sure my mother was a Scipling—but my grandmother told me she didn't approve the match." He recalled how Thorarna had told him about the dangerous powers of the Alfar until his young mind had been impressed with their treachery and mystery.

Jotull stood up quickly. "Mixed marriages are not uncommon, but they're never a good idea. From the evidence of that natural power of yours, I had suspected something of the sort. As long as it plagues you, you'll never be able to consider yourself a normal Scipling; and until you learn to control it, you won't be a very successful Alfar, either. In my opinion, it would be better to get rid of it entirely."

Sigurd scarcely listened to him. His mind still reeled. He remembered Ragnhild mentioning mixed marriages. He thought of his possibilities, once he mastered his capricious power, which was now plucking the threads from the hangings on the walls.

"How do I learn to control it, Jotull?" he asked.

Jotull scowled, but Bjarnhardr cackled with glee. "Yes, how indeed? It might be useful when Halfdane comes after you." Bjarnhardr suddenly dropped his jovial attitude and his eyes began to shine with a feral gleam. "Jotull! I've had the most splendid idea," he said, with a different sort of chuckle.

"Spare me the details," Jotull retorted. "Don't you think I haven't thought of it already? It occurred to me long ago at Hrafnborg that Halfdane would go to any lengths to retrieve Sigurd and this box. I fully expect that he's not far behind us at this very moment. He's going to rush right into Svinhagahall like a bull to the shambles, all unsuspecting that Sigurd has led him to his doom." He darted Sigurd a speculative glance to see if any hesitation remained.

Sigurd banished his doubts and fears for the moment by saying carelessly, "Then let him bear the responsibility for any grief that befalls him. I didn't ask to be taken to Hrafnborg, and I didn't ask for him to follow me here. I refuse to submit to being duped and used as a pawn by him. He's aggrieved me enough that the next time I see him it will be as an enemy."

"Good for you!" Bjarnhardr shook his hand warmly and proceeded from that moment to make up for all the deprivations and hardships Sigurd had been forced to endure at Hrafnborg. Sigurd was given a small chamber of his own, as comfortable as a roaring fire, fleece, and furniture could make it. He was at liberty to sleep all day if he chose or to take a torch and servant to prowl around the chilly corridors of the ancient fortress, marveling at the industry which had been spent to erect it when a simple firehall would have been quite adequate.

He sat for hours beside Rolfr in the adjoining room where his friend was suffering some ill effects from his wound and

spending most of the time in a drugged stupor or restlessly
raving nonsense. Otherwise there was little to do except scratch
the itching of the new beard Sigurd had decided to grow or to
sit in the company of Bjarnhardr and Jotull.

At rare intervals, Sigurd poked his nose outside and saw
nothing but snow, darkness, and the sentries shivering over
their posts. Several times he saw Gunnolfr, cold, pinched, and
envious. The other chieftains looked little better when they
came to Bjarnhardr to report or complain. Sigurd suspected
that the lot of the common soldier was not quite as comfortable
as his own, and probably not as good as that of the horses. He
chose not to dwell on his observations, however.

Bjarnhardr kept Sigurd's attention distracted by a host of
amusements. There was nothing less agreeable to Sigurd than
this fulsome flattery, and he would not have tolerated it, if not
for the necessity of waiting for Rolfr to recover from his injury
before they could resume their journey to Svartafell. He chafed
at the delay.

Bjarnhardr, too, found the delay irritating, and every cunning glance at Sigurd's box seemed to aggravate him further.
Loudly he complained to Jotull when his bondmen were driven
back across the Bedariver. When the darkness at midday paled
to hopeful twilight, Bjarnhardr lamented that the winter was
almost over and Halfdane was still undefeated. Jotull, undisturbed, retorted that the winter was far from over yet; once
they returned from Svartafell, wondrous feats of destruction
might yet be realized.

Covertly Jotull and Bjarnhardr had tried to persuade Sigurd
to leave Rolfr behind, that they might depart immediately, but
Sigurd refused to consider the idea. He said it would be a
coward's deed to abandon his friend, but secretly he knew he
relied upon Rolfr as an ally against two powerful rivals. As
soon as Rolfr was fit, it would take all their strength to resist
and think up some way of losing Jotull and Bjarnhardr. Sigurd
seized every opportunity of poring over their maps until he
knew vaguely the location of the dvergar regions that lay over
the lowlands to the east, where the mountains began again. He

grimly hoped that two riders could make it that far without
falling prey to trolls or other enemies.

Sigurd made no mention of his plans to Rolfr, knowing that
someone was certain to overhear. The only safe topics were
Svartafell and how soon Rolfr would be strong enough to travel.
Rolfr had been considerably wasted by the fever, almost to a
shadow of his former robust self. Daily he gingerly practiced
bending his bow; but, judging by his trembling and pained
grimaces, it would be many weeks before he could be thought
deadly with his arrows.

Sigurd and Rolfr seldom missed a chance to survey their
surroundings during the few hours of pale twilight when the
sun appeared on the horizon. The view from the fortress parapets was dismal enough—nothing but stark snowy fells, frozen lakes and rivers, and the wretched deserters dangling from
the gibbets. Svinhagahall itself, with its rotting towers and
broken walls, was not a sight to cheer the hearts of two young,
homeless men who both gazed southward toward Hrafnborg
for long silent periods without saying what they were thinking.

The sun hung reluctantly overlooking such a scene for a
short space, then slid gratefully back into oblivion, and the
land fell again into darkness. As Sigurd and Rolfr descended
the crumbling stairway, they met Jotull coming quickly up in
search of them.

"I've been looking everywhere for you," he said, breathless
and impatient. "You shouldn't wander off without telling anyone where you're going. It's not as safe as you think it is in
Svinhagahall. I've got some news for you, Sigurd, most unwelcome news indeed. Just before noon, while it was still dark,
someone sighted an old friend of yours who has come hunting
for you."

Sigurd stopped. "Not Halfdane, surely!"

"No, no, although it wouldn't surprise me much," Jotull
said in a tone of peculiar satisfaction. "Come along, don't stop
now. It simply isn't safe prowling around this old ruin."

"Why not?" Rolfr demanded. "You never said anything
before. We should have nothing to fear—unless Hross-Bjorn

has somehow made a reappearance." He looked hopeful until Jotull nodded grimly.

Sigurd smothered a groan of despair. "It always comes along just when I feel that I'm making progress."

Rolfr trod on his foot warningly and Sigurd closed his mouth. Lately, to relieve the boredom, Rolfr and Sigurd had been practicing what little magic they knew between them in an effort to get Sigurd's power under control. They mentioned their experiments to no one and carefully concealed their mistakes.

"The longer we delay in Svinhagahall, the better the chance that Hross-Bjorn will find you," Jotull continued. "There are a thousand hiding places in this wretched old catacomb. I can't protect you every instant, especially if you persist in wandering away. By the end of the week, I want to be away, whether Rolfr is ready to travel or not."

Immediately Rolfr said, "I shall be ready. I can travel, although I won't be much good with my bow. What I would like to know is why you can't get rid of the sending. I always thought you had power enough to do just about anything, Jotull."

"Why bother? We'll just leave it behind." Jotull sounded impatient, so they followed him down with no further questions.

The sending lost no time in making its presence known. It became the terror of the half-dozen guards, and stalked any lone stragglers wandering about the walls and earthworks. The gibbets on the earthworks earned a fresh reputation for horror after the sending took up residence in the charnel pit nearby and gnawed upon the frozen carcasses of the deserters as they hung in their chains.

Sigurd learned to hate Svinhagahall with a bitter loathing during the last days before their departure. He thought he heard Hross-Bjorn slinking after him around every corner, and the wind flapping a hanging startled him inordinately. Sigurd's nerves became raw, and he realized he was scarcely better than a prisoner. The only time he felt truly safe was standing outside, gazing at the sun when it came up to throw its golden gleam and long, black shadows behind every object. The sending preferred darkness to work its mischiefs on him, when he felt the most insecure.

When he thought he could stand it no longer, he cornered Jotull alone one day and said in a low voice, "We both know the sending is yours. What's the use for it now, Jotull, since you've got me and the box away from Halfdane?"

Jotull's eyes belied his wary caution. "That's rather a dangerous accusation to make, isn't it? I don't think you'd care to offend my honor, would you?"

"No one else is listening, so your pride is still intact. Will you get rid of that sending or not?" Sigurd stared back at Jotull with the concentration lent him by anger and determination. His natural power overturned a chair and started launching small bits of peat at Jotull's ankles. The wizard glowered around the room warningly.

"No, I won't get rid of the sending," he replied. "I shall keep it from hurting you if you stay near me. The least you could do is allow me to keep the box safe for you. If the sending got it, he might give it to Bjarnhardr, for all we know."

Sigurd turned away, clutching the box under his arm. He always carried it with him now. "You'll have to do better than that, Jotull. Halfdane was far more successful than you in winning my foolish trust, though Halfdane wasn't half clever, I'm beginning to think. You know more about fear than trust, don't you?"

Jotull permitted himself a small, dark smile. "It works as well, if not better, I should think. At least I know you're not going anywhere without me."

"Even Bjarnhardr is more clever than you, Jotull. Look at these fine clothes he gave me, besides the new saddle and that shield. Tonight he's going to give me something more valuable, he said. I'm starting to believe he's rather pleasant, in spite of being so ugly." Sigurd smiled as Jotull's looks blackened. "He says he plans to get rid of you as soon as you're not useful to him any more."

Jotull chuckled dryly and settled himself again into his chair. "That's not news to me, so you needn't think you can play us against each other. I'll warn you now that any gift of Bjarn-hardr's is likely to have very long and stout strings attached. You'll be sorry if you get yourself under any obligation to him."

"And you are much more honest, with your simple coer-cion," Sigurd observed ironically, as Jotull stretched out more comfortably by the fire.

"Precisely," the wizard replied, shutting his eyes.

Sigurd noticed later, when Bjarnhardr presented him with the gift, that Jotull was not so carefree as he pretended. Jotull followed them watchfully as Bjarnhardr led the way to a heavily locked and barred door which opened into the warlord's treasure room. Sigurd gazed around in silent admiration at Bjarnhardr's loot, stolen from his vanquished enemies. Every imaginable object that could be made of gold or studded with precious jewels lay in carved chests, with swords, axes, knives, spears, helmets, and other useful items scattered among the ornaments and baubles.

Bjarnhardr unlocked an elaborate funeral chest and gingerly lifted out a sheathed sword. "This I give to you as a token of our friendship. I insist that you take it, or I shall be grievously offended." He grinned and winked like a merry little troll. "If Halfdane comes looking for you, it will be wise to meet him with a sword in your hands. A bad day it will be for Halfdane, eh?" He grinned and winked even harder at Jotull, who looked away in disgust.

Sigurd took the sword and examined it, silently estimating how much such a fine implement was worth. Its hilt was heavily chased in gold and the blade was bright and sharp. Bjarnhardr watched him speculatively, and his eyes also were bright and sharp.

"Well? Does it meet with your approval?" he asked slyly. "If you don't like it, I can find you another one—not so fine, and not so perfectly suited to your purpose, I fear."

Sigurd had no delusions about Bjarnhardr's gift. It was a payment, and nothing more, for a service Bjarnhardr hoped he would render. Sigurd smiled to think that Bjarnhardr was going to be disappointed, besides giving away an excellent sword.

"It's perfect, and I thank you," he said, sheathing the sword. "I hope I can repay you somehow, by whatever means I have."

Bjarnhardr shook his head. "No, no, it's merely a gift, a small gesture of esteem, and nothing more. Take it and be welcome."

"And may it serve you as well as it has its past owners," Jotull added, exchanging a glance with Bjarnhardr, who scowled at him with a flashing eye.

Rolfr was looking over his arrows when Sigurd made his appearance with the sword. He unsheathed it for Rolfr to look at, tossing it on a fleece where Rolfr sat. "Have a look at this. Bjarnhardr gave me this as a token of friendship and nothing more. Or so he says. What would you say it means—friendship, or is it another bribe?" He admired the runes etched from hilt to point.

Rolfr stared at the sword twinkling in the firelight. His eyes widened as he gazed. Dropping his arrows, he covered his eyes with his hands and fell back, pale and trembling. "Take it away, Sigurd! I can't look at it another moment!" he gasped.

Hastily Sigurd sheathed the sword and hid it under an eider. "Whatever is the matter, Rolfr?" he demanded. "Did you see something in those runes carved into it? Are you sure it wasn't just a trick of the firelight? They're old runes; they can't mean anything for us."

Rolfr shook his head, still trembling. His eyes were still glazed with shock. "I know what I saw. The runes twinkled and twisted like flames, and for an instant I could read them. Every Alfar is entitled to extraordinary perceptions now and then, and what I saw—" He stopped and dug at his eyes with his knuckles, as if he could remove the images they had seen.

"What? What did they say?" Sigurd demanded, torn between a desire to comfort Rolfr and the urge to fly across the room and tear the sword from its sheath to stare at the runes.

Rolfr sighed resignedly. He gazed at the fire. "It said, 'By this hand you die.' It was my own death I saw. It was with that sword—and at your hand."

# Chapter 10

❖❖❖❖❖❖❖❖❖❖❖❖❖❖❖❖❖❖❖❖❖❖❖❖❖

"No—you must be mistaken. Old swords always have these dire sayings. Rolfr, your brain is still fevered if you think I'd ever kill you. I'd rather die first." Sigurd glanced toward the place where he'd hidden the sword. "Surely the message wasn't intended solely for you, Rolfr."

"But it was, I know it was. I looked at those tangled runes and thought nobody could ever make sense of them. Then the next thing I knew, the firelight seemed to pick out certain ones, and I read their message. I can't escape it, Sigurd."

Sigurd stepped quickly to the doorway to see if anyone might be listening outside. He heard a scuttling noise, but it was only the rats. "I'll give it back to Bjarnhardr and tell him to break it. It's rather a nice sword, though—I'd hate to see it ruined. I can't see how a sword can decide whom it's going to kill. Surely, Rolfr, you must have imagined it." He needed a sword, and good swords weren't easy to get, especially since he had no gold to trade for one.

"No, I know what I saw. That sword has marked me for death."

"But why? What did you do to deserve special magic runes? I ought to be the one it wants to destroy, because I have the box and everyone wants to get it. Perhaps the message was meant for me, do you suppose?" He and Rolfr stared at each other. Then Rolfr shook his head.

"No." He sighed. "Much as I would like to believe otherwise, it was meant for me. I have that feeling of doom."

"It gave me rather a cold feeling when I first saw it, and then Jotull said something strange that made Bjarnhardr look as if he wanted to cut Jotull's throat. Something about the sword serving me the same as it had served its past owners. Jotull was rather provoked about the whole thing, as if the sword were no great thing. But I think it has a curse on it. I'm going to give it back to Bjarnhardr and tell him what I think of anyone who would give a cursed sword as a gift to someone who is supposed to be his friend. Maybe I was right to doubt and fear both of them. Maybe I should—"

Rolfr reached out and grabbed his arm. "Sit down, you idiot. You'll not say anything to them to make them suspicious of us. You don't even dream what a situation we're in. If you were an Alfar, you'd know more what really goes forward here, but perhaps it's best to be unaware sometimes of the real danger. Listen to me, Sigurd, and do as I tell you, or, I promise you, you won't be sorry; you'll be dead. Now I know you're going to say it isn't as bad as all that and that you can take care of both of us; but perhaps there is a way we can do what Bjarnhardr wants and still survive. Therefore, it's best to be as friendly as possible to him and Jotull for a while. Continue as you started; regard the sword as a great gift of friendship. Who knows, maybe they are genuine in their friendship for you. You've certainly not disappointed them in your hatred for Halfdane."

"But the curse on the sword," Sigurd interrupted. "What about that? Why would they give it to me, if their intentions weren't evil?"

Rolfr sighed and scowled. "I certainly felt a curse on it for me, at least, but it probably won't harm you. Curses on old swords such as that one are as common as fleas on sheep. It might have been the mildest curse on any sword he possessed. Maybe he simply doesn't know—but Jotull would know. Jotull can smell a spell a hundred miles off. I had the same dread feeling when I saw that carved box, Siggi, and I knew then that something bad would happen if I mixed up my fate in the fate of whatever is inside that thing."

Sigurd thought of the box, which he had packed in his saddle pouch. "I think that I hate it already without even knowing what it is," he said bitterly. "It was in that box waiting for me before I was even born. It's simply not fair. Look at all the trouble it's caused already. I don't think I want to open it any more, for fear of worse troubles. Talk about a curse—an entire settlement was deserted because of it, my grandmother died prematurely, and I've always suspected something strange about poor old Adills' death."

"But there has been one benefit," Rolfr said with a wan smile. "Without the curse of that box, you and I would never have become such friends—for however long it may last."

Sigurd found little comfort in Rolfr's words. He took the sword and hid it where he wouldn't have to look at it. With unusual reluctance, he joined Bjarnhardr and Jotull in the main hall. Their friendship and hospitality had never seemed so genuine, however hard he might try to see the evil in them. When Bjarnhardr perceived his sober countenance, he at once limped to his side, sat down to inquire earnestly what was troubling him, and poured him a cup of mead to cheer him up.

"It's that sword you're worrying about, isn't it?" Bjarnhardr tapped his nose thoughtfully and looked rather sly. "You're afraid you can't repay my favor someday, aren't you?"

Sigurd attempted to shrug off his mood as general low spirits or somesuch nonsense, but Bjarnhardr would have none of his evasions. Before very long, Sigurd told him the entire story about Rolfr and the sword. Bjarnhardr threw himself back in his chair, with an expression of great astonishment.

"A fine picture, giving a man a sword with a curse on it!" he exclaimed, shaking his head as if he were in deep pain. "I can't believe you'd think it of me. You know I'm completely honest with you. Haven't your cares become my cares, and your journey mine also? I wouldn't leave Svinhagahall for any cause except one I felt to be almost as important as my own life is to me.

"I don't wish to be the cause of ill feelings between two such friends as you and Rolfr, but I might remind you that he still feels loyalty to Halfdane and it would be a great credit for him if he were to bring you and the box back to Halfdane. You must also remember that the poor fellow has been desperately ill and may suffer from a diseased brain for the rest of his life.

I'm glad you brought this matter to my attention, so we can make allowances for Rolfr's condition. It would be better if we could persuade him not to come with us on this journey, which is certain to be hazardous for such a weakened constitution. If he does depart with us, I greatly fear he shall not return."

Sigurd knew there would be no persuading Rolfr to stay behind. "But about the sword—you're quite certain there's no such curse on it that might require me actually to kill Rolfr with it?"

Bjarnhardr shook his head emphatically. "Upon all that I hold sacred in my life, I swear there isn't. I would never put such a weapon into the hands of a friend." He clutched the arms of his chair as he followed Jotull with a baleful eye. "That wizard would like nothing better than to see bad blood between you and me. Perhaps he did something to the runes. He made that Hross-Bjorn, you must know. You've got to watch out for him, my lad, or he'll steal that box away from you."

"No, he won't," Sigurd answered. "I escaped from Halfdane, who wanted it just as badly."

For a moment, Sigurd and the battered warlord measured each other warily. Then Bjarnhardr rapped on the floor with his peg and laughed. "You're a match for Halfdane, indeed. That's why I gave you the sword. When you've done for Halfdane, you can kill Jotull, can't you?" His eyes gleamed with malignant delight.

"Then all I'll have left is you," Sigurd answered without a trace of humor, looking steadily at Bjarnhardr.

When the time arrived for their departure, snow and wind howled around Svinhagahall with no sign of abating. Jotull stalked up and down the broken parapets with the snow hissing around him and plastering his beard. When he returned to the hall, he flung off his cloak irritably and declared, "There's magic involved in this storm or you can have my staff and satchel. You saw how it comes from the south—from Hrafnborg? If it's that measling rat Mikla, I'll hang him up by his heels for the next fifty years."

Rolfr brightened at the mention of Mikla, but Sigurd felt a

chill of dread at the possibility of adverse magic being directed at him from Hrafnborg. The door shook in its frame and he thought he heard the sending snuffling under the door. He put his hand on the hilt of his sword, and the wind seemed to chuckle mockingly at the idea of one lone Scipling challenging the sweeping fury of the storm.

"Can't we leave anyway?" he asked. "It's only a spring storm and not likely to last long."

"No indeed," Jotull replied, looking into his satchel intently. "We're going to counter their blizzard with another spell, one which I hope will rattle them to their boot soles." He snatched up some devices and an assortment of small objects and strode hastily toward the narrow winding stair that would take him to the high parapets of the fortress, an ideal place for hurling counterspells.

Sigurd fumed and fidgeted while Rolfr and Bjarnhardr sat opposite one another by the fire, pretending to doze but in reality exchanging suspicious stares. Several times Sigurd went to the door to listen, thinking he had heard muffled shouts of alarm, but he didn't dare open it for fear of the lurking sending. He sent the servants out instead, one by one, but the perverse creatures did not return. Slyngr was the last to go, after much arguing and complaining that it wasn't his duty to run errands— his duty, as far as Sigurd was able to surmise, was to do nothing but humor Bjarnhardr and insult the chieftains when they came for their orders.

The useless fellow was gone only a few moments, and Sigurd had scarcely fastened the last of the many bars on the inner door when Slyngr threw himself against it in a flurry of kicking and pounding and screeching. He fell inside the moment Sigurd opened the door, skewered through by a Ljosalfar arrow but still alive. Bjarnhardr scuttled across the floor, clutching his sword, but Sigurd had the door shut and locked in an instant.

"They're here," Slyngr gasped, staring around in horror. "Like white wolves in the snow. Silent—dreadful—arrows!"

"It's Halfdane," Bjarnhardr said grimly, his features split by a fierce grin. He clapped Sigurd on the shoulder. "This time

I shall have someone to fight for me who won't fail. That sword against Halfdane's gauntlet will be better than an even match. I knew I survived with this crooked back and wooden leg for a reason, and that reason will be vengeance—sweet and precious and final vengeance."

Rolfr looked up from the pale-faced, dying Slyngr, who was staring with an accusing gleam in his eyes toward Sigurd. "You're not going to fight Halfdane, are you? Remember, he saved your life twice, Siggi."

Sigurd listened to the hushed tramplc of feet approaching the outside door and trembled with the anticipation of battle. "If he thinks I'm going meekly back to Hrafnborg as his prisoner, then I'll fight him. I'll fight him to the death, if he thinks he can take the box away from me. I know that's what he's come for."

Bjarnhardr drew his own sword and positioned himself behind Sigurd. "I'm not much good, but I'll protect your back as much as I can, Sigurd, as a true friend should." He darted a malignant glance at Rolfr, who remained beside Slyngr.

"I'll not lift a hand against Halfdane," Rolfr said flatly. "Sigurd, it will be much to your discredit if you fight him."

Sigurd paid no heed. The door suddenly shuddered under a battery of blows, and a chorus of voices demanded that the door be opened. Bjarnhardr blanched and withdrew a few more paces toward the doorway to the narrow stair leading upward.

A voice outside silenced all the others. "Hold your noise. We'll blast the door open if we have to. Halloa! Sigurd! Are you in there?"

Sigurd crept up on the door. "I'm here. That sounds like Mikla, the apprentice."

"It is, you fool. Now open this door before I burn it down. We're rather out of patience with you, Sigurd."

Sigurd was about to make a hot-tempered reply when Jotull suddenly descended the stair and burst into the room with a bound. He took the foremost position at the door, ignoring Bjarnhardr's relieved exclamations and pretending not to have noticed the warlord attempting to sneak up the stairway.

"So it's Mikla, is it, who is wizard to Halfdane now?" Jotull

boomed through the door, using his spitting staff's head to
unlatch several of the locks. "You sound far too brave for a
lowly apprentice. You're not a wizard yet by any means. I
can't suppose that even you would have the rash ill judgment
to wish to match me with magic or face me even at swordpoint."

His reply was a thunderous assault on the door. "Open it,
or we'll bury you with this door for your coffin," the voice of
Halfdane rumbled. "You alone are the one I hold responsible
for this folly, Jotull. When we have the time, we shall settle
the matter and leave one of us dead."

Jotull nudged the final bolt almost off and leaped to a better
defensive position. The next assault from outside sent the door
reeling half off its hinges and Halfdane surged inside, halting
at a respectful distance from Jotull and Sigurd with his sword.

Bjarnhardr sat down in his chair with a wide grin, as if the
situation were conceived solely for his amusement.

"Good evening, Halfdane, my old enemy and rival," he
said, tapping his peg on the ground to call everyone's attention
to himself. "Isn't this like old times, when we used to burst in
on each other more regularly to fight it out? I've missed the
old Hrafnborg in the lowlands quite dreadfully. Every time I
see its ruins, it gives me a not-unpleasant pang, I assure you."

Halfdane advanced into the room, lowering and snow-cov-
ered, an uncouth contrast to the assured Bjarnhardr. "I wish
nothing but the pangs of premature death for you, Bjarnhardr.
It seems that the most useless creatures are the hardest to kill,
like snakes and Dokkalfar. Shall I have to kill you this time,
so you can join your guards and wall-watchers in their recent
unfortunate fate? I've come here for the Scipling whom Jotull
abducted from Hrafnborg, and I won't leave without him."

"Well, then, you'll have to discuss that with Jotull and the
Scipling," Bjarnhardr said, still grinning as he played with his
sword.

Sigurd and Halfdane exchanged an unfriendly glower. Jotull
leaned on his staff and said, "I don't believe you understand
that Sigurd came away without the least persuasion, so you
can't accuse me of abducting him."

"You influenced him," Halfdane retorted with a fiery glare.

"You knew you could convince him of almost anything you found it convenient for him to believe. If he wanted to leave Hrafnborg, you certainly did nothing to coax him to stay."

"Stay!" Sigurd exclaimed. "For what? It wouldn't take you long to kill me, once you decided that I wasn't going to give you the box. I know you were plotting something against me."

Halfdane turned his angry gaze upon Sigurd. "And do you think that Bjarnhardr and Jotull aren't? You can't suppose that they are totally honorable men who care for nothing but your welfare?"

"No, I don't," Sigurd replied. "There's no one I trust anymore. Not you, not them. I'm going my own way about opening that box and I'll take it extremely ill if you attempt to interfere. Your intention is to get the box from me. You've tried to deceive me, and I don't trust the motives behind anything you do."

Bjarnhardr interrupted, "Those are fighting words, Sigurd. Why don't you just call Halfdane a liar and be done with it?"

Halfdane took a step toward Bjarnhardr. "Keep your tongue silent, or I'll finish the job of killing you this time. You're not all that pleasant to look at and never were, so your removal would be a favor to everyone. I shall settle with you later for your part in this dispute. But for the present, the issue is between me and the Scipling."

Sigurd gestured toward the door with his sword. "Then the argument is finished, if that's true. I refuse to go back to Hrafnborg under any circumstances with a man who is certain to be my assassin."

Bjarnhardr chuckled as a half-dozen Dokkalfar slunk down the narrow stair and crept behind his chair, swords and axes ready. "The odds are getting more even every moment, Halfdane. You must know you can't take the Scipling and the box out of here without a fight. It's obvious that he doesn't want to go, and I don't think he shall. After all, he's a guest at Svinhagahall and I'm obliged to prevent his falling into the hands of ruffianly outlaws such as yourselves. With much sorrow and regret, I fear you must depart without Scipling or box, and which of the two is the greater loss is up to you to decide.

Will you retreat like a reasonable man, Halfdane, or shall we be forced to make it messy and unpleasant?" He smiled and nodded toward the dark, waiting figure of Jotull, who looked from Sigurd to Halfdane and on to Bjarnhardr with the calm, intent gaze of a bird of prey watching its target.

Halfdane answered by tossing his cloak out of the way of his sword, and the Ljosalfar instantly stood on their guard for battle. Jotull drew his sword and held his staff in his left hand.

"No, no," Bjarnhardr said, waving Jotull aside. "I have a new follower to fight for me. Sigurd is more than anxious to match wits with you, Halfdane. I gave him that sword, and this will be the time for him to try it out. Nothing could delight me more than seeing your blood on the blade that I put into his hand."

Halfdane's black brows were scowling as he glanced from Sigurd to the sword and back to Bjarnhardr. With a contemptuous snort, he sheathed his own sword and folded his arms. "I refuse to fight when the match is so unequal. It would be nothing short of murder."

"That's not true!" Sigurd's eyes flashed as he stepped closer, brandishing his sword menacingly. "I'm no novice, nor was I before I came to your realm. Your refusal to fight is an insult to me, and I challenge you to defend yourself or die. Besides this insult, I also have Thongullsfjord to avenge. I defy you to deny that you caused the trolls to drive everyone out and caused the blame to be put upon my innocent grandmother, so that she died of the shame."

Halfdane swelled with anger, but still he did not put a hand on his sword. "I do deny it and I still refuse to cut short your career of stupidity and ignorance. Get yourself ready to go back."

"My lord," Dagrun said, stepping forward. "He doesn't mean to come away peacefully. I think this is the time to tell him your secret."

"No indeed, Dagrun, not in this place, and not at swords' ends," Halfdane replied impatiently.

"Keeping secrets is bad policy," Dagrun muttered, stepping back reluctantly, still scowling anxiously.

"It's no secret to me," Sigurd retorted. "I heard you boasting that you could get the box into your hands with no struggle at any time you chose. Remember talking to Dagrun one night in the small horse barn? I was there and I heard everything. You can't deny that you were plotting to trick me and perhaps eventually to kill me if I didn't hand the box over to you."

Halfdane and Dagrun exchanged a startled glance, as if they were trying to recall exactly what had been said.

"We plotted no such thing," Dagrun began furiously, but Halfdane bade him be silent. He looked at Sigurd, dark with brooding menace.

"We've wasted enough time. We're taking you back with us, and one day I hope you'll thank us for it. You've been blinded by a lot of gifts and flattery, not to mention your own natural arrogance. And even that sword which you're trying to provoke me with is an evil trick on your gullible disposition. I recognize the sword and I promise you that no one who was a true friend would give that sword to you. It has passed through the hands of several owners, all of whom committed atrocious killings with it. It has a curse on it that compels its owner to infamous deeds. The best thing you could do with it is to return it to its source, preferably sticking it through his heart."

Sigurd glared into Halfdane's eyes, burning with shame and indignation that Halfdane would speak to him as if he were a green youth who didn't know how to live his own life. Rolfr's reaction to the sword surged through his memory, which made him all the angrier at all Ljosalfar, whose sole object seemed to be the disappointing of all his ambitions. The sword in his hand almost quivered with his rage and yearning for battle, yet Halfdane's steady eyes threatened to stare him down.

Bjarnhardr's voice was taut with excitement. "You'd better put on your gauntlet, Halfdane. I think he means to kill you, and he could do it, too, if you're not careful."

Halfdane made no move to put on the gauntlet in his belt or to draw his sword. Sigurd had never hated anyone so fiercely as he hated Halfdane at that moment. The sword did not waver; the room seemed to dim around him as his heart began to hammer in his chest and his breathing deepened. He recognized the choking feeling of impending murder and succumbed to it wholeheartedly. He swung the sword at Halfdane, feeling the metal bite into flesh as Halfdane threw up one arm in an effort to protect himself from the blow, which caught him fairly off guard. He had barely cleared his sword from its scabbard when Sigurd ran him through. With a final incredulous look at Sigurd, he collapsed to the ground. No one was more amazed than the watching Ljosalfar, who broke into a sudden bereaved howl and charged forward with the object of instant and gratifying revenge upon their warlord's slayer. Sigurd retrieved his sword and leaped away. Bjarnhardr's Dokkalfar surged forward to protect him, and the hall echoed with the clamor of swords on shields and voices raised in fury and mortal pain. Sigurd scarcely knew with whom he fought; he slashed away with a berserkr blindness until the last of his opponents turned and skipped over the litter of weapons and bodies in pursuit of the retreating Ljosalfar.

Jotull sheathed his sword and chuckled in the sudden silence, looking around for Bjarnhardr, who had been defending himself rather desperately in the stairway. The warlord limped forward, wheezing and coughing but still grinning.

"We foxed them, Jotull," he gasped, sinking down in his chair to catch his wind. "And Sigurd killed Halfdane. Oh, wasn't it splendid? The fool had no idea what was coming to him. Sigurd! Where are you? You've earned that sword a thousand times over, and I shall forever be in your debt. Where's Halfdane's carcass, Jotull? The gauntlet is mine."

Sigurd began to look around him, after he had sheathed the sword. All but one of Bjarnhardr's men lay dead or severely wounded, but if any of Halfdane's men were killed, their companions must have carried them away, including the body of Halfdane. Jotull cursed as he searched and Bjarnhardr's triumphant grin faded into a petulant scowl.

"Then follow them, Jotull! They can't be far away yet. I wonder if Rolfr had something to do with spiriting his body away so speedily. If he has, I'll—"

The person in question obligingly presented himself from his hiding place in an old storeroom. "I didn't wish to fight against my own friends and relatives," he said. "I prefer to stay neutral as long as possible. But I didn't take Halfdane's body away; how could I, hiding in here all the while?"

Sigurd didn't quite know how to look at Rolfr or speak to him. His initial fierce elation dissipated quickly, but he felt obligated to maintain a certain swagger around Bjarnhardr and Jotull, so he pretended to be vastly disappointed that the Ljosalfar had carried away Halfdane and his gauntlet. Bjarnhardr's mood remained nasty, and Jotull departed in ill humor to organize the battered defenders of Svinhagahall into a pursuit party.

"We can't leave until they get back," Bjarnhardr growled, flinging himself into his chair and rubbing his maimed leg like a bear nursing a wounded paw. For the rest of the day, he drank himself into a stupor, and when he awoke hours later he fell into worse temper upon discovering that Jotull and the others had not yet returned.

Sigurd and Rolfr kept out of his way, particularly when he began threatening his attendants with his sword every time they came near him. He raved and roared far into the nighttime hours, but his noise was not the only cause of the Scipling's wakefulness.

Sigurd sat by the fire in his comfortable room, feeling chilled and lonely. At last, he went in search of Rolfr, unable to bear his misery in solitude any longer.

"Rolfr, are you asleep?" he whispered gruffly at the door, where a faint gleam of firelight showed.

A dark figure near the fire stirred and answered without looking around. "No, I'm still awake. You might as well come in. It sounds as if Bjarnhardr is still savage. We won't be getting any sleep tonight."

Sigurd sat down on a stool near Rolfr and stared into the coals for a long while in silence, matched by a despondent silence from Rolfr. "I know you have a right to hate me, Rolfr," he finally said. "I guess this is a good reason for us to part, and I certainly wouldn't blame you. I imagine you've been thinking thoughts of revenge for Halfdane, haven't you? At the very least, you'll probably leave me here and go back to

Hrafnborg—something I can never do now. Ragnhild will wish my sending had drowned me that night, and I'm not so sure it wouldn't have been for the better of everyone. I wish I hadn't done it, Rolfr," he added in a sudden burst of regret. "Something about holding that sword in my hand made me feel like murder. I haven't really felt at all proud of myself, when I think about how Halfdane tried to help me—and he did save my life twice."

Rolfr sighed and hunched his shoulders. "You'll soon get over it, Sigurd. With Jotull and Bjarnhardr to urge you along, you'll probably forget about Halfdane. Don't worry about me, I'll stay with you until—until what I foresaw comes to pass. What's done is done, Sigurd, so there's no use in torturing both of us by looking back and wishing you hadn't done it. If you don't stop brooding about it, you'll have to go through the rest of your life with things falling down from the walls or shooting around the room, as that poker is doing." He nodded toward a sooty poker which Sigurd's natural power was pushing across the floor in erratic patterns. Most of the objects hanging on wall pegs had fallen to the floor with Sigurd's inadvertent glances.

"I'm an enemy even to myself," Sigurd said bitterly, as a hot coal leaped out of the fire with a loud pop and burned a hole in his pants before he could brush it away. "It seems that everyone I come near loses his luck. Maybe you'd be better off to leave me, Rolfr. It might lengthen your life."

"No, Siggi, you might not know it, but you need me." Rolfr thoughtfully stirred up the fire and glanced at Sigurd. "There is a way you could partially repay the Ljosalfar for Halfdane's death, if you cared to do it."

Gloomily Sigurd rubbed the burned place on his knee. "I haven't got anything worth having, except my life, and that's not worth a great deal when you consider there's a sending following me that seems determined to destroy me. But go ahead and tell me your idea. It can't be any worse than handing myself over for their revenge."

Rolfr's eyes were bright and intent. "You could keep Bjarnhardr and Jotull from having whatever it is inside your box.

It's very valuable to them, and Halfdane apparently thought it was worth keeping away from them, if he was willing to lose his life coming to get you and the box. We can escape from Svinhagahall without much trouble, because so far you've showed no inclination for leaving. We could find our way back to Hrafnborg and get Mikla to help us get to Svartafell. If you could somehow fill Halfdane's place, the Ljosalfar will forgive you, and Halfdane won't have died for nothing."

Sigurd listened to Bjarnhardr roaring irritably at his servants and calling for Slyngr, who would never answer his summons again. He thought of the plentiful food and fires and ease which he had grown accustomed to and he thought of Jotull's black powers ranged against him if he did decide to escape. He also thought about the sending, which kept him a prisoner within the safe walls of Svinhagahall more effectively than locks and bars ever would have done.

"I don't think we could survive, just the two of us alone in the dark," he said. "You can't shoot and neither of us knows the spells for discouraging trolls. I think we're safer to pretend to go along with Bjarnhardr's plans, and I'm not altogether certain there won't be someone somewhere who will refuse to settle for anything less than blood for Halfdane. Someone like Ragnhild." He shuddered suddenly, with the strange feeling that she might be thinking about him at that moment. Having her for an enemy could be unpleasant. The braided chain of her hair around his neck felt more like a noose than a token of esteem. He took it off quickly and would have thrown it into the fire except that he stopped to save her little ring, which fitted his least finger; then it occurred to him that an extra bowstring was never unwelcome, so he shoved the braided hair into his pocket instead of burning it.

Rolfr turned back to gaze into the fire without speaking. After a long interval, he said, "Halfdane must have been right when he said that your sword leads its owner to commit infamous deeds. The killing of Halfdane was the first and I am likely to become the next. I wonder what's going to become of you, Siggi." He poked at the fire without looking up.

Silently, Sigurd agreed with him, but he said nothing. He

and Rolfr passed the night listening to Bjarnhardr's intermittent outbursts and marking the hours by the changing of the watchmen in the ruined towers above, who tramped down the narrow stairway and exited through the main hall entrance. Once Sigurd thought he heard the triumphant cackling of Hross-Bjorn and the thunder of its hooves on the hall doors, but he might have dreamed it.

After that, sleep even in the smallest of cat naps was impossible, although the morning watchmen had not yet relieved the midnight watch. Sigurd left Rolfr sleeping in an uncomfortable knot beside the cold hearth and went prowling through the labyrinth of Bjarnhardr's subterranean fortress, looking for someone to question about Jotull. His lamp was dim, the grass wick almost gone, and he saw only a few scuttling rats and Bjarnhardr's hounds, who wagged their tails, stretched, and decided he was as good a person as any to accompany on a jaunt through the cold corridors. He came upon a few servants dragging bundles of wood, but they scuttled away from him almost as readily as the rats, recognizing him as the wielder of the cursed sword. He found the infirmary in the lowest and dankest of the subcellars, but no one there was in any condition to talk to him. Halfdane's surprise attack on the previous day had taken a heavy toll among Bjarnhardr's guards, which no doubt was part of the reason for the warlord's disagreeable humor.

Thoroughly chilled by this time, Sigurd hurried back to the main hall, where a skinny old thrall was heaping up a generous fire in preparation for Bjarnhardr's morning appearance. The old fellow started when he saw Sigurd and apprehensively exclaimed that the breakfast wasn't ready yet, adding in rather an accusing tone that the hour was early, and no one else was awake.

"I don't mind waiting," Sigurd said. "Go on about your duties. I'll watch the fire and mend it if it needs it."

"Good. Then you won't mind letting in the morning watch when they knock at the door, will you?" the thrall inquired hopefully, rubbing his knotty hands together near the flames.

Sigurd agreed, and the ragged creature disappeared into the

dark passageway, leaving Sigurd to be the first one to discover what sort of mood Bjarnhardr was in after a night of drinking and bellowing for Jotull or Slyngr. He hadn't waited long when the morning watch tramped up to the door and knocked respectfully. With gruff mutters of thanks, they marched into the hall, and the last one ushered in another fellow in a snow-laden cloak.

"Says he's a messenger. Knows something of Jotull's whereabouts, if he's to be believed," the guard announced, giving the stranger a poke with his bow in passing and eyeing the fire enviously.

The messenger positioned himself before the fire and shook off the snow so his cloak could steam in the welcome heat. Sigurd sat down in a chair and rested his chin in his hands, taking no further notice of the messenger. The servants came in to place the eating things on the table. The moment they were gone, the messenger pushed back his hood and turned to Sigurd, who was idly examining the hilt of his sword and trying to decipher the runes carved into the handle. When Sigurd glanced up at the messenger, he recognized a scowling and vengeful-looking Mikla.

# Chapter 11

❖❖❖❖❖❖❖❖❖❖❖❖❖❖❖❖❖❖❖❖❖❖

"What are you doing here?" Sigurd asked, putting his hand on the sword. "Do you want to get killed?"

"No more than Halfdane did," Mikla replied bitterly. "I came to get you and Rolfr and bring you back. The others have gone ahead with Halfdane to the nearest house of healing."

"Then he's not dead?" Sigurd gasped.

Mikla shrugged. "There may yet be a chance that a bit of

life still lingers, but I myself have very little hope. Where's Rolfr?"

Sigurd nodded toward the passage. "Asleep. Why don't you get out of here before someone discovers you, Mikla? If Jotull found you here, he'd make cats' meat out of you."

"Never mind that. Come on, Sigurd, don't you want to escape from here?" Mikla glanced nervously toward the passage.

"I'm not a prisoner," Sigurd snapped, without much conviction as he thought about the sending. "And when I do leave, it won't be to go back to Hrafnborg, not with all those vengeful Alfar waiting to shed my blood for Halfdane. I'm going to Svartafell to see the maker of this box and ask him to open it."

"Then I shall go with you. If I have anything to do with this matter, I won't allow Bjarnhardr or Jotull to get control of what you carry in the box. Once either of them gets control of whatever that thing may be, we may as well seal the doom of the last of the Alfar."

"Outlaws, you mean. You're all Alfar," Sigurd said, still toying with the sword. "It seems to me that I've allied myself with the side that has the best chances of survival. Just look around and compare Svinhagahall to Hrafnborg and you'll see why I have no intention of forsaking what I have for the privilege of freezing to death with you on the way to Svartafell. Even if we did succeed, it would still be a losing battle to try defending little hill forts like Hrafnborg against something like Svinhagahall."

"So that's your decision? You'll join with the side that looks the strongest, whether right or wrong? Listen, I've looked around Svinhagahall and I've seen enough to convince me how much better off we are at Hrafnborg. Did you ever see anyone freeze or starve there? Did Halfdane eat meat when there wasn't meat for his men? Maybe his hall wasn't opulent, but there wasn't any meanness there, at least. Svinhagahall reeks of meanness, Sigurd, and I'm shocked that you can't smell it, too."

Sigurd felt his temper rising, particularly when he realized he couldn't find much to say in defense of Bjarnhardr's method of leading his men. Bjarnhardr liked to keep his people dependent upon him for their survival. While such a situation was rather harsh on some when they fell into disfavor, Sigurd thought he was above their plight—at least, until he earned Bjarnhardr's displeasure.

"Mikla, I don't know why you're wasting your time here," he said. "I'm not leaving with you, and you can't force me as long as I've got this." He half-drew the sword, threateningly.

Mikla glowered at him. "Oh, indeed? You're just a Scipling, Sigurd, and I'm very nearly a fully adept wizard. I daresay I can pretty well take you anywhere I think you should go and I'm going to take you and Rolfr to Svartafell despite your best efforts to bluster and make a fool of yourself. We haven't much time, so go wake Rolfr and get yourselves together ready to travel. I've got your horses saddled and waiting."

Sigurd stood up and drew the sword. "This is my answer. You'd better leave now before I get angry enough to kill you, too."

Mikla raised his staff. "Oh, you've acquired a taste for killing your friends, have you? Put that sword away or I'll melt it and your hand with it, without much regret at all."

"Spoken like a true friend," Sigurd replied with a snort. "I know who my real friends are, and you're not one of them, Mikla."

"Yes, I am, you idiot, and you're too stupid to know it," Mikla retorted.

Sigurd blazed with fury, and he had never wanted anything as much as he wanted to kill Mikla. "Those are words a man never forgives," he said, and made a deadly thrust at Mikla, who had learned from Halfdane's example to expect treachery and saved himself by twisting away. Only his cloak was pierced by the gleaming blade.

Mikla leaped over the table and raised his staff for a spell. Sigurd would have followed, but suddenly the back of his head seemed to explode and he staggered a few steps across a wildly tilting floor before collapsing. Rolfr peered into his face anxiously while the room whirled around giddily.

"Are you all right, Siggi? I hope I didn't hit you too hard."

"No, I'm all right, nothing's the matter," Sigurd said a little thickly, sensing a terrific lump rising on the back of his skull. He looked at Rolfr reproachfully, feeling terribly betrayed.

Sigurd rose rather shakily to his hands and knees and made no protest when Mikla pounced upon his sword with a vengeful grunt, sheathed it, and tucked it away in his belt. By the time Sigurd felt like standing up, Rolfr had stowed their possessions in two saddle pouches, stolen a fine cloak and new boots for Mikla, and taken possession of most of the food on Bjarnhardr's table. He draped Sigurd's cloak around his shoulders, careful not to jar his tender wound, and announced, "We're ready. Let's go, Mikla."

They each took one of Sigurd's arms and marched out the door and down the long dark passageway to the outside, where the guard tending his miserable fire scarcely looked up at them as they hurried importantly by. When the guards at the earthworks stepped forward to question them, Mikla replied in an irritable shout, as a person of consequence would do, and set spurs to his horse.

They galloped away into the thinning darkness, and nearly half a day of sunshine put them that much ahead of their pursuers. Mikla and Rolfr were exultant. Sigurd still sulked, and every turn of his head was another reminder of Rolfr's perfidy. After a few days of travel, he began looking forward to the sunlight hours and condescended to speak to Rolfr and Mikla.

The first thing he demanded of Mikla was his sword, but Mikla replied, "I've got it in a safe place where it won't do any harm. You really don't want that sword back, Sigurd. I read its runes and it's cursed to any hand that bears it. It says "Three treacheries I do commit.' The runes are Dvergar— probably the Dokkalfar captured a smith and forced him to make a sword of power for them, and this was the way the smith got even with them. Dwarves are excellent fellows sometimes, but they carry a grudge forever. When we get to Svartafell, we'll ask Bergthor if he can destroy this sword so no one else will be killed."

Sigurd sighed and stared into the fire that was heating their meager breakfast. "I don't admit it often, but it's always true—

I'm a fool. Jotull and Bjarnhardr set it up so Halfdane would be enticed into Svinhagahall where I would have this sword to kill him."

"Yes, Bjarnhardr made sure the message arrived at Hrafnborg," Mikla said. "Halfdane suspected a trap, but I'm sure he never thought it would be you. I can't exactly place all the blame on you, but it will be difficult for you to redeem yourself. I hope that box holds something marvelous to make up for the loss of Halfdane."

Rolfr stoically pulled on his sodden boots. "I can't help wondering where Jotull is. Did he continue after the fellows with Halfdane, or is he following us? Which prize does he think the most valuable—or the easiest to capture?"

No one cared to answer his question, but it was the one that they all thought about as they mounted up and rode into the darkness. Each day the sun came up earlier and lingered longer, which seemed to have a disheartening effect on the trolls, and considerably delayed their pursuers from Svinhagahall. On cold, frosty nights they could hear the clatter of horses' hooves over stone several miles away, and Mikla wove his best spells to thwart the Dokkalfar. He raised fogs so thick that breathing was almost impossible and caused snowstorms and thunderstorms to cover the tracks of their horses and to confuse their pursuers. He experimented with illusions, such as a brightly lighted hall and merry voices singing, which led the Dokkalfar from fell to fell until they realized it was only a ploy to put them off the track. His best spell was the illusion of a deep crevice in the earth barring the Dokkalfar from their prey, which led them far aside when they tried to find a way around it or through it. Sigurd began to look upon Mikla with new respect when he conjured an awesome, fiery spectacle in the sky to discourage their following enemies further.

One circumstance, however, could not be alleviated by magic. Their meager stock of food had dwindled almost to nothing, and, according to Mikla's maps, they were scarcely one quarter of the way to Svartafell.

"Why can't you magic up some food for us?" Sigurd grumbled one supperless night as they huddled, wet and disheart-

ened, in a shallow lava cave while the spring rain poured down
outside.

Mikla shook his head. "It wouldn't do us any good if I did.
There's no substance to conjured food. What we'll have to do
is stop at some of the settlements and farms along the way and
work for food. Being around other people will make it harder
for Jotull to locate us with his spells. We'll alter our course
slightly westward, and in two days' time we'll be at a farm
called Thufnavellir, where we hope they'll need some help for
sheep shearing. After that, we can stop at Kvigudalir, Myrk-
dhal, Skardrsstrond, Fljot, and Gunnavik. By then we'll be at
the foot of the fells where Bergthor lives in his Svartafell."

Sigurd tugged thoughtfully on his beard and frowned. "I
didn't realize there were so many farms and settlements between us and Svartafell. Won't that mean more eyes and ears
to do the seeing for Bjarnhardr and Jotull?"

"Alfar are independent by nature, and Dokkalfar are no
exception," Mikla replied. "It may be a surprise to you, but
Bjarnhardr and Jotull won't be popular among the farming folk
where we are going. They won't hasten to sell us over."

Sigurd comforted himself with thoughts of a real roof between him and the rain and some half-decent food instead of
starvation. Even if Bjarnhardr somehow captured them, he
thought he could soon win back the warlord's favor. He had
left against his will, after all. If any one thing was obvious, it
was the fact that the three of them could not survive alone,
just as he had told Mikla, and that was a source of satisfaction
to Sigurd.

They found Thufnavellir at the close of the short early-spring
day. The rain had dissolved most of the snow, filling the riv-
erbeds with roaring torrents of boistrous water, and the smooth
hills around the farmstead were already beginning to turn a
faint green. Smoke curled invitingly from the chimney of a
large turf house, which was surrounded by smaller huts and
stables and pens for the livestock. From the blattering of sheep
and the barking of dogs, Sigurd guessed that the shearing was
already in progress.

As Mikla had predicted, the farmer at Thufnavellir was glad

for more help with the shearing. Kambi Coalbrow, the farmer, made no great show of hospitality when they finished their work for the day and went into the hall to eat, but the food was generous and the manners of the family and servants were cautiously polite.

"We don't get many visitors," Kambi said, puffing gently at the pipe within his huge gnarled fist. "Not to say you're not welcome, but perhaps you noticed certain warning signs of the nature of Thufnavellir, and you might not care to stay and work for as long as you might wish."

His bright eye gleamed through the scowling hedge of his thick, curling eyebrows and fastened immediately on Sigurd with such a knowing glance that Sigurd was chilled and put on guard as surely as if the man had said to him that he knew all about him. Sigurd had the wit to realize at once that Kambi was no ordinary farmer, in spite of his rather crude and loutish appearance.

Mikla also studied the farmer. "Yes, I noticed an unusual number of barrow mounds around the farm and I had a chilly feeling that it might not be a pleasant place on a moonless night. I've had a bit of teaching in a few wizard crafts, and I'd be glad to try settling your walking dead, if that's the problem."

Kambi's wife and daughters looked up from their stitching and exchanged glances of wary interest. Ulfrun, the wife, looked not at all pleased. She said to her husband sharply, "There now, it's just like you to frighten away three good workers, when there's no chance of getting any more. You'd better keep silent, Coalbrow."

"No, I won't, you old vixen," Kambi returned. "I knew another wizard when I saw him." He looked at Mikla, sighed, and shook his head. "I've lived here man and boy all my life and never thought it a peaceful spot, but I never knew how bad it could get until my father died a year ago. He was the wizard Vigbjodr, a most excellent wizard and an enemy to Bjarnhardr all his life. When Vigbjodr died, Bjarnhardr sent a necromancer to raise him from his grave and get control of his powers, and now Vigbjodr wreaks Bjarnhardr's vengeance upon this farmstead and all within. We don't dare occupy this hall at midnight because of my father's draug. It has killed several visitors it found sleeping in his bed, and others have simply disappeared, I suspect they were carried into his grave and became milignant ghosts to play further evil tricks upon us. We've had a fjylgjadraug tormenting us since Thufnavellir was settled. The wretched little creature spoils our milk and curds and kills our livestock from time to time, but otherwise it's more of a nuisance than a danger. You'll see him, a small ragged boy in a russet shirt, and I daresay you'll feel his spite, if you stay here long."

Sigurd looked at Mikla with a wry smile. "Do you still think Bjarnhardr will have a hard time finding us here? We couldn't have picked an easier place."

Rolfr shuddered and edged away from a pile of bones that were to be used as firewood, and Ulfrun cackled unkindly. "You'll have to get used to them, young man; there's bones under every tussock of Thufnavellir. Kambi's ancestors had the great foresight to build their farm right in the middle of an ancient burial ground, so the plow turns up bones with every furrow. Stupidity began in Kambi centuries ago and has reached its full flower in this last representative you see here before you. If only Kambi would have the sense to go over to Bjarnhardr while he still lives, we'd all live more comfortably, I'm certain."

Kambi scowled at his wife and plucked at his heavy nether lip. He arose solemnly and announced, "It's time we left the hall. I'll show our guests to the cow house, which is truly the best accommodation we can offer you, I'm sad to say."

"And even that is likely to be cold and wet if it rains," Ulfrun said hopefully.

Sigurd's spirits sank at the mention of the cow house. He looked around at the comfortable hall with its soft beds and warm fire and glared resentfully at Mikla. "I don't want to sleep in a cow shed. You may, if you want to, but I'm going to stay here where it's comfortable. I think," he added in a whisper, "that story of a draug haunting the hall is just an excuse to put their guests in a miserable place to sleep."

Rolfr shook his head vigorously. "No, no, the cow house is good enough for me. I don't want to share a place with any draug or a fylgjadraug, thank you."

"Then I'll sleep here by myself," Sigurd said stubbornly.

"You won't survive the night if you do," Kambi replied. "I won't be the one to blame for your death."

The turf roof groaned suddenly, and a fine sifting of dust powdered Kambi's shoulders. "You see," he went on sadly, "it starts already. Probably it's Mori, the fylgjadraug, trampling around up there plotting a mischief."

Mikla peered up into the gloom of the rafters, where the stars shone in through the smoke hole. "Has your cow house a good stout door?" he asked. "One that a horse couldn't kick down?"

Kambi shrugged his thick shoulders and looked even more sad. "One poor farmer can't be expected to do everything, can he? The door is a door, and that's about all you can say for it."

"Then we shall sleep here in the hall tonight and take our chances with Vigbjodr and Mori," Mikla said decisively. "I fear we may have brought something just as bad with us to Thufnavellir." He glanced around as he said it to make sure Ulfrun and the others had gone out. "We are no friends to Bjarnhardr either, and he has followed us with a sending."

"Then you are Ljosalfar, too," Kambi said with gloomy satisfaction. "I was almost sure of it, but one doesn't like to ask questions of strangers. We are sadly fallen since the destruction of Snowfell, my friends. I fear you will come to no good at Thufnavellir, but if you think it best to sleep in the hall, then I shall leave it to you. Bar all the doors securely and don't let anyone come in, no matter what he says. I wouldn't sleep in the best bed, either; that's Vigbjodr's bed and he hates to find anyone sleeping in it." Bidding them farewell, he left the hall to them and trod heavily away toward the small, smoky hut where he slept.

Rolfr looked around the empty hall, clutching his axe when a stray gust of wind from the smoke hole stirred a cloak hanging on a peg. In the silence, they heard the roof timbers creaking

as something moved across it to the edge and leaped to the
ground with a grunt. In a moment, three muzzles snuffled
eagerly under the door. After sampling the door frame with its
teeth and kicking the door until it shook, the sending trotted
away with an irritable growl.

Rolfr let out the breath he had been holding. "I'm sure I
won't sleep a wink as long as we're at Thufnavellir," he said.
"We won't stay here long, will we, Mikla?"

"We're committed to help him finish shearing, at least,"
Mikla said, "and that should take us nearly two weeks. He's
got sheep at his farms in the fells that need shearing, too. By
then we'll have earned a bit of food to carry away with us
when we go."

"But what if Jotull finds us in the meantime?" Rolfr lowered
his voice and glanced toward the door. "And Bjarnhardr surely
has powers to find us somehow, doesn't he?"

Mikla made himself comfortable beside the fire. "We have
crossed running water many times since leaving Svinhagahall,
and that will make Bjarnhardr's powers considerably less useful. Jotull will have difficulty tracing us after all this rain. It
will take him awhile to find us. Now then, who's going to
stand the first watch? Sigurd, if I remember right, it's your
turn."

Sigurd looked around indignantly at the stout walls and roof.
"Why? We're perfectly safe, as long as we keep the door shut."

"No, someone ought to watch," Rolfr insisted, still eying
the cloak on the peg. "With Hross-Bjorn and a host of draugar
prowling around, I won't sleep unless I know someone has his
eye upon them."

Sigurd took the first watch. Mikla and Rolfr curled up beside
the fire and soon fell into exhausted slumber. Sigurd listened
for the draugar of Thufnavellir, who obligingly howled and
called from the barrow mounds. While Sigurd was trying to
get a look at the creatures through a small crack in the door,
he heard a rustling at the smokehole overhead, and something
plummeted through it to land on the floor not far away. Sigurd
grabbed his axe and poised himself to defend the hall. The

thing shook itself like a bundle of old rags and, turning around, caught sight of Sigurd.

"Why, halloa! So it's you!" the creature declared, with a wide grin cracking its wizened little face, and it shook with glee as it stuck out one paw for Sigurd to shake reluctantly. "I'm so pleased to meet you. We hardly ever have guests anymore. I am Mori. Doubtless old Coalbrow has told you about me." He shook hands with himself, snorting and chuckling as if he were drowning.

Sigurd drew back in revulsion. Mori was no bigger than a two-year-old child and as shriveled and wrinkled as an old dried apple. He wore no garment other than a ragged, coarse shirt with the sleeves and hem raveling away in tatters. Various other rags were tied around him here and there to cover the worst of the holes in his attire, and a most disreputable old hood sagged into one eye or the other as he grinned up at Sigurd like a horribly sage and ancient infant.

"How—how do you do," Sigurd said warily, still clutching his axe and wondering what the sending would do.

"How do I do? Why, I does just about anything I pleases." Mori cut a caper and cackled maliciously, keeping his bright little button eyes fastened on Sigurd. "I've just been to the dairy house, where I spoiled all the cheese curds with horse dung. Those stupid women forget to set out my share, so that's how I teach 'em not to forget poor old Mori. Tomorrow I'm going to flay Coalbrow's bull to the knees if they forget again."

"Well, there's food here in the hall, if you're hungry," Sigurd said, nodding toward the kitchen.

"Hungry!" Mori cried, rolling his bloodshot eyes. "I'm always hungry! Imagine yourself left as a poor little babe to starve on the fell as I was, and you'll see why I simply can't eat enough!"

Sigurd glanced at his sleeping friends, then followed the creature to the kitchen annex with waves of horror washing over him, not unmingled with a healthy dose of curiosity. Mori promptly seized the leftover haunch of lamb and greedily devoured it in less time that it would have taken Sigurd to eat a fraction of it. Tossing the bones on the floor, Mori stuffed curds, skyr, and cream into his mouth with both hands, wasting almost as much as he ate. Whole loaves of bread met a similar disgusting fate, and the sending did not stop his gluttonizing until all the food in the pantry was eaten or ruined.

"Is that all?" Mori asked, wiping his mouth on his dirty sleeve and looking around hungrily. "Ulfrun is the stingiest housekeeper I have ever encountered. Look at my poor stomach. It's still as flat as an empty sack." He pulled up his shirt and showed Sigurd the shriveled hollow of his belly, with the ribs standing out under tight, yellow skin. Sigurd shuddered in renewed horror.

"Nothing but skin and bones," Mori said proudly. "Not much to look at, eh? Eh?" He nudged Sigurd and winked furiously.

"No, there's hardly anything to you at all," Sigurd said in confusion, but it seemed to be what Mori wanted to hear. The little beast flung himself on the floor in a desperate fit of laughing and wheezing, as depraved a sight as Sigurd had ever beheld.

"But there you're mistaken," Mori said suddenly, bouncing to the center of the kitchen table, where he wiped his grimy feet. "A sending made from a dead infant abandoned on the fell by its mother is a most nasty sending indeed, especially if you can get it just before the last breath leaves its body." Mori leaned forward to speak into Sigurd's face, leering and twisting up his features in a manner that would have given fits to a lesser constitution. "I was scarcely dead when a wizard found me and turned me to his purposes, the first of which was the opportunity for frightening my wicked mother out of her wits and encouraging her to break her neck on the cliffs of Huskavik. These miserable rags were the rags she left me in. But I got my revenge on her." He showed his teeth at Sigurd in a menacing grin.

"To be sure, she certainly deserved it," Sigurd stuttered.

"Ah! I'm glad to hear you say so!" Mori turned a handstand on the table. "I believe you and I are going to be great friends, as long as you let me wreck the kitchen every night. You've brought me a fine assistant from Bjarnhardr, that Hross-Bjorn.

Only that wizard of Bjarnhardr's could be clever enough to think of such a beast. It changed itself into a flayed cat and suffocated a thrall earlier tonight. Tell me, what did you do to earn Bjarnhardr's hatred so thoroughly?"

Sigurd could scarcely think with Mori's hard, bright eyes boring into him. "I don't know, exactly. I'd thought Hross-Bjorn was from someone else—"

"Oh, no, no, he's not! It takes a sending to know a sending, I always say, and I know a Svinhagahall sending when I see one. Here's one now." Mori hugged himself.

Just then the front door shook under a heavy, single knock, and Sigurd seized his axe. Mori cackled at Sigurd. "There's old Vigbjodr wanting to get in. He'll go away in a minute and you'll hear the other night-walkers. We get old Skuma shrieking for help behind the sheepfold, where she was murdered about fifty years ago. In a moment, she'll be scratching at the door and pleading most pitifully for you to let her in, but if you do, she'll drag you away to her grave and that will be the last we'll see of you—alive, anyway. And the infants that died of exposure on this farm scream the loveliest choruses—"

Sigurd's hairs lifted in terror as the draug Skuma began scratching and moaning at the door, begging to be let in so she wouldn't die. When her desperate cries finally faded away, he heard other wails and shrieks coming from the barrows surrounding the farm buildings.

Another heavy, single knock jolted the door in its hinges, and Mori chuckled appreciatively. "Vigbjodr is getting impatient. Would you like to let him in?"

"No! Don't!" Sigurd gasped, as the sending made a move toward the door. "I don't fancy wizard draugar any more than I do you—I mean to say—if he was manufactured by Bjarnhardr—"

"It's the gold he wants to come to look at, you know," Mori whispered, with a wider grin than ever. "Ha! I see by your eyes that you do fancy gold. But there's something there that you'll like better. I know a great deal about you, my friend, and because I like you, I'll tell you what it is and how you can get it. But first you've got to promise not to say a word to your nosy friend Mikla. Him I don't like at all. Do you promise?" He leaned forward suddenly to glare malevolently into Sigurd's face.

Sigurd edged away slightly. "Well, suppose you tell me first what it is that I want so dreadfully, and whether it will be very hard to steal. I've never stolen anything from a draug before, and there's only one thing I'd even consider worth the risk—"

"What is it?" Mori demanded, leaning farther forward and grinning horribly.

"A sword," Sigurd said, and Mori fell off the table in another laughing fit. When the paroxysm passed, Mori climbed up the table leg and solemnly shook hands with Sigurd.

"A sword it shall be, then, my friend," Mori said with an unpleasant leer. "To fight that Hross-Bjorn, I wager! What a battle that will be. But you promise not to say one word to your wizard friend Mikla? He's mighty young for the kind of power he wields, and you don't like him much anyway, do you?"

"I don't like him at all. He stole my sword and refuses to give it back to me. If I could get another one, I would do almost anything, even steal it from a draug. I give you my word I won't say a thing to Mikla." Sigurd shook hands again with Mori, whose grin couldn't be stretched wide enough.

"It's a pact, then, between the two of us. I'll help you get your sword from Vigbjodr's secret treasure trove, and you shall help me be a nuisance to Coalbrow and his family. Ha, listen to old Vigbjodr knocking away at the door! Tomorrow night we'll let him in and you shall see your sword. And just for the fun of it, why don't you sleep in his bed?"

"Because he'll kill me if I do," Sigurd said in alarm.

"Ridiculous. He'll only kill you if you don't do what I say. Take a bunch of knives and arrange them around the bed so all the points go inward, and he won't touch you."

Sigurd answered with a skeptical grunt. "I'd be safer sleeping on the floor, wouldn't I? Not that I doubt your word, but—"

Mori sat down and crossed his stumpy legs. In a reproving tone he said, "Now, you should know that I wouldn't lie to you. I'm a friend of your friend Bjarnhardr. Come on, I dare you to try it. The door will be shut, so old Vigbjodr won't get in. I'll help you arrange the knives. Bjarnhardr wants you to have this sword."

Reluctantly Sigurd agreed to try it, as soon as Rolfr took his place watching, and politely suggested that Rolfr might not be as friendly to sendings as he was; if he saw Mori upon awakening at midnight, he was liable to scream and wake up Mikla. Mori took the hint. "Then I'll be going. I don't like Mikla. I'll have to make some mischief for him, to be sure I will. Good night, my dear friend. Watch for me tomorrow night. Don't forget the knives, points aiming inward. Farewell!"

Sigurd felt rather foolish lining the edges of his bed with sharp knives, and hoped he wouldn't forget they were there or thrash out in his sleep and cut himself. Rolfr stared sleepily at his preparations and went away to wake himself up in the cold draft coming in under the door.

"Did you see anything strange, Siggi?" he mumbled, with a yawn.

"No, nothing at all," Sigurd answered, from the depths of the extraordinary eider on Vigbjodr's bed. "Just some rats in the kitchen, I think." He was suddenly so sleepy he couldn't keep his eyes open another instant. Helplessly he listened to a loud snore from Rolfr's post at the door, which was echoed by a snicker from the smoke hole in the roof, where a wizened old infant's face was peering down into the room. Even Mikla was so drugged by sleep that he never heard the bolts on the door slide back and the hinges creak slightly as the heavy door swung ajar.

# Chapter 12

◇◆◇◆◇◆◇◆◇◆◇◆◇◆◇◆◇◆◇◆◇◆◇◆◇◆◇◆◇◆◇

A great shout jarred Sigurd from his sleep. He leaped out of the bed, barely remembering the knives in time to avoid slashing his legs to ribbons.

"Halloo! Is anyone alive in here?" Kambi Coalbrow bellowed, holding up a lantern to look around from his position in the doorway.

It was dark, but Sigurd knew it was morning. "We're still here," he said rather snappishly. "Is this the way you awaken your people every day?" He saw Rolfr leap up from his cramped sleeping position with a guilty expression on his face.

"The door was standing wide open," Kambi declared. "Surely you had the good sense to lock it last night after we left."

"Of course we locked it," Mikla said, lighting the fire with a quick flick of his hand. "Rolfr, it was locked when you stood watch, wasn't it?"

Rolfr was silent with misery. "It was before I fell asleep. I don't know what came over me, but all at once I couldn't keep my eyes from closing. I've never slept on guard duty before."

"It was Mori," Kambi said gloomily. "That's his idea of a joke. What good luck none of you were killed."

"The draug of Vigbjodr didn't appear then," Sigurd said with a sigh of relief, and started to step down the steps of the bed.

"Stop! Don't come forward!" Kambi shouted suddenly, sweeping the light of his lantern across the floor. "There, do you see that dirt? It looks like footprints coming into the hall and across it; they stopped beside the bed."

Sigurd looked at the lumps of mud tracking across the floor

167

and his skin crawled. Mikla shone the light of his staff at the dirt and said, "It's grave-mold. Whoever steps into that will be in the draug's power." He stared at Sigurd, his face owlish and pale in the flickering light. "What I can't understand is why Sigurd is still alive at this moment. The draug stood only a few inches away from him."

Sigurd sank back into the bed carefully. "Knives," he said rather weakly.

"A clever trick," Mikla said. "I wonder if it will work next time." He looked suspiciously at Sigurd and seemed on the point of asking him some questions, but Kambi was anxious to get on with the day's work. He was obviously accustomed to the capricious pranks of the draugar inhabitants of his farm, and since there was no harm done, he was ready to forget it.

During the dark hours of the morning, Sigurd kept a watchful eye turned for signs of Mori. He saw Hross-Bjorn roosting on a ridge above the sheepfold and watching him with baleful eyes, a black shadow against the struggling pale dawn. Sigurd thought he had never seen such a gray and desolute place as Thufnavellir that morning, and he earnestly wished they hadn't come here. Even some of the fences were made of bones, huge stark whale ribs, as if a monster had crept up to the hall and died. Sigurd decided to go up on the hillside a little way from the shearing and sit down to rest a bit, in a hopeless effort to cheer himself up by talking to Tofa, one of Kambi's daughters. Scarcely had they begun to talk when Tofa stopped suddenly and pointed down the hill. A stray gust of wind was blowing some dead leaves and a dried lump of dung, which came tumbling merrily up the hillside toward Sigurd and Tofa.

"It's Mori," Tofa said nervously. "He follows my father around like that all the time. I think I'll go back down to the others, if you don't mind. We can talk later."

Sigurd could only gape in astonishment and dismay as the ball of dung tumbled to rest against his boot.

"Mori! Is that you?" he whispered sternly, making sure nobody could see him talking to it.

With a curious swirl of dust and rags, Mori appeared before his eyes, squatting in the dirt and turning a few somersaults for good measure. "Why, hello! How did you sleep last night, my friend?"

"Very cold, especially when Vigbjodr stood beside my bed and breathed his cold draug's breath on me. That wasn't a friendly thing to do, opening our door that way." Sigurd felt much bolder, knowing the sun would be up in a half hour or so.

Mori grinned and winked. "But he didn't touch you. I was right, wasn't I? Tonight I'll give you a look at the sword—unless you're afraid, of course. You're not frightened, are you?" He giggled tauntingly and made faces.

"Certainly not," Sigurd snapped, not certain at all.

"I thought you weren't," Mori answered, rolling himself into a ball again and preparing to tumble away. "Be ready when I put your friends to sleep, and I shall be there when Vigbjodr sounds his knock. You'd better have something for me to eat or I'll make a mischief for you." With a final, wheezing cackle, the ball of horse dung rolled away down the hillside. When Kambi plodded around the corner of the barn in his heavy manner, the sending made a sharp turn to follow at his heels.

During the day, Sigurd saw several examples of Mori's work, which Tofa pointed out to him. Something frightened the sheep and they bolted away into the fell, where one broke its leg. One of the other daughters cut her hand, and the gates to the sheepfold would never stay shut, so the sheep were always escaping or getting mixed with the wrong flocks. A neighbor had trouble with his horse when he came to collect his sheep that had mingled with Kambi's sheep, and nothing he could do would persuade the horse to go through a certain gate. When the afternoon waned toward twilight, the neighbors who had come for their sheep hurried away anxiously, glad to escape from Thufnavellir before darkness descended.

When the day's work was done, everyone walked toward the hall, where Ulfrun had cleaned up the mess in her kitchen, loudly lamenting the folly of her youth which had persuaded her to marry Kambi Coalbrow of the haunted Thufnavellir. Sigurd walked beside Rolfr, who also was too tired to talk. As they passed through the gate where the farmer's horse had

refused to pass, something struck Sigurd a staggering blow in
the chest and knocked him over backward into Mikla, who had
been at least five steps behind. Gasping like a beached fish,
Sigurd sat up and looked around incredulously to see what he
had run into, thinking vaguely that he had walked into the
closed gate, but he could see it was standing open.

Chattering in concern, Kambi's family gathered around him,
but Mikla suddenly leaped through them with a great shout,
brandishing his staff like a madman. The girls scuttled away
in alarm, except Tofa, who was a large, stout girl and quite
capable of hauling Sigurd to his feet and half-dragging him to
the shelter of the cow house. Looking out the door, Sigurd saw
Hross-Bjorn standing on the roof of the hay barn, shaking its
heads in a haze of blue phosphorescence and pawing the air in
an excess of pure evil spirits. It snarled and grunted, reaching
down to snap at Mikla's staff.

Mikla blasted it with a gout of fire, which caused it to sail
across the intervening space to land on the roof of the cow
house. The four girls cringed, too terrified to shriek, as the
roof sagged and the cows bellowed and plunged around in their
stalls. Kambi rushed into the barn from the small back door,
narrowly avoiding being trampled by a huge bullock that crashed
from its stall. The sending leaped off the roof in pursuit of the
bullock and they both vanished into the ravine behind the hall.

Kambi sent the girls to the hall, but he beckoned Sigurd
and Mikla and Rolfr to remain in the cow house. They helped
him soothe the cows, and then he sat down beside his latern
and slowly stuffed and lit his pipe. When his thoughts were
sufficiently collected by the comforting puffs of fragrant smoke,
he looked at Sigurd and said, "That's a very annoying sending.
It's going to make your life wretched unless you do something
about it."

"That's nothing exactly new to me," Sigurd said impatiently. "But this is the first time it's attacked me directly. I
wonder if that means that Jotull is getting closer. You two are
the wizards. Why don't you do something about the sending?
I thought magic was supposed to be much more useful than
what I've seen. If you're such a wizard, Kambi, why do you

tolerate this walking burial ground you're living in? And that Mori—" He didn't quite dare continue, for fear Mori might be somewhere near listening and grinning.

Kambi continued smoking his pipe. "I've been thinking about it for a few years, but I confess I'm rather slow in doing anything about the draugar of Thufnavellir. I've grown accustomed to them. The easiest way to live with draugar is simply to make the necessary allowances for them. Mori has lived on this farm more than a hundred years, and Vigbjodr was my own father, you recall." He stroked his chin sadly. "But perhaps I could help you get rid of Bjarnhardr's sending."

Sigurd did not protest that he thought the sending was from Halfdane or Jotall. It no longer mattered to him who had made it, when each breath he drew caused such an ache in his chest from the wallop the sending had dealt him. "I'm all in favor of that. What can we do?" he asked.

Kambi rolled back, looking up with a laborious sigh. The sending tramped up and down on the roof turves, making the timbers underneath creak dangerously. "I shall think about it," he finally said.

Throughout the evening Sigurd watched Kambi with great impatience, but the placid fellow showed no signs of recalling what he had said about turning back the sending. Sigurd hid his disappointment when Kambi and his family finally adjourned to their little hut for the night. Mikla tried to persuade Sigurd to sleep on the floor instead of Vigbjodr's bed, but Sigurd smugly arranged his knives and pulled the eider up to his chin, pretending to go to sleep. Mikla paced up and down the hall, a model of vigilance, while Rolfr unashamedly went to sleep.

Sigurd lay awake for a long time, wondering where Mori was. The hall was silent. Mikla sat beside the door, nodding and yawning and futilely trying to keep himself awake. After a day of chasing sheep and throwing them on their backs to be sheared, staying awake half the night listening for ghosts was nearly impossible.

Vigbjodr's first knock startled Sigurd bolt upright, but Mikla was sound asleep and scarcely twitched at the sound. Another

single blow jolted the door after a long silence, and it startled
Sigurd almost as much as the first one had. After a long time,
the third knock startled him again. Then he heard another sound,
a sliding of wood through metal braces, and the main bolt of
the door slid to the floor with a clatter. The top and bottom
bolts likewide eased themselves from their moorings and crashed
to the floor without awakening Mikla and Rolfr. Then the fist
of Vigbjodr struck the heavy door open, and Sigurd saw a dark
shape so large that it blocked most of the doorway. The draug
lurched forward with a muddy clump-clump of leaden feet,
advancing upon Sigurd in the bed. Sigurd slowly shrank himself
down to the smallest lump possible, unable to take his eyes off
the towering shadow. It advanced to the foot of the bed and
looked within at Sigurd, who didn't dare blink his eyes for fear
of the noise he might make. He felt like a rat trapped in a
cupboard and swore he would never again sleep in an enclosed
wall bed. The hulking shadow of the draug took another dragging step, and Sigurd felt it groping at the foot of the bed. He
snatched his feet away in horror. Then he heard one of the
knives catch in fabric or flesh, and the draug drew back with
a rumbling growl. Still muttering, it turned its eyes upon Sigurd, two dull red lights in a face that seemed more bone than
flesh, with matted tufts of beard hanging down on the draug's
breast like strands of filthy wool. Just when Sigurd thought he
couldn't stand another moment of staring into the creature's
eyes, it turned and shuffled away slowly to fumble around on
the wall across from the bed. It lit a lamp after much jumbling
and dropping things. By its light, Sigurd saw that the lamp
base consisted of half a human skull. All he could see of the
draug was its back, with its clothes earthy and half-rotten, as
it opened a narrow door in the turf wall hidden behind a hanging. He heard the ring of gold pieces and ornaments as the
draug counted them over.

"Isn't this fun?" a voice whispered in his ear, causing him
to straighten up so suddenly that he knocked his head against
the top of the bed. Beside him in the bed, Mori grinned at him
and pulled the eider up under his dirty chin. "In a moment

you'll see the sword. Would you like to know what you have to do to get it?"

Sigurd spared an instant from his fascinated study of the draug and the treasure. "Hadn't we better keep quiet?"

"Oh no, there's nothing to worry about. The old dolt isn't going to get past those knives. How do you like the lamp? Very clever, isn't it?" He nudged Sigurd and cackled. "It's burning human belly fat, the best sort of fat for any kind of devilment. It always burns steady, but very dim, very dim. There now, look quick, he's holding the sword."

The draug slowly drew the sword and let it gleam a moment in the dull light. "Tomorrow night," Mori whispered, "the sword shall be yours. Listen carefully and I'll tell you how we'll trick him." He whispered into Sigurd's ear, and Sigurd listened in growing dismay and revulsion.

"I can't do that," he exclaimed. "How will I explain it to Mikla? He won't let me wander around outside alone after dark—and I don't know if I want to do it myself, either."

Mori grinned until his eyes were pulled almost shut. "You won't be alone. Not at Thufnavellir. Besides, I'll be right there with you. I think we can arrange to deceive Mikla. I can dispose of him completely, which might be the easiest."

"Are you stronger than Mikla?" Sigurd asked, frowning. The draug had put away the sword and was counting its money again.

"Oh, bother Mikla! He's nothing but an apprentice. You'd think he was your master. Don't you trust yourself?" Mori tittered until he had to smother himself with a mouthful of eider. He chewed off a corner of fabric and spat out the feathers. "He's a sly one, that Mikla, but Bjarnhardr will get him, too, just as he finally got Vigbjodr, and as he'll get Kambi one day when he happens to die. You'll die, too, presently, my dear friend, but you can postpone the horrible day if you can get Vigbjodr's sword. Will you do as I have told you, or shall we stop being such good friends?" He took another ripping bite out of the eider and snorted among the feathers.

Sigurd watched Vigbjodr count the last of the gold and

extinguish the gruesome lamp. "You're positive it will work, Mori?"

Mori snapped his fingers. "Just like that. After everyone is asleep, I'll come to get you." He nodded five or six times for emphasis and rolled himself away in a small whirlwind of feathers, straw, and dried dung.

The draug slowly plodded through the hall again and out at the door, without bothering to shut it. Sigurd eyed the grave-mold on the floor and did not stir from his bed until morning, when he was awakened from some dreadfully unpleasant dreams by Kambi's worried shout. Mikla awoke very stiff and cha-grined, and Sigurd pretended to be upset that nobody had awak-ened him for his turn at watching, so it couldn't really be his fault he had missed his shift.

"Mori must be responsible," Kambi said, shaking his head gravely. "He likes nothing better than making more trouble for anyone he can. I have the feeling a very great mischief is afoot." He looked straight at Sigurd as he said it, and Sigurd again had the uncomfortable sensation that old, slow Kambi knew far more than anyone gave him credit for.

No mention was made of turning back Hross-Bjorn until after noonday, when everyone had eaten and Kambi sat con-tentedly smoking his pipe and looking up at the blue sky. After making several peaceful remarks—that spring was not far away, it would be summer before any of them knew it, and lambing and shearing would soon be finished—he put away his pipe and looked soberly at Sigurd, Mikla, and Rolfr. In a lowered tone of voice, he said, with uneasy glances toward Ulfrun, "Tomorrow I'll begin making preparations. I have certain things I need to gather first."

Ulfrun soon divined his intentions despite his precautions. She was already in a quarrelsome mood after discovering that Hross-Bjorn had killed her best bullock in the ravine and had frightened the cows so badly that they gave scarcely any milk.

"Pooh, what sort of wizard do you think you are? Ever since Vigbjodr died, you've kept saying you'll do something about him, but he's still here haunting us. Not to mention the other draugar, of course, who are practically hoary with a long tradition of making Thufnavellir the most miserable spot in Skarpsey." She continued to mutter throughout the day, finally summing up her dissatisfaction with a threat. "Coalbrow, if you foolishly attempt to turn back that sending, I shall be so angry that I'll never speak to you again."

Kambi brightened visibly at the prospect. Soon after supper that evening, he took a spade and a large sack and strode away by himself with a touch more purpose in his usual aimless, deliberating manner.

Sigurd arranged his bed on the platform as far as he could get from Vigbjodr's bed and bore the playful taunts and jokes of his friends with the knowledge that he had earned them. He didn't feel much like joking when he thought of the experience that awaited him tonight. Several times he almost decided it wasn't worth it for any sword, but each time he resolutely reminded himself that a man was not a man without a sword. He rested his head on the little carved box for a pillow and told himself that Mikla would not dare attempt taking this sword away from him. If Mori was to be believed, Bjarnhardr had somehow divined Sigurd's plight and was doing his best to help him through Mori. Or so it might seem. He could get himself killed by trusting a fylgjadraug.

He did not intend to sleep that night, but the next thing he knew, Mori was poking him awake and grinning horribly into his face.

"Shh! It's almost time for Vigbjodr to knock," the sending warned. "After I open the door for him, we'll nip out and pay a visit to Vigbjodr's barrow. You haven't changed your mind, have you?" He glared closely into Sigurd's face and began to laugh.

Sigurd glanced at Mikla and Rolfr, who were both sound asleep, in uncomfortable positions where the spell had caught them. Mikla looked as if he had just reached for his staff, and the intent scowl was still on his face.

"I haven't changed my mind and I'm not afraid," Sigurd lied, flinching at the first echoing thump on the door. He crouched in his dark corner as the bolts slid back and the draug shoved the door aside. It stalked stiffly into the hall, straight to the wall bed, where it looked in a moment and groped at the foot to be sure no one was there. Mori snickered and bumped Sigurd with his elbow, making all kinds of grimaces and contortions to convey his idea of a fine joke upon the other sending.

While Vigbjodr was occupied with counting treasure, Mori tugged Sigurd to his feet and prodded him out the open door with much grumbling and derision at Sigurd's natural caution. "What an old worrier you are! They're nothing but draugar. Come on, come on, it's going to take us until dawn at this rate!"

He led Sigurd to a barrow mound not far up the ravine behind the hall. It was a fairly new mound, and someone had ringed it with stones to form the shape of a ship. Sigurd could see that the portal stood wide open, and every ounce of his common sense cried out a warning against Mori's plan. In spite of the cold, frosty night, Sigurd felt the sweat trickling down his spine, as if something with icy breath were breathing behind him. He glanced back frequently and was not reassured when he saw nothing. For the first time he thought about Hross-Bjorn, instead of his shame at appearing as a coward. He stopped, suddenly much more sensible than he had been in a very long time.

"Listen here, Mori, this is the greatest piece of foolishness anyone has ever talked me into," he began impatiently. "I don't care what you do, I'm not going to crawl into that old barrow and wait for Vigbjodr. He can keep his sword; it's not worth that much to me."

Mori grinned unpleasantly and hugged his sides with both arms, which were far too long for his body. "But the barrow mound is closer than the hall now, and it looks to me as if you're going to need a bit of protection." He waved a paw at a huge black shadow that detached itself from the dark ravine, trotting slowly toward them with all six ears pricked forward attentively. After a few more paces, Hross-Bjorn assured itself that it really was Sigurd, and broke into a gallop, lashing its tail over its back in delight and uttering three tones of savage little grunts. The bluish nimbus encircled its head like a cloud of gnats, causing its eyes to gleam as if in anticipation.

Sigurd raced for the barrow without another moment's thought. Mori yapped at his heels in the form of a scruffy little black dog, and together they tumbled into the open barrow, which was muddy from the spring rains. Hross-Bjorn arrived a moment later and lowered its three heads to peer inside. When it saw Sigurd, it lifted its lips and snarled like a mad dog. Mori, still in his dog form, leaped forward with all the bravery and tenacity of a small mongrel defending its property. For a moment the two sendings lunged and snapped at each other with a horrible wrangling, snarling war cry, and Sigurd expected to see Mori snatched away and shaken to shreds. But it was Hross-Bjorn who finally backed away, snorting phosphorescent clouds and raking its huge, hairy hooves in frustration.

Mori changed himself back to his own form and taunted Hross-Bjorn triumphantly. "Now we'll see whom this Scipling really belongs to! I've taken him for myself, Hross-Bjorn, so you may as well go back to whatever bog you came out of and let the maggots finish eating you, or put yourself to a truly useful purpose and let Ulfrun burn you for firewood."

Hross-Bjorn plunged at the barrow opening a few more times to bellow and growl and make a show of digging them out with its hooves. In the midst of all its fury, it stopped and tossed up its head to listen intently. In the sudden silence, Sigurd heard the dragging steps of the draug approaching the barrow. With a snort, Hross-Bjorn arched its tail and trotted away contemptuously, darting its glowing eyes over its shoulders several times to look at Vigbjodr.

Mori clapped both hands over his mouth and turned a few backflips in his excitement. "He's coming, he's coming! Remember what I told you to say? Don't forget a word of it!"

The slow footsteps of the draug halted outside the barrow. Sigurd wondered if Vigbjodr was listening to the hammering of his heart. He didn't know what sort of outburst to expect, so after the ranting and roaring of Hross Bjorn, the draug's low, wretched groan stood his hair on end. The groan rose into a rending howl of such misery and despair that Sigurd covered his ears in an attempt to silence it. Mori punched him viciously until he regained his composure to the extent that he unplugged his ears and slapped Mori out of the way.

"Say it, say it, you fool!" Mori snapped, kicking him.

"What do you want?" Sigurd roared out at the draug.

"My barrow," the draug moaned. "Get out of my barrow."

"I won't get out until cockcrow," Sigurd replied, after a vicious gouging by Mori's sharp elbows.

The draug uttered another chilling cry and Sigurd clapped his hands to his ears, certain it would drive him mad if he heard it again. Mori pounded him with both fists until he uncovered his ears. "I won't get out! You can't have your barrow back!" he shouted, despite the fact he was more than willing to let the draug have it.

"Gold," the draug whispered. "I'll give you gold. It's almost time for cockcrow. I can't bear the light of day. Take my gold and let me get back into my grave."

"I don't want your gold," Sigurd answered, truthfully enough. "What else do you have?"

The draug muttered to itself, as if trying to remember. "Jewels. Armor. Magic tokens. Weapons."

"Weapons? Give me a sword and you can have back your barrow," Sigurd said, with Mori to prompt him.

The draug moaned again and shuffled away, returning to the hall. Mori leaped up and down, hugged himself, and hugged Sigurd with such strength that it left him breathless and disgusted. "Mori, I don't see what you'll get from all this nonsense," Sigurd said suddenly. "I'll be leaving Thufnavellir next week when the shearing is done, and I'll take the sword away with me. You'll have nothing you didn't have before."

Mori put his face close to Sigurd's. They could see each other quite well in the half-dark of the early-spring night. "Oh, I'll have my reward," the sending replied with a leer. "There's nothing I enjoy like doing someone a favor." He chattered other nonsense which Sigurd couldn't really pay attention to while listening for Vigbjodr's return. Finally he heard the slow, dragging steps. He looked out the portal anxiously and saw the bulky shadow approaching, bearing a sword in its arms.

"It's nearly time," moaned the draug. "Here's your sword.

Now let me get back into my barrow." It dropped the sword at the entrance and Mori snatched it inside immediately.

"Make him beg," Mori whispered. "Make him crawl on his hands and knees!"

Sigurd wrestled the sword away from Mori. "There's no time for that. I won't make him beg; even a draug has its dignity. Vigbjodr! Thank you for the sword. Now withdraw to the next barrow while we leave this one."

"You forgot something," Mori said tauntingly, folding his arms. "But I'm not going to tell you what it is. You'll just have to discover it for yourself."

Sigurd unsheathed the sword to look at it in the dim starlight. Having a sword in his hands again was very good. "I don't care, Mori, and I don't care much for you, now I've got myself a sword. A man with a sword in his hands can't make very many mistakes." He admired the cool slimness of the sword and put it away in its sheath. With a wary glance around to make sure Vigbjodr had retreated to the next barrow, he stepped outside the mound to hurry back to the hall. Already he was thinking of Mikla and Rolfr and how he was going to explain the acquisition of a fine sword overnight, without anyone's by-your-leave. He resolved the dilemma with a shrug and decided to hide the sword until they were well away from Thufnavellir.

Mori accompanied him back to the hall, in a fine fettle with the secret he supposed he was keeping from Sigurd. "Farewell, my dear friend, my dear, dear friend! I do hope you'll enjoy using that sword," Mori called to him from the peak of a roof, saluting him facetiously. "I shall expect you to let me in tonight to ruin Ulfrun's kitchen again. I hope you won't be sleeping too soundly."

# Chapter 13

◆◇◆◇◆◇◆◇◆◇◆◇◆◇◆◇◆◇◆◇◆◇◆◇◆◇◆◇◆

Sigurd hid the sword in the wall bed, correctly supposing that nobody would want to do much prowling around
a sending's bed. He had scarcely lain down after carefully
barring the door again, when suddenly the voice of Kambi
was hallooing them awake. Mikla awakened instantly. "The
door is still shut," he said in triumph, but then his eye fell
on the grave-mold and he stifled a groan. "I fell asleep
anyway. There's something peculiar about that, when I was
so determined not to. Sigurd, did you see anything strange
last night?"

Sigurd did not have to pretend being still tired and very
annoyed with Kambi, who still knocked and hallooed outside
the door. Rolfr stood up to let him in, and Sigurd called out
sharply, "Watch out for the grave-dirt, Rolfr!"

Mikla stood up to look at the dirt and the locked door. "Now
our draug is learning to lock the door behind himself," he said
grimly. "There's more than draugar prowling around this hall
at night."

Alarmed, Sigurd sat up. "You should know that sendings
can do almost anything they please. Mori must have locked
the door."

When Kambi was let in, all the same questions and answers
had to be given again, and Kambi did an unprecedented thing
by sitting down to smoke a pipeful before breakfast. While he
was thus occupied, Sigurd picked up his muddy boots and tried
to creep outside unnoticed to clean them off, but Rolfr bawled
out, "My, what a mess you're making, Sigurd. You should

180

have cleaned your boots off better last night. You're as muddy as old Vigbjodr."

To Sigurd's relief no one seemed to notice that the mud on his boots was barrow-mold instead of black, healthy bog mud. He hurried outside to scrape the stuff off, already beginning to hate himself for tricking his friends.

He felt even more guilty and ungrateful that day when Kambi gave him a fine little amulet to hang around his neck. Even Mikla spoke to him cordially, and Rolfr's steady loyalty never wavered. All during the day, as he clipped the heavy coats from the sheep, safe and dry in the barn, Sigurd felt guilty about the sword hidden in the sending's bed.

As the gloom of evening deepened, his fearful anticipation was heightened by the approach of a storm. Later that night, when the storm was lashing Thufnavellir in full force, Kambi knocked at the door of the hall and Mikla hurried to let him in, along with a fierce gust of wind and rain that swept the fire up the chimney in a guttering roar.

"Tonight is a good night for working magic," Kambi said to Mikla, his usually dull gaze bright with excitement and his ponderous manner was definitely brisk. "The forces that we harness are the liveliest on a stormy night."

"But so is Hross-Bjorn," Sigurd added. Before the door closed, he pointed toward the barrow mounds, and they all saw Hross-Bjorn in the lightning flashes atop a barrow, standing on its hind legs to defy the elements crashing around it.

Kambi barred the door. "We shall soon be rid of Hross-Bjorn. Mikla, take this bag and put it in a safe place."

He gave Mikla a large sack and took his place beside the fire. After making several appropriate gestures to summon the attention of the magical powers he called upon, he assembled an array of magical objects on a small silver tray— a bit of gray fleece, an axe amulet, a fishhook with the barb pointed outward, a dead mouse, and a bloody handful of chicken gizzards. Kambi threaded everything onto the hook and cast the whole mess into the fire, which blazed brighter and higher. He gazed into the fire until he seemed to be in a trance, muttering long incantations as if he were talking in his sleep.

"The elements are very propitious," Kambi droned, his eyes on the fire. His distant and preoccupied manner was enlivened by a sudden "Ah!" as if he had seen something significant and unexpected. Sigurd thought of the sword with a guilty burst of apprehension. He glanced toward the wall bed where the sword was hidden, wondering what exactly Kambi could see in his trance. Maybe he knew what Sigurd had hidden in the wall bed. Nobody else might look there, but Kambi might, and it was the first place Vigbjodr would look. As he gazed at the bed in the panels, his capricious power left off pothering among the hangings on the walls and clattered the doors of the bed violently back and forth with an appalling racket.

"Stop it!" Sigurd whispered furiously and the uproar subsided, leaving him alternately hot and cold with his guilty secret. He even considered giving it back, but it was a brief consideration. Hastily he poked more peat into the fire to cover his mortification, hardly noticing the human bones entangled in the fuel. The peat began to steam and dry, and Kambi's eyes rolled upward in his head as he muttered and mumbled in his trance.

Outside, the storm descended on the valley of Thufnavellir with terrifying ferocity. The hall trembled under the onslaught of wind and rain. After a particularly heavy crash of thunder, Kambi's eyes flicked open. "Now we're ready to begin work," he said. "Mikla, open that bag I brought. I hope you know somewhat of the construction of witches' bridles."

Sigurd withdrew slightly, but not so far that he couldn't watch as Kambi and Mikla made three bridles, using the most abhorrent materials Sigurd could imagine. Kambi didn't say where he had got them, but the pieces of the bridles were various parts of corpses. The cheek pieces were hip bones, the reins were skin, a bone from the throat formed the bit, and pieces of scalp were used for the crown pieces of the bridles. Sigurd was awed into complete silence, knowing he was seeing magical apparatus taking form before his eyes.

As they worked industriously, something scratched at the door and moaned. Instantly Sigurd leaped to his feet, thinking of Vigbjodr creeping from his barrow with vengeance as his object. His three companions looked up at each other a moment before returning to the absorbing task of the bridles. Sigurd could not keep his eyes off the door, checking a hundred times to make sure it was indeed barred.

"My jawbones!" a voice whimpered just outside the door. Sigurd's hair lifted. "I want my jawbones!"

Somewhat accustomed to Thufnavellir's draugar, Rolfr replied in a shout, "We haven't got your jawbones! Go back to your grave!"

"My jawbones!" the draug called more insistently.

"Just ignore it," Kambi said, without looking up from his grisly chore. "It will lose interest in us in a moment and go away."

"My jawbones!" the draug shrieked. "In the fire!"

Mikla leaped up and raked a set of jawbones and teeth from the fire. "Open the door, Sigurd! How can I work with all this nonsense going on!" When Sigurd hesitated, horrified, Mikla exclaimed, "What are you afraid of? Open the door!"

Sigurd unbarred the door and opened it a small crack while Mikla tossed the bones outside. Evidently contented, the draug did nothing more to make its presence known. Sigurd could not stop thinking about Vigbjodr, however. Every time the door rattled, he experienced a nervous thrill of sheer dread. He wondered if he ought to take the sword back as soon as it was daylight.

The wind howled around the corners like a choir of draugar and rattled at the door with the utmost urgency to get in. Suddenly the door shuddered under a series of thundering knocks. The occupants were startled, but one became accustomed to mysterious knockings at Thufnavellir. Mikla remarked that it sounded like rather a large draug this time, and Rolfr looked a little concerned. Sigurd began to sweat with the worst fear he had ever known—the fear experienced by the truly guilty under imminent exposure. He had no doubt that it was Vigbjodr out there knocking.

Another salvo of heavy knocks echoed in the hall, followed by an angry shout. A voice muttered indistinguishably, then came another attack on the door until it rattled. Sigurd rejoiced in the thick turf walls and the stout door until he thought of the malicious Mori, whose idea of fun might be to open the door and let the angry draug in. The furious roars and bellows on the other side of the door did not remind Sigurd in the least of the pitiful draug of last night who had wanted nothing but to reclaim its usurped resting place.

The roars and screams became distinguishable as words. "I want my sword! Give it back! Thieves!" The last word trailed away into a wild howl that gave Sigurd gooseflesh. He glanced covertly at Mikla and Kambi to see if they suspected anything.

"Pay no attention to him," Kambi instructed his guests, not looking up from his stitching. "He can't harm us as long as he can't get in. We'll be finished with these before much longer if we keep at it."

Kambi did not look at Sigurd, but Sigurd was certain Kambi knew about the sword. He resolved to give it back tomorrow, or as soon as Kambi demanded its return. Kambi, however, gave all his attention to the bridles.

Sometime after midnight, the storm cleared away and Thufnavellir was strangely silent. All the draugar had likewise disappeared. The moon shone through the clouds, peaceful and brilliant in the pale northern sky. Kambi nodded his head and fastened the last stitch. "The elements are helping us," he said approvingly.

Sigurd left the safety of the hall with utmost reluctance, but he knew it would look absurd to protest. Glancing around on all sides for Vigbjodr lurking in any of the shadowy corners of Thufnavellir, he clung to Kambi's heels as they set out to search for Hross-Bjorn. They did not have to search very long before they spied three sets of sharp ears just barely showing over the peak of the cow house roof.

"Now then, there he is," Kambi said. "I don't believe we'll have any difficulty coaxing him down from there. We'll move over to the hay meadow where there's plenty of room for him to tear around."

"There's not much shelter," Sigurd grumbled. "What if your bridles don't work?"

Unruffled, Kambi pointed out the jutting heap of rock in the center of the meadow in case of any emergency and began his incantations. Hross-Bjorn listened and watched disbelievingly as its enemies walked out into the open field. Grunting, it scrambled after them, switching its tail with great interest. Its huge, round feet plopped down faster and it broke into a gallop, uttering a series of fierce growls as it bore down on its target. Mikla, Kambi, and Rolfr stood their ground, chanting away at the incantation, but Sigurd made a feint toward the rocks as the sending came hurtling toward him. He could hear its teeth gnashing viciously and he put on a burst of speed, but suddenly the sending sprawled in a heap, knocked over backward by Kambi's rebuffing spell. Wheezing and gasping, the sending got to its feet, glaring a moment from Sigurd to Kambi before bolting away at a gallop, lashing its tail furiously and snorting clouds of reeking steam.

Kambi looked at Sigurd in gentle reproof, and Sigurd guiltily resolved to stand his ground next time.

Hross-Bjorn made several rushing charges at them, always stopping short skittishly and bolting away before Kambi could get close enough with his spells.

"He's suspicious," Kambi said, after the ninth attempt.

"He certainly came after Sigurd the first time," Mikla said. "Perhaps we could hide in the rocks and let Sigurd walk toward him for a short distance to lure him in close enough."

"You must not want to find out what's inside the carved box," Sigurd replied. "If I should die tonight, no one would ever know where I've hidden it."

"You aren't going to die," Mikla answered. "Just walk out into the field far enough to get Hross-Bjorn to make a pounce at you. We'll be right behind you, in case anything happens."

Sigurd was not reassured, but he walked a few paces away from the boulders. Hross-Bjorn spied him immediately and came trotting from the dark ravine, heads held high warily. It halted a moment to survey the situation, then came forward at a cat-footed stalking pace. Sigurd backed away, wishing he weren't so far from the shelter of the rocks. The sending quickened its strides, eyes gleaming intently. Sigurd turned and bolted just as the sending gathered itself for a mighty spring forward. Its teeth snapped behind him like three huge traps, one after the other. Sigurd zigged to one side, then the other, with Hross-Bjorn lunging after him in wide arcs, but the arcs were steadily narrowing. With a final desperate dive, Sigurd reached the safety of the rocks, and Hross-Bjorn came plunging after him like a monstrous dog chasing a rat.

Kambi rose up suddenly from his concealment, both hands outstretched as he intoned the words of his spell. The sending stared at him warily, growling, then whirled to flee at top speed. Mikla exclaimed in disgust. The sending, however, made a few lunging strides and came to a trembling halt, its sides heaving and its eyes glaring. With tremendous effort it tried to lift its feet, but they might as well have been mired in one of the stickiest of Thufnavellir's bogs. Kambi nudged Mikla and Rolfr and began to creep closer.

Hross-Bjorn flattened its ears and snarled horribly, but Kambi walked forward, still reciting his spells. Hross-Bjorn's ghastly heads began to sink, and the snarls sounded more like snores. The lashing tail hung limp and the furious quivering vanished with a long, peaceful sigh. Sigurd held his breath. Kambi approached the unsightly beast and began fastening the bridle on the nearest nodding head.

Suddenly, with a convulsive heave and a snort, Hross-Bjorn snapped out of its trance, hurling one of the bridles backward into the air. Kambi leaped away as Mikla rose up with a derisive shout to distract the sending. Hross-Bjorn lunged at Mikla, teeth snapping and eyes gleaming fierily. Kambi seized the opportunity of plunging his sword between the sending's ribs, which slowed its attack on Mikla. It stood on its hind legs with a terrible scream, took a few lunging steps toward the ravine behind the hall, then fell headlong down a gully, rolling in a tangle of legs.

"Is it dead?" Sigurd gasped in the sudden calm, unable to believe such luck.

Kambi shook his head and sank ponderously to his knees to catch his wind. "It's not that easy to kill a sending, since those things aren't really alive," he said. "It's a spell one must break, a most treacherous one. We'll go look at him as soon as I've caught my breath."

"It's too dark," Sigurd protested. "Let's wait until dawn."

"No, let's have a look at him now," Kambi insisted.

They climbed carefully down into the gully where the sending lay. Mikla lighted his staff so they could see it, lying on its side with the sword still between its ribs. It looked and smelled as if it had been dead a long time, and all its eyes were tightly shut. Sigurd went closer for a good look at it, but Rolfr grabbed his cloak and pulled him back, shivering. "It doesn't look as if it's dead to me," Sigurd whispered. "What if it's only shamming?"

Kambi pulled at his lip worriedly. "Be ready for anything when I pull out the sword." He put his foot against the beast's ribs and pulled on his sword. Instantly, with a convulsive heave, the sending came to life like a cyclone almost under their noses. It seized Kambi and shook him furiously and threw him away to make a charge after the others, who had fled—Rolfr and Mikla in one direction and Sigurd in the opposite. The sending rushed after Rolfr and Mikla until it discovered that Sigurd wasn't with them, then it turned and came looking for him.

He crashed wildly through the bushes in the gully, not knowing whether to hide or to outdistance the beast. He clambered up the steep side of the gully with the vague idea of somehow gaining the safety of the hall, but Hross-Bjorn, snorting up behind him, abruptly convinced him there was no time for that. He was certain he was doomed. He took his axe from his belt and chose a slight elevation to mount his defense. Just as the sending burst from the gully, looking around for him eagerly, Mori appeared on a nearby barrow, leaping up and down and shrieking "In here, in here! Come on, Sigurd!"

Sigurd raced to Mori's mound without a moment's hesitation. Mori beckoned to him from the opening of the barrow, laughing delightedly when Hross-Bjorn's huge hooves thudded down the space Sigurd's body had wriggled past just an instant ago. Mori rolled around in the soft earth in a fit of glee, gasping, "Oh, what fun, what fun! Another instant and he would have smashed your brains out!"

Sigurd slumped wretchedly against the moldy wall, not even minding the bones he was sitting on. He was too distraught to think of anything, except the way the sending had tossed Kambi away over its shoulder, torn and bleeding.

"My bad luck has struck again," Sigurd moaned, watching Hross-Bjorn's teeth clipping and foaming in a frenzy to get at him.

"Don't be discouraged," Mori said. "He's still got Mikla and Rolfr to kill off yet. When you run out of friends, you'll really be in trouble." The idea was so droll to Mori that he fell into a fresh fit of writhing and gasping.

"You're disgusting," Sigurd said. "Get rid of Hross-Bjorn so I can go back and see if Kambi is still alive."

Mori wiped his eyes, still chuckling. "I hope he's dead. I hope you stay here for a long time indeed, my dear friend. You're the finest misfortune ever to befall this unlucky place."

"No, I'll be glad to leave," Sigurd snapped. "The sooner the better, too."

"What a pity. I'm getting quite attached to you. But old Vigbjodr is the fondest of you, and he's not as obliged to stay at Thufnavellir as I am. I wonder how you'll like traveling with that vengeful old draug haunting your footsteps. He's got dreadful powers and he wants his sword back. It was very foolish of you to forget to swear him to stay below the ground after you took his sword."

"Foolish! You never told me to make him swear anything!"

"Didn't I? How careless of me! What a dreadful mistake. But it will be more peaceful here at Thufnavellir without Vigbjodr, and Ulfrun will thank you for taking him away with you. She can also thank you for the removal of her husband from her life, courtesy of Hross-Bjorn." Mori laughed until he was so tired he could only pant and kick.

Sigurd wished he had the sword as he glared at Mori murderously. His natural power buzzed around Mori like a flock of hungry carrion flies. "Why did you do this, you wretched piece of dried corruption? Was it Bjarnhardr that put you up to all of it? What could you possibly have to gain from it?"

Mori grinned horribly. "Nothing at all. I like to make people suffer. It's so amusing. In your case, it's so easy. You said you'd do almost anything for a sword, and look at what you've accomplished—Kambi dead, Vigbjodr thoroughly aroused and furious, and Ulfrun almost as upset as Vigbjodr. She'll be even madder now, since it was your fault Kambi turned to magic and got himself killed by that sending."

Sigurd knew it was true. "Bjarnhardr must be behind this somewhere," he said bitterly. "I couldn't make such a mess of things by myself. I know now that he was never trying to be a friend to me. All he wants is that box. But you can tell him, you revolting little carcass, that I don't care this much for him." He snapped his fingers under Mori's desiccated nose.

"Ho, ho, indeed! Does this mean you want to put back Vigbjodr's sword? That's fine gratitude, even for a Scipling. Bjarnhardr has gone to a lot of trouble to help you." Mori giggled, his sunken little eyes fastened maliciously on Sigurd. "Are you afraid?"

"You heard what I said. Now get rid of Hross-Bjorn so I can leave. I've earned that sword. I owe Bjarnhardr nothing."

Mori snorted and chuckled, then set about discouraging Hross-Bjorn. When the sending finally made its abrupt exit with two snouts full of porcupine quills, Sigurd squeezed out of the barrow and hurried toward the hall.

He found Mikla and Rolfr there before him, assembling Kambi's thralls and paid workers and arming them with hay knives, pitchforks, sticks, and rocks. Very unwillingly, they followed Mikla to the ravine to look for Kambi. To everyone's astonishment, they found him alive, and no one was more astonished than he was, although the sending's teeth had left ugly wounds. It would be a long time before Kambi could throw a sheep and shear it.

Ulfrun lost no time in seizing the uncontested rule of Thufnavellir. The next day after the accident, she sent for her three brothers to help her run the farm, supposedly until Kambi recovered, but Sigurd secretly wondered. Ulfrun never openly invited the three unwelcome visitors to leave, but she made it plain that she blamed them for Kambi's injury and the further aggravation of Vigbjodr, who had become a terror every night. Mori's tricks also became much more dangerous and destructive, and many of them centered on Sigurd. Ulfrun began to perceive Sigurd as an immensely unlucky object to have around. Her discerning, ratlike eye discovered Sigurd to be the source of all misfortune, and Sigurd himself could not disagree.

After the arrival of Ulfrun's brothers, who similarly bore the family traits of parsimoniousness and incivility, Mikla, Sigurd, and Rolfr decided to depart. They asked permission to bid Kambi farewell, and Ulfrun grudgingly allowed them to see him for the last time. She kept him a virtual prisioner in his bed, feeding him a prisoner's rations of gruel, boiled turnips, weak tea, and other nourishing substances.

Kambi greeted them weakly, but he was glad to see them. Ulfrun hovered nearby, begrudging them even a farewell, as she had begrudged the pay they had earned and the supplies to carry them on their journey. She inserted as many answers to their questions and statements as she possibly could before Kambi could arrange his slow thoughts and get his mouth open, but he did manage to say he was sorry to see them leave before Hross-Bjorn was turned back, and he regretted the behavior of his father's draug, since Vigbjodr had been friendly and hospitable before his death. Then, as Ulfrun was sternly ejecting them from the sickroom, Kambi called out, "I hope you have the bridles, Mikla. I shall expect to hear soon that you have succeded in destroying Hross-Bjorn. You won't give up, will you?"

"Of course not," Mikla said, resisting Ulfrun's efforts long enough to shake Kambi's hand. "We'll undo him or send him packing back to Bjarnhardr. I don't believe you'll have to worry much about Vigbjodr once we're not here to annoy him any longer."

Kambi's eyes rested upon Sigurd with a benevolent, anxious expression. "It's a long journey to Svartafell," he said thoughtfully. "And very dangerous. But remember that I am your friend, and you can always come back to Thufnavellir, no matter what has happened."

Sigurd was spared making an answer because of Ulfrun's haste to see them on their way. With deepening shame, Sigurd thought guiltily of the sword, and how easy it would be just to leave it, but he hated to concede the battle, now that it had progressed so far. As long as he must fight for the box anyway, he might as well have the sword to fight for, too. It would also be wise to keep it as a weapon, since Mikla refused to let him use the other one.

A day's journey took them past several of Kambi's near neighbors and brought them to Kvigudalir, where they were politely informed that no more workers were needed. Sigurd, astonished and suspicious, noted that the farmers were even farther behind in their shearing than at Thufnavellir, and the master had only three hired men to help.

"Our reputation has become known," Mikla said in a low voice, when Sigurd told him what he thought.

The hospitality of Kvigudalir, offered somewhat reluctantly for one night, was of such a parsimonious nature that Sigurd was almost glad they weren't able to stay longer. The farmer pointed out a corner in his hall where the unwelcome guests might stable their horses and a platform rather far from the fire where the travelers might sleep. The food was plain and ungenerous. The inhabitants of the farm, from the master to the least thrall, seemed to slink around with a frightened, conciliatory manner that puzzled Sigurd almost as much as it angered him.

"What's wrong with them?" he whispered to Mikla that night as they stretched out uncomfortably to sleep. "Surely they know we'll be leaving as soon as we can. I've never seen such inhospitable Ljosalfar. They scarcely even talk to us."

"Surely they've dealt with sendings before," Rolfr muttered.

Mikla leaned on one elbow. "It's not the sending they're afraid of. They're afraid of angering Bjarnhardr and Jotull against them, and it's well known that we are running away from Bjarnhardr. Kambi is known as a rebel, and fearful folk such as these have no wish to be tainted with any unwelcome suggestions of insurgence."

Sigurd snorted. "I think Kambi was far happier and twice as much the man for his independence as this sniveling Geirmundr is for his craven loyalty to Bjarnhardr."

"I'll certainly be glad to leave them to themselves," Rolfr replied. "They're more like daytime Dokkalfar than real Ljosalfar. I'm sure they'll find the means of sending word to Bjarnhardr where we are. I wish we hadn't stopped here, Mikla."

Mikla shook his head. "It will be all right. I once asked Kambi if it would be safe, and he told me to cast a spell on them in the morning to make them forget we were ever here." He chuckled in satisfaction.

"I wonder if any spell is strong enough to make them forget Hross-Bjorn," Rolfr said with a sigh. Sigurd entertained some private worries about Vigbjodr, whose sword was concealed underneath him now. By day he wore it behind his back under his cloak, but he knew he couldn't expect to hide it much longer.

Near dawn, Hross-Bjorn and Vigbjodr arrived at Kvigudalir. The hall door suddenly thundered with Vigbjodr's furious knocking, and the sleeping hounds began to howl in terror. With a rending of wood and palings, the cattle escaped from their pens and bolted away like mad things while Hross-Bjorn brayed atop the cowhouse. Geirmundr and his craven sons cowered as Vigbjodr battered at the door and they beseeched Mikla to do something to preserve them. Mikla obligingly cast a few spells, but Vigbjodr replied with spells of his own that threatened to shake the house down. The eventual diminishing of the dark into silvery predawn finally discouraged the draug's attacks. As soon as they could ready themselves, the travelers departed with no breakfast and a curt refusal of their help in gathering the strayed cattle.

Sigurd rode with a feeling that the silence of Mikla and Rolfr was somehow accusatory. He knew Kambi must have told Mikla about the sword, and he fervently wished he had never let Mori tempt him into stealing it from Vigbjodr.

"What did we ever do to earn Vigbjodr's following us?" Rolfr finally demanded bitterly, when they stopped to rest the horses at the top of a steep green fell. Kvigudalir lay far below.

Mikla said nothing, nor did he even look suspiciously at Sigurd. "It will all come out in a while," he said rather ominously.

"Vigbjodr won't want to get far from Thufnavellir," Sigurd said hopefully. "His grave is there, and the people Bjarnhardr sent him against."

"But Bjarnhardr might have changed his mind and sent him against us," Rolfr said.

"No, that's not it," Mikla said stubbornly. "But we'll all have to suffer until the truth comes out—not to mention the fright and distress of the farmers we hope to work for until we get near to Svartafell. I am afraid that the matter is not in our hands." He looked at Rolfr as he spoke, and Sigurd hoped his own mortification was not as apparent as he felt it to be.

In the next five days, they stopped at three farms, where they were gladly received until the advent of the two sendings. Some of the farmers were sympathetic, some were loyal to Bjarnhardr, but none were interested in having their farms torn up and their livestock terrorized by Hross-Bjorn. The travelers earned barely enough pay in food for the little work they did to take them to the next farm. They quickly learned that spending their nights in the open was nothing short of warfare all night long. Without the magical knowledge of Mikla, either of the sendings would have easily overpowered them. Mikla became exhausted; by the time they reached Gunnavik, he looked almost ill. As they always calculated to arrive at a new farm early in the morning, they were able to work a full day. Mikla ate nothing that night and fell asleep on his pallet directly, despite the rather jovial company. The master of the farm, Gunnar, a pugnacious little fellow with a bristling red beard, made no secret of his hatred of Bjarnhardr and was fiercely indignant when Sigurd ventured to warn him in advance of the sendings.

"Sendings! We're not afraid of Bjarnhardr at Gunnavik," he declared, his eyes sparkling in anticipation of a battle of any nature. "My brother-in-law is a first-rate wizard and he'll rattle those sendings down to their toes. I'll tell my men to be ready for them and we'll catch them up short, indeed we will!"

His enthusiasm was only slightly dampened when he later learned that his brother-in-law the wizard was visiting at another farm and not expected to return for three days. Sigurd began to look at Mikla with more apprehension as the night deepened. Gunnar also looked at him, cocking his head to one side like a stout, elderly bird looking at something with one eye.

"He's got a fever," Gunnar said decisively, summoning a servant to come and attend. "I don't think he's going to do much good against those sendings tonight, my friend. He's half out of his head already, and I don't expect him to get any better for quite a while. Drat that wretched Snorri! What did he have to go to Gautrvellir for at a time like this? Well, never you mind, we'll still show those sendings that Gunnavik is not a place where Bjarnhardr can frighten us. We're good honest Ljosalfar and not afraid of a fight." He strode around, giving the orders in a brisk, cheerful manner, but Sigurd could only sit and stare at the delirious Mikla with the heaviest feelings of impending doom and dread.

# Chapter 14

❖❖❖❖❖❖❖❖❖❖❖❖❖❖❖❖❖❖❖❖❖❖❖❖

When Hross-Bjorn made his appearance around midnight, he found a stableyard securely locked, barred, and bolted with all the beasts within. Gunnar's sons, hired men, and thralls waited with arrows and lances behind walls and under doorways. When Hross-Bjorn triumphantly settled himself upon the stable and commenced to roar and scream, the archers stood up and filled his grizzled hide with arrows. Not accustomed to such mistreatment, Hross-Bjorn took flight, growling and snarling, with his arrogant tail tucked under his haunches. When he reached a safe distance from the archers, he stopped to paw the ground and scream in pain and fury as he bit at the arrows sticking to him.

Vigbjodr was not to be put off so easily. He shambled into the farmyard and hammered at the door of the hall as expected, but in reply to the burst of arrows that descended upon him, he conjured up gales of wind and sleety snow to baffle his assailants. Inside the hall, Sigurd knew the plans had gone awry. Rolfr looked grim and unsheathed his axe.

"I don't know what good it will do, but I'll chop him to pieces if he comes through the door," he said, nodding toward the door in question, which wasn't very strong. Only a handful of defenders waited inside the hall, listening apprehensively to the confused shouts of the men outside and the shuddering crashes at the door.

Behind Sigurd, Mikla lay in the grip of a shivering, sweating fever, flinching at the crashing and shouting outside. "Sigurd," he whispered. "Give back the sword."

"What sword?" Rolfr looked baffled as Sigurd hesitated.

Sigurd stood irresolute a moment, then he confessed, "I stole a sword while we were at Thufnavellir. It's Vigbjodr's and he wants it back."

"Siggi. Whatever prompted you to do such a thing? Kambi was so kind to us, in spite of Hross-Bjorn!"

Sigurd nodded unhappily. "I know, it was terrible of me to steal it, but all I could think of was getting my hands on another sword. That wretched Mori led me into it."

"Well, you didn't have to let him lead you. Give the thing back to him, Sigurd." Rolfr cringed as the door made a splintering sound.

"It's too late!" Sigurd fell back away from the door. "What's done is done. It will take magic to turn the draug back now, and Mikla's in no condition for it." He glanced worriedly toward Mikla's pallet, where Mikla lay scarcely aware of his surroundings. "I know now I shouldn't have let Mori trick me. I'm sure they're all in league with Jotull and Bjarnhardr, but what can I do now?"

He whirled as the door splintered again, this time revealing an ugly blunt axe chopping a hole in the door. Sigurd dived toward his own possessions in the corner, groping for Vigbjodr's sword. In an instant, it was in his hand. Rolfr leaped aside as the door burst open in a shower of ice and splinters, and the hoary old draug of Vigbjodr lurched into the hall with a deafening bellow, swinging his axe like a scythe. His hooded head almost touched the rafters, and his arms were twice as long as Sigurd's. When he saw Sigurd confronting him with the sword, he let out a powerful roar and lashed at Sigurd with the axe. His movements were ponderously slow.

Sigurd and the defenders darted out of the way, and Sigurd slashed at the draug's leg as he dodged. The sharp metal met little resistance in the dried skin and rotten cloth and very nearly took the leg off at the knee. Sigurd boldly cut at the draug's arm, severing it with a single whack. Vigbjodr roared more furiously and swung his axe wildly. Staying away from the axe, Sigurd hacked off the wounded leg, which did not greatly discomfit the draug, who scarcely noticed his losses until Rolfr chopped his other leg from under him.

With the draug down to their level, they soon made short work of him, despite their amazement when Vigbjodr still hacked at them with his axe without benefit of a head to guide it. Quickly, they finished chopping the draug to pieces. With difficulty, Sigurd pried the axe out of the dismembered hand, which still searched and grasped around as if it were alive.

In a fine state of horror, the defenders of the hall bundled up the pieces of the draug in a sack with a heavy stone in the bottom, which someone carried to the firth and dropped off the cliff into many fathoms of cold blue water. When Rolfr and Sigurd felt like speaking again, they did not congratulate each other and indulge in the usual boasting after such a victory. Sigurd told Rolfr about stealing the sword, rather dully and greatly ashamed of his folly. Rolfr solemnly agreed as Sigurd berated himself for his selfishness and stupidity, which had cost many farmers some of their best animals; and now Mikla was lying gravely ill because he hadn't confessed his crime earlier.

"Let's just be grateful that this is the end of Vigbjodr, at least," Rolfr finally said. "And you've got yourself a decent sword now, although the cost was rather high. You should be content, Siggi."

"I know I should, but I feel too guilty," Sigurd replied.

"You wouldn't, if you'd stop doing things you know are wrong," Rolfr said.

Throughout the day as Sigurd worked, Gunnar stopped by frequently for a kind word with him, which restored his spirits greatly. Gunnar assured him that they might stay as long as they wished after Mikla was well again, and he would have his brother-in-law put his wits to work and get rid of Hross-Bjorn. Gunnar's eyes shone at the mention of Hross-Bjorn, and Sigurd suspected with amusement that the rotund little farmer looked forward to another clash with the beast. Had his size matched his ferocity and love of battle, Gunnar would have been a perfect giant.

Sigurd was further encouraged that evening by the news that Mikla was much better. This, added to the growing assurance that the draug was truly destroyed, made Sigurd feel almost cheerful. If Hross-Bjorn returned that night, he would get more of the same ill usage before he had much of a chance to do any damage.

Little to Sigurd's surprise, Hross-Bjorn did not approach the farm too closely that night, but preferred instead to lurk in the ravines and hills to the north, uttering plaintive bellows like a lost heifer in an attempt to lure someone to destruction. Gunnar, however, had accounted for all his cattle and warned everyone to stay within doors after dark, unless he required their services with their bows and arrows.

On the next day, Mikla was improved enough to want food and a little company. Sigurd went to him and told him about the sword. Mikla felt well enough to speak rather sharply, remarking, "It's no surprise to me. I knew about it from the very instant you started to plan such treason with that mortified relic, Mori. I could have told you what the consequences would be, but I thought it would be better for you to suffer. You need to have your great unbridled arrogance humbled a little now and then."

Sigurd swallowed an angry retort. "You're quite right," he said, forcing the words out. "In the future, I'll try to think less of myself and how to get what I want, come weal or come woe. I can see where I've been stupid. Mikla, I want your advice more often. You'll help me if I ask, won't you?"

"You won't ask, and if you do, you won't follow it." Mikla looked searchingly into Sigurd's face and sighed gloomily. Relenting, Mikla shook Sigurd's hand. "Of course I'll help you, Sigurd, but it won't always be pleasant advice, and you won't want it when you hear it."

Sigurd reflected a moment and thought that was probably true. "Well, remind me that I asked for it, then, and perhaps it won't be so hard to take. By the way, Rolfr and I both thought we ought to make another attempt to bridle Hross-Bjorn when Snorri returns. He's a ripping sort of a fellow, if you can believe the tales Gunnar tells."

Mikla shook his head. "I think we'd better hurry on to Svartafell as soon as I'm strong enough to stay on a horse.

Gunnar would be delighted to have us stay here a month or two, but the matter of the box weighs upon my mind."

Sigurd tried to hide his disappointment. "It might not take very long," he began. But Mikla's weary, knowing look seemed to say, "You see, you don't want anybody's advice! What did I tell you?"

Sigurd departed, hating the taste of swallowed pride. He comforted himself by sharpening his sword a bit, admiring it, and telling himself that circumstances hadn't really turned out too badly after all.

Gunnar called a celebration in honor of his guests that night, and it continued far into the late hours. Guards were set out for Hross-Bjorn, but all they had to report was sighting the creature roosting in the cliffs above the firth, making all manner of dreadful screams, but not daring to approach any nearer. The boldest of the guests offered suggestions for killing Hross-Bjorn and volunteered their services, if it ever came to that, but Sigurd didn't doubt that they earnestly hoped it wouldn't.

When all the guests had gone home, except for a few of the less-disposed who had fallen asleep under the tables, Sigurd and Rolfr banked the fire at their end of the hall and comfortably went to sleep on the platforms on either side. Mikla had gone early to a cozy hut where he could expect to get some sleep instead of roistering.

Sigurd had slept only a few moments, he thought, when he heard something thump rather heavily nearby. He listened a moment, but it wasn't repeated, so he composed himself again for sleep. Almost at once, he heard another thump. Suspiciously, he stared around in the darkness, seeing nothing extraordinary in the dim moonlight sifting through the smoke holes in the roof. While he was looking, the hole overhead was suddenly darkened for an instant and something fell with a heavy thump into the ashes of the fire.

"What was that?" Rolfr whispered across the hall.

Sigurd stepped off the platform, skirting the area near the fire, and joined Rolfr on the other platform. He carried his sword with him, and didn't like to admit to himself that he felt a huge lump of fear threatening to choke him.

"Can you make a light, Rolfr?" He tried to sound casual.

Obligingly Rolfr lit a small lamp and held it up. "Look at that!" he gasped, almost dropping the lamp.

A disembodied hand and two parts of a leg lay in the ashes. For a moment, they could do nothing but stare in shock. Sigurd felt his hair rise on end and his blood seemed to turn to ice.

Then Rolfr laughed shakily. "This must be Mikla's idea of a joke," he whispered. "He's probably up there on the roof chucking down pieces of an old body, hoping to scare us."

Sigurd smiled, relieved, but he couldn't help flinching when another piece dropped through the hole. More pieces followed.

"I don't think much of his joke," Sigurd growled uneasily, taking the lamp to hold it closer. "Ugh, here's a hand. It looks—" He suddenly uttered a yell and leaped back onto the platform, spilling the lamp and nearly setting Rolfr's eider afire. "It moved, Rolfr!" he gasped. "I saw it, I swear it!"

Rolfr groped around for another lamp. "You must have imagined it, Siggi," he said in a voice that had a distressing tendency to quaver. He found a lamp and lit it, holding it aloft. As he did so, something slithered across the floor from the other end of the hall. When they looked in that direction, they saw nothing but sleeping hulks of men, and Gunnar's contented snores grumbled soothingly inside the panel bed. Then Sigurd saw a movement. "A rat," he said in disgust, but in an instant, when he got a better look at it, he had to stifle another wild yell. It was Vigbjodr's axe, which he had taken away and thrown in a corner several nights ago. Now it came hurrying along the ground toward them, first one end, then the other, jumping along as if someone were pulling it by a string.

Rolfr moaned thoughtfully at the sight of it and turned his light on the pieces of corpse. Skillfully, they sorted themselves out and fell into place. The right hand reached out for the axe. Even before the corpse sat up with a fiendish grin, Sigurd knew it was Vigbjodr. He yelled the news at the top of his lungs, awakening nothing but the echoes. Dogs and men slept heavily, without a twitch.

"Wake up, you fools! It's the draug!" Sigurd implored as the ragged creature stood up and faced them, rumbling a chal-

lenge. Vigbjodr was so tall that he had to stoop, and his arms
seemed like tree trunks. The axe whistled as it bit through a
rafter that was in the draug's way, and a bench crunched into
splinters as he trod upon it. Sigurd and Rolfr retreated, watching
the creature battering around in the rafters like some huge
childhood nightmare, an impression enhanced by their inability
to awaken anyone else in the hall. Finally they made a concerted
rush and hacked away one leg with difficulty, but the parts
scuttled back together almost instantly, and the draug was more
savage than before.

The next time they parted the body from one of its limbs,
Rolfr hurled the piece across the hall and positioned himself
to prevent its return while Sigurd pressed the advantage. A
hand or a foot or leg always managed to dart past Rolfr just
as Sigurd had the creature down to a manageable size, so it
seemed a never-ending battle to the exhausted warriors. They
fought until their arms ached, realizing remotely that morning
must be approaching because they could see more light filtering
in through the holes in the roof and around the cracks in the
door.

Someone was pounding and shouting at the door, but no
one could reach it to open it. Sigurd thought he recognized
Mikla's voice. In another moment, the locks and bars began
falling away, and suddenly the door burst open, letting a rec-
tangle of sunlight into the dark and dust-filled hall. The light
fell on Vigbjodr as he raised himself on one elbow to take a
swing at Sigurd, who had successfully hewn his last leg from
under him. The axe flew wide across the hall and buried itself
to the haft in a thick timber. In years to come, Gunnar never
tired of showing off this relic of the battle with the sending,
although he never mentioned that he had slept through the entire
fight.

The sending sank to the earth with a peculiar rocky clatter,
the head, arm, and shoulders turned to stone in the sunlight.
The remaining parts seemed to shrink back to mere bits of dead
limbs in the shadowy light of the hall. Mikla stepped inside
warily, with his staff poised. Gunnar and his family awoke
from the spell at once; after a few moments of pure astonish-

ment, they gathered around the remaining bits of the draug and peppered Sigurd and Rolfr with questions.

Sigurd jostled his way through the admiring, congratulating crowd and seized Mikla. He had only one question. "Is this the end of him, Mikla?"

Mikla politely detached himself from Gunnar, who seemed to think that some mighty spell had been worked, a spell even more wonderful than anything his brother-in-law Snorri could have conjured.

"I simply don't know for sure," he told Sigurd in a low voice. "Gather up all the remaining parts and the stones, also. We'll put them in a bag and say some proper sending-laying spells over him and take him back to Thufnavellir and hope for the best."

Sigurd nodded and unbuckled the belt of the sword, not without regret. "I'll put this with him, too, and maybe he'll be content to stay in his barrow." It was a mighty struggle, and very painful.

When all the pieces were collected and put into a bag, Sigurd quickly put the sword in without pausing to look at it. Mikla said his solemn spells and performed certain rituals, such as driving needles into the soles of the sending's feet to prevent Vigbjodr from walking again. Thus reassured, Gunnar promised that he would have the bag delivered to Kambi at Thufnavellir. At the mention of Kambi, Sigurd thoughtfully rubbed the small talisman the wizard had given him; a similar one hung around Rolfr's neck, as if Kambi had known they would need protection against the walking dead. Sigurd felt ashamed of himself, realizing Kambi had known that he had taken Vigbjodr's sword. What made Sigurd smart the worst was remembering Kambi's unabated kindness to him despite his theft.

When they finally left after Snorri had returned, they departed as heroes, with many injunctions to return for a longer visit. Gunnar gave them enough supplies and three extra horses, which would take them at least as far as Svartafell. He knew stories of the mountain where Bergthor worked his marvelous craft, and he and Mikla and Snorri spent hours poring over sheaves of maps, trying to find the one that must be Svartafell. Gunnar wanted most desperately to accompany them, but he didn't like to leave his farm while Jotull or Bjarnhardr were searching for Sigurd. Their arrival at Gunnavik was not to be missed. Snorri's face was doubly regretful when the three travelers departed.

Hross-Bjorn had learned caution from the fate of Vigbjodr, and the lengthening days decidedly handicapped his usual style. The sight of the three grisly bridles hanging from a pole near the camp was usually enough to keep Hross-Bjorn at a respectful distance, where he snorted and roared in an attempt to lure away the six horses—a ruse foiled by Mikla, who plugged the horses' ears with beeswax. The travelers also learned that Hross-Bjorn had other tricks.

Sigurd was alone in the camp one silvery evening while Mikla and Rolfr were picketing the horses in a nearby ravine. Suddenly he heard a voice shouting in distress farther down the ravine, below the camp. Listening a moment, Sigurd was almost certain it sounded like Rolfr. Seizing his axe, he plunged away down the ravine, leaping over boulders and dodging bushes and small trees. He jumped over the small, icy streamlet, slipping on the mossy rocks in his haste. The cries for help continued below the lower part of the ravine. He wondered briefly how Rolfr had traveled so far in such a short time after leaving with the horses and Mikla, but his anxiety to save his friend soon overwhelmed the small nagging thought.

He ran and scrambled down the ravine until it suddenly occurred to him how dark it was around him. Halting suddenly, he realized he should have found Rolfr in his distress much sooner. He had been so wrapped up in the idea of appearing the hero that he had greatly overrun his common sense. As he started to turn back, feeling an icy brush of fear sweeping over him, he heard a splash not far away and the grinding of two rocks being stepped upon. He froze, listening, and again the shrill cry rang out in the ravine. Now he was close enough to realize the eerie sounds were not words but cleverly cadenced shrieks that he had tricked himself into hearing as words.

Swiftly, he turned and ran down the ravine, followed by

Hross-Bjorn's triumphant, rumbling chuckle. Several times he stopped to listen, hearing each time the stealthy padding of Hross-Bjorn's hooves over the mossy stones, or the crackling of branches as the sending bulled his way through thickets. Despairing, Sigurd hurried on through the deepening darkness. Whenever he tried to climb the walls of the ravine, the sending anticipated him and appeared above him, grinning and snarling over the parapet. Once Sigurd thought he had escaped, but his groping fingers suddenly touched the sending's muzzle, and he narrowly avoided the creature's viciously snapping teeth.

Just before the sky darkened entirely, he found a cave and crept cautiously inside on his hands and knees. It was dry, even it it wasn't very deep, and Hross-Bjorn was too large to fit in, unless he changed his shape. To forestall that possibility, Sigurd gathered a pile of wood and made a fire at the mouth of the cave, telling himself that Mikla would surely see it and come to his rescue. He listened disconsolately to the complaining of his empty stomach as he fed sticks into the fire, and he cursed his hasty overreaction to the trap Hross-Bjorn had cunningly set for him. Looking through the flames, he saw the nimbus that glowed around the sending's heads, and three pair of eyes gleamed at him coldly across the ravine. He looked at his supply of wood and hoped it was enough to last the night. As the flames died down, Hross-Bjorn crept closer, retreating only when Sigurd added more wood.

When the night was perhaps half over, Hross-Bjorn seemed to lose interest in his game and wandered away down the ravine with much snorting and trampling back and forth. After his departure, Sigurd heard a few trolls hunting not far away and hoped earnestly that they wouldn't see or smell his fire. A deluge of rain shortly before dawn put an end to the gruff calls of the trolls. Gratefully Sigurd abandoned his cave when he thought it was light enough to deter the attacks of trolls and sendings and rushed up the ravine.

The farther he traveled, the more uneasy and puzzled he became. He passed six forks in the ravine, any one of which might have been the one he had descended the night before. The rain had obliterated any trace of his passage, and it had been nearly dark. He could have wept in frustration. He shouted many times, but never received an answering shout. He sat down and concentrated on sending a mental message to Mikla or Rolfr, trying until his temples ached. The only obvious result was the rampaging of his natural power, which ever lurked one step behind him to guide his foot into a nettle patch or lead his hand into a place where two rocks were sure to pinch it.

Ultimately, there was nothing to do but continue up the ravine, attempting to choose the way that seemed to feel right. He tried to remember the lessons Adills had taught him about finding lost things and using his instincts to guide him. It seemed that when he felt the most certain he was on the right track, the ravine suddenly ended at an unfamiliar wall of rock or a waterfall.

By midday he was ready to admit that he was lost. He was also hungry. Wearily he sat down to nibble a handful of early-spring herbs he had recognized and gathered without much expectation of relieving his hunger. The most sensible thing to do was to wait to be found, but it was difficult just to idle away the afternoon without the least indication of whether or not Mikla and Rolfr were going to find him. He climbed the side of the ravine to watch for them and saw nothing but mile upon mile of green, folded landscape, stitched with a thousand streams, pools, and rivers that collected from the melting of the winter snow. It was depressing to be so dreadfully alone and insignificant.

Before evening arrived, Sigurd began to hunt for another cave to hide in. To his growing dismay, he found nothing suitable. He stumbled along in the shadows, doggedly searching for any sort of niche that might deter Hross-Bjorn's attacks. The sending followed him, perhaps two bends behind, seemingly appreciating his plight and finding it tremendously humorous, judging by the chuckling.

At last Sigurd stumbled upon a tiny grotto between two stones, with a third forming a crude roof. Hastily he scrabbled together an armful of wood and squeezed himself into his inadequate shelter. He reached into his pocket for his tinderbox, but it wasn't there. For a long, dumb moment, he stared at nothing until the realization sank in that he was almost defenseless. Fiercely, he searched all his pockets, glaring around wildly for inspiration. His miserable cave held out no opportunities or advantages, and the ravine might well have been a sterile desert for all the help it offered. Sigurd took a good grip on his axe and wiped the sweat from his face on his sleeve, knowing he and the sending had come to their final confrontation at last, however unprepared he might be.

Hross-Bjorn trotted into view, ears forward and tail waving like a banner. In the dying daylight, he looked confidently aware of Sigurd's helplessness. Sigurd ground his teeth and wished for Bjarnhardr's berserkr sword, which made him able to attack and kill almost anything. The sending stopped and posed ceremoniously, acknowledging Sigurd and his axe with a defiant snort.

Sigurd, much to his annoyance, observed his capricious natural power tugging at his cloak and making it flap. The power nudged at him like an anxious young billy goat, and even pelted him with a few small pebbles, exasperating him to the point of cursing at it and telling it, "You've been nothing but a nuisance from the very start, and now that I'm about to perish in a most horrible fashion, you want to torment me, too. Stupid, useless bad luck is all you've ever been to me. When I'm dead you'll have no one to bother." He took his eyes from Hross-Bjorn long enough to glower around at the invisible influence, which had been tweaking at his beard.

Hross-Bjorn advanced a few dancing steps, with his foremost head turned playfully to one side, grinning in horrible delight. Sigurd took a step, balancing his axe. A breath of wind fanned his cheek, and suddenly a fist-sized rock struck the sending right between the eyes of the right-hand head. The beast fell back on his haunches astonished, as another rock struck full in the chest with a great thud. Staggering backward, the beast roared with pain and indignation. Sigurd stared around carefully and saw no one who could be throwing rocks. The sending suddenly charged at Sigurd, digging his hooves into the soft earth and hurling up clods in his wake. Sigurd crouched, ready, but he was spared again by a small avalanche of rocks flying down from above.

Hross-Bjorn tried to swerve to miss a keg-sized rock bouncing at him and leaped over a volley of smaller stones; after tripping and stumbling on the rolling rocks, he skidded on his side into a pool of water at the foot of a small waterfall. As he dragged himself out, more rocks flew through the air with deadly accuracy to hammer on his ribs and knock against his skulls. Large, stationary boulders rolled ponderously from their resting places as if intending to block his escape, jostling together with an ominous rumble and striking sparks from one another. Hross-Bjorn cleared them with a series of desperate flying leaps and disappeared at full gallop down the ravine, followed by a deluge of hurtling rocks.

When the last pebble had fallen, Sigurd looked around slowly at the disordered rocks lying at his feet with their green caps of moss torn off and jagged with new fractures. "I don't understand it," he said aggressively to the silent darkness, "but thank you." His power nudged him gently, and suddenly he had the feeling he wasn't alone any more, and it was a warm, comforting sensation. He knew he no longer needed to hide in his miserable cave, so he stepped into the ravine silently, requesting his power to find Mikla and Rolfr. It responded with a definite push upstream along the ravine, so he trudged forward, glancing back often for Hross-Bjorn.

The moonlight shone brilliantly all that night. Hross-Bjorn followed almost silently, staying just out of the range of Sigurd's power. Tired and miserable as he was, Sigurd couldn't help being delighted with the ability to move things with a glance of his eye; a purposely directed thought fired a stone at Hross-Bjorn like a catapult. He did not know the precise instant when his natural power submitted to his control, but he suspected that it had to do with his realization of his certain death if something extraordinary didn't happen. The power soothed his fears, guided his feet to the spots where they wouldn't slip, and assured him that he would find Mikla and Rolfr, who were probably searching for him in the higher reaches of the ravine.

Thus it was that Sigurd was feeling tremendously confident

and capable when he rounded a curve in the streambed, and
something rose up before him without a sound and grabbed
him in great hairy arms. He tore himself away, smothering a
yell of fright and ran a few yards down the ravine before he
realized nothing was chasing him. Breathing hard, he stopped
and looked back.

"Hello?" a faint voice called. "Is someone there, someone
other than a draug or my imagination? Probably just a dream,"
the speaker added, with a heavy sigh that became a moan.
Sigurd heard a chain rattle.

"Who's there?" he called gruffly.

"Bless me, someone is here! Hello! Help! I'm caught in a
trap here and I'd gladly pay you to free me! Please help me.
I've been here for three days and I'm about to starve to death.
Worse yet, the person who set this trap is likely to come by
at any time and make an end of me. I assure you, I've done
nothing to deserve such a fate. I've never done anything violent
in my life, and to die like a common troll is an outrage to my
dignity."

Sigurd listened to the voice in amazement. It was a hoarse,
rather fussy voice which reminded him of the petulant and
comfortable old retainers of Halfdane who liked to sit by the
fire in the hall and boast of their past deeds.

"Who are you?" he asked, stepping closer. "What sort of
trap are you caught in?"

"My name is Grisnir, and I'm caught in a troll trap, of
course," exclaimed the voice impatiently. "I don't know much
about it besides that, and it's hurting my leg dreadfully. If you
won't help me, just go away and stop tormenting me with the
hope of escaping. I'll abandon myself to despair!" Grisnir suddenly uttered a terrifying howl and rattled his chain.

Sigurd crept forward for a look, since the fellow apparently
couldn't attack him with his leg in a trap. Warily, Sigurd peered
around the rock and saw a large troll sitting in the middle of
the ravine with a metal contraption with some large, savage
teeth clamped onto one leg.

"You're a troll," Sigurd said stupidly.

Grisnir folded his arms across his chest. "To be sure I am,

since this is not a man trap or a fox trap or a bird trap, but indeed a troll trap. Did you ever hear of a troll being trapped with anything else? This one is an excellent style forged by Vigasmid, the smith who lives in Sleggjavellir, and I can recommend it from personal experience. There is no way a troll can escape from it, once captured. I believe you can have one made for about two and half marks."

Sigurd came a little closer, and the troll looked at him with gleaming eyes. "But if I were to free you, I think you'd probably kill me for a meal almost immediately, wouldn't you?" Sigurd asked.

Grisnir sighed and hunched his shaggy shoulders. "I am not the sort of troll who eats anything undiscriminatingly. I have a rather delicate digestion and I understand that you Alfar carry a great number of diseases, not to mention the plague. No offense to you, but I prefer beef, nicely roasted over an open fire and basted with its own drippings."

Sigurd's mouth watered at the thought of it. "I'm more than a little hungry myself—but I've always been told you can't trust a troll's word."

Grisnir shifted impatiently. "Listen, my friend, you like gold, don't you? I know all Alfar love it. I'll give you more than you can carry away with you, if you'll only help me get out of this trap. I'll give you all you can eat of my beef and venison, too. My house isn't far from here. A treacherous thing to set a trap almost on my doorstep! Come, can't you see I'm not interested in killing you or anybody? My leg hurts dreadfully, and all I want is to get safely underground again where I can nurse it. It's such a small thing for you to free a troll from a trap, but I assure you it's terribly important to me."

Sigurd felt his power give him a nudge forward. He approached the trap and looked at it. Grisnir raised his wizened face from his paws hopefully, gritting his teeth in pain as Sigurd examined the trap.

"I fear your leg is broken," Sigurd said. "There'll be no hunting for you for quite a while. I suppose you have a chieftain who won't be pleased to feed a useless troll."

Grisnir straightened his shoulders. "I am a solitary troll, not an animal who hunts in a pack. I earn my food and gold by selling my advice, knowledge, and spells to the farming and fishing folk who live near my mountain. Thus it is that I am particularly aggrieved that the Alfar I have trusted so long have turned against me and commenced setting traps for me. It puts me in a very low frame of mind, I assure you."

"Where is this contraption's trigger?" Sigurd wrestled the trap around and finally got both feet placed on it to exert the necessary pressure to open its vicious jaws. With a whimper of relief, Grisnir pulled his broken and badly lacerated leg from the trap and crawled toward the water which he hadn't been able to reach for three days. Sigurd offered him his drinking cup, after a moment's consideration. He helped Grisnir wash his wounded leg. They bound it up in some fragrant leaves the troll directed him to pick from the damp walls of the ravine and wrapped the whole business in a large piece of the long, frayed cloak the troll wore over one shoulder. Then Sigurd helped him to his feet, directing him to lean on his rescuer's shoulder, which was a good ways lower than that of Grisnir. The troll grimaced and moaned with each painful step, stopping often to catch his breath and mop his hairy face, which was sweating profusely.

"I shall reward you with gold and jewels for your help," he said. "It's not much farther now. You'll see a great rock lying over two others like doorposts and a lintel. My door is directly underneath."

In a short while, Sigurd saw Grisnir's landmark. With a last staggering effort, they crept up the steep path and collapsed under the huge porch, puffing, gasping, and grinning at one another in triumph. "I have a couple of friends who would be greatly amazed to see me now," Sigurd said with a laugh, shaking his head. "This must be one of the more insane things I've done yet."

"Humane, not insane," Grisnir said with a faint chuckle. He separated a key on a chain from his furry chest. "Shall we go inside? There won't be a fire nor much to eat, I fear, but I trust we shall find something to suit us."

# Chapter 15

◈◈◈◈◈◈◈◈◈◈◈◈◈◈◈◈◈◈◈◈◈◈◈◈◈

Sigurd helped push open the heavy door; a small hallway led to a short flight of wide steps upward. Grisnir pointed out a lamp and a tinderbox. In a moment, the soft glow of whale oil showed Sigurd a big, comfortable room hewn from the native stone, complete with a hearth. A large pedestal table and chairs, carved from stone, faced a tremendous pillared bed, which Grisnir crept into with thankful groans. Sigurd looked around with increasing delight, seeing all manner of fine little figures carved out of the stone, placed on shelves and niches around the room. He lit a crackling fire in the hearth, and Grisnir directed him to a beautifully carved trunk which held the food supplies. The first thing Sigurd cooked was a huge panful of eggs, with bread toasted over the coals.

When their hunger was slightly relieved, he set about cooking some meat. His eyes kept drifting back to the trunk. "I have a little carved box which you'd like," he said, knowing that Grisnir must be the craftsman who had done all this carving. "It was done by a dwarf, Bergthor of Svartafell, and it's very nearly as fine as the work you do."

Grisnir sat up straight. "Bergthor, eh? It's not surprising you think my work looks almost as fine as his. He was my teacher many years ago, and it was he who convinced me that life alone inside a mountain is very pleasant indeed. I sustain myself by my crafts and skills—at least I did until three days ago. I don't know if I shall ever trust any of those Alfar again." He frowned and tugged at his long, pointed ears by their pendulous lobes. "Well, never mind about them. Give the meat a last turn and go look inside that small chest on the shelf. You

211

can take from it whatever you wish, or take all of it and be welcome. Gold and valuables are things that mean very little to me, except as a means of barter for what I want. Yesterday at this time, I very much wanted someone to come along as you did to free me from that trap."

Sigurd's heart thumped as he looked into the little chest. It was almost full of gold pieces and gold jewelry, as well as precious gems. He wondered how much of it he should take, then he wondered how he would carry it. Even a small amount of gold was very heavy. He looked back at Grisnir, reclining on his stone bed with a huge cup of mead, which he was slowly draining, looking at Sigurd kindly between sips.

Sigurd chose only one stone, a large, twinkling red one that reminded him of Ragnhild. It would look splendid fastened around her pale throat, if he could manage to give it to her somehow without letting his presence be known. Probably she hated him, but he took the stone anyway.

"Nothing more?" Grisnir exclaimed.

"I can't really carry it very well," Sigurd said. "Not where I have to go. I'd like this red stone to give to a girl I know, if I ever see her again." He glanced at her ring on his least finger and thought gloomily of his past misdeeds.

"Yes, I thought you wouldn't stay long," Grisnir said. "Not with that thing following you. I don't know what it is, nor do I particularly wish to get better acquainted. But I owe you a favor; before you leave, I would like to repay you, if there's any way I can. You mentioned Bergthor." He continued no further, too polite to ask any inquisitive questions of his guest.

Sigurd sat down on a stool near the troll. "My friends and I are traveling to see Bergthor on a peaceful mission. All we want is for him to open the small, carven box I mentioned before, and we wish him no harm. I'm sure you know how difficult Svartafell will be to find; but if you were his student at one time, perhaps you could draw us a map. Also, if you've encountered a pair of Alfar and six horses who seem to be searching for someone, well, the someone is me, and I'd greatly appreciate finding my friends again."

Grisnir rubbed his scratchy chin with one paw. Almost without appearing to think about it, he picked up a knife and a wand of wood. His awkward-seeming paws suddenly became quick and dextrous. He carved a few faces and some runes as he thought. "Well, I hope there's no harm in you," he said at last. "It seems that any one of almost any species is good-natured enough, taken individually; it's only in numbers that any of us are bad. I believe you are honest and won't do any harm to Bergthor, so I shall give you a map in gratitude for saving one miserable old troll against your better judgment. If you should ever need my help again, you'll know you can find me here."

Sigurd accepted the carved wand, thinking at first it was a gift, but in a moment he realized it was the map, naming mountains and peaks as landmarks. He smiled gratefully at the old troll. "Then you've decided to trust your farming and fishing folk again, after the nasty trick someone played you?"

Grisnir waved a paw and shut his eyes. "Oh, I can find out who set the trap and why he did it. Someone must have a grudge against me, but I'm not the sort to run away from a confrontation. This mountain and these valleys belong to me, too. I'm a tough old rogue, and it will take more than troll traps to discourage me from dealing with my old friends. I still like them, although someone wishes me evil. You needn't worry about me—no, indeed. It's more important that we find your friends before they decide to give up searching for you. While I was lying in the ravine, hiding by day as best I might for fear of the sun, I thought I heard a number of horses pass by overhead. In my delirium, I assumed it was a band of draugar or a wild hunt or sheer imagination, but now I think it might have been your friends. Tomorrow, if I were you, I would go back and look for their tracks near the place where I was trapped." He showed his large, broken teeth in a friendly smile. "Now then, is the meat done? It looks exactly perfect. One's stomach revolts from overcooked meat, as I'm certain you are aware."

On the morrow, Sigurd took his leave from Grisnir with pleasant regret, after many assurances of lasting gratitude and promises that he would stop again on his return journey from

Svartafell. Grisnir showed him where he hid an extra key under a stone inside the porch, if Sigurd should happen to arrive when Grisnir was not at home. Sigurd promised that he would make himself at home, find something to eat, and dry his clothing, if he had been rained upon.

"Nothing is more unhealthy than sitting in wet clothes," Grisnir admonished him, raising one large paw in farewell. "I wouldn't recommend getting one's feet wet in early-morning dew, either, not even at your young age. Good luck to you on your journey, Sigurd."

Sigurd thanked him again, and the door in the mountain was quickly closed as the sun showed a sliver of itself over the mountainside. Feeling warmed and hopeful from Grisnir's news of Mikla and Rolfr passing near him, he hurried back to the place and searched around until he found the tracks. They were probably about two days old, he decided, but he didn't let that discourage him. He set off in the same direction, certain that Mikla would search each ravine thoroughly until he found him.

By midday, he was beginning to wonder if Mikla and Rolfr hadn't secretly coveted the box all along and were glad for an excuse to be rid of him. Tiredly, he sat down on a moss-blotched boulder to eat the lunch Grisnir had insisted on packing for him, assuring him that his digestion would suffer if he got into the insalubrious habit of missing his dinner. He smiled at the thought of the old troll lecturing him about keeping his feet dry and not sleeping on the damp earth if he could help it. When he was finished with his meal, Sigurd stretched out on the moss to rest, look back on the valleys where Grisnir's farming and fishing folk lived, and wonder if they were loyal or defiant to Bjarnhardr.

He fell into a light doze, induced by the softness of the fragrant moss, the songs of the birds building nests in the ravine beside the chuckling water, the soft sunlight, and the feeling that he was completely alone and safe lying on the side of the fell.

His power suddenly awakened him in the form of an angrily buzzing bee making dives at his face. He looked around quickly to see where the danger lay before announcing himself with a movement. Above him, outlined against the sky, stood a horseman. Sigurd eased himself into the shelter of a small bush and watched the fellow, who was too far away to recognize. Although he hoped desperately it was Rolfr or Mikla, his common sense told him it might well be someone from the nearby settlements who might think he ought to be killed or hauled before the chieftain and priests. When the horseman finally turned and disappeared behind the hillside, Sigurd felt intensely disappointed, and his power was so annoyed with him that it kept shoving his hood into his eyes and dropping rocks into his boots as he walked carefully away in the opposite direction.

After sitting down for the fourth time to dig a rock out of his boot and grumble aloud at the rash of tricks his power was tormenting him with, it suddenly occurred to him in a burst of revelation that it was trying to tell him he was going the wrong way. After a moment of intense consultation with himself, he decided he probably had seen Mikla or Rolfr. He rushed back to the place where he had seen the horseman. Two fells away, tiny with distance, a procession of six horses and two riders plodded along the black gash of the ravine. Sigurd gave a great whoop and waved. In a moment, they all turned around and came cantering toward him like a beautiful dream, sinking out of sight into the swales and appearing suddenly much closer, the horses' manes and tails catching the light like pale plumes. When he heard the thud of hooves on the soft earth and the creak of leather, the dream became reality and he rushed forward to meet them. The horses jolted to stiff-legged halts all around him, and Rolfr leaped on him joyously with a welcoming yell.

"Where were you? What happened?" Rolfr demanded delightedly, echoed by a not-so-pleased Mikla, who still sat on his horse scowling.

"It was the sending," Sigurd said. "I heard it calling and I thought it sounded like you, Rolfr, shouting for help, so I chased it down the ravine until I realized it was a trick."

"That ought to have been the death of you," Mikla said

reprovingly. "I'm still amazed to see you alive. Did you have to fight with Hross-Bjorn?"

Sigurd thought of the discovery of his control over his power and smiled. "Yes, and I shall tell you about it later."

"Later?" Rolfr exclaimed. "I want to hear about it right now. Mikla, let's stop awhile for a little celebration. Sigurd, you must be half starved."

Mikla sighed and consented, shaking his head in exasperation. Rolfr uncorked a flask of Gunnar's fine ale, and they sat down and passed it around while Sigurd talked. Rolfr interrupted with frequent exclamations of astonishment and glee, and even Mikla forgot his disapprobation long enough to add an interjection or two.

"I must say we're both very relieved to have you back," Mikla said when Sigurd had told about Grisnir. "I certainly wouldn't know what to do with this." He knocked on the lid of the carven box. "Well, is everyone ready to proceed again?"

The thing that really saved Sigurd from a tongue-lashing was the rune-stick map which he had received from Grisnir. At the sight of it, Mikla's entire attitude had undergone a dramatic turnabout, and for a while he could only shake his head and gently turn it over in his hands.

As they rode into the fells, Rolfr told Sigurd how they had returned to the camp and discovered his absence. For a long while, they had waited; then they became alarmed, but it was too dark to search, and they didn't want to move camp too soon and definitely lose Sigurd. The next day they searched and found no traces of footsteps after the rainfall, and on the next day they were awakened before dawn by faint shouts from higher above in the ravine.

"The sending," Sigurd said immediately, and Rolfr nodded.

"Mikla dowsed you out as lower, but we could hear these cries above us, so we went upward. I certainly wish I could have met Grisnir. Who would ever have imagined a troll choosing to lead a decent life like that? I hope we can stop on the way back. My, isn't it splendid to be back in the fells at last? I wouldn't like to live in the lowlands, no indeed."

As they continued toward Svartafell, Sigurd thought more

often about the box, and his curiosity about what lay inside it began to pique him quite fiercely. For some reason, he also thought more about Bjarnhardr's sword, which Mikla carried. Perhaps now that he had his errant power under his control to strengthen him, he could possess the sword and use it without falling under its influence.

Hross-Bjorn had lost his arrogance and confidence after his rout at Sigurd's hands. At night, he prowled warily around their camp, well out of the reach of any spells, rumbling and growling to vent frustration when no one was deceived by his voices and altered forms. Sigurd perceived that the sending seemed almost desperate; in the scanty light of dawn or dusk, Hross-Bjorn looked almost haggard. He was no match for the power and Mikla both, and the knowledge of it must have cankered his wicked soul.

Watching the sending's resentful trampling and pawing one evening, Mikla observed, "Bjarnhardr must be almost as angry, if he's aware of our progress, and I'm sure he must be."

Sigurd thought of the Dokkalfar who had pursued them, and wondered aloud if they were still following, inexorably picking up the clues and information they needed from the farms were the three friends had stopped to work. "And what about Jotull?" he added, frowning in the puzzlement of his mixed feelings about the wizard. "Is he just awaiting his chance, do you suppose?"

Rolfr shivered. "Oh, yes, I'm almost sure of it. He isn't holding back out of any fear of us, I assure you."

"He'll wait for the best opportunity," Mikla said. "Jotull is not one to give up easily, and I doubt if Bjarnhardr will allow him to return to Svinhagahall without that box. I've been expecting to see him again, and the only thing that astonishes me is the fact that we haven't seen him yet."

"But I wouldn't stop looking," Rolfr added hastily, with a nervous glance behind him. "Jotull's no fool."

"But he doesn't know the way to Svartafell," Mikla said. "He's relying upon us to show him. You recall that the box is as useless to him as it is to us, until it's opened. I'm sure he has a plan in mind, but whatever it is, Rolfr, you may be sure that it calls for the removal of you and me."

Rolfr grimly flexed his arm. "I think it's about ready to pull a bowstring—a little stiff perhaps, but I'm no longer useless."

Sigurd looked at Mikla. "And I would feel far better if I had a sword to help defend all of us. Surely I'm stronger now that my power is my ally, Mikla, so why don't you give it back?"

Mikla's eyes promptly retreated under his scowling brows. "No, never," he said instantly. "I had a very close call with that sword myself and I might not be so lucky the next time."

"You don't trust me," Sigurd retorted, rising to stalk away.

"It's not you I distrust, it's that sword and its curse," Mikla snapped.

"It's the same thing," Sigurd replied angrily. "If you trusted my abilities, you wouldn't be afraid to give the sword back to me. You're saying that I'm incompetent to handle it."

Mikla returned his accusing glower. "Why should I be willing for you to experiment, when I'm the one who would suffer the most if you lost your temper? I wouldn't really think you'd be willing to make another mistake, Sigurd, if your power failed to control the curse."

Sigurd turned his back and walked away, partly to prove that he could control his temper and partly because he was afraid he was going to lose it again. If he had learned anything, it was the futility of arguing with Mikla, who was so unreasonably stubborn that nothing would ever change his mind; trying to negotiate with him only set him all the firmer in his convictions. The more foolish they were, the more solidly he insisted upon them.

Sigurd remained cold to Mikla for several days. They were traveling in rougher country, which necessitated a slower pace and more stops to rest the horses. Sigurd and Mikla refused to speak to each other, leaving Rolfr to do most of the talking. Rolfr urged them individually to stop quarreling, and Mikla might have been persuaded to put an end to the dispute, but Sigurd vowed he wouldn't speak to Mikla again until his sword was returned to him. Traveling with two companions, each of

whom refused to acknowledge the other's existence, was trying
even for someone of Rolfr's amiable disposition.

Bad luck added to everyone's discouragement. Several times
they went astray and had to backtrack, using Mikla's dowsing
pendulum to find the way. Frequently they had to forge through
deep snow and skirt gaping crevices in the earth, where the
water thundered below and churned itself to spume on the teeth
of the jagged rocks. At night, they were cold and often wet as
they huddled in the scanty protection of a rocky overhang or
shallow cave, and everyone's thoughts dwelt on the green,
sheltered lowlands they had left behind.

Sigurd felt more sorry for himself with each passing mile
as they climbed into the higher mountains. The snow was
deeper and the wind blew colder over the icy rocks in the
exposed places. They descended from a long traverse of a
windswept scarp into a deep, narrow valley, which was clogged
with a massive snowdrift. Glad to escape the claws of the wind,
the horses halted and put their heads down to nibble at the few
wisps of winter-crisped grass struggling between the stones.

Mikla dismounted and stood awhile, looking back the way
they had come, with an intent frown on his face. For several
days, Sigurd had been upon the point of breaking his resolve
and asking Mikla if he thought someone was following, but at
the last minute he decided to uphold his pride and refrained
from speaking. Rolfr looked back uneasily also, after watching
Mikla, but he said nothing and looked anxious and puzzled.

Mikla turned sharply, focusing his attention on the snowdrift
ahead of them. Thrusting his staff into it, he hoisted himself
up to its crest to survey it. He called back to the others, "I'm
going to walk across it and make sure it's not just a bridge
over a fissure. Bring the horses up here and wait until I give
you the signal from the other side."

Sigurd sighed, irritated and cold. "I don't know why he has
to do this every single time we cross a snowdrift or glacier,"
he growled to Rolfr. "There's probably several hundred feet
of ice below us, but that's not nearly enough for Mikla."

They coaxed the horses onto the snowdrift and watched
Mikla striding across the gleaming white expanse before them,

prodding each step ahead with his staff. Then Sigurd heard a sound like a sigh. Mikla stopped an instant and then began to run. The snow sagged slowly in a large circular depression covering nearly a third of the glacier. Sigurd and Rolfr raised an involuntary shout of horror, and suddenly the snow bridge vanished with a sighing groan, taking the small figure of Mikla with it into a vast blue chasm in the ice below.

After a moment of frozen shock, Rolfr and Sigurd desperately drove the horses off the edge of the snow, slithering and scrambling in sudden panic. Halting the plunging horses on a nearby knob of barren rock, they looked back at the glacier and the fissure, where more snow crumbled silently into the great crevice, leaving edges as sharp and clean as if something had sliced it. Rolfr clenched his hands and stared helplessly, shaking his head and repeating, "I can't believe it. He's gone—just like that. Here one moment, then just gone."

"It might have been all of us," Sigurd said in a shaken tone, and suddenly he felt so weak around the knees he could hardly stand. He sat down on a boulder and leaned his head in his hands, wishing that he and Mikla had parted on more friendly terms. "Is there any sense in trying to get close enough to look down into it?"

Rolfr shook his head with painful slowness. "It's more likely we'd go down, too. The snow will be unstable and very dangerous. The fissure looks terribly deep, and so much snow fell in that he's sure to be buried." His voice faltered and broke, and he walked away a short distance.

Sigurd stood by the horses, who gathered around him with alarm in their large clear eyes, tossing their manes and snorting warm breaths as if they scented the recent death. After a while, Sigurd also felt the urge to leave the desolate spot and he called anxiously, "Rolfr, we've got to go. I don't like the feel of this place anymore."

Rolfr swung around immediately, his grief forgotten. "You're right. Let's go back the way we came so we won't get lost. We'll have to go higher to get around this place. We don't have a map now, you realize."

It was an unpleasant shock. Sigurd's eyes traveled to Mikla's horse, which trotted along nearby with its reins flapping on its neck. The map had fallen into the fissure with Mikla, but his satchel and the sword were still fastened to his horse. Sigurd thought of the sword reluctantly, yet with growing excitement. Like Rolfr, he began to look back often.

At the end of the day, they stopped and set up their camp. Sigurd quietly claimed the sword by untying it from Mikla's possessions and putting it with his own saddle. Rolfr gave him a troubled glance but said nothing. He was drawing another map on the side of a leather pouch. Between the two of them, they managed a fair duplicate of the map on the rune stick, which they had studied often enough to memorize. But that wasn't much comfort in their present situation. Sigurd gloomily wished they had studied it more intently and recalled more accurately the distances between landmarks. Rolfr was fairly certain they had remembered all the landmarks, which was as much as they could do for now.

Hross-Bjorn, emboldened by the loss of Mikla, tormented them that night with faint shouts that sounded like a man calling for help, which was almost more than Rolfr could resist. He strode up and down in anguish, shaking his head and muttering to Sigurd, "I know I can't leave my live friend to try finding the one we know must be dead. You won't let me, will you, Siggi? Help me keep my wits, or I fear I may do something dreadfully rash."

"Sit down at once then," Sigurd commanded obligingly. "Have some tea. You know it's only Hross-Bjorn trying to lure you out there. Nothing must happen to you, Rolfr. Then I and the box would be alone." He shivered and poked more wood onto the fire, despite its scarcity. Their campsite was sheltered in a small cirque, with little waterfalls hissing down its steep sides. Rocks clattered down occasionally, probably dislodged by Hross-Bjorn's prowling hooves. It was as safe and secure as any previous campsite, but Sigurd admitted to a desolate feeling of vulnerability, which Rolfr wholeheartedly seconded. They both stayed awake most of the night, taking turns dozing between Hross-Bjorn's crying. Once Hross-Bjorn crept close to the camp in an attempt to frighten the horses into breaking their picket lines and bolting away madly, but Sigurd's power rose up and darted a fiery explosion at the sending.

"A small one, but very admirable for a first attempt," Rolfr declared, after a moment of astonishment; Sigurd was far more astonished. "You've learned a great deal for a Scipling, Siggi. It seems to come almost naturally to you. With a little practice, you'll be turning a rather noisy and smoky explosion into a very deadly dart of pure flame like a lance. I confess I'm rather jealous. The best I can do is a few sparks and a great deal of smoke. Tell me exactly how you did it."

Sigurd thought a moment, then shrugged. "I just don't know. I was mad enough at Hross-Bjorn at the moment to kill him, if he'd been within reach. I thought about it and it happened, that's all I know. Do you think he's sufficiently frightened to leave us alone for the rest of the night?"

Rolfr yawned and shivered. "I hope so." He paused a long moment. "You do have that sword you could use if he dared attack us outright."

"Yes, I suppose," Sigurd said, looking at the sword which lay sheathed across the saddle with a small glow of pride. He had been right and Mikla wrong about having enough power to possess the sword without being compelled to do any evil violence with it. His late experiences, he reflected, had made him wiser, sadder, and considerably stronger. Thinking about his own improvement soon soothed him into complacent slumber, undisturbed by any further demonstrations from Hross-Bjorn.

For several days, Rolfr's spirits remained low, and Sigurd supposed it was Mikla's death that depressed him. Rolfr spent a lot of time watching their backtrail, perhaps expecting to see Mikla following them, miraculously safe and unhurt. Since a great part of each night consisted of several hours of twilight, Rolfr had ample opportunity for perching himself on a high point to gaze back over the way they had journeyed that day. Finally Sigurd climbed up to him, determined to convince him that it was useless to hope after nearly a week since the accident on the glacier.

"Rolfr, what are you watching for?" he began, rather impatiently. He would rather spend his evenings resting and eating—with only two to feed now, there was more food. "If you think Mikla may still be alive and trying to catch up with us—"

"No, no, it's not that. I only wish it were something so agreeable as forlorn hope that forces me to keep watching. Siggi, don't you feel it, too? Isn't there something amiss with your peace of mind?" Rolfr frowned and pulled his cloak tighter against the cold wind that was howling dirges in the jagged cliffs nearby.

"Well, I hadn't thought about it lately," Sigurd said. "Since I got my sword back, I felt more confident; but yes, I felt a little uneasy in that place where we lost Mikla. What do you think it is? Now that you mention it, I do feel unaccountably uneasy—but that may be Hross-Bjorn's influence. I can always tell when he's near."

"This feeling is another influence you should recognize," Rolfr replied, with a significant glance at Sigurd.

"You mean Jotull?" Sigurd scanned the wasteland of twisted rock and ice below. An approaching storm draped the scarps one by one with a mantle of misty gloom. "I hadn't felt threatened, exactly, in the same way you seem to be." He frowned, thinking that the reason for that might be that Rolfr had always regarded Jotull and Bjarnhardr as enemies, but Sigurd's feelings were still confused.

Rolfr sighed, his breath making a cloud. "Let's go below and start a fire in the cave instead of freezing on this rock. Even Jotull would have better sense than to travel on a night like this. We'll see it snow before dawn."

The cave where they camped had been a shelter for travelers for countless years, which seemed to promise that they were on the right track for Svartafell and the other Dvergar settlements to the north. Fires had blackened the cave's walls and unknown hands had inscribed the walls with runes and messages for other travelers. From the wood left behind by others, Sigurd built a crackling fire, and the horses outside crowded around the cave mouth to be near the light and warmth.

Rolfr studied their map in the firelight. "We're getting near," he said hopefully. "Tomorrow, if all goes well, we'll start down

the north side of these fells into the Dvergarrige. I'll feel somewhat safer there, since the Dvergar are no friends of Bjarnhardr,
who doesn't quite dare to try routing them from their mountain
halls. This time tomorrow we may be in a dwarf's dwelling,
instead of shivering in a miserable cave and looking forward
to sleeping in the dirt and rocks. Then it will be free sailing
to Svartafell and Bergthor.''

He put the map away and stretched out by the fire, where
the wall made a natural curving reflector for the heat, but his
expression was not altogether content. It seemed to Sigurd that
Rolfr was listening to the sounds outside the cave, but all Sigurd
was aware of was the approaching storm, which suggested a
feeling of excitement. Sigurd kept getting up from his pallet
to look out at the deepening cobalt gloom which had filled all
the valleys below and was now creeping toward their little cave
with gusts of its rainy breath.

He turned back and sat down for the fifth time, after a look
at the horses to be sure they wouldn't stray in the storm. Then
he stood up again, listening intently. Rolfr met his eyes and
reached for his bow.

"It's only Hross-Bjorn, up to his usual tricks," Sigurd said,
but Rolfr slowly shook his head, motioning Sigurd to be silent.
In a moment, a faint voice hallooed from the top of the next
ridge south.

"Hross-Bjorn," Sigurd insisted.

"No," Rolfr said, extinguishing the fire with a quick spell.
"It isn't Hross-Bjorn, and if you'd think about it, you'd know
it isn't Hross-Bjorn either. Get your axe and be ready, if they
can find our cave in the dark."

Sigurd picked up the sword, but he put it down again in
favor of the axe. The rain pattered down outside with increasing
force and he heard a grumble of thunder booming from cliff
to cliff in the valleys below.

"I can't see a thing," he muttered, "so I'm certain whoever
is out there can't see us, either."

Almost as he spoke, a brilliant bolt of lightening shuddered
across the sky, illuminating the landscape in its stark, white
light. The horses tugged at their picket ropes restlessly.

"It's useless, they'll find us," Rolfr said grimly. "Be ready to fight, Siggi. We're not giving up the box this close to Svartafell. I wish I'd thought to burn that map, so they wouldn't learn the way." He scratched around in the dark, moving rocks, and Sigurd supposed he was hiding the map drawn on the pouch. "They'll probably keep us alive with the thought of torturing the directions out of us, but it would be better to be dead than to consign that box to their hands."

"Jotull and Bjarnhardr?" Sigurd squinted against the rain whipping into his face as he peered out into the storm. "Rolfr, I think you've lost your common sense. Jotull wouldn't be traveling on such a dog's night, let alone Bjarnhardr—"

Someone shouted again, much nearer to the cave, and another burst of lightning pierced the darkness with its lurid flickering. Rolfr made no reply except to fit an arrow into his bow. Sigurd looked outside again sharply, thinking he had heard the sound of hooves on the rock. Suddenly he knew he heard something, but the rumbling of the thunder prevented him from identifying the sound, and the restive pawing and squealing of the horses helped confuse him. In the next flash of lightning, he saw a dark, flapping figure framed against the opening of the cave. Rolfr leaped up with a warning shout, at the same instant as Sigurd raised his axe, but the figure collapsed before he could strike.

With an oath and a spell, Rolfr lit the fire again with a roar of heat and light, illuminating the huddled heap beside the opening. Together they bent to examine their unbidden guest, who was shaking with cold and soaked through by the icy rain, which had frozen to sleet on his cloak. They carefully turned him over, making a few signs to ward off evil.

It was Mikla. After an instant of shock and self-reproach, they hauled him close to the fire and began feverishly drying his clothes and trying to make him comfortable. Both his clothing and his person were mercilessly battered from his ordeal; one crudely bandaged arm might have been broken, and his boots were worn from five days of walking. Rolfr shook his head and repeated that he'd never forgive himself, never, for not trying to rescue Mikla from the maw of the glacier.

"Very commendable," a voice said suddenly, from behind them. "Now that you've cared for the apprentice, how about the master?"

# Chapter 16

◇◇◇◇◇◇◇◇◇◇◇◇◇◇◇◇◇◇◇◇◇◇◇◇◇◇◇◇◇◇◇

"Don't stare, Rolfr," Jotull continued, seating himself with his usual grace beside the fire and throwing aside his wet cloak. "It's pleasant to see you again, Sigurd. You left Svinhagahall without telling a soul farewell—very bad manners, you realize."

Sigurd recovered from his confusion quickly. He glanced at Rolfr, who was white with fury. "We didn't leave under our own volition, but—"

"Yes, I know it was Mikla who took you away. He's caused me no end of trouble, but the penalties for rebellious or runaway apprentices are rather severe, so I hope he's learning a lesson." Jotull crossed one foot over his knee as if he were completely at home, despite Rolfr's furious glowering and Mikla's groans.

"He might have died," Rolfr snapped. "I can't imagine you being anything less than savage when you have the opportunity, and I daresay Mikla was in no condition to defend himself when you found him. How many of these bruises and cuts are yours?"

Jotull smiled and shook his head pityingly. "Why, if I hadn't come along when I did, he'd still be in that crevice, frozen hard as a rock. A bad apprentice is better than none, so I took him out, not without great difficulty and danger. I hope he'll be grateful to me in the future for the risks I took in saving his wretched life. He owes me a tremendous debt for preserving him. Stubborn as he is, I believe he's not quite so haughty now, eh?"

"You've treated him very shabbily," Rolfr went on, still angry. "A bad master is far worse than a bad apprentice, particularly when the master is a liar, as well as a traitor and a spy."

"Sigurd," Jotull interrupted, "tell your friend he's going too far for such a lowly thrall as he is." He smiled lazily at Sigurd, whose blood was chilled at his glance.

"Rolfr, shut up," he said at once.

"Good, Sigurd. I hope your readiness to follow my orders will be an example to these other two friends of yours. Now then, get me something hot and decent to eat; and when you're done, go attend to my horse." He took a familiar rune stick from his belt and held it up admiringly. "I trust you are keeping the carven box safe?"

"Yes, I've got it," Sigurd answered nervously. "I'm keeping it safe until we reach Svartafell." A touch of defiance crept into his tone despite himself.

"Keep it, then," Jotull replied with a weary sigh. "You've done well enough protecting it so far, I'd say, although I thought for certain you'd lose it at Gunnavik, as well as your life, when old Vigbjodr came back after you'd chopped him to pieces."

Rolfr looked up from the preparation of Jotull's food. "If you were there, you might have helped. And while we're talking about sendings, why don't you do something to get rid of Hross-Bjorn? I assume you've attached yourself to us now, so there's no need of the sending to annoy us."

Jotull's dark eye flickered with displeasure. "Rolfr, your attitude has become rather impertinent—and imprudent. You have seen the way I dealt with Mikla's overweening behavior. If you don't wish to become acquainted with my wrath in a similar manner, you'd better mend your demeanor."

Rolfr stalked away to look at Mikla, who had stopped shivering and was now sleeping heavily. "If Mikla were in any condition to speak, I know he'd say we don't care for your attitude or demeanor either. What gives you the right to half-kill Mikla and to force yourself into our camp with all manner of threats and black looks? You've done nothing to help us along our journey when we were nearly starving and no place would take us in; now we're almost there, and you move in as if you'd been in command all the time. We won't surrender to you and Bjarnhardr so easily, Jotull. I'm not one to be inhospitable, but, unless you want to be killed, you'd better go back out into the storm." He drew his sword and advanced a step, putting himself between Mikla and Jotull.

Jotull raised one eyebrow and got to his feet in a leisurely fashion. "Surely you realize how absurd you're being. You've never even begun to be a match for me in a fair fight."

Rolfr's eyes flashed as he brandished his sword. "Fair fight? When have you ever fought a fair fight, Jotull? Your only success is in how well you cheat."

Jotull scowled angrily at Sigurd, who was too amazed by Rolfr's fierce speech to do more than stare from Rolfr to Jotull. "Sigurd! If you value the life of this puppy, you'd better tell him to stop his snarling before he gets himself killed. I daresay you've not turned against an old friend like me, have you? I know I can count on you, Sigurd, not to turn me out in the storm."

Sigurd looked from one furious countenance to the other and drew a deep breath. Carefully he said, "I wouldn't want to turn anyone out into such a storm as this, even though it might well be one of your own creations. What I propose, if you'll both listen to me, is that Jotull will leave in the morning and promise to go back to Svinhagahall without doing anything to prevent our journey to Svartafell. The box and its contents are mine, Jotull, and I'm the one who will decide what to do with them—and whatever I do, it won't be giving them to Bjarnhardr or anyone else."

Jotull shook his head and sighed. "I've never mentioned Bjarnhardr, or giving up the box to me or anyone. I'm merely trying to protect you so you'll survive long enough to get that confounded box open. I don't want it, and I don't want Bjarnhardr to have it, either. I couldn't be more glad to see it in your hands. Perhaps I have spoken too harshly, but I've traveled a long way with very little rest and I'm very much out of temper. I may not have been very sympathetic to Mikla; he ran away and betrayed his master in a most dastardly way, after all, but I didn't put him into the terrible condition you see him in now. He was in wretched shape when I found him, and I certainly wouldn't want to do anything to make him more of a burden than ever. What would that benefit me? Now then, let's forget this ridiculous quarrel for tonight, at least, and take it up tomorrow when we're all better rested. Isn't that a reasonable suggestion?" He looked appealingly to Sigurd, who found himself nodding and agreeing.

"We'll settle it tomorrow," he promised, very much relieved. "Come on, Rolfr, be reasonable. You wouldn't want to turn a dog out into such a storm as that."

Rolfr turned away in disgust. "You're a bigger fool than you were before, Sigurd, if you believe you'll be rid of him so easily."

Sigurd's anger swelled after such an affront, but he swallowed his angry retort. "I know you don't mean that, so I'll forget you said it," he said rather stiffly. For the rest of the evening, Rolfr refused to speak to him, choosing instead to watch by Mikla. Sigurd talked amiably with Jotull, who quickly assured him that their friendship was in no way impaired by his unexpected removal from Svinhagahall; even Bjarnhardr was as kindly disposed toward him as before and understandably anxious for his safety. Jotull asked to see the sword and seemed glad to see it when Sigurd showed it to him.

In the morning, Mikla awakened weak and peevish, but glad nevertheless to see his friends. The return of Jotull he accepted with bitter resignation, eyeing his old master with such a look of smoldering hatred that Sigurd wondered why Jotull tolerated it. Jotull returned Mikla's scowls coldly, remarking that he hoped Mikla's strength would return soon so he could resume his old duties.

"I'd rather have died," Mikla muttered sullenly, looking venomously at Sigurd as he fastened the sword around his waist. "As if we didn't have troubles enough, now we have to worry about you losing your temper and killing all of us. Remember that I warned you, Sigurd."

"I can take care of myself," Sigurd retorted. "Somehow I'd hoped that nearly losing your life would have made you a more pleasant fellow to be around, Mikla, but I can see you're as spiteful as you ever were and maybe worse." He threw the last of his tea in the fire.

Mikla would have snapped back at him, but Jotull told him to be silent. "Much as I despise reviving unpleasant topics, I must do so, with the earnest hope that you have done some reconsidering in the night and are no longer adverse to my accompanying your party to Svartafell. I hate to be so insistent as to stoop to coercion, but you might as well know that I have this." He held up the rune stick carved by Grisnir.

"That belongs to Sigurd," Rolfr declared, flushing with anger. "You took it from Mikla, like a common thief. A friend gave it to Sigurd, and you'd better return it to us, or—"

"Be quiet," Jotull said, in a voice of deadly calm. "How was I to know if Mikla was dead or alive? When I found him, it was anyone's guess how long he would survive."

"If you're so honorable, you'll return our property to us," Rolfr said, disregarding Sigurd's signals to be silent, "without attaching any conditions to it. I know what your conditions are, and I tell you now we reject them. We can find Svartafell without the rune stick or you."

Jotull shrugged. "Certainly, you can find Svartafell. But how can you be sure Bergthor will even consent to talk to you? Dwarves are suspicious creatures by nature, and you might be killed or thrown into a dungeon first, with questions later. This stick, however, has a message on it from Grisnir to Bergthor, telling him he can trust the bearer. If I know dwarves, I think I can fairly promise you that you won't get near an important dwarf like Bergthor without some sort of authorization or recommendation from someone known to him." He smiled in his superior manner and took up his staff. "Well, Mikla, are you ready to depart? This is likely to be your last look at your old friends, so remember them well."

"You won't give them up so easily," Mikla said, with a

jaundiced glower at Sigurd and Rolfr. "You'll go to Bergthor and you'll invent a plot to trap them." He gave Rolfr a warning scowl.

Rolfr's eyes narrowed. "Then we'll have to have that rune stick. If he won't hand it over after reasonable threats, then we'll have to kill him somehow." He drew his sword before Sigurd could stop him. "If you're a friend to me, Sigurd, you'll help defend me."

"Rolfr! Are you crazy? We can't kill him! We'll have to take him with us," Sigurd exclaimed. "Now put away your sword and be reasonable!"

"I won't," Rolfr said, making a flourish with his sword. "I told you last night we wouldn't be easily rid of him. He wouldn't leave us for anything, Sigurd, and you're a fool if you don't know it."

Jotull backed warily toward the opening. "You're wrong, Rolfr. I shall leave and I'm taking your only chance of seeing Bergthor along with me." He held up the rune stick and laughed, shoving Mikla outside behind him as he went. "Goodbye to your only piece of luck!"

"Wait! Jotull, don't leave!" Sigurd started to follow, but Rolfr stepped in front of him, still with the sword in his hand.

"Sigurd, don't stop him! You're being an idiot! You're letting him get you under his control!" Rolfr hissed.

"No, you're the one who's being a fool!" Sigurd retorted, with a shove. "Get out of my way! We've got to have the rune stick!"

Rolfr responded to the shove by knocking Sigurd flat with a heavy blow from his left fist. Sigurd rolled up and twisted out of the way, reacting as he had been taught. He drew his sword as he regained his feet, lunging forward to meet the figure advancing upon him with sword in hand. The fury of the curse was upon him as well as his own indignation, making him totally forget it was Rolfr he was attacking. The swords clashed in the tight quarters of the cave, striking sparks from each other that hissed and sang.

Sigurd was beginning to be surprised at Rolfr's ability with a sword. But suddenly Rolfr misjudged the lowness of the roof and struck the stones a jarring, resounding stroke that sent his sword spinning out of his reach. Sigurd wavered an instant, but the curse impelled him forward to finish the fight. As he raised his sword, a fist-sized rock flew at him from nowhere and struck him in the pit of his stomach with staggering force. He fell over backward, gasping for breath painfully. For a moment, he forgot about the fight, and Rolfr immediately seized the opportunity. He trod heavily on Sigurd's wrist and twisted the sword out of his grasp, not minding that he cut his hands in doing so. With a warning shout, he rushed from the cave and scrambled nimbly up the side of the skarp, evading the determined pursuit of Sigurd. At the summit of the cliff, Rolfr swung the sword around his head and let it fly in a spinning arc out over the ranks of jagged pinnacles and chasms hundreds of feet below. It flashed like a needle before plunging downward out of sight. Neither Rolfr nor Sigurd heard it strike the stones below.

Sigurd could not look at Rolfr. Gruffly he said, "I'm glad it's gone. Sorry I was such an ass. It was senseless of me to think I was stronger than the curse."

"Yes, you were an idiot," Rolfr agreed angrily. "Sometimes I think the only thing good about you, Sigurd, is your natural power. You would have killed me if it hadn't stopped you. Just as I foresaw it in Svinhagahall."

"It's gone now," Sigurd said, shuddering and hating himself. "Neither of us has to worry about it any more."

Jotull clambered up the face of the rock and seemed startled to find them both sitting down talking. He looked quickly from one to the other, then out over the pinnacle to the depths below. "Gone?" he inquired of Sigurd, with a lowering glance at Rolfr.

Sigurd nodded, and Jotull shook his head, as if such irresponsible behavior was beyond his comprehension. "Well then, I only came to say farewell, and I wish you the best of luck in getting to Bergthor."

"No, don't leave just yet," Sigurd said, starting to follow him down. "Let's talk some more about the rune stick. We were friends once, Jotull, if you recall."

Jotull inclined his head. "Yes, I recall our friendship, and it seems a pity now that we should fight over this little stick of wood. I realize now that we are equals, you and I, no longer the great wizard and the admiring little Scipling. I must admit that I admire the way you have outwitted Bjarnhardr, as well as myself, for as long as you have. You have great power, Sigurd, and it's a shame if we can't come to an agreement together that will benefit both of us."

Considering Jotull as an equal seemed to remove much of his threat. "Well then, if we can't get rid of you, I suppose we'll have to take you as well as the rune stick. But I want you to swear that you won't attempt to trick me out of the box and its contents, and I demand that you put a stop to Hross-Bjorn."

"I promise that I won't attempt to steal the box and whatever is inside," Jotull replied. "May I be stricken by all the powers of darkness if I do. But as for Hross-Bjorn, that's a problem. You see, I did manufacture that sending, I am ashamed to admit, but I gave its control to Bjarnhardr. There's nothing I can do to stop him in his treachery. He would kill me in an instant, and I bitterly regret my misplaced trust in him. But I know I can trust you, Sigurd. You can be as great as Bjarnhardr or Halfdane one day and I know you are far more worthy to be a leader of the Alfar."

"You should know me too well to try flattery," Sigurd said. "I might be worthy of such power someday, but right now the task before us is finding Svartafell, so I propose we get to it." He thought that sounded rather fine and dignified, but the effect was ruined by a hoarse laugh from Mikla, tottering against the rocks below.

"The task before you, Sigurd, is finding out how gullible you really are. You'll give the box to your enemies next. What will it take to open your eyes?"

Jotull and Sigurd exchanged a glance, and Jotull sighed. "You can believe whomever you choose, Sigurd. I won't try to force your decision—but it was a very good point you mentioned about you and Rolfr not being able to continue alone."

"I've decided," Sigurd said. "Rolfr? Surely you understand

that it's the best choice for us, don't you? These past nights worrying about whether Hross-Bjorn will get to us or not have very nearly been the death of us both. Come on, don't look so sulky. You wouldn't want to lose Mikla either, would you?"

Rolfr glowered at Sigurd and Jotull and turned away to seek another path down. He looked rather pale and shaken, now that his anger had drained away. "I don't think my opinion matters much, Sigurd. All I want is an end to all this fighting, one way or another."

"This is the best way for us," Sigurd assured him anxiously, but Rolfr did not look back or halt his descent. "I'm sure Jotull will give us a better chance at seeing Bergthor."

The weary voice of Mikla interposed. "Promises! What foolishness! What could you possibly know about anything concerning Jotull?"

Sigurd chose to ignore Mikla. He felt he had done the only logical thing despite the fact that both Mikla and Rolfr maintained a flinty silence for the rest of the day and stared at him with cold, accusing eyes whenever his back was turned.

He found himself thinking of the sword throughout the day, and Jotull mentioned it several times, as if he couldn't forget about it either. Sigurd was glad it was gone before it had fulfilled its grim prophecy of three villainous killings—one killing was more than enough for Sigurd's conscience to bear.

That night they camped in a small, green dell on the downward side of the mountains, where the snow still lingered in tall, weeping drifts, pooling into a thousand icy little ponds where the grass and moss were green around their edges like bowls of emerald. The horses were glad for the grass, and Sigurd was glad to be out of the high-altitude winds. Most comforting of all was the possession of the rune stick, which Jotull had presented him with in a handsome gesture of faith, so they now knew exactly what directions to take. Highly pleased, Sigurd attempted to compensate for the frigid silence of Rolfr and Mikla by chatting with Jotull as they used to do in Hrafnborg. However, he forbore to ask any questions about the events of Svinhagahall. He didn't want to renew the subject of Halfdane's death. Nor did he wish to question the wizard too closely about Hross-Bjorn. He knew he had to be exquisitely careful, or he might arouse Jotull's volatile temper once again.

After the evening meal was eaten and the guard posted, Sigurd remembered that he ought to look at one of the horses' hooves to check on the healing of a stone bruise. Elfradr, Ragnhild's horse, nibbled at his beard by way of a friendly greeting, and Sigurd found himself thinking of the horse's owner, reflecting that his days spent at Hrafnborg had been a happy time, if only he had had the sense to know it then. He shrugged, supposing it did no good to brood about it.

When he returned to the campsite, he passed Rolfr, who returned his greeting with a dispirited grunt, which Sigurd took as an encouraging sign that the siege of silence was drawing to an end. He flung himself down on his pallet after a nod to Jotull, who was busy with his boots in the firelight. Mikla was already asleep, very tired after a day of travel. Something hard poked Sigurd in the back, as if some careless person had thrown something on his bed. Muttering, he grabbed the thing to throw it aside, and it rang with a metallic clamor against the rocks where it landed. Sigurd clutched his hand as if it were burned, not believing what his senses had told him. He groped around in the rocks and prickly scrub until his hand touched cold, sharp metal again.

"Jotull!" he called, backing away. "Is this someone's idea of a bad joke? I don't find it amusing in the least degree. When Rolfr threw that sword away, I was glad to see the last of it and its mischief. After nearly killing my two friends, I'm not yet ready to make jokes about it." He stood up, glaring at Jotull and Rolfr.

"Whatever are you talking about?" Jotull shut his book in irritation and got up to confront him. "My humor doesn't lend itself to joking."

Sigurd looked at Rolfr, who slapped his own sword. "I've been standing guard since sundown right on this spot. As a near victim of that cursed sword of Bjarnhardr's, I swear by my own honest sword that I haven't attempted anything by way of joking about it. What do you mean, Sigurd?"

Sigurd backed down a little from his indignation. "Someone

put a sword on my eider tonight, as if to make me think Bjarn-hardr's sword had somehow followed me. It's a very poor sort of joke, and I know someone must have done it." He eyed Mikla, who had been asleep almost since supper was finished, which would seem to exclude him from suspicion.

Jotull scowled in the flickering firelight. "You're certain it was a sword?" he asked sternly. "Let's have a look at the object. Where did you throw it?" He plunged into the bushes where Sigurd indicated, casting about with the lighted tip of his staff. "Here it is!" he called in a voice of amazement. "It does indeed seem to be—Sigurd, where are you? Help me fetch it out; it's fallen into the water."

Sigurd backed away, his heart pounding with horror. "Then leave it there. It's Bjarnhardr's sword; I know it by the terrible feeling it gives me. Don't touch it, Jotull, or the curse may affect you!"

"Nonsense. I'm quite safe. The curse is only upon the person who first draws it from its sheath after its last fulfillment of its three murders. I didn't draw it, nor has it fulfilled its prophecy, so it won't get me under its influence. Bring me its sheath, if you still have it." Jotull lifted the sword carefully from its rocky resting place to carry it back to their camp. It gleamed in the dim light, perfectly familiar to Sigurd and perfectly terrifying.

"How did it follow me?" Sigurd almost moaned, groping in his bag for the sheath, which he had thriftily saved. "Rolfr, you did throw it away up on the top of Yslaberg, didn't you?"

Rolfr stared as if in a trance. Then he backed away, making all the signs he knew to ward off evil. "I threw it all right, and it fell where no mortal man could find it again deliberately. It has followed you by magic, Siggi. I should have known I wouldn't escape my doom quite so easily as that. Didn't I tell you in Svinhagahall that there was nothing we could do to prevent my fate?"

Sigurd watched Jotull sheath the sword. Grimly he said, "It may have followed us because I kept thinking about it all day. I don't really know what things are possible with this power of mine, but it seems to me that we can do something to stop the sword from following or being drawn. Jotull, what do you think? Can we put a huge boulder on the sword to hold it?"

Jotull replied, "If your power can draw the sword after you, then it can push a boulder aside—if it is indeed your power that is drawing it. If it is Bjarnhardr, then the matter is very different and much more grave."

"Surely you're wizard enough to stop it from following us," Sigurd said challengingly. "I don't much care who is making it follow, but it's up to you to see that it is stopped. I'm sure you're the equal of a one-legged, maimed runt of a warlord like Bjarnhardr."

Jotull's eye flashed dangerously, but he spoke calmly. "Yes, I can probably prevent the sword from following us, if that is what you think you wish."

Sigurd was certain, and he did not feel safe until Jotull had buried the sword under an avalanche of huge lava shards, which he dislodged from the cliffs with spells. During his turn at watching that night, Sigurd found his eyes drawn repeatedly to the heap of sharp slabs and rubble. He hoped earnestly he had seen the last of the cursed sword. With his own eyes, he had seen it buried under tons of rock; and should it be drawn out again, it would be by a more powerful agency than his own puny powers.

The sword did not reappear that night, and Sigurd fell asleep confident that it was still buried. In the morning, however, he awoke to find it cradled in his arm, glinting in the pale morning light. With a shout, he leaped away from it, as if he had nearly put his hand into a set trap. Rolfr greeted the news of the sword's return with a fatalistic sigh and shaking of his head, and Mikla smiled in wry triumph.

"Might not the next object of the curse be Jotull?" he whispered to Sigurd maliciously. "Since he is your dear friend, it's only logical that you'll try to kill him next. If that's the case, then I vote we keep the sword against that happy eventuality."

Sigurd told him what he thought of such advice. When he regained his temper and his composure, he renewed his appeal to Jotull to get rid of the sword again. This time Jotull wove spells over the sword and wrapped it in a bag made of a foal's

caul, and then he threw it into a deep pool where the bottom
was lost in the black depths of the earth.

"He looks as if he's trying," Rolfr observed, watching Jotull
over his spells. "One would think he didn't want the sword to
follow, but I certainly wonder if he wouldn't like to have you
and me out of his way, Mikla."

Mikla shrugged and looked askance at Sigurd. "What possible interference can you or I be to him, Rolfr? In spite of all
our best efforts, Jotull has exactly what he wants."

"I don't think you can say what Jotull actually wants,"
Sigurd protested. "He's not an easy person to judge, nor are
you being strictly fair to him. He did pull you out of that crevice,
you know."

Mikla turned to Sigurd and snapped, "You're the wrong
person to talk about judgments. Halfdane saved your life twice,
yet you never were fair to him. Don't get self-righteous with
me." With a particularly sharp glance at Sigurd, Mikla stalked
away toward the horses.

Sigurd soon forgot his doubts in the realization of how near
they were getting to Svartafell. They passed many signs of the
industrious mining operations the dwarves employed in the
fells, casting up enormous mounds of shattered rock excavated
from the hearts of the mountains. Twice they passed the portals
of great halls dug into the sides of heavily wooded fells, but
they saw no sign of the dwarves who occupied them. Dwarves,
as Jotull explained, preferred the underground and the hours
of darkness, although the sun did no more damage to them
than making them rather cross and uncomfortable—unlike the
effect on trolls or the Dokkalfar, to whom the touch of the sun
spelled instant death.

As soon as the sun sank from the sky for several hours of
twilight, the dvergar began to bustle to and from the mines,
and the travelers were frequently hailed and called to account
for themselves. The dour-faced miners gathered around the
horsemen, examined the rune stick, and demanded to see the
carven box as final proof. Then, with much head shaking,
nodding, and muttering among themselves, they directed the

travelers onward and stood staring with imperturbable rudeness until the strangers rode out of sight.

Finally the travelers encountered a lone drawf plodding along the road beside a large, rattly cart being drawn by a stout, shaggy pony who looked far too small for the cart, but was far too stubborn to be daunted by such an immense load. Firewood had been piled on the cart until another stick would have almost certainly toppled the whole business over, pony and all.

"Halloa!" the dwarf exclaimed at the sight of the strangers overtaking him, and he and the pony stopped dead to stare. Sigurd had thought he could stare down almost anyone, but the dwarves, he soon learned, were masters at the art of staring a stranger completely out of countenance.

"Halloa!" the old fellow said again with particular emphasis. "Now what might you Alfar folks be doing in the Dvergarrige? Seems to me you leave us alone well enough until you want to start trouble, and trouble usually starts with the appearance of one of you wizardy fellows. You're as wizard as any wizard I've seen, just as sure as I'm as much of a woodcutter as you fellows have ever seen."

While Jotull explained, Sigurd eyed the old fellow's huge gleaming axe, which was carried over one thick shoulder. The dwarf's clothing was rough and ill-assorted, and his white hair and beard grew wild and long. The dubious eyes which he cast upon Sigurd were hooded with wrinkled folds of swarthy, unwashed skin, but Sigurd detected no meanness in the woodcutter's gaze.

"Well then, so you're a-seeking old Bergthor, are you?" The woodcutter rubbed his ear with his axe, and Sigurd wondered if he might not accidentally take it off sometime when he was scowling and thinking so intently. "As it happens, this here load of wood is for Bergthor's forge. I'm taking it to him myself." The words came out like a hard-wrung confession; even more reluctantly, the old dwarf added, "I could guide you there, since it is a dreadful chore to find the place, if you folks was of a mind to travel with such equipage as this." He jerked a thumb at the creaking cart and the diminutive pony, who peered through his thick forelock, like a weasel in a hedge.

"That's a very kind offer," Jotull said, "but I fear we'll only be an impediment to you. Our horses have traveled all day and are nearly spent, so we'll be stopping presently for the night. I'm sure you've just begun, and we couldn't ask you to stop when you've scarcely started your journey."

The woodcutter shook his head. "Makes no matter to me. I was going to stop at Drafdritrshof for a draught of ale anyway, and that could take all night and the next day, too, if I want it to. Bergthor can wait for his wood easier than I can go without my ale. I expect you can convince Drafdritr that he ought to put you up for the night and give you something to eat." His tone suggested there was not much hope of Drafdritr's hospitality.

"Well, we don't wish to hamper your journey," Jotull replied, "nor do we wish to intrude upon your friend Drafdritr, if he's not the sort who likes unexpected guests. Perhaps we'll ride on to the next settlement instead of stopping there with you."

The woodcutter shrugged and looked at the sky speculatively. "Makes no difference to me what you do, but the next settlement is considerably out of your way if Svartafell is where you want to go. I'm not one to try interfering with other people's plans though, so go ahead to Eyjadalir. Drafdritr runs a house of refuge for travelers so he sees enough custom not to miss yours too much. I shall tell him I sent you on so you wouldn't have to suffer from the discomfort of his hall and the badness of his beer."

"You might have mentioned earlier that he ran an inn," Jotull said impatiently.

"You didn't ask," the woodcutter morosely replied, with a chirp to the small pony, who lunged into his collar and bore the huge creaking load away, followed by his slouching master, bearing the axe.

After discussing the matter a few moments, the travelers decided to risk the questionable hospitality of Drafdritrshof, hoping that bad beds and poor food would be better than none at all. They found Drafdritrshof quite easily, immediately recognizing the immense load of firewood reposing in the doorway, minus the sharp-eyed pony. Somewhat to their astonishment, they were welcomed with great courtesy by Drafdritr and his sons, whose ages were indistinguishable one from another, and in a short time they found themselves comfortably provided for in one of the most hospitable houses Sigurd had ever encountered. He couldn't help looking at the old woodcutter drinking his ale in a dark corner. The old fellow shook his head gloomily and whispered noisily behind his hand. "I told you it would be bad, didn't I? You can't blame me for not trying to warn you." He blinked his eyes, which became more inflamed-looking as the evening progressed, but no amount of ale or fine singing could relieve his contrary disconsolation. Sigurd later learned from one of his hosts that it was a point of great pride with the old woodcutter that he hadn't found anything pleasant to say about anything in well over sixty years.

In the morning, the woodcutter's great clumping boots awakened the house at a much earlier hour than usual, and his muttering prompted the travelers to hurry themselves. Sigurd wondered how he could even move, after drinking such prodigious quantities of ale last night, but, by the time they were ready to start, the creaking cart and pony had been waiting with much impatience for what the woodcutter said was half the morning.

Jotull fumed inwardly at having to suit their pace to so slow a conveyance, but when he attempted to persuade the woodcutter to tell him the directions, the stubborn creature merely scowled and shook his head as if Jotull had sunk very low indeed in his estimation.

"No need to be in such a devil of a hurry," the woodcutter growled. "We'll be there soon enough, probably too soon for your liking. Bergthor's a rude old churl, and his hospitality would scandalize the trolls. You'll get nothing but what the rats don't want there. I always thought you lowlanders might be somewhat strange, coming all this way just to see a smith. Now don't tell me about it; there's nothing I hate worse than knowing someone else's business." He scuttled away to the other side of the pony, which move put him in no danger of any unwanted confidences.

By the end of the day, they had passed through most of the mining area and ascended a winding rocky track higher into the fells. Several times they all had to push the overloaded cart, despite the woodcutter's grumbling that the pony could do it himself, and wasn't it like a smith to put himself in such an out-of-the-way location.

At sundown, they halted in the desolate refuse of an abandoned mine, and the woodcutter announced with grim satisfaction, "This is where we part company. Goodbye." He started to lead the pony toward the gaping mine portal, which was inscribed with crumbling runes.

Jotull strode after him. "Wait a moment, you old ruffian. You said you'd show us the way to Svartafell. This certainly doesn't look like the dwelling of an important man like Bergthor. Is this your notion of assisting strangers in your land— to lead them to a deserted spot miles from the nearest settlement in the hopes they'll lose themselves? If that's what you have in mind, my friend, I can promise you some very bitter regrets which will make your present complaints sound like the mere squeakings of a mouse." His eyes gleamed with a deadly light that Sigurd didn't like to look at.

The woodcutter turned to glower threateningly at Jotull. "I only said that you might follow me to Svartafell, as this load of wood was for Bergthor's forge. I never said Svartafell was where I was going to. You were presumptuous, my fine fellow."

Jotull clutched his staff. "You mean to say you never intended to lead us to Svartafell?" he inquired, trying to keep his voice calm.

"Well, I brought you here, didn't I?" the woodcutter countered.

"Yes, but this isn't Svartafell," Jotull snapped.

"Oh, aye? Isn't it?" The woodcutter feigned great surprise.

"You mean this is Svartafell?" Jotull exclaimed.

The woodcutter pondered, but could see no way of denying the truth. "Some say it's Svartafell," he said grudgingly.

"Then why didn't you just come out and say so?" Sigurd demanded.

The woodcutter eyed him disapprovingly. "You didn't ask."

# Chapter 17

◇◇◇◇◇◇◇◇◇◇◇◇◇◇◇◇◇◇◇◇◇◇◇◇◇◇◇◇

"I can't believe a person of any importance would live in a place like this," Jotull growled as they picked their way down the dark mine tunnel toward a glowing light ahead. Heaps of unrefined ore were flung here and there with no regard for the path where people might have to walk. Unfamiliar implements used for mining loomed in the dim light, rusty and menacing. As they neared the forge, they heard the snorting and stamping of horses and voices shouting and cursing in the manner reserved for men who were trying to induce a fractious and powerful horse to do something against its wishes.

When they came into view of the forge area, they saw an immense, shaggy, gray horse plunging with half a dozen men clinging to its neck and muzzle, trying to stay out of the way of the lashing hind heels and the pawing forefeet. The horse carried the men into seven other big gray horses that welcomed the opportunity to rear and lunge against their halters. After a great deal of wild struggle, someone brought the horse under control by biting its ear, and the beast subsided, legs braced and trembled indignantly. When the smith's apprentice picked up one hoof, the entire kicking, cursing battle was repeated. Eventually the horse was thrown on its side and secured with a network of ropes, and the apprentice began trimming its huge hooves.

Then Bergthor, the stoutest and sootiest of all the men, realized that he had strangers in his forge. He folded his arms and scowled at the woodcutter for an explanation. The woodcutter jerked his thumb over his shoulder and grumbled, "I brought your wood, and these Alfar fellows followed me. I don't know who they are or what they want, but if you ask me, strangers are always trouble."

Bergthor took off his thick gloves and shoved them under his belt. He was a thickset, powerful man in the prime of his life, rather taller than the other dwarves Sigurd had seen, and his beard and hair were black and bristling from repeated singeings at the forge. "Well then, strangers, have you come for business with me? I am Bergthor of Svartafell." His voice boomed over the angry snorting of the thrown horse and the puffing of the bellows as another apprentice heated the iron to shape the horseshoe.

Jotull stepped forward with a stiff bow. "I am the wizard Jotull, and I have brought this Scipling Sigurd for you to examine a piece of your handiwork to see if you can make a key to open it." He motioned to Sigurd, who stepped forward with the carven box.

"You made the lock, I believe," Sigurd said, "quite some time ago. You see your name carved into the box itself."

Bergthor brushed past Jotull to take the box gently in his huge, black-seamed hands. A look of delight and astonishment replaced the black scowl. "Wherever did you get this? I made this a long time ago, before the mining trade became so profitable. Now I spend much of my time shoeing these villainous horses and mending machines. I used to work with beautiful things like wood and silver and gold, but now all I have time for is iron." He sighed and shook his head. "Let me think—I made this box for a lady as a wedding gift. This is no place to talk, though. Come with me and we'll have something to drink while we remember."

The woodcutter brightened at the mention of drink and gladly stumped along after them down a narrow tunnel to a smaller room, very rough and jumbled, filled with smoke from the incompetent roasting of a large piece of meat. Bergthor sat on a large, black chair that creaked ominously under his weight, and he placed the box before him on the table.

"It has been a long time since I used a little chisel and a small hammer to carve with," he said fondly, then summoned the serving girl with a shout and directed her to bring them ale. "We must not be in any hurry to open it. I wonder what's inside it." He shook it, listening to the soft rattle inside.

Jotull's eyes burned. "Its contents will be of no interest to you. The box has been in the Scipling realm for many years and whatever has been put inside is probably of no significance."

Sigurd and Rolfr looked at the wizard in silent astonishment, and Mikla smiled grimly. Jotull darted them all a covert, warning glance.

"Then what do you want to open it for?" Bergthor smiled and rubbed his broiled-looking nose with one large forefinger. "If it wasn't something valuable to you, why did you come all this distance to have me open it?"

"What I meant to say," Jotull replied gracefully, "was that you probably wouldn't think it was worth much. Obviously, it's not gold or jewels, or we'd hear a different sort of sound. Therefore, it can't be anything worth coveting."

Bergthor grinned, showing great white teeth like a horse's. "I understand. You're afraid I might want to take it from you. Well, my friend, you're safe with me. There isn't much that I covet anymore. I'm not so young and greedy now as I was when I made this box."

"Was it a very long time ago?" Sigurd asked. "Perhaps you made it for my grandmother."

"Perhaps I did, but I don't remember doing any work for the other realm at that time. Now and then I do something for Sciplings who have a little power, but this box now, I made it for a lady. Was she an Alfar lady? No, wait—she was a Scipling. Ha, now I remember her. She was beautiful and she was about to marry an Alfar warlord. Her name was Ashildr. This lovely little box was a gift from her husband to hold her jewels and precious things. Ah, but she was a dainty little thing to look at, and she came here with him, she did, because she wanted to have a look at a black dwarf."

Sigurd put down his horn cup excitedly. "She was my mother. I never remembered her, because she died and my grandmother took me to raise. If she was married to an Alfar, that means that I am half of this realm and half of the other. That explains why I have a natural power." He grinned at Rolfr, who beamed at him and winked knowingly. "What else do you know about my parents, Bergthor? You can't imagine how I've yearned to know about them, and my grandmother died before she could tell me anything at all." He leaned forward eagerly, his attention riveted on the smith.

Bergthor's genial eyes misted over and he shook his head gently. "Imagine you coming all the way from the other realm with this box to find your father. There's probably not another soul who could tell you his name, and I'm honored and touched to be able to tell someone such news that it will gladden both our hearts for the rest of our lives. His name, lad, was Half-dane."

Sigurd leaped up with a yell he couldn't stifle, knocking over the bench beneath him with a crash. He slammed his fist on the table and shouted into Bergthor's blank face, "No! That's not his name!"

"Why, what's the matter?" the smith demanded, rising to his feet with a flicker of outrage in his puzzled tone.

Jotull leaped up. "Sigurd, sit down. It might not be the same one, you know. Halfdane is a very common name in this realm. I've known five or six men in my lifetime who bore that name. Sit down and calm yourself. What a fool you're being."

Sigurd sat down, covering his face with his hands to hide his shame. He was shaking with a horrible fear. "I'm sorry, Bergthor, terribly sorry to have been so rude, but it was a— a shock when you said that name. I owe you an explanation, painful as it is to me. You see, I killed a man named—of that name—just lately, more by accident than anything else. You must understand what a jolt it gave me to hear you say—well, never mind. I think I'd like to walk around a bit before we open that box. Maybe you could use another hand in nailing the shoes to those eight gray horses."

Bergthor scratched his chin ruefully. "That I certainly could, but I don't know if it's good manners to ask a guest to risk his life and limbs with those stallions. Whenever they come in to be shod, I wonder if I'll get my brains kicked out."

Sigurd stood up resolutely. "That sounds like exactly what I need. Rolfr, are you going to join the fun?"

Rolfr looked white, and his eyes were staring. With a shake of his head, he broke whatever trance he had slipped into and said, "Why not?" He stumbled along to the forge, and he and Sigurd did not speak to each other for the rest of the night. When the horses were finally shod, they were glad to fall into the beds which Bergthor indicated. Sigurd fell asleep, too exhausted even for nightmares.

In the morning, he awoke with the knowledge that the box had to be opened, and the dread of it almost choked him. When he joined the others beside the fire in Bergthor's main room, another unpleasant surprise was awaiting him. Bjarnhardr's sword lay on the table. "I found it where you had left it beside your door last night," Bergthor told him. "You shouldn't be so careless of such a finely crafted blade. I'd keep it in its sheath if I were you."

Sigurd only nodded dumbly, staring at the bright metal of the sword, twinkling at him mockingly in the firelight. He had little appetite for the breakfast which Bergthor's housekeeper prepared for them. He looked at the carven box reposing in a place of honor on a shelf and wished he had never found it in Thorarna's trunk.

After breakfasting on several more pots of ale, the woodcutter went out to unload his cart. Sigurd offered to help him, but the woodcutter only stared at him and said that no one laid a hand on his firewood except himself, since not every fool could unload a cart, and away he stalked in high dudgeon, shaking his head and muttering.

"I've changed my mind," Sigurd said, when Bergthor lifted the box down. "I don't want to know what's inside it."

Jotull darted him a venomous glance. "Don't be a simpleton,

Sigurd. You have to open it now. I haven't spent all my time coaxing you along and strengthening your will just to have you go sour on me at the last moment. You will open that box and you will accept whatever you find inside. I'm afraid I over-estimated you, and you're going to disappoint me. It hasn't been easy to get you this far, Sigurd, and you've a long way before you, but as long as you listen to me I can promise you'll prosper. If you don't do as you are bidden, you'll be cast aside. We'll provide for you as long as you conduct yourself according to our plans. I shall show you what happens to those who get in the way." He took a small parcel from his satchel and un-wrapped the cloth covering. Sigurd shrank back as the wizard placed a dead bird before him—it was a sparrow hawk, with its eyes sunken and its claws shriveled.

"Adills!" Rolfr gasped in a muffled voice. "Then you did kill him, just as I suspected!"

Jotull nodded, his eyes watching Sigurd with a hard, bright stare. "Yes, I killed Adills. This isn't an innocent game you've become involved in by bringing that box here, and Adills isn't the first or last to die because of it. We've been searching for it for more years than you've existed. When we found it, we wasted no time on sentiment and softness. You saw what hap-pened to Thongullsfjord; Bjarnhardr and I would kill a thousand more for the contents of that box. To think—all these years when we were searching for it, all that stood between us and it was one old woman and a brat of a boy. Take another look at old Adills, and see if there are still doubts in your mind about whom to obey."

Sigurd shoved the dead bird away angrily without looking at it. "So this is what we've come to, Jotull. You haven't befriended me for friendship's sake. All you've wanted is to get control of whatever is inside this box. You know what it is, don't you?"

Jotull no longer attempted to keep his features arranged pleasantly. "Of course I do, you fool," he snapped. "Now before we open the box, I demand that you swear an oath of fealty to me to ensure your future obedience, or your life will be forfeit."

"I won't do it," Sigurd retorted, putting a hand on his axe. "Why should I give up my freedom to you and Bjarnhardr, when the box and its contents are no one's but mine? Bergthor, we're not going to open that box as long as Jotull is in Svartafell. He's no friend of mine, and never was." He glared at Jotull with the white-hot anger of one betrayed.

Bergthor clutched the box under one massive arm and looked at his guests in consternation. "Now, let's speak a little more calmly, my friends," he said. "This talk of killings and swearings and threatenings is serious. It seems to me that the young man does indeed have the best claim to the box, and you, wizard, are attempting to seize what you have no right to, despite all the years you've spent coveting it. I don't like to see a fellow being badgered in my own home, especially by someone who claims comradeship with Bjarnhardr. I'm afraid my hospitality is no longer offered to such a one as you, Jotull, if you persist in threatening Sigurd."

Jotull transferred his haughty glare to Bergthor. "What do I care for your hospitality or you?" he answered with a sneer. "You'll do as I tell you, or there won't be another horse shod in Svartafell. This dispute is between Sigurd and me, and we don't want your clumsy interference. Get yourself busy finding a key to that lock or make one or smash the lid in. I don't care how you do it, but you must open that box immediately."

Bergthor placed the box on the shelf again and folded his arms with a sinister smile. "A smith of the Dvergar has no need to fear a wizard of the Dokkalfar, even though you once were Ljosalfar. I have heard the story of your treachery to Halfdane of Hrafnborg. There is no place in my sympathy for such a murderer as you."

Jotull raised one eyebrow and looked at Mikla and Rolfr. "Which one of them told you? One of them is going to die for this."

Mikla declared promptly, "I told him. I've waited a long time to avenge myself, Jotull. I knew from the first day you arrived in Hrafnborg that you were Dokkalfar in your heart."

"Rolfr, get the men from the forge," Bergthor commanded, taking the hammer from his belt. "We'll take this spy to trial for his crimes, and it will be a bright day for the memory of Snowfell when we hang him and stake his carcass in the bog."

Jotull stood up, staff in hand, with an incredulous smile. "You can't think you can be more powerful than a full wizard of the Dokkalfar? I may as well warn you that being a traitor has distinct advantages. I know the spells of both Alfar, and neither the sun nor dark earth hold any terrors for me. If your sooty dwarves lay their hands upon me, I shall instantly kill them." He conjured a blue plume of flame at the end of his staff and waved it contemptuously under Bergthor's nose, almost close enough to burn his beard.

Bergthor raised his hammer and struck at the staff, causing an explosion of hot, red sparks and an impact that made Jotull stagger. A fiery halo surrounded the smith's hammer and the mighty arm that wielded it. Bergthor advanced a step, motioning Rolfr to conduct his errand. "You must have forgotten, wizard," he rumbled in a voice of menace, "the smiths of the Dvergar are the priests of Thor. I am the master smith and I have three other smiths besides three apprentice smiths. There are other arts which we practice besides the hammering of iron." He reached out his hand, and suddenly it appeared to be full of cherry-red coals, with orange and blue flames lapping through his fingers. "Sit down, wizard, and put your staff on the table where we can watch it."

Jotull hesitated, measuring Bergthor's potential powers of destruction against his own. With no abatement of his scorn and pride, he sat down and laid his staff across the table, a choice influenced perhaps by the arrival of the other six smiths armed with their hammers.

"Dyri, we'll need a chain capable of holding a wizard," Bergthor said. "A chain with powers. Have you got one that will do the job?"

Dyri snorted into his scorched red beard. "Have I got a chain to hold a wizard? I've got one that will hold the Fenrir-Ulf, if I was of a mind to go a-hunting wolves." He stalked away to fetch it from the forge, and Jotull glowered haughtily at Bergthor.

"You needn't think this will stop Bjarnhardr from getting

that box," he snarled. "And you, Sigurd, you've still got Hross-Bjorn following you, and you've still got two murders to commit with that sword. It won't leave you alone until you do what you know you must. If you want to be rid of the sending and the curse, order Bergthor to get rid of these hulking idiots and proceed immediately with opening the box."

Sigurd shook his head. "I know what you are, Jotull. I'll never trust you again."

Rolfr and Mikla nodded at him, their eyes alight with encouragement, and Mikla heaved a great sigh of relief. "I thought he'd never open his eyes," he whispered to Rolfr.

Suddenly they all heard Dyri give a shout from the forge and the sound of running feet, followed by scuffling outside the door. It burst open before anybody could reach it to see what the trouble was. A fence of Dokkalfar swords surged into the room. The smiths met them with a battery of hammer blows; but at a shout from Bergthor, they left off and retreated.

"Before we fight, I want to find out who we're fighting and what for," Bergthor thundered, striding into the center of the room, his hammer held aloft and flaming. The Dokkalfar at the door shrank back and presented the sharp tips of their swords. "Who are you? What business do you have here?"

They glowered at him from under their helmets and backed away until a solitary figure stood between them and Bergthor. With a stumping gait, the figure advanced a few steps until the gleaming of Bergthor's torch illuminated his features.

"It's Bjarnhardr!" Sigurd exclaimed, covering his dismay by adding, "The berserkr!"

Bjarnhardr turned his menacing smile upon Sigurd. "Is it you, Sigurd? I might have known you'd be the first to know me. What's the cause of this conflict? What are these great fellows doing in here looking so grim and evil, when they ought to be working?"

Jotull leaped up. "I'll be glad to explain! They were holding me prisoner and they had the presumption to think they could put me on trial for treachery to Halfdane. Sigurd refuses to assist us and won't let Bergthor open the box. If you hadn't been so slow in getting here, we might have avoided any bloodshed, but right now I don't see how we can avoid killing the lot of them. It would save us a great deal of trouble later." He bent a cold, gloating gaze upon Sigurd, Rolfr, and Mikla.

Bergthor shook his head like an angry bear. "If you harm any of them, I'll see to it that no one ever opens that box without being struck by curses and plagues that will lay the lands barren for a hundred years."

"No, no, there's no need for that," Bjarnhardr said anxiously, pegging closer to Bergthor. "Now sit down here and let's discuss this like rational men. Let me explain to you why you must open this box for us—"

"I won't open it for anybody but Sigurd," Bergthor declared, folding his arms and looking away from Bjarnhardr, but still holding his hammer in one fist.

"Come now, surely you realize Sigurd is nothing in this game," Bjarnhardr pursued. "He's as good as lost right now, and you will be, too, if you don't follow the rule—which is that the least powerful had better submit to the wishes of the most powerful if they want to continue surviving. Not only you are in question here, but these other smiths. Think what a wealth of knowledge and power will be wasted when they die."

"They won't die in vain. The least I can do is smash your skull before I die," Bergthor replied placidly. "That would leave Jotull in command at Svinhagahall, if he escapes, or some lesser churl if he doesn't. We may as well as die and leave the curse of this carved box to the next person who finds it."

"Is that what you're resolved upon?" Bjarnhardr inquired. "A senseless slaughter, with none of us profiting and all of us losing?"

"If you lose, then I profit," Bergthor growled, swinging his hammer lightly. "The realm will be well rid of vermin such as you, and I suppose there are more smiths to take my place in Svartafell."

Bjarnhardr shook his head. "You aren't following the rules, my dear fellow. In this sort of game, we are supposed to compromise to reach an agreement. Suppose I were to pay you in gold to open that box? What would you say to that?"

"I would say it's Sigurd's box, and you'd better pay him your gold if you're so anxious to get rid of it," the smith replied.

Bjarnhardr turned his fox's grin on Sigurd. "Well, old friend, surely you realize you've lost everything by now anyway, so why don't you cease to be a complication and order that box opened? It might save your life. I wouldn't object to letting you live, as long as you keep out of Jotull's way. Surely you realize there's no sense in resisting any longer, don't you? Weren't we always good friends, Sigurd? Trust me once more when I tell you to open that box for us, and I'll see to it you come to no harm." He smiled with easy confidence and cast a sly wink in Jotull's direction.

Sigurd stood still, hesitating. He looked at the stricken faces of Mikla and Rolfr, who waited anxiously for his answer. "Before I say yes or no," he began slowly, looking intently at Bjarnhardr, "I want to know something more about the history of this box, Bjarnhardr. What do you know about it—without telling me what is inside?"

Bjarnhardr shrugged. "It's a commonplace history, but I'll tell you about it for the sake of wasting time so you can make up your mind. It was made by this same scowling Bergthor for a very famous warlord who had the misfortune to marry a Scipling woman, whose beauty must have charmed his natural caution, or he might have known what a weakness she would be to him. For her sake, he gave up much of his fighting against his enemies, such as I undeniably represent. She even took from him half of his powers and locked them away in a little box as a surety he would give up warfare as an occupation.

"Strangely enough, he agreed that he would hold and defend what he had, instead of conquesting for more of the fallen kingdom of Snowfell. This was noble of him, but rather foolish. One evening while he was gone from home, a band of Dokkalfar attacked his home fort and burned it to the ground with every person inside—no, not quite every person.

"The lady's mother, a veritable witch in her own right, had made nothing but trouble for the pair since they were married, and it was later said that she escaped from the flames with the warlord's infant son and the box—very sensible of her to save them, but infinitely troublesome for us, since she promptly returned to the Scipling realm and lost herself for more than twenty years. However, we found her again last year. There now, is that enough dull history for you, or would you like me to continue? The warlord's story has a most amusing ending."

As Bjarnhardr talked, Sigurd was hot and cold by turns with the realization of how the words applied to him. He covertly clutched the edge of the table with hands to resist the impulses that threatened to overwhelm him. "No, that's enough. Bergthor, I want you to open the box now."

Bergthor's black brows crawled incredulously. "Now? With these wolves waiting to grab your birthright away from you the instant they see it?"

Sigurd darted a glance at Rolfr and Mikla, who stared at him in silent appeal and mute despair. "Yes, Bergthor, I'm ready to deal with them upon the terms they know best. Do as I ask you, please?"

Jotull and Bjarnhardr exchanged a triumphant wink, and all the Dokkalfar watching relaxed their grim expressions and leaned on their swords as if they no longer expected to use them at any instant. Bergthor gazed at Sigurd in uncomprehending anguish, then slowly lifted the box off the shelf and put it on the table, every movement betraying his deep disappointment and sorrow. With a reproachful glance at Sigurd, he delved into the pouch hanging at his belt for a massive ring of keys, which he examined one by one. The keys were flat bits of metal with two holes punched to correspond with the locking mechanism inside the box. Finally he found one and tried it, but it did not work the lock. His large, skillful fingers moved as slowly and clumsily as he dared, with Jotull and Bjarnhardr leaning over his shoulders to watch impatiently.

At last, he could no longer avoid finding a key that fitted. He slipped the key in place and pushed it to the other end of the lock slot with a significant clicking of the mechanism inside. Without touching the lid, he pushed the box across the table to Sigurd, even as Bjarnhardr made a grab for it. Sigurd put his hands on it protectively and stared back at Bjarnhardr and Jotull.

"There's only one more detail in your story, Bjarnhardr," he said. "What was the name of this unlucky warlord whose wife and home you wantonly destroyed?"

Bjarnhardr grinned and drew back in mock surprise. "Why, haven't you guessed it yet? It was Halfdane of Hrafnborg, your own father, and you killed him with your own hand!"

Some of those in the room stood stock-still in astonishment, then turned to their neighbors to exclaim over it. In that moment, Sigurd opened the box, snatched out the contents, and hurled himself across the room to the shelf where he had placed Bjarnhardr's sword. His chest was so tight he could scarcely breathe as he drew on the black gauntlet, the mate to the one Halfdane had carried under his belt and used to confound Jotull and Hross-Bjorn. In an instant, he felt its power; when he grasped the cursed sword, the effect was like putting red-hot metal into water.

With a yell that bespoke all his years of yearning for a father and a name, he leaped across the table straight into an icy blast of Jotull's that shattered around him like arrows glancing off armor. Not at all deterred by the blast, Sigurd's next leap carried him face to face with the astonished Jotull, whose last word was the beginning of the escape spell, and whose last glimpse was of Halfdane's long-missing gauntlet grasping the sword that was dripping with his own blood. Mortally wounded, Jotull fell against Bjarnhardr.

Bjarnhardr scrabbled desperately to get away from Jotull's limp weight before Sigurd could reach him. The stunned Dokkalfar churned forward, but the smiths halted them with hammers and fire. Sigurd chopped at Bjarnhardr as he scuttled for the protection of his Dokkalfar, who seized their warlord and ran from the awful sword and gauntlet that scythed down anyone foolish enough to linger in its path. The few brave Dokkalfar who attempted to withstand Sigurd's wrath delayed him long enough that Bjarnhardr and the others reached their horses and fled into the night, badly reduced in number and totally stripped of pride.

Sigurd would have taken one of the gray stallions and raced after them, but Bergthor gave orders to close the outer doors.

"Let the cowards go for now, Sigurd. You'll know where to find Bjarnhardr when you want him. There's not enough of us to pursue them, and they could hurt you with a spell. Come now, you got Jotull; that should be a comfort to you."

Sigurd slid down from the back of the gray stallion, still holding the sword, which had fulfilled its curse of three murders several times over. He strode to the forge where the coals still burned hot and red beneath the ash. Thrusting the sword into the coals, he beckoned to one of the apprentices to apply himself to the bellows. Then he turned to a puzzled and aghast Bergthor and said, "There is no comfort. I killed my own father with that sword."

Bergthor gazed at him in great sorrow, but could find nothing to say. Rolfr and Mikla likewise were silent, pitying Sigurd in the horror of his situation.

"Melt the sword down," Sigurd commanded in a strained but steady voice. "Make sure that no piece of it will ever find its way into human hands again, or bad luck is sure to follow whoever tries to use it."

Bergthor nodded. "I know of a deep fissure that reaches the fires and molten stone of Muspellheim. No one will ever reclaim the metal if I drop it down there."

Sigurd nodded rather vacantly, looking at the gauntlet still on his hand and suddenly feeling hollow without his terrible anger and despair. He began to experience a different sort of anger, which was directed against himself. Slowly he removed the gauntlet and tossed it on Bergthor's cluttered workbench, too drained of strength even to watch as his slain enemies were hauled away. He slumped on a low stool and watched dully as the sword was heated and bent and hammered into a shapeless lump by Bergthor's capable hands.

"Tomorrow I'll take it to the fissure and dispose of it properly," Bergthor said, looking sweaty and much more cheerful. "Nothing like a good bit of work to soothe one's spirits. I'm ready for food and drink; how about you, Rolfr? Mikla? Sigurd?"

Rolfr and Mikla promptly agreed, but Sigurd shook his head.

"You fellows go on ahead. I just want to sit here and stare at the coals in the forge for a while. Then I think I'll go to bed."

"Aye, it's getting late," Bergthor agreed. "I wouldn't mind sitting by the forge for a while myself. I've always thought it was a good place to be after a day's work, sitting beside the anvil and watching the coals glowing in the dark. I'll have the housekeeper fetch us our supper and we'll eat it right here."

Sigurd only shrugged without looking at him. Rolfr and Mikla ate their supper, and the soothing warmth of the forge soon put an end to their desultory conversation and sent them to sleep. Presently Bergthor too nodded and dozed, finally succumbing to sleep after a long battle to stay awake. He slept heavily, dreaming wretched dreams, and suddenly awakened when a cool draft touched him. He started awake with a snort and glanced around suspiciously, thinking perhaps a bad dream had awakened him. Then he leaped to his feet and shook Rolfr and Mikla awake.

"Get up and get ready to go out," he commanded, and bestirred an apprentice or two for good measure. "Sigurd's gone, leaving his box and gauntlet behind."

# Chapter 18

◇◆◇◆◇◆◇◆◇◆◇◆◇◆◇◆◇◆◇◆◇◆◇◆◇◆◇◆

Sigurd's first idea was to find Hross-Bjorn and let him finish the task Bjarnhardr had him created for. He found the sending easily enough, once he had left the safety of Svartafell's forge, but Sigurd's own natural power rebuffed the attacks of Hross-Bjorn. The creature had learned caution, and the precipitous withdrawal of Bjarnhardr and his Dokkalfar seemed to have further alarmed Hross-Bjorn. After a few rushing charges, which were more for effect than for real intent to do any murdering, the sending retreated to a watchful distance. Hross-Bjorn kept his distance throughout the following days of Sigurd's wanderings, but never allowed the man to escape his surveillance, hoping perhaps for an opening when Sigurd's natural power was weak or off guard.

Suspecting that his well-meaning friends would search for him, Sigurd sought out the most isolated and dangerous region of the Dvergarrige to lose himself in. By day he skulked in pursuit of small game, after discovering to his disgust that he even lacked the will to starve himself to death, and by night he discouraged the predations of hungry trolls. By the time winter returned, he was almost as wild and fierce as the trolls who stalked him—no longer for food, but as a rival.

By Midwinter Sigurd had allowed his desire for mere survival to supercede his self-hatred for killing Halfdane. Food was scarce in the harsh fells, so the trolls moved their hunting grounds nearer the Dokkalfar settlements in the lowlands. Sigurd followed, knowing his survival depended upon attacking the trolls and stealing their stolen booty from them. Sigurd felt no remorse at eating the mutton of the Dokkalfar farmers who had turned him and his companions away when he had first passed their way.

The trolls feared him with almost supernatual awe, a feeling which the furious demonstrations of Hross-Bjorn certainly fostered, particularly when the sending had the good fortune to get his teeth into the hides of several trolls. After killing perhaps a dozen of them, Hross-Bjorn earned for himself the status of a virtual deity of destruction, a principle much appreciated by the trolls, despite the fact that they were the ones who suffered.

When the crisis of the dark, hungry winter was at its apex, and the easiest prey had been taken and eaten long ago, Sigurd and the trolls began to experience the desperation of imminent starvation. With food scarce and wild game nonexistent, the trolls stalked Sigurd. The ensuing battles provided both stalkers and prey with an abundance of roast troll, a tough but hearty fare which promised to last until winter's end, as long as Sigurd was able to defend himself with Halfdane's axe and Hross-

Bjorn had teeth and hooves to batter the attackers into lifeless lumps.

Thus it was that Sigurd finally managed to kill the leader of the trolls, a huge, shaggy beast with both ears chewed off and one eye missing from a recent confrontation with Hross-Bjorn. Sigurd had need for a good warm cloak, so he thriftily skinned the troll leader and slung the hide over his shoulders while the remainder of the trolls watched him from a respectful distance. Backing warily into a cleft in the rocks, Sigurd watched the trolls industriously carve their fallen leader into steaks and chops for roasting, wasting nearly as much as they salvaged. After the fire was built and the meat more or less cooked, Sigurd was astonished when the trolls made offers of peace to him, along with a sizable hunk of roast meat, which was as tough and flavorless as Sigurd had suspected it would be. The numbers of the troll band had decreased to the point where even they realized that something else would have to be done if any of them were to survive until spring. What they wanted was a clever leader to help them prey upon the Dokkalfar of the lowlands. After a moment's consideration, Sigurd agreed to be their new leader.

For the rest of the long winter, Sigurd and the trolls ruled the lowlands with a reign of terror, sparing only the farms of the rebellious Ljosalfar. The trolls grew fat and gathered many recruits, and Sigurd took increasing satisfaction from tormenting the Dokkalfar. He thought of Bjarnhardr in Svinghagahall with increasing frequency, and began to wonder if he could move his troll band westward next winter.

The Dokkalfar did not submit gracefully to being plundered. They set traps and organized massive hunting parties. Word spread of a man who ruled the trolls, which gave rise to all manner of dreadful and totally false legends about him. A reward was posted for his capture by Bjarnhardr himself, which was not nearly as effective as the threats which soon followed if the troll-man were not captured without further delay.

The increased vigilance of the Dokkalfar might have been an inconvenience, but the winter was drawing to an end and the fells were again alive with natural game to sustain the trolls between attacks on the settlements. Sigurd planned carefully and managed to attack when most of the Dokkalfar were hunting for him elsewhere and thus unable to defend their sheep and cattle.

His luck came to an abrupt end one spring night, however, when his band ran unexpectedly into a group of troll hunters lying in ambush in the cliffs above the trolls' habitual path. In the following barrage of arrows and spears, Sigurd was wounded in the leg with an arrow. He couldn't keep up with the retreating trolls, who abandoned him without much regret in true troll fashion when they discovered his efficiency impaired, and the magic of his unassailable leadership vanished almost instantly.

Left alone, Sigurd tied up his wound with the remains of his very ragged shirt and hobbled down the ravine away from his pursuers as fast as he was able to go. During the day, he hid by a small waterfall and rested. While he lay there, he let his thoughts travel backward over his past follies and acquaintances, wondering if this would finally be the end which he had once so much sought. Hross-Bjorn hovered nearby, watching and waiting with unflagging patience while Sigurd grew weaker. Sigurd eyed the sending, thinking of Bjarnhardr and the revenge he ought to have taken upon him. Sadly he thought of Rolfr and Mikla, wishing that he had realized from the beginning that they were his true friends, not Jotull and Bjarnhardr. With even more bitter regret, he thought of his father, Halfdane, and of Ragnhild, forever removed from him now because of his stupid, blind pride. It seemed to him as he lay helplessly bleeding to death among the unforgiving boulders of the ravine that he had betrayed every person he ought to have trusted and he had allowed his enemies to flatter and deceive him with ridiculous ease. Dying miserably like a wounded troll would be a fitting end for him, particularly if the vengeful Dokkalfar were lucky enough to find him still alive.

By nightfall, his condition was much worse and he was scarcely conscious, imagining himself back at Hrafnborg or in his grandmother's house at Thongullsfjord. Instead of his grandmother, however, the person he imagined beside him was Ragnhild. He had kept the bowstring made from her hair, the ring she had given him, and the red jewel, thinking many times that he ought to have thrown them away. As he lapsed in and out of consciousness, he thought he saw Ragnhild bending over him, but her face always seemed to change into a troll's face. Then he thought his enemies must have found him and were carrying him away to his doom, slung like a half-empty sack over the back of a shaggy horse, jogging and jouncing over the stones in the ravine. The last thing he remembered thinking was what peculiar feet the horse possessed, large and hairy, with great black toenails instead of hooves.

When he finally awakened, he was astonished to realize that he felt as if he might live after all. The next thought uppermost in his mind was to see where he was and who had carried him there. By the light of a low fire, he saw dozens of small, laughing faces peering at him from the shadows, and they gave him a great fright until he realized that they were only carvings of little creatures made of wood or stone. A memory struggled for recognition in the depths of his weary brain.

Then he saw an old heap of motley skins shift itself slightly. A long, stringy arm reached out to stir the contents of a black kettle hanging over the fire. A troll, Sigurd told himself with surprise, wondering if his troll band had decided to return for him after all. But his trolls had possessed no snug shelter with a hearth and shelves hewn into the stone, and certainly not a fine bed such as he was lying in, with carved pillars at the four corners and coarse clean linen.

"Grisnir!" He fell back, relieved and exhausted after solving the puzzle, and closed his eyes with a sigh of almost contentment.

Grisnir shuffled near the bed and laid one furry paw on Sigurd's brow. "The fever's gone," he rumbled. "And you recognized me for the first time. It looks as if that poisoned Dokkalfar arrow isn't going to do its evil work, after all."

Sigurd opened his eyes and couldn't help returning the old troll's fearsome, grimacing grin of delight. Nothing could be quite as ugly or as welcome as Grisnir's battered countenance with almost every tooth bared in pleasure.

"Grisnir. I must be dreaming you," Sigurd said, wishing he didn't feel like such a weakling. "How's the leg?"

"Crooked and gimpy and aches like a bear's got his teeth in it when the weather's wet," Grisnir replied promptly, "but I'm not complaining. At least I'm still alive and able to repay you your debt for saving this old troll. Now it's my turn to be doing the good deed for you, and what a pleasure it is! It seems that old ravine is a bad place for legs, at times," he added, as a gentle hint that he would like to know more about how Sigurd came to be wounded.

Sigurd's brief happiness faded. "Perhaps it's no favor you're doing me, or anyone else, Grisnir. If the valley people ever found out that you preserved the life of the hated troll-man, they'd hunt you out and nail that old hide of yours to a barn."

Grisnir only grinned the wider and rubbed his hands together. "Then you're the troll-man who has caused so much havoc among the Dokkalfar? Nothing could delight me more!"

"Let me finish. I became a troll because of a horror, one which I'll never forgive myself for as long as I live. It is a fearful burden. I killed my own father. I was used like a mindless tool by his enemies. When I die, I won't be sorry for myself and I don't think anyone else will be sorry, either." He stared at the ceiling of the cave, not wanting to see Grisnir's joy turn to scorn.

Grisnir said nothing for a while, digging into his ear with one thick finger. "I hear voices from time to time," he muttered in irritation. "Voices took me to you the night I found you in the ravine, and they've plagued me ever since. There's a Mikla, and a Rolfr, and a Ragnhild who are calling for you. Are they enemies of yours, Sigurd? If they are, all you have to do is command me to defend you, and I'll perish in the attempt. Indeed, you have done a tragic thing, but I won't turn my back. The sorrow is mostly yours, so I don't wish to add to it. You can stay here with me as long as you wish—forever, if you like."

Sigurd did not doubt his sincerity. "Grisnir, I'm nothing but a burden to you. I'm a burden to myself, so how can you be so kind?"

Grisnir shrugged and cast his eyes upward to think a moment. "A part of my heart will belong to you as long as you live, and there's nothing much you can do to shake my friendship for you. Would you like for me to get rid of these three people who are calling for you? I can, if you wish it."

Sigurd closed his eyes again, exhausted. "No, Grisnir, they're my friends, too. True friends, like you. I still think I wish all of you would allow me to go my way and be a troll or die— or whatever hard fate I deserve."

Grisnir shook himself. "No, no, we can't permit that. I see you are tired now, so I recommend you go to sleep. It will take your other friends a while to find you here, and you'll have to be strong and well by the time they get here."

Sigurd relaxed willingly. "I want to stay here, Grisnir. I don't want to go back with them."

"Not just yet, no," Grisnir replied soothingly, and tiptoed back to the pot of broth simmering over the fire.

The last days of winter passed, and it was well into spring before Sigurd felt that his strength had returned. His wood carvings, which had occupied him so well during his convalescence, lost much of their charm after the sun returned to the land. He knew he had to take care to avoid being seen by anyone who still harbored a grudge against the troll-man, but he couldn't resist being outside the dark cave on a warm, bright day.

"My old cave is getting a little small for you," Grisnir noted, with a sage wrinkling of his large forehead. "It won't be long until your friends hear you sending for them."

Sigurd shook his head, still anxious. "No, I don't see how I can ever face them again," he said, but in his heart he knew he wanted something more than hiding in a troll cave for the rest of his life.

"I saw another friend of yours last night," Grisnir went on thoughtfully. "That sending Bjarnhardr and Jotull put on you knows you're still alive, and he's waiting for you. Someday you're going to have to do something about him, Sigurd."

"I know, I know," Sigurd muttered. "Do you really want

to get rid of me so badly, Grisnir? I know you're used to being alone—"

Grisnir interrupted with a huge snort. "Get rid of you, indeed! I said you may stay forever, if you wish it. But I can plainly see that you're beginning to look around, and you know you've got more important things to do before you salt yourself away to hide."

Sigurd sighed, then smiled wryly. He gave the old troll a couple of hearty thumps on the back and said, "Yes, I know you're going to say it will be good for me and I'll be happier in the long run, and all you really want is for me to be satisfied."

"Why, how did you know? You took my very words!"

"Maybe my powers are becoming more acute," Sigurd said, "but one doesn't share a cave with a troll without coming to a very strong acquaintance."

Grisnir had instructed Sigurd in the use of his natural powers during the winter, and by spring Sigurd could do things by the power of his mind that would have amazed him a year earlier. With more instruction, Grisnir assured him, he would be as Alfar as any Alfar born, thanks to his excellent heritage of innate powers from his father Halfdane. He knew how to summon Mikla and Rolfr, after Grisnir had taught him to listen for them calling him. To his surprise, he heard Ragnhild more frequently, particularly when he concentrated on her ring and her bowstring, and it was to her he sent his first call through the vast uncharted spheres of the mind's magic. Then he called for Mikla and Rolfr, whose signal was stronger and often mingled with an unfamiliar one which might have been the smith Bergthor, still searching for him.

"They're coming," Grisnir announced one evening as they sat watching the shadows descending the surrounding fells.

"Yes, I feel it, too," Sigurd answered, with more gladness and excitement than he had anticipated.

"I wonder if Hross-Bjorn will be as glad to see them," Grisnir said slyly. "I suspect they'll bring his doom with them."

For a moment, they both studied the sending, which occupied a hilltop considerably out of the reach of Sigurd's power. Hross-Bjorn no longer caracoled in ecstasies of arrogance and power. He lurked around Grisnirsfell, lean and deadly, waiting to play his tricks when he thought he saw an opening. While Sigurd was ill, the sending had tried to get into the cave through a variety of disguises which hadn't fooled Grisnir for an instant. Hross-Bjorn no longer wasted his energy in useless displays of fury; he concentrated on ways to get to Sigurd. Sometimes he changed his form to several wolves or other dangerous predators, but of late he had shifted his tactics to more devious schemes. Once he slipped under the door, disguised as a shaft of straw, but Sigurd swiftly tossed him into the fire, where he roared up the chimney with a deafening howl of wind. The sending changed himself into a furious storm, which caught Sigurd a mile from the cave and kept him under a rock for several hours until he discovered how to rebuff the sending with his own powers. It was no wonder that Hross-Bjorn began to be frustrated and so desperate that he restorted to tricks, which Sigurd and Grisnir only laughed at.

The sending did its best to thwart the arrival of Mikla and Rolfr, causing rains and floods and blizzards of snow, but finally the travelers arrived with a great thundering at the door. Sigurd hurried to open it, and they fell inside laughing and half-killing him with buffets, bear hugs, and punches to assure themselves he was truly alive and not an illusion. Grisnir closed the door against the driving blizzard, adding his admonitions to get out of their unhealthy wet cloaks and boots and to sit down by the fire while their dinner cooked.

When the uproar subsided somewhat, Rolfr exclaimed, "Sigurd, I can hardly believe it's you. There are two streaks of gray in your beard, just like an old man, and you've got a limp. What have you done to age yourself so dramatically almost overnight?"

"It was a long, hard winter," Sigurd replied with a smile, thinking how Rolfr would stare when he told him about living with the trolls.

"Well, the hard times are over," Mikla declared with all of his customary earnestness and desire to be perfectly understood. "Nobody blames you for what happened at Svinhagahall. You had no control over those events. If you were to explain it completely to the men of Hrafnborg, they would forgive you and cherish an even greater hatred for Bjarnhardr. You must come back to the place where you belong, Sigurd, instead of hiding your shame among strangers."

He seemed prepared to argue, but Sigurd surprised him by saying, "You're quite right, of course, Mikla. You always were right in your judgments. I've been thinking for a long time that I ought to face the men of Hrafnborg and take what censure they decide to deal out. But first, there's a thing I have to do. Did you bring me my box and the gauntlet inside, Rolfr?"

Rolfr's eyes began to sparkle. "I certainly did. Are you going to claim the gauntlet, Sigurd?"

Sigurd let his eyes rest upon the box as Rolfr pulled it from his saddle pouch. "I shall be its humble servant and allow it to use me for whatever good I can do with it. It seems almost too much to hope that they might want me back at Hrafnborg, but I have an idea that might win them over. Tomorrow night, if it is fair, I'll begin the final working out of my revenge upon Bjarnhardr."

The following night was peaceful and overcast with silver clouds reflecting the starlight in a soft glow that made it perfectly easy to see. Sigurd drew the gauntlet from his belt and put it on as Hross-Bjorn greeted them with a contemptous snort from his perch among the rocks above Grisnir's cave. Warning his friends to stay at a safe distance, Sigurd chose a level space on the other side of the ravine while Hross-Bjorn watched with interest, uttering a growl of suspicion.

"Hross-Bjorn, I challenge you and your creators to honorable battle," Sigurd called. "You're a cowardly, craven beast, and Bjarnhardr's another. If you have any regard for yourself or your name, you'll come down here and fight with me. Unless you do, I'll tell all of Skarpsey what a nithling you really are, that you're nothing but a heap of old bones and hide with three empty heads that make a great deal of noise, but there's no courage beneath it all. Come now, sending, surely you're not afraid of me, are you?"

Hross-Bjorn answered with a fiery snarl, raking his hooves on the flinty earth and shaking his heads until his manes writhed like snakes. Fire gleamed in his eyes and surrounded him like a pale nimbus. He reared aloft on his hind legs to answer Sigurd's challenges with roars and bellows and much clashing of his deadly fangs. Then he charged down the rocky slope at Sigurd, necks outstretched, teeth bared, and his hooves thundering with destructive fury. Just as it seemed Sigurd would be run down, Sigurd stepped aside and struck the sending in the middle on his back with a gloved fist.

"Bravo!" Rolfr shouted, as the sending rolled head over heels and lay gasping.

In an instant, Hross-Bjorn was on his feet again, as angry as before. After much preliminary pawing, tail-lashing, and similar displays meant to frighten his intended victim, Hross-Bjorn charged again. This time Sigurd struck the beast in the throat of the right-side head, which checked his rush so abruptly that the creature plowed along on his knees and ended up by flipping over in a somersault. If Sigurd had chosen to fight with his axe, he might have finished the sending then and there; but for the sake of fairness, he allowed Hross-Bjorn to get to his feet without further damage. Wheezing, the sending eyed his opponent and thoughtfully raked one hoof.

"He's contemplating a shape-shifting, Sigurd," Grisnir called worriedly. "Don't let him deceive you. Are you sure you don't want some help?"

"Quite sure," Sigurd replied, without removing his eyes from Hross-Bjorn. "Let him shift if he wants to, but he knows this gauntlet is more powerful than anything he can change to. Either fight or run away, Hross-Bjorn. But I shall find you one day and finish the job that I started tonight."

Hross-Bjorn shook his head and charged, halting at the last instant and changing himself to the lake monster Sigurd had seen at Hrafnborg. The creature towered above him, spitting poison and lashing a forest of tentacles. Sigurd snapped off one appendage that wrapped around his arm, then seized a long, snaky neck and began to twist it. The sending gave a screech, floundering to get away. Sigurd suddenly found himself twisting the neck of the sending's original shape, with the huge hooves pounding and slashing at him and the other two horse heads reaching over to bite him. Grimly, he maintained his hold and struck the nearest head a heavy blow between the eyes, which staggered the beast. Another smash on the other head's nose sent the creature to his knees, and Sigurd twisted the horse's neck until the head was halfway around and shrieking for mercy.

Mikla abandoned his safe post and dashed to Sigurd's side, tearing open his satchel. "I've still got the bridles!" he exclaimed, pulling a tangle of strange objects out of the satchel and beginning to fasten one of the bridles on the sending.

"Give them to me!" Sigurd puffed. "Get out of the way, Mikla, before you get hurt!" Hross-Bjorn began lunging and kicking.

"No, I'm all right." Mikla rubbed a kicked leg. "There's no sense wasting a perfectly willing assistant. There, it's on! Now for the others!"

The bridled head thrashed about desperately, but could do no harm. The instant Sigurd released it, the creature leaped to his feet, plunging and kicking like the gray stallions in Bergthor's forge, but Mikla held fast to the reins, despite the fact that he spent more time in midair than on the ground, with the sending's great hooves flailing around, trying to reach him. Sigurd gave the beast another thump on the back and yanked one of the back legs from under him when he staggered. Hross-Bjorn went over again in a heap of scrambling legs and threshing necks.

Sigurd pounced on the foremost head, which was bigger and more vicious than the side ones and also strong enough to throw him off his feet when he attempted to wrestle with it. Two sets of horribly snapping teeth came lunging at him, and the beast threw himself over on his side in an effort to roll over Sigurd and crush him. One set of teeth fastened itself suddenly on Sigurd's foot as he leaped to get away, but in an instant the beast released him with a frightful howl as Grisnir came hurtling from his doorstep to wrap himself around the sending's neck and sink his sharp yellow teeth into Hross-Bjorn's ear. Grisnir's reward for his efforts was a severe pounding as the sending tried to dislodge him.

Sigurd calmed the beast with a terrific blow between the ears of the foremost head. The beast reared back on his haunches, maddened and desperate, and Sigurd clung to the thick neck with his hand clamped over the beast's nostrils. Gasping for air, Hross-Bjorn opened his mouth, and Mikla thrust in the bit and swiftly fastened the bridle on the foremost head. Not to be left out, Rolfr rushed forward to seize the reins. Much subdued, groaning, Hross-Bjorn made very little struggle as the third bridle was buckled into his last free muzzle, which was considerably battered from pounding Grisnir on the ground. The troll, unharmed, removed his teeth from Hross-Bjorn's ear and untwined his arms from the beast's neck.

"Now we've got him," Grisnir declared, stepping back as the sending lurched to his tottering legs and stood with bridled heads trailing almost to the ground. "What shall we do with him?"

Mikla wrapped a set of reins around his fist, looking a bit wild and untidy from his struggles, but highly pleased. "He's going back to his master—Bjarnhardr—and he's taking a wonderful cargo with him. Sigurd, what curses do you want to inflict upon your old enemy? You name it and I can put Hross-Bjorn to it. How about a fire curse, or shall we let Hross-Bjorn follow Bjarnhardr and kill him, as he tried to do with you?"

Sigurd jerked at the bridle he held so he could look into the sending's lusterless eye. "No, that's not quite good enough for Bjarnhardr. Or the Dokkalfar who have infested the lowlands that once belonged to Snowfell. What I want is a plague, Mikla, that will move from Dokkalfar settlement to settlement, sparing none and leaving nothing behind but empty buildings and the barrows of the dead. Bjarnhardr will hear about its approach and he will flee, but the plague will follow him until there's not a Dokkalfar left aboveground on all of Skarpsey. The Ljosalfar shall be spared from the curse, and Snowfell will be rebuilt."

Rolfr gazed at Sigurd in awe. "That's wonderful, Siggi. That will be the end of our outlawry and exile. We won't need to hide in hill forts any longer."

"It will take time," Mikla said, after considering the plan

for a long moment. "When the plague starts moving westward, so will the Dokkalfar. We'll need to fortify ourselves against traveling bands of marauders, who will be hungry and desperate. We'll need powerful leaders." He and Rolfr looked toward Sigurd standing beside the huge, subdued beast.

Sigurd nodded, still studying Hross-Bjorn. "I would like to be there when Hross-Bjorn finally catches Bjarnhardr. I can't imagine Bjarnhardr dying with much grace or courage, and I foresee that he'll be all alone, since he's not one to inspire loyalty in his followers. A most wretched and lonely death will be his." He looked back at his companions, breaking off his reverie. "Well, Mikla, when shall you begin our plague curse?"

"At once, of course." Mikla opened his satchel to begin.

When he was done with his spells, which involved the collection of some strange and rather gruesome specimens, he built a small fire almost under the sagging noses of Hross-Bjorn and burned the little dried creatures, herbs, and bones, making marks in the earth and calling upon the powers of the earth to assist him. The smoke roiled around Hross-Bjorn's red-rimmed eyes, climbing thick and fast into the pallid night sky and making a smell like a thousand open barrow mounds. Hross-Bjorn began to moan and strain, tugging at the bridle reins until they could scarcely hold him down.

"Now, let him go," Mikla said at the end of a long chant, with a note of triumph in his voice. "Look, he's going, he's going!"

The sending rose into the air, a massive black shape that seemed to expand into a huge bank of cloud, towering and spreading across the sky until the silvery clouds were blanketed with menacing black. Slowly, the blackness traveled westward like a great pall falling over the face of the island.

"It's done," Sigurd said with satisfaction. "Now let's get back to Hrafnborg."

# Chapter 19

◈◈◈◈◈◈◈◈◈◈◈◈◈◈◈◈◈◈◈◈◈◈◈◈◈◈

They walked their tired horses for the last miles to Hrafnborg. The first watchman they encountered rode away at a wild gallop with the news of their return, notifying the next post, who would carry the word to the next watchman, and onward to the hill fort. They had heard about Sigurd's plague, which was filling the lowlands with its deadly pestilence already.

As they plodded wearily toward the last watch post, Sigurd almost wished he would never get there. He had taken suitable revenge upon Bjarnhardr and all the Dokkalfar for Halfdane's death, but there still could be someone who might not think it atonement enough, and that someone was Ragnhild. He dreaded meeting her, dreaded the scorn that she would always bestow upon him for his weakness. Even his possession of Halfdane's other gauntlet could not rectify the loss of Ragnhild's esteem.

"There's someone coming to meet us," Mikla reported, his manner brightening. "We're home, finally home."

The horseman approached at full gallop. Sigurd's heart knocked worriedly; the rider was clad in red, the color always worn by Ragnhild. In an instant he knew it must be Ragnhild, from the slight build and the long, fair hair flying behind her.

She halted the horse with a skidding plunge, leaping to the ground and almost falling in her haste. Sigurd quickly dismounted, thinking she was probably going to run at him with a knife in her hand, and he would have a better chance of defending himself on the ground. He would get a good grip on her until her fury subsided a bit, and then he would turn her over to Mikla and make his escape. For a brief moment,

271

he thought it would have been better to have stayed away than to return to see her hatred.

She came stumbling and running over the bristly fellside, laughing, much to his astonishment. Sigurd could see no knife in her hand, and her face was brimming with welcome. He took a few wary steps forward, still not trusting her entirely, and she plummeted into his arms, like a hawk buffeting the wind out of its quarry. Her arms locked around his neck; he felt her tearstained cheek against his face. This was welcome, he realized with a searing stab of humility, and he clasped Ragnhild gratefully in his arms.

"I never expected this," he said, as she wiped her eyes on his frayed cloak, still half laughing and half crying.

"Look at you, you're nothing but tatters," she said, with a last sob in her throat, followed by a delighted laugh at the sight of the mending job he had done on his shirt. "I'm glad I made you a new one. I must have known how badly you'd need it. I see you've still got my little ring—and the bowstring?"

"Still here." Sigurd indicated the vicinity of his neck. "But— there's something—I know I can't be forgiven. I almost didn't think I should come back here, after—my father, you know."

The merriment faded in Ragnhild's eyes, and she smiled with an expression of both sadness and warmth. "I think you've changed, Sigurd."

"I hope I have," Sigurd answered, with a shudder and a glance at Mikla and Rolfr who were hovering nearby, looking on with weary contentment.

Ragnhild studied him carefully. "Your beard has grown in at last, but it's grown in gray here and there. This past year must have been the worst trial you've ever endured, to leave such marks upon you. Halfdane will hardly know you."

Sigurd felt his face turn white. "What did you say?" he asked in a half-whisper.

Ragnhild turned to look across the fell, back the way she had come. "You can see for yourself what I said," she replied, nodding toward the approaching rider on the slow-pacing black horse.

Sigurd scarcely knew how he walked forward to meet Halfdane. He put one hand on the crest of the horse's neck, unable to find any words to speak, and his mouth was almost too dry for words. Halfdane looked the same—stern and bleak, and his eyes were wary. He kept his injured arm covered inside his cloak, and he kept his shoulders hunched suspiciously.

Sigurd grasped a handful of mane, knowing that he would have to be the first to speak. "Can I—do you want me to come back?" he finally asked.

Halfdane's shoulders relaxed somewhat. "Only if that's what you want," he replied in a gruff tone. "I'll no longer try to hold you where you don't want to stay."

"Mikla and Rolfr—they never told me you still lived. They never even hinted! It was your signal I heard and didn't recognize. I thought it was Bergthor!"

"I forbade them to tell you," Halfdane explained. "I didn't want you coming back because you felt you had to face me. Only if you came of your own will, not to apologize, were you to return."

"Why didn't you tell me at first who I was?" Sigurd asked. "I might have believed you, if you had told me."

Halfdane shook his head, withdrawing a small flat key from a chain around his neck. He held it out to Sigurd. "This is the key that fits the box. Several times I thought about giving it to you, but I was afraid of what Jotull had done to your mind. The consequences might have been disastrous to Hrafnborg through no real fault of your own. If you had turned against me then, knowing that I was indeed your father, the pain would have been far worse than the wound I received in Svinghagahall."

Sigurd averted his eyes. "I'm thankful you weren't killed."

Halfdane pulled an amulet from his throat, a small hammer made of gold. "Adills once gave me this as protection. I don't know if that saved my life, or the healing physicians of Arnljotrshof. It's no easy thing to kill tough old warlords such as I am. If you'd practiced harder, you might have done it. However, it was near enough."

"You're being too kind. I was a stupid fool and you knew it. I realize now that what I overheard in the horse barn was only Dagrun telling you that you should tell me who I was, but—" He halted with a bitter sigh. "I don't suppose I would have believed it then."

"No, I didn't think you would, if Jotull could help it," Halfdane replied. "He could have easily convinced you that I was lying, even if I had opened the box and shown you the gauntlet."

Sigurd nodded his head. "How could I have been so weak?"

"Not weak, just deceived. It happens to everyone sometime. If not for Jotull's clever lies, I believe you would have seen the truth easily. But Jotull convinced you that you were abused and he was the only person who befriended you. And I, too, made a mistake. I was too proud and too fearful that you wouldn't want to be my son. I waited too long for the right time to tell you—a severe tactical error for an experienced warrior." He knit his brows as he considered his mistake in a military aspect. "I should have told you the first time I saw you on the fell in the rain that day, but your grandmother had told me that Ashildr's son had died long ago. I, too, have difficulty recognizing a lie when it comes from someone I trust."

Sigurd looked away to the west, thinking of Thongullsfjord. "It wasn't her fault. She was afraid I would leave her alone. I was all she had after my mother died."

Halfdane sighed in his heavy, moody way. "Yes, poor Bergdis never wanted her daughter taken away by an Alfar, and she fixed the blame on me for her death. I came to take you back with me as the tradition demands, knowing that Bjarnhardr would be looking for you and the gauntlet soon. When matters worsened in Thongullsfjord, I began to suspect the truth. Bjarnhardr's trolls drove away everyone who might have protected you, but still Bergdis did not ask for my help. I don't believe even now that she meant to be so bitter, but she never forgave me for my wrongs. Much could have been averted if I had been at Hrafnborg when Bjarnhardr arrived with his mob." His face darkened with the memory. "And Jotull. I wished a thousand times for just a jot more proof and I would have cut him down in an instant. It's hard to tell about wizards. I was a fool to think he wouldn't try spiriting you away to Bjarnhardr at the first opportunity."

"Jotull was repaid," Sigurd answered. "And Bjarnhardr won't escape either." He took the box from an inner pocket and turned it over in his hands a few times, looking at it. "This belongs to you. I'm returning it now. The gauntlet is inside."

"No, it's yours to use however you wish." Halfdane's gaze was hard and bright as he looked toward the lowlands. "It will take both of us to reclaim what we once lost. That has been my dream since the day you were born. Now my dream has become Bjarnhardr's nightmare." He gathered up his reins and nodded to Rolfr, Mikla, and Ragnhild. "A hero's welcome is awaiting you in Hrafnborg. Dagrun was the only one who knew from the start who the Scipling really was." His face, lined with griefs and hatreds, softened into a cautious smile.

"I don't feel like any sort of a hero," Sigurd replied rather anxiously. "Are you sure they forgive me?" He scowled toward Hrafnborg, clinging to its rocky perch on the fellside.

"I'm sure," Halfdane answered, extending his hand to Sigurd. "You have my word of honor."

Sigurd returned his handshake fervently. Looking into his father's face at last, he did not doubt that their future as father and son would be one of mutual satisfaction, in spite of the disputes that were sure to surface between two characters who shared so many of the same personality traits and faults.

The plague raged in Skarpsey, driving the contaminated remnants of the Dokkalfar back to their underground retreats, carrying the contagion with them. The prosperous settlements and mining areas were all but deserted, except for the most stubborn of the luckless Dokkalfar, who inevitably sickened and died. Some still fled before the approach of the plague, but the places that were not already cursed were growing fewer and fewer as the months passed. After a year, a Ljosalfar could ride almost anywhere in Skarpsey without much fear of the sickly and scarce Dokkalfar he might encounter, and after a year and a half the word spread that not a single Dokkalfar remained aboveground. The few who had prudently never abandoned their old tunnels for Bjarnhardr's promises were not likely to risk catching the plague by prowling around aboveground.

Not without some regret, the Alfar of Hrafnborg made preparations to return to the lush valleys of the lowlands and rebuild their old way of life. The first objective they planned was the reconstruction of the original hall at Hrafnborg, which Bjarnhardr had burned. Halfdane's courageous warriors would become his retainers, sworn to follow him in the defense of their homes, fields, and flocks, should danger arise again.

In the midst of packing carts, sledges, and horses—and the goodbyes which came almost daily, along with promises that almost everyone would soon reunite at the new Hrafnborg— a grim reminder of the past arrived on Sigurd's doorstep. Ragnhild, his wife of nearly a year, opened one of the back doors early one morning and nearly tripped over a wretched bundle of rags huddled in the scanty shelter of the doorway. She took one swift look at it and hurried back inside to find Sigurd and Halfdane. They looked up from their conversation with Rolfr and Mikla in some surprise as she spoke.

"There's a dying creature at the kitchen door. It looks to me like a very old Dokkalfar with the plague." She spoke calmly, but the mention of the plague always made everyone feel uneasy, even though they knew it was destined to curse only the Dokkalfar.

"I'll have the creature sent to the stable to do his dying," Sigurd said, rising to summon Dagrun from the main hall, where once he had taken his meals with the rest of the men.

"No, wait. Let's have a look at him first," Halfdane said, his brows drawn down in a familiar scowl, a reminder of the old days when he'd done a great deal more scowling than he had of late. "I have the most singular impression—but no, what a ridiculous notion. Come along, Mikla, what are you waiting for? Let's examine this creature. It may be the last Dokkalfar we see for a long time."

"And there's nothing wrong with that, if you ask me," Rolfr declared a little nervously.

"Then you can sit here by yourself, if you wish," Mikla

replied, "but it would be better for your reputation if it weren't known that Ragnhild is braver than you are." He grinned at Rolfr and gave him a push toward the kitchen, where Ragnhild was stooping down to look at the dying Dokkalfar, her fists cocked on her hips critically.

"He looks as if he used to be a person of some importance," she announced to Sigurd. "Let's carry him in beside the fire."

Sigurd frowned. "What, and carry the plague into our house? Isn't the stable quite good enough for him, Ragnhild?"

"Let me see his face first," Halfdane said, kneeling beside the ragged, huddled creature and turning the emaciated body slightly so its wasted countenance was exposed. "It's the plague, of course; you can tell immediately. This one seems to have been a cripple to start with, a hunched shoulder and—" His voice trailed away as he observed that one of the fellow's legs was a worn wooden peg.

The Dokkalfar's papery eyelids fluttered open and the cracked lips whispered, "Halfdane? Is it you?"

"Bjarnhardr!" Sigurd gasped, and Halfdane echoed him.

"Aye, it's Bjarnhardr," the wretch wheezed, with a shiver. "I've come to die with my enemies, since my friends are already dead—if I ever had any. Are you here, too, Sigurd? This will be a happy day for you, I believe, seeing the end of me and the sending you turned against me. Are you still as stupid as you used to be?"

"Yes, but now I know it," Sigurd retorted, "so it's not such an inconvenience any more. Is there anything we can fetch you to ease your last moments? Even I would hesitate to add to your torment, much as I would have liked to at one time."

"There's nothing like triumph to make a man generous," Mikla grumbled. "We don't want to make him so comfortable that he decides not to die, Sigurd."

Bjarnhardr shook his head slightly and shut his eyes. "Oh, you needn't concern yourselves about my lingering on," he whispered. "You should know that, once a curse of yours has got its fangs into a body, there's no road back. But I wouldn't mind dying with a last taste of good stout ale, Halfdane. There are no regrets between us, are there now? We did our best to destroy one another, and you have won. Ah well, so it goes."

"Yes, so it goes." Halfdane cradled his old enemy's head on his arm and poured the ale down his throat, although Bjarnhardr was able to swallow very little of it. Sigurd looked on with amazement as Halfdane made Bjarnhardr as comfortable as he might be under the circumstances and watched beside him for the rest of the day. When Sigurd returned from an errand at sundown, he learned that Bjarnhardr had died.

Halfdane ordered a fire to be built; Bjarnhardr was burned and the ashes were scattered to the four winds by Halfdane and Mikla, who had watched all the proceedings with a slightly disapproving eye.

"You certainly made it easy for him at the last," Sigurd observed. "And we've all lost too much sleep keeping the fire going." He looked at Ragnhild scattering the hot coals briskly, scolding Rolfr vehemently for falling asleep during the long watch.

"We're finished now." Halfdane leaned upon a staff to watch the rising sun coloring the low-hanging clouds. "It's true, he didn't deserve to die with someone watching over him, someone to give him a decent burning or burying. But it wasn't so much for him I did it, as for myself. I'm no sentimental idiot. I wouldn't have minded seeing the crows and foxes picking Bjarnhardr's bones."

"Then why—" Sigurd bit off his inquiry when Ragnhild bestowed a warning look upon him, which she often did when Sigurd demanded too many answers to questions he probably oughtn't ask. With a grunt, he changed the subject. "It's too bad we burned the earth here so drastically. It looks as if it had been blasted, doesn't it? I wonder if it will ever be green again."

Halfdane looked at him fondly. "Oh, it will heal." He prodded at the deeply charred and barren earth. "It will heal."

# ABOUT THE AUTHOR

Elizabeth Boyer began planning her writing career during junior high school in her rural Idaho hometown. She read almost anything the Bookmobile brought, and learned a great love for Nature and wilderness. Science fiction in large quantities led her to Tolkien's writings, which developed a great curiosity about Scandinavian folklore. Ms. Boyer is Scandinavian by descent and hopes to visit the homeland of her ancestors. She has a B.A. from Brigham Young University, at Provo, Utah, in English Literature.

After spending several years in the Rocky Mountain wilderness of central Utah, she and her ranger husband now live in a rural Utah community. They met on a desert servival trip in the canyonlands of southern Utah, which they love accordingly and visit often. Sharing their home are two daughters, and an assortment of animals. Mrs. Boyer enjoys backpacking, cross-country skiing, and classical music.

Dear Reader,

Your opinions are very important to us so please take a few moments to tell us your thoughts. It will help us give you more enjoyable DEL REY Books in the future.

1. Where did you obtain this book?

| | | | | | |
|---|---|---|---|---|---|
| Bookstore | ☐1 | Department Store ☐4 | Airport | ☐7 | 5 |
| Supermarket | ☐2 | Drug Store ☐5 | From A Friend ☐8 | | |
| Variety/Discount Store | ☐3 | Newsstand ☐6 | Other_____ | | |

(Write In)

2. On an overall basis, how would you rate this book?

Excellent ☐1    Very Good ☐2    Good ☐3    Fair ☐4    Poor ☐5    6

3. What is the main reason that you purchased this book?

Author ☐1    It Was Recommended To Me ☐3    7
Like The Cover ☐2    Other_____

(Write In)

4. In the same subject category as this book, who are your *two* favorite authors?

_____ 8
9
_____ 10
11

5. Which of the following categories of paperback books have you purchased in the past 3 months?

| | | | | | | |
|---|---|---|---|---|---|---|
| Adventure/ | | Biography ☐4 | Horror/ | | Science | |
| Suspense ☐12-1 | | Classics ☐5 | Terror | ☐8 | Fiction ☐x | |
| Bestselling | | Fantasy ☐6 | Mystery | ☐9 | Self-Help ☐y | |
| Fiction ☐2 | | Historical | Romance | ☐0 | War ☐13 | |
| Bestselling | | Romance ☐7 | | | Westerns ☐2 | |
| Non-Fiction ☐3 | | | | | | |

6. What magazines do you subscribe to, or read regularly, that is, 3 out of every 4 issues?

_____ 14
15
_____ 16
17

7. Are you:    Male ☐1    Female ☐2    18

8. Please indicate your age group.

Under 18 ☐1    25-34 ☐3    50 or older ☐5    19
18-24 ☐2    35-49 ☐4

9. What is the highest level of education that you have completed?

| | | | |
|---|---|---|---|
| Post Graduate Degree ☐1 | College Graduate ☐3 | Some High | 20 |
| Some Post Graduate | 1-3 Years College ☐4 | School | |
| Schooling ☐2 | High School | or Less ☐6 | |
| | Graduate ☐5 | | |

(Optional)

If you would like to learn about future publications and participate in future surveys, please fill in your name and address.

NAME_____

ADDRESS_____

CITY _____ STATE_____ ZIP _____ 21

Please mail to:   Ballantine Books
DEL REY Research, Dept.
516 Fifth Avenue — Suite 608
New York, N.Y. 10036

F-12